About the Authors

Alison Roberts lives in Christchurch, New Zealand, and written over sixty Mills & Boon Medical Romances. As a qualified paramedic she has personal experience of the drama and emotion to be found in the world of medical professionals, and loves to weave stories with this rich background—especially when they can have a happy ending.

When Alison is not writing you'll find her indulging her passion for dancing or spending time with her friends (including Molly the dog) and her daughter Becky, who has grown up to become a brilliant artist.

Lynne Marshall used to worry she had a serious problem with daydreaming, then she discovered she was supposed to write those stories! A late bloomer, Lynne came to fiction writing after being a Registered Nurse for twenty-five years and when her children were nearly grown. Now she battles the empty nest by writing stories from her heart which always include a romance with a touch of medicine for both Medicals and True Love.

To find out more about Lynne, please visit her website: www.lynnemarshallweb.com

Kate Hardy lives in Norwich, with her husband, two young children, one bouncy spaniel, and too many books to count! When she's not busy writing romance or researching local history, she helps out at her children's schools. She also loves cooking—spot the recipes sneaked into her books! (They're also on her website, along with extracts and stories behind the books.)

Writing for Mills & Boon has been a dream come true for Kate—something she wanted to do ever since she was twelve. She loves writing Medical Romance for over ten years now.

Kate also in to he

Hot Single Docs

COLLECTION

July 2018

August 2018

September 2018

October 2018

November 2018

December 2018

January 2019

February 2019

Hot Single Docs: London's Calling

ALISON ROBERTS

LYNNE MARSHALL

KATE HARDY

MILLS & BOON

Published in Great Britain 2019
by Mills & Boon, an imprint of HarperCollins*Publishers*
1 London Bridge Street, London, SE1 9GF

HOT SINGLE DOCS: LONDON'S CALLING © 2019 Harlequin Books S.A.

200 Harley Street: The Proud Italian © 2014 Harlequin Books S.A
Special thanks and acknowledgement are given to Alison Roberts for her contribution to the *200 Harley Street* series.

200 Harley Street: American Surgeon in London © 2014 Harlequin Books S.A
Special thanks and acknowledgement are given to Lynne Marshall for her contribution to the *200 Harley Street* series.

200 Harley Street: The Soldier Prince © 2014 Harlequin Books S.A.
Special thanks and acknowledgement are given to Kate Hardy for her contribution to the *200 Harley Street* series.

ISBN: 978-0-263-26833-1

09-0119

MIX
Paper from
responsible sources
FSC™ C007454

This book is produced from independently certified FSC™ paper to ensure responsible forest management.

For more information visit: www.harpercollins.co.uk/green

Printed and bound in Spain by CPI, Barcelona

200 HARLEY STREET: THE PROUD ITALIAN

ALISON ROBERTS

CHAPTER ONE

WINNING WAS SUPPOSED to be what mattered.

And it was. The end justified the means, didn't it?

Of course it did. That couldn't be doubted for a heart-beat in this case. The blanket-wrapped bundle in Abbie de Luca's arms was the absolute proof of that. The battle had been hard fought and gruelling enough to have almost destroyed her but she had won.

No. *Ella* had won. Her precious baby, only just a year old, had fought the killer disease of acute lymphoblastic leukaemia at an age where the greatest challenge should have been learning to sit up and take her first steps. The fact that they were being sent back from the only place in the world that had offered the new and radical treatment so that Ella could continue her recuperation at the Lighthouse Children's Hospital in London was proof of having won the battle. It meant she was a huge step closer to going home.

But was the 'home' they'd left behind still there?

For either of them?

Being escorted off the flight from New York before any other passengers and fast-tracked through customs at Heathrow airport like royalty should be making the triumph of winning all the sweeter.

So why did Abbie feel as if she was stepping onto a new battlefield? One that was only marginally less significant than the life-and-death struggle that had represented most of the three months she had been away with her tiny daughter.

'There's an ambulance waiting for you, Mrs de Luca.' The customs official eyed the wheelchair beside Abbie that the steward from the plane had been pushing. 'Is this all going with you?'

'No. It's going back on the next flight.' Abbie unwrapped Ella just enough to unhook the electrodes from the monitoring equipment. 'It was only a precaution. We didn't even need the oxygen.' They hadn't needed a medical escort either. One of the rare positive aspects of having a paediatric surgeon for a mother, although the negative side of knowing too much had outweighed that far too many times already.

Ella stirred in her arms but didn't wake. Abbie took a moment to check the connections of the central line the baby still had under her collarbone and made sure the syringe driver attached to the tubing hadn't run out of the drugs that were still a necessary part of treatment. Then she tucked it securely back into the folds of blanket and gave Ella a kiss on the few stray wisps of hair she had somehow retained.

As Ella relaxed back into sleep a tiny hand came up to touch her mother's cheek, as if she was reassuring herself that she was safe. She was probably smiling, Abbie thought, watching the crinkle deepen around the tightly closed eyes. Shame nobody could see it because of the mask needed to protect the baby from airborne infections.

The gesture had been enough to melt hearts around her anyway.

'Aww…' The burly customs official was smiling. 'What a wee pet.'

'Adorable…' The steward was blinking hard. 'I'm so happy she's going to be all right now, Abbie.'

'Thanks, Damien.' Abbie had to swallow the big lump in her own throat. Happy didn't touch the sides of how she felt about her daughter's new prognosis. 'And thanks so much for taking such good care of us on the flight.'

'It was a privilege. Have you got someone meeting you now?'

Abbie nodded. 'The ambulance is here. They're taking us to the Lighthouse. That's the children's hospital I work at.'

But the steward was shaking his head. Frowning. 'No… I meant… You know…'

Abbie did know. He meant someone with a personal attachment. Like Ella's father?

'Maybe. It was a bit of a last-minute rush and we weren't sure we'd get onto this flight. The New York team obviously managed to arrange the transfer but I'm not sure who else knows about it.'

She'd tried to ring Rafael but his phone had gone to his message service. Mr de Luca was in surgery all day, she'd been informed. Could they take a message? No, Abbie had responded. She'd be seeing him soon enough.

Or maybe that should be too soon? She'd walked out

on her marriage to fight this battle. Maybe that was why success wasn't tasting as sweet as it should.

Maybe the price had been too high.

'Abbie…' The man who'd been allowed into this private area of the customs hall and was now striding towards them wasn't an airport official.

'Oh, my…' Damien clearly appreciated the attributes of the tall, sexy newcomer. 'Is that Ella's daddy?'

'No.' Abbie shook her head, bemused. 'He's more like my boss.' And clearly a commanding enough presence, even out of a medical environment, to have had rules broken for him.

The steward was grinning as he started to manoeuvre the wheelchair out of the way. 'Tough job,' he murmured, 'but I guess someone's gotta do it.'

Abbie felt her lips curve as she raised her voice. 'Ethan…what on earth are you doing here?'

'I happened to field a call to Rafael about your arrival time and the ambulance transfer. He's caught up in Theatre so I thought I'd come for the ride and make sure you had a welcoming committee.'

And who could be more appropriate than one of the Hunter brothers, the owners of the prestigious London plastic-and-reconstructive-surgery clinic that employed both of Ella's parents as specialist paediatric surgeons. The clinic that had made it financially possible for Ella to go to the States and undertake the risky, experimental treatment that had been her only hope of a cure.

'Does…does Rafael know we've come home?'

'Not yet.' Ethan's gaze gave nothing away. 'The case he's operating on today is putting him under considerable pressure. I…didn't want to distract him.' The hint of a smile was sympathetic. 'I'll let him know the moment he comes out, I promise.'

Abbie simply nodded. There was a subtext here. That Rafael would need prior warning before seeing her again? Hearing her voice, even, given that their minimal communication of late had been via text and email? That, without some kind of intermediary, his Italian pride might be enough for him to refuse to see her at all? Maybe their first meeting would involve a solicitor and official documents outlining shared custody agreements for their child. How sad would that be?

'You're good to go.' The customs official stamped their passports and nodded towards someone near the door. 'Mr Hunter shouldn't really be in here. They'll show you out to where the ambulance crew is waiting. Your luggage will be sent by taxi as soon as it's offloaded.'

Ethan picked up the cabin bag by Abbie's feet but his gaze rested on the bundle in her arms. 'You okay? Would you rather I carried Ella?'

Abbie shook her head. 'I'm good.'

She wasn't about to hand her baby to someone else to carry, despite her precious burden feeling heavier by the minute. She was exhausted, that was all. These last few months had taken their toll, physically as well as emotionally, but she couldn't afford to stop being strong.

Not when she was stepping onto a new battlefield.

At least she had an ally. Given what Abbie had heard about his heroic stint in Afghanistan, it was probably overkill in any protection stakes, but there was also the history of the bad blood between the Hunter brothers. If she and Rafael did need an intermediary, someone who was experienced in negotiating the kind of tension that represented the dark side of a loving relationship was ideal.

Not that Ethan gave much away. The slight limp he walked with, which was a legacy of his army days, attracted more than casual stares as they walked to where the ambulance was parked, but he gave no sign of being aware of the curiosity.

And when they were tucked up in the back of the ambulance, on the M4 and heading into the city, he gave no hint that Abbie might be facing any escalating complications in her life.

He and Rafael were friends but they were men. Had they shared anything more personal in the time she'd been away? A late-night card game and plenty of whisky, perhaps, along with commiseration over their disastrous love lives? Maybe Ethan had reminded Rafael that the odds had been stacked against his marriage succeeding anyway. Sure, they'd been very much in love with each other but they'd barely had time to get to know each other properly, had they? They may have chosen to get married themselves but others would no doubt have viewed it as a shotgun wedding when they'd known that a baby was already on the way.

That baby was still asleep, bless her, now safely cocooned in the baby seat strapped onto the stretcher. Ella and Ethan sat facing her, the ambulance crew happy to sit up front, chatting, knowing that their transfer patient had a privileged level of medical supervision in the back.

The traffic slowed as they joined the flow on the Great West Road. A perfect opportunity to test the

water, Abbie thought, but…good grief…she felt ridiculously nervous about it. She knew she couldn't just dive
straight in with what was foremost on her mind but, to
her dismay, her voice still came out unmistakably shaky.

'H-how are things going at the clinic?'

'Good. Very busy. You would have seen some of the
publicity over our latest charity case?'

'Ah…no… Sorry, I'm a bit out of touch. I haven't
seen much news for ages. Is it a paediatric case?'

'Yes. A ten-year-old Afghan girl—Anoosheh—who
was noticed when her orphanage was evacuated. She
got abandoned on the doorstep as a toddler when her
disease became more extreme. Now she's got a neuro-
fibromatosis that's the size of a melon and has disfig-
ured half her face to the extent that she was being used
as a servant and kept well hidden from any prospec-
tive adoptive parents that visited the orphanage. Not
only that, she's probably lost the sight in one eye and
is gradually losing patent airways.'

'Oh…poor thing.'

'Today's surgery won't be the last but hopefully the
result will be enough to show people that there's a little
girl in there who just needs to be loved. There's huge
media interest and there's been some offers of adoptive
homes in the UK already. I imagine there's a pack of
reporters waiting to pounce on Rafael as soon as he's
out of Theatre. I'll try and head them off but it's just
as well he can cope with that kind of pressure while
he's operating.'

'Yes…he's good at that.'

Because he could detach himself from his own emotional involvement and see the bigger picture?

The way he had even when he'd been dealing with the trauma of his own daughter's prognosis?

Abbie's heart was thumping in her chest. She took a deep breath. 'So he's…um…okay, then?'

'Seems to be.' There was a short silence, as though Ethan was debating whether to say anything more, and then he slid a brief, sideways glance at Abbie. 'I don't think I've ever seen anyone try to bury themselves in their work so effectively before. He's taken on every difficult case he could possibly squeeze into his schedule. And then some. I've barely seen him.'

Oh…no confessions of heartbreak over a card session, then. No admitting that he might have made a terrible mistake by issuing the ultimatum that if Abbie insisted on taking Ella to the States then their marriage was over.

But the argument he'd felt so passionately justified in upholding had been that their daughter's quality of life outweighed its quantity. That they didn't have the right to put her through so much extra suffering when the chances of success were so small.

Surely the fact that it *had* worked was enough to justify her decision to go? Wouldn't Rafael be so thrilled to have the prospect of Ella's long-term survival that that ultimatum was now irrelevant?

Maybe. But there was more to it, wasn't there? He was her husband and a proud man. How much damage to their relationship had she done by refusing to respect his opinion and openly defying him?

And worse than that—much worse—she'd taken a sick baby away from her adoring father. She'd seen the pain in Rafael's eyes as she'd walked away with their

daughter in her arms. He hadn't expected to see her
alive again. How painful would that have been? He had
every right to hate her for that.

Abbie had had Ella in her arms and she'd still cried
all the way to New York.

So Rafael had shut himself away. She'd guessed that
by how distant he'd sounded when she'd tried to call
him. By how impersonal his email correspondence had
rapidly become. He'd buried himself in his work to the
extent that when Abbie had reached out in the darkest
days, so far away and so lonely and so desperate for
support, the response she'd received had seemed cold
and clinical. As if his emotional involvement with both
herself and Ella was a thing of the past.

Was it all over?

It wouldn't be fair to try and get any further clues
from Ethan.

It was Rafael that Abbie needed to talk to.

Needed to *see*. The longing was getting stronger by
the minute, as if her body realised that the distance between them was closing rapidly. She still loved her husband. Yes, they had pushed each other away and there
was a lot to forgive on both sides, but the love was still
there. It always would be.

Rafael would welcome Ella back into his life, she had
no doubt at all about that. But would *she* be welcome?

The prospect of the rift between them never healing was terrifying.

With a huge effort, Abbie tried to find some inner
strength. To feel positive. She even managed to find a
smile to offer Ethan.

'So what else is happening? Have Leo and Lizzie set a date for the wedding yet?'

'Yes. It's going to be the last Saturday in April.'

'What? Good grief…that's only a couple of weeks away.'

'Tell me about it. A quiet affair might have been easily organised but the kind of splash that goes with a high-society wedding at Claridge's? I'm trying to stay well out of it all.'

Abbie smiled. 'Good luck with that.'

Ethan snorted. 'Yeah… I haven't been entirely successful. Lizzie's managed to talk me into being best man. And that means I'll have to come up with some kind of speech.'

'I'm sure you can do it. Even with a tight deadline. But why are they in such a rush?'

Ethan shrugged. 'Guess they didn't want to wait. They're in love.'

There was something in Ethan's tone that made the conversation dry up completely at this point. Abbie didn't know the story behind why the Hunter brothers had been estranged for so many years but, like everyone else associated with the clinic, she was aware of the tension that still lingered between the men. The fact that Lizzie had been the one to persuade Ethan to be best man was evidence that things still weren't easy.

Was that all there was to whatever was remaining unspoken? Was Ethan happy for Leo or did he have doubts that the marriage would succeed? Maybe she and Rafael were being seen as an example of marrying in haste and repenting at leisure.

The lump in Abbie's throat made it too hard to take

a new breath. To try and distract herself she leaned over Ella and stroked her baby's cheek softly with her forefinger.

The welling up of love she had for her child wasn't enough to distract her completely. She and Rafael had been in love like that once. Not very long ago, in fact. They should still be in the honeymoon phase of their marriage but look at where they were now.

What should have been a perfect union so quickly blessed with a beautiful child had been blown apart by a cruel twist of fate.

And now Abbie was returning to where it had all happened.

The pieces of that perfect life were going to be in the same place again.

What remained to be seen was whether it was going to be possible to put them back together again.

A glance through the tinted glass of the ambulance windows showed that they were passing Regent's Park. There were taxis and double-decker buses nose to tail around them. Definitely London. Home. God, it was good to be back. She could even see the big square brick building on the end of Harley Street coming up—a close neighbour of the Hunter Clinic.

Ethan followed her line of vision.

'Have you missed it?'

'So much.' But it felt distant. Like part of previous life. How hard was it going to be to find her way back?

'Are you ready to come back to work? We desperately need you as soon as you can manage and I know that they've been holding their breath to get you back on board at the Lighthouse.'

'I could start tomorrow.'

'Really? That would be terrific. But won't you need time to get Ella settled?'

Abbie's smile was poignant. 'The oncology ward at the Lighthouse is more of a home for Ella than anywhere else. She's spent most of her life in there. And the staff are like a huge collection of aunties and grannies. The sooner we get things back to normal, the better for both of us, I think.'

For all of us, she amended silently.

Rafael de Luca stripped off his bloodied gloves and dropped them in the bin. Then he pulled at his mask, breaking the strings and bending the wire that strengthened the top hem as he sent it after the gloves.

Finally, he could take a deep breath of unfiltered, fresh-feeling air. Not just because the mask was gone but because the gruelling surgery that had kept him on his feet for so many hours he'd lost count was over.

They'd done well. The team he'd gathered around him to perform this complex operation had been outstanding. In an ideal world they were maybe not exactly who he would have chosen to work so closely with but the choice of his perfect partner had been taken away when Abbie had gone, hadn't it?

The 'dream team,' they'd been known as at the Hunter Clinic. Such perfect partners in the operating theatre, it had seemed inevitable that they would find they were a perfect match outside work hours as well.

Ha…

So much for fate. And so much for a distraction from his modus operandi these days. That momentary flash of recognising what had been missing from his theatre today was as far as he would allow it to go. And that had only happened because he was so incredibly exhausted. His back ached abominably from standing in one position for far too long. His eyes ached from peering through microscopic lenses for the fine work and a generalised ache in his head from such prolonged and fierce concentration was gaining vigour.

With his gown removed and balled up to join the other disposable items in the bin, Rafael could push open the double doors and exit Theatre. With some time in hand before checking on young Anoosheh in Recovery and no concerned family to go and talk to, he could do what he most wanted and go and stand under a hot shower for a considerable period of time. He needed a shave, too.

There would be reporters anxious to hear how the surgery had gone but nobody would expect him to front up to a camera until he'd had time to clean up properly. And maybe he wouldn't have to do it at all. Rafael could see Ethan Hunter waiting outside Theatre. Far better that the media dealt with the man who was not only one of the owners of the Hunter Clinic but in charge of the charity side of the business and directly responsible for Anoosheh being brought to London for her life-changing surgery.

'Rafael… How did it go?'

'Good.' He nodded his greeting. 'As good as we could have hoped for. The tumour is gone. She has a titanium plate in her jaw and we've reconstructed her nasal passages. There's more work to be done, of course. When she's recovered from this.' The finer work of removing excess scar tissue and repositioning facial features. The kind of work Abbie excelled at.

Letting his breath out in a weary sigh, Rafael rubbed at his forehead and pinched his temples with a thumb and third finger as he screwed his eyes shut. *Dio,* but he was tired.

'And the eye?'

Rafael opened his. 'They think it may still be viable. Time will tell if she can see out of it now that the obstruction is cleared.'

'Good. That gives me enough to update the media.'

'Grazie.' Rafael found a smile. 'I appreciate you doing that. I'm going to hit the shower and then head home.' He found himself staring at Ethan's odd expression. 'What? You want me to face the cameras after all?'

'No, it's not that. It's...'

'What?' Rafael's smile was fading.

'Abbie,' Ethan said quietly.

Rafael's heart skipped a beat and then thudded painfully. Something had happened. To *Ella*? Oh, no...not that. *Si prega di dio,* not that...

'She's here, Rafael,' Ethan said into the stillness. 'They're both here. Ella's been transferred to the paediatric oncology ward here to finish her recuperation.'

Rafael could only keep staring. Why hadn't he known about this? Why hadn't Abbie contacted him? Because she couldn't even bring herself to *talk* to him any more? Was that how things were going to be now?

'It was a last-minute decision, apparently.' Ethan wasn't meeting his gaze any longer. 'The call came in after you'd started the surgery on Anoosheh. I decided it was better if you weren't distracted so I took it on myself to go and meet them at the airport. I'm sorry you didn't get the message when it was intended.'

Rafael made a noncommittal sound. This wasn't Ethan's fault. Surely the decision to transfer Ella would have been made days ago. Abbie could have let him know. Or maybe she had... He'd been so focussed on this major surgery that he hadn't checked his personal email in a day or two. He hadn't even checked in with his message service since yesterday.

And what did any of that matter anyway?

They were *here*.

Just a floor or two and a few long corridors away.

The two people who meant more to him than anyone else on this earth were in the building so what the hell was he doing, standing here?

'I have to go,' he snapped. 'I have to see them.'

The relief that a long, hot shower could provide was forgotten. Unnecessary. A new surge of energy coursed through Rafael as he took the stairs rather than wait for a lift. Made him pick up his pace until he was almost running through the corridors in his theatre scrubs and plastic boots, earning startled glances from people who clearly thought he was on the way to an emergency.

It wasn't until he was close to the open doors leading to the paediatric oncology ward that his pace faltered. Seeing Abbie standing in the corridor outside one of the private rooms felt like he'd just run into an invisible wall.

Twelve weeks since he'd seen her.

The woman he'd married. The love of his life. The mother of his child.

But the last time he'd seen her had been when she'd

walked away from him, taking their child with her. When she'd refused to bend to his ultimatum and had chosen to go against his wishes, even if it meant the end of their marriage.

When his marriage had ended.

He'd been wrong to issue that ultimatum. Wrong to deny Ella the chance that the treatment had offered. He knew that and the knowledge was a knife that had twisted inside him for weeks now. Ever since the possibility of success had become apparent.

He also knew that Abbie had been through hell on the other side of the Atlantic and he hadn't been there to support her. He'd made her do it alone because he couldn't back down enough to find a way to apologise. Not through an email or text anyway, which had become the only way Abbie had wanted to communicate.

She must hate him for making her go through all that alone.

She hadn't seen him yet. She was looking through the window of the room. Watching to make sure Ella was asleep, perhaps, so that she could go and take enough of a break to have a meal?

She'd lost weight.

The shapely curves of her body that had first caught his eye when they'd started working together at the Lighthouse had all but disappeared. Her jeans looked too big for her legs and even from this distance he could see how prominent her collarbones were above the scooped neck of her sweater. Even the thick tresses of her glorious, honey-blond hair looked as if they'd lost volume by the way they were lying in a subdued and limp ponytail against the top of her spine.

A spine that looked a little less straight than he remembered in the strong, independent woman he'd fallen in love with and married.

How hard had this all been?

Rafael could feel his heart breaking. His every instinct was to rush forward and gather Abbie into his arms. To hold her against his heart and whisper promises. That everything would be all right. That he would always love her. That he would never allow life to be so hard for her again.

But how could he? The distance between them couldn't be resolved simply by him walking close enough to put his arms around her, and what if she pushed him away? His pride was already in tatters. Had been ever since she'd walked out on him. And, besides, there was only one of those promises that he could make with any certainty.

That he would always love her.

Would that be enough?

Maybe he was about to find out.

He never felt this nervous pushing open the doors to enter Theatre, even when he knew that the challenge was going to be huge.

His mouth never felt this dry.

It was hard to make his voice work. So hard that only a single word came out.

'Abbie...'

CHAPTER TWO

'ABBIE...'

She knew it was Rafael well before she turned to face him. It had always been unique, the way he said her name. It wasn't just the Italian accent or the smooth, deep voice. It was the subtle note of...wonder, almost. Or reverence? As if she was the most wonderful woman on earth and that made her name special, too.

Unique. One of a kind. Like Rafe.

Abbie braced herself, as she turned, for the first sight of her husband in what suddenly seemed a vast amount of time.

Three months.

But, at this moment, it felt like three *years*.

What would she see in his face? The joy of knowing she'd brought his daughter back to him? Anger that had burned away to leave a residue of resentment?

Echoes of the unbearable pain she'd seen before she'd turned her back and defiantly taken Ella away from him?

When she had turned and found herself facing Rafael with only a few feet between them, Abbie had to brace herself all over again.

How could she have forgotten the effect this man had on her? It was so much more than purely physical. More than emotional, even. It was a visceral thing. She was facing the part of her own being that had been torn free.

It stole her breath away. Made her heart stammer and trip.

'Rafe...'

Abbie tried to smile but it wasn't going to happen. Her lips simply wouldn't co-operate. She could only stare, drinking in this first glimpse, anxiously scanning his body and face to try and collect her impressions.

Dear Lord, but he looked so tired. As though he hadn't slept well for weeks. As though he hadn't even shaved for more than a day or two. He hadn't had a hair-cut for a while either, and... Had he just come straight from his stint in Theatre? Black curls were flattened in places and still looked damp with sweat. Were his scrubs a size larger than he usually wore or had he lost weight?

Yes. He looked exhausted. And wary but not angry. He looked...

Wonderful.

Tall and commanding and every bit as gorgeous as the first time she had laid eyes on him. Despite every-thing, Abbie could feel a curl of sensation deep in her abdomen as her body responded to being this close to him, but this overwhelming awareness wasn't anything as simple as physical attraction.

They knew each other so well. On so many levels. They made up two halves of a whole.

They *loved* each other.

At least, they had.

If only Rafael would smile. Or step closer. Hold his arms open so that she could fall into an embrace that would magically erase the pain they'd caused each other and make everything all right again.

But he wasn't moving. He seemed to be staring back at her with a mirror image of her intense scrutiny of him.

'How are you, Abbie?'

'I'm...' The word 'fine' tried to form on her lips but it wasn't true. Abbie didn't feel fine at all. She felt overwhelmed and unsure. 'I'm...okay. A bit tired. It's been a big day.'

A big twelve weeks.

A traumatic journey that she'd had to take *alone*. Abbie swallowed hard as she felt the hurt coalesce into the shape of the painful rock inside her chest that she'd lived with for so long now. 'And you? How are you, Rafe?'

'I'm...also okay...I think.' The familiar gesture as Rafael raked his hair with his fingers made the rock shift a little and sent a painful shaft through Abbie's heart. He was as overwhelmed as she was with this reunion. Unsure of what to say. Or do. 'I...wasn't expecting this. It's...'

'Sudden, I know.' This was weird. To feel the hurt this man had caused her and yet to feel so much compassion for him at the same time. 'I would have let you know sooner but it...just happened.'

He didn't believe her and Abbie could understand that. The possibility of sending Ella back to her home town to continue her recuperation had only been talked about in the last few days. She was still fragile. How much organisation had been needed to send a sick baby to another country?

'They only started to make enquiries first thing this morning. And things just fell into place. There was space available on a flight and a bed here at the Light-house and they didn't have to arrange a medical escort. And...when her results came through later, looking so good, Dr Goldstein just looked at me and smiled and he said...he said, "How 'bout it, Mom? Would you like to go home today?" And...'

And Abbie's voice was shaking now. Could she tell him that the first thing she'd thought at that point had been how badly she'd wanted to see *him* again? That the picture in her head of Rafael holding his baby daugh-ter again and seeing how much better she looked had filled her heart with so much longing that it had felt like it might burst?

No. She couldn't tell him because he had started speaking himself. She had to stop saying anything. Ra-fael had to repeat his question.

'What results? What were the tests?'

Did it matter? This was a doctor talking, not a fa-ther. Was he still that distant? This was what had caused their separation in the first place, wasn't it? The way he could remove himself from the emotional involve-ment of being a parent. To step back and see the big-ger picture through a professional lens. To decide that the quality of what would be a very short life was more important than the desperation to keep your own child alive as long as humanly possible.

'They took a bone-marrow biopsy yesterday. And bloods. We already knew she'd got through the dangerous cytokine release syndrome that the treatment caused. What we didn't know was whether the T cell therapy was really working.'

'And...' It looked as though Rafael was having to swallow a large lump in his throat, judging by the way the muscles in his jaw and neck were working. 'It's looking good?'

That was more like it. The doctor would want the exact figures. A copy of the test results, like the one Abbie had ready for him in her bag. But for a father? Knowing that the results were *good* would be enough to create such a wash of relief and hope for the future that the numbers were irrelevant.

Abbie nodded. It took a moment to trust her voice. 'She still needs protection for her immune system and she'll need another bone-marrow biopsy at the three-month mark but...' She took a deep breath as she blinked back tears. 'It's looking good, Rafe. As good as I hoped it would. The treatment's worked.'

As good as *she'd* hoped?

The choice of pronoun pushed him away. Just as Rafael had been about to pull Abbie into his arms so that they could celebrate this miraculous milestone together as Ella's parents.

To rush into the room they were standing outside and see for himself that Ella wasn't the critically ill baby she'd been the last time he'd seen her.

But it was true. He deserved to be dismissed as having been one of the hopeful parents. As soon as Abbie had heard about the experimental treatment that took T cells from the blood and reengineered them in a laboratory so that they could be put back into the body to find and kill the cancerous leukaemia cells, the hope had been born on her side.

All Rafael had been able to see had been how experimental the treatment was. That the success rates with adults had not been consistent and it had *never* been tried in a baby. That the risks were enormous and going through with the treatment would only cause so much more suffering that would probably still end in Ella's death. And he'd been right. The new T cells had caused an illness that had come within a heartbeat of killing Ella. She'd hovered between life and death in a paediatric intensive-care unit for weeks.

And *he* should have been there but he hadn't been able to bring himself to travel so far in order to watch his baby die. And, yes…even though it shamed him to admit it, part of what had kept him here had been that it seemed like a fitting punishment for Abbie for taking his beloved child away from him.

So much pain. On both sides.

What would Abbie do if he tried to take her in his arms right now? Push him away? Flinch?

He couldn't bear it if that happened.

But somehow he had to try and find a way to bridge this awful gap between them.

'It's been so long, Abbie. So…*hard*…'

So hard. It had been a nightmare ever since their precious baby had hit the headlines at becoming one of the rare cases of ALL being diagnosed at such an early age. Gruelling months of chemotherapy that had failed to produce remission, let alone a cure. And having them both disappear from his life had only plunged him deeper into his personal hell, especially in the wake of the fights over whether it was the right thing to do.

Missing his wife every day but being so angry at the way she'd made things so much worse. Missing his child with an ache that had gone even deeper than his bones. Sleepless nights and days waiting for the phone call that would deliver the dreaded news that the battle had been lost. Days when a fierce focus on his work had been the only thing that had kept him sane.

He heard the way Abbie's breath left her lungs in an incredulous huff. The pain he could see in her eyes hit him like a physical blow.

'How would you know, Rafe? You weren't *there*.'

Would they ever be able to get past this?

'I'm here now.' His voice sounded as raw as it felt. 'Isn't that enough?'

Abbie just stared at him for the longest time. He could see her lips tremble as her hands gripped the opposite arms, crossed over her breasts as if she was defending her heart.

'No,' she whispered. 'I don't think it is.' She took a ragged, inward breath. 'We…needed you, Rafe. And you…you weren't there.'

Dio, but this was hard. Did they have to go through it all again? Every impassioned fight? He'd never felt this tired in his life.

'You know why.'

'Yes.' Abbie's voice was tight. 'I know *why*. But I still don't *understand*. How could you not be there if you really love someone?' There were tears on her face now but Rafael couldn't move to brush them away. He'd lost the right to offer comfort because he'd caused the pain.

'You weren't there,' Abbie said again. 'For me *or* Ella. And…and it was *awful*, Rafe… You have no idea….'

'That's not true.' He couldn't help the hard edge that made the words clipped. But it seemed like they did have to go over the old ground just to get to a place where they could talk to each other again. 'I have a very good idea. That's why I didn't want you to go. To put Ella through that.'

Flashes of pain from other, long-ago cases were never far away. Especially cases like little Freddie…. Years ago, now, but it was still an effort to push the memory of that particular little boy away. Rafael had started in paediatric oncology determined to beat death for those innocent children but he'd learned the hard way that there had to be limits. That fighting *too* hard could only make things worse for everyone involved. Including the surgeon. He'd had to leave the specialty in the end because the toll it had taken on him personally had been too great.

'And if I hadn't, we wouldn't be here now. Ella wouldn't still be alive.'

'No…' The word was a weary sigh.

This was also true. And suddenly nothing else mattered. Ella was still alive. She was in the room right beside him. He couldn't stay out here a moment longer. Taking a step closer to the door brought him a step closer to Abbie, but she moved a little. And now Rafael could see through the window of the room.

He could see *Ella*.

Sitting in a cot and playing happily with a toy.

A toy he recognised. Called Ears. A soft pink rabbit with disproportionately long legs and ears. A silly toy he'd bought when she'd first been sick and been admitted here, which had fast become her 'cuddly.'

Ella was holding Ears in one hand as she knelt in the cot and then pulled herself up using the side of the cot. He could see the nasal prongs supplying oxygen taped to her face and one arm was bandaged, keeping the IV line that went to the port beneath her collarbone safe from being tugged. It didn't stop her getting to her feet, though.

Dio…she was strong enough to stand?

It didn't stop Ears being dropped over the side of the cot either, but Ella didn't burst into instant tears, like most children her age would. She just looked down at the floor and then up, perfectly confident that help would not be far away.

And then Rafael could really see her face for the first time. Those big, dark eyes were looking straight at him.

For a long, long moment they stared at each other. Rafael could remember the first time he'd held this baby and the overwhelming need to protect her. He could remember the feel of her downy skin. The smell of her when she'd been freshly bathed and fed. The sound of her voice when she'd been learning her own baby language.

But would she remember anything at all about him?

It seemed that she did. Her eyes got even bigger and those rosebud lips curled and curved into a smile. And Ella held up her little arms, which was enough to make her lose her balance and sit down on her padded bottom with a thump, but she was still smiling.

Still holding out her arms to her father.

And nothing else mattered.

Without even another glance at Abbie, Rafael rushed into the room.

Abbie stood and watched through the window.

It had been only a few minutes since she'd been doing exactly this, watching to see if Ella would be happy for a few minutes while she went to… What had she been going to do? Go to the bathroom? Make a coffee in the staffroom?

Whatever her intention had been, she'd forgotten it the moment she'd heard Rafael call her name and she'd had to brace herself for their reunion.

And now it was over.

They'd seen each other again. They'd talked.

But had anything been resolved?

If anything, Abbie felt more unsure than before.

Slow tears were leaking from her eyes and rolling down the side of her nose as she watched Rafael gather up his daughter into his arms and press his cheek against the top of her head. He had his eyes closed so he couldn't see that she was watching. And…oh, God…did he have tears tracing the edge of *his* nose, too? No…Rafael would never cry. But if he ever did, his face would look exactly the way it did right now.

The love he had for his daughter was almost as palpable as the wall Abbie had to reach out and touch for support.

He'd never expected to be able to hold her again, had he?

Or to see her smile. To hear that noise she made when

she was really happy—a kind of cross between cooing and giggling that sounded like water going out of a sink.

Being a plughole, they'd called it. *Ella's being a plughole*, they'd tell each other and then they'd both hold each other's gaze and smile because they knew it was such a happy noise and it had been such a rare thing amongst the pain and sickness. Those poignant smiles and the silent communication of eye contact had been moments of connection that had given them strength to go on. That had made them feel that sharing this heart-breaking journey was making their relationship stronger. But, in the end, like it did so often with this kind of unimaginable stress, it had torn them apart.

Yes. Rafael still adored his daughter. She could see him rocking her now and hear his voice as he spoke rapidly in Italian. She caught the word *fiorella*. Ella's proper name. His little flower. And he was singing now. Softly. Still in Italian. Stroking the odd patches of wispy hair on Ella's head so gently. It was one of the things she loved about this man, that he could be so passionate. So demonstrative.

And for a moment when he'd been out here with her, he'd looked as if he still loved *her* like that, too.

Just before he'd stupidly said how *hard* it had been for him.

He hadn't been there. Hadn't sat for countless hours amongst the bank of monitors in the intensive-care unit, wondering if each breath Ella took would be her last.

Maybe she shouldn't have taken the bait and reignited the old conflict but…it still *hurt*, dammit.

It wasn't going to just go away by itself.

Being together in the same place wasn't enough because it felt like there was no common ground between them.

Or if there was, the only person inhabiting it was a baby called Ella.

CHAPTER THREE

'I CAN'T BELIEVE you're starting back at work so soon.' Ella's nurse for today, Melanie, was watching Abbie spoon morsels of breakfast into her daughter's mouth. 'You've only just set foot back in the country.'

'I just want to get back to normal.' Abbie's smile was a bit of an effort. Getting Ella back to London had been a huge step closer to getting back to a normal life but she had no real idea what 'normal' was going to be from now on.

She caught an escaping dollop of porridge with the edge of the plastic spoon and waited until Ella opened her mouth so she could pop it back where it belonged. 'And I've had far too much time away already,' she added. 'You know what they say, Mel. "Use it or lose it."'

Melanie looked up from the drugs she was preparing for Ella's syringe driver. 'You won't go straight back into full time, though, will you?'

Abbie's headshake was swift. There was no way she could suddenly cope with that kind of punishing schedule—the long surgery hours at the Lighthouse, outpatient clinics, ward rounds and the travel time and consultations at the Hunter Clinic. A schedule that Rafael had apparently ramped up to an unthinkable level while she'd been away. No work–life balance there but she could understand escaping like that. And her own life had been just as one-sided. For a very long time.

'I haven't been genuinely full-time for ages,' she said aloud. 'We started scaling things down when I got to about six months pregnant and then things got even more disrupted after Ella was born, of course.'

Melanie's nod was sympathetic. She clicked the syringe into the driver. 'You must be missing your work, too. You don't get to be as good as you are if you don't really love what you're doing. Are you in Theatre today?'

'No. It's just an outpatient clinic this morning. They're easing me in gently.'

'That's good.' Melanie was making an exaggerated happy face at Ella. 'You done yet, chicken? Ready to have a wash and get dressed and face the day?'

Abbie wiped Ella's face with a damp cloth. 'I think we both are.' With a final cuddle she handed Ella to Melanie. 'Be good, sweetheart. I'll be back as soon as I can.'

Setting off to the Lighthouse's outpatient department, she realised how nervous she was feeling. Maybe it was because she was out of her jeans for the first time in ages and wearing clothes more appropriate for her job. A neat blouse tucked into a long, swirly skirt that reached the top of her boots. An unbuttoned white coat as a jacket. The bright name badge that had a cute flower with a smiley face for a centre that told the world she was 'Doctor Abbie.'

Or maybe it was because people would be bringing their precious children to her to have decisions made about potentially major surgery. She would have to weigh up the risks versus benefits for other people's children when she was so acutely aware of how it felt to be a parent herself. What the repercussions of those risks might be.

Oh, for heaven's sake, Abbie scolded herself. 'It's only an outpatient clinic. Hardly life or death.'

There was an expectation, however, that she would start again with the really high-pressure work as soon as possible and get up to reasonable speed so that she wouldn't lose the skills that had won her such a prestigious position in the first place. The expectation wasn't just coming from the Hunter brothers or the head of the paediatric surgical department at the Lighthouse Children's Hospital.

It was coming from Abbie herself and that was why she'd told Ethan that she would start again so soon.

The passion that had led her into this career represented a part of herself that she had no intention of losing. First and foremost, it was who she was. Being a wife and a mother might be just as important but that part of her couldn't survive in isolation. Not happily, anyway, and if she wasn't happy she couldn't do her best. *Be* her best.

This nervousness that made her stomach churn was very unfamiliar, though. Disconcerting. It was only an outpatient clinic she was heading for, she reminded herself again. One of her favourite parts of her job, where she could spend time with young patients and their families, either exploring the possible routes they could take to make a positive difference in their lives or checking up on progress and getting the satisfaction of seeing that difference.

Why was she so nervous?

Because she felt rusty from being away from the action for too long? Those kinds of nerves might be expected when she was back in Theatre with a scalpel in her hand but they would be welcome then because she'd know they would keep her focussed and would evaporate as her confidence returned.

This was different. This was the first time she would be working with Rafael since she'd accepted the ultimatum that meant their marriage was over. Would working together make things better or worse? Could it break through the polite distance they'd ended up in last night before Rafael had excused himself to do a post-operative check on his most recent patient?

Apparently not.

Rafael had arrived before Abbie and, against the background of a crowded waiting room, he was sorting files with the clinic's nurse manager, Nicky. Like Abbie, he was wearing an unbuttoned white coat over his professional uniform of tidy trousers and a neat shirt and tie. He had a name badge on his pocket, too. Nothing as frivolous as a smiling flower, though. His was a far more dignified standard issue with the tiny lighthouse logo and his full name.

Abbie hadn't even offered to get him a fun badge when she'd had her own made. She'd always known the limits to which his pride would let him bend.

Or she'd thought she'd known. Until it had come to the crunch.

Both Rafael and the nurse manager looked up as Abbie approached.

'Abbie.' Nicky's smile was welcoming. 'It's so good to see you. I was delighted to hear that you'd be sharing the clinic this morning. I'll bet your registrar was delighted as well.'

Rafael's smile wasn't nearly as welcoming as Nicky's but at least it *was* a smile. One that was at odds with the wary look in his eyes. Surely Rafael wasn't nervous about working with *her* again? No...

She'd never known him to be nervous about anything. Excited, certainly, like he'd been when they'd seen the stripes on the pregnancy test stick that had meant they were on the way to becoming parents. Fearful, maybe, like he'd been when they'd been waiting for those first test results to come back and explain why their newborn baby was failing to thrive in such a dramatic fashion. And angry, definitely, like he'd been when she'd refused to accept his decision that enough was enough when it came to putting Ella through any more misery.

But nervous? This was disconcerting. Abbie had to force herself to return Nicky's smile of welcome.

'I did hear that you've been incredibly busy. It's lovely to see you, too, Nicky.'

'And I hear that Ella's doing well. That's such good news.'

'It certainly is.' Abbie slid a sideways glance at Rafael but he seemed absorbed in the list of patients. He eased a set of patient notes out of a pile and put it to one side.

'How long before you can take her home?'

Rafael's head jerked up at this query and Abbie could feel the intensity of his glance and it felt...accusing? This wasn't something they'd had a chance to talk about last night. How could they, when Abbie wasn't even sure whether she *had* a home to take Ella back to?

'Um...it'll be a few weeks, I think. We need to see how things go. Certainly no decision will be made until she's had her T cells checked at the three-month mark.'

Which gave them some breathing space at least. Time to sort out where they were as far as their marriage went. Or how they might share Ella's parenting in the future.

The noise level in the waiting room was increasing. A scuffle had broken out near the toy box and more than one child was crying. A woman carrying a well-wrapped baby was standing near the door and looking as if she would prefer to turn around and go out again. Her partner was trying to persuade her to take a seat. Nicky surveyed the scene and squared her shoulders.

'We'd better get this show on the road. I'll get the first patients into the consulting rooms. I've put you in Room 3, Abbie.'

'Cheers.'

As Nicky moved away, it felt as if Abbie and Rafael were almost alone, sandwiched between the waiting-room chaos and the rest of the staff, who were busy organising the rooms for the consultations and tests that were scheduled.

'Hi...' Abbie offered a smile. 'You okay?'

'I'm fine.' Rafael smiled back. Another polite smile. 'And you? That chair in Ella's room can't be that comfortable to sleep in.'

'I'm used to it. I've been sleeping in one of those chairs for so long now that a bed will probably feel weird.'

And there it was again. A slap in the face. A reminder of where she'd been for the last three months. An echo of the awkward moment last night when Rafael had asked if she would come home to sleep and she'd said that changing something that big in Ella's routine was out of the question just yet.

'How is she this morning?'

'Good. She ate a little stewed apple and porridge for breakfast. It's great that she already knows so many of the nurses on the ward. She's got Melanie today and I don't think she even noticed me leaving to come here.'

'I'll get up and see her as soon as we've finished here. I...wasn't sure whether to disturb your early-morning routine.'

Keeping his distance? Abbie stifled a sigh. 'She's your daughter, Rafe. You can spend as much time with her as you want.'

His nod was almost curt. He reached for a pile of notes and slid them along the counter. 'Here are your patients for this morning.'

It wasn't rocket science to see that her pile was much smaller than his. Or that the names on the list had been divided far more equally. Abbie raised her eyebrows. Rafael shrugged.

'I've added some cases to my list. It's your first morning back, Abbie. I wanted to make things a little easier for you.'

Abbie stared at him. 'If I didn't think I could cope, I wouldn't be here.'

The words came out a little more vehemently than she'd intended but it was bad enough feeling nervous about her own performance. She didn't need other people doubting her abilities.

He mirrored her raised eyebrows and gave another one of those subtle shrugs that was part of what kept people so aware of his birthplace. *As you wish*, it said. *It's of no importance to me.*

Except it had been of importance or he wouldn't have done it. And it was a generous gesture when he probably had too much to do today anyway. Maybe she should compromise. Abbie scanned the list rapidly.

'I'd like to keep this little girl.' She tapped the list. 'Grade-three microtia. That's one of my favourite things to do.'

Rafael knew that. He'd been in Theatre with her more than once as she'd tackled the delicate surgery to create an ear from the birth deformity that had left nothing more than a peanut-shaped blob as an outer ear. Life-changing surgery for a child who was being teased at school, and this little girl was seven years old.

'And this one...' She pulled another set of notes from the pile. 'Seven-month-old ready for repair of his cleft lip and palate. Oh...it's Angus. I remember us seeing him for his first consultation. That's another one I'd love to do...'

Her voice trailed away. The sometimes massive surgery needed to correct this kind of birth defect was a procedure that both she and Rafael were known to be exceptionally good at. Together. Rafael's skill at shifting bones and moulding features in conjunction with her ability to join tiny blood vessels and nerves and then suture to leave almost invisible scars had made them a team that people came from all over the country to consult via the Hunter Clinic.

Would she want to do it by herself?

'Maybe I'll leave this one for you.' Abbie couldn't bring herself to look up at Rafael. 'I'll take Harriet back, though. I've been wondering how those burn scars are settling. She must be due for her next surgery.'

Rafael simply nodded, took the first set of notes from his pile and headed to the first consulting room. Abbie took her first set and went past his door to Room 3. Separate lists. Separate rooms. Separate operating theatres even? Was this how it was going to be from now on?

Even when they'd seen different patients in the past, they'd always been popping into each other's rooms to get a second opinion or simply brainstorm a case. This felt wrong but it was also a relief. Perhaps they needed time to get used to working together again. Or maybe they actually needed to find out if they *could* work together when their personal lives were in such disarray. Being too close too soon could well mean that it would never happen.

There was no reason why they couldn't define some professional boundaries and make it work. Was there?

Apparently there was. The message Abbie got later that day, asking her to attend a meeting at the Hunter Clinic, had all the undertones of a 'Please explain.'

'Urgent message, Mr de Luca.'

'What is it, Nicole?' The expression on the young woman's face suggested that his secretary was anxious. She was right behind him as he kept moving into his office.

'A meeting at the Hunter Clinic at five p.m. With Leo and Ethan Hunter. In Leo's office. Gwen said she's checked your calendar and you're available, so...'

The sentence was left hanging but Nicole might as well have finished it. The unsaid words were that no excuses would be acceptable short of the direst emergency.

'Did she say what it was about?'

'No. Shall I order a cab for you?'

'I suppose you'll have to,' Rafael growled. He didn't have any consultations booked at the exclusive Hunter Clinic that he could think of so he had no idea why it was suddenly so important to meet with the Hunter brothers this afternoon, and if he did have a space on his calendar, he'd much rather be spending that time with Ella.

Now he'd barely have time to eat the sandwich he'd just bought on the run for a late lunch. He dropped the plastic triangular package on his desk, along with the other purchase he'd made in the gift shop beside the café.

'Oh, what's that?' Nicole's face lit up with a wide smile. 'It's gorgeous.' She reached out to pick up the huge teddy bear that was wearing a sparkly pink tutu and had pink ballet shoes on its feet. She hugged the bear. 'I love it. It's so soft and squishy. And *huge*. It must be just as big as Ella is now.'

'Almost.' It wasn't really a baby's toy either, but his Fiorella was growing up, wasn't she?

'I heard she was back. And that she's doing well. That's wonderful, isn't it?'

'It certainly is.'

Nicole put the bear down with some reluctance. 'She'll want to be a dancer when she grows up after she sees this. Look at those cute ballet shoes. Oh…I would have loved something like this when I was a little girl.'

A little girl. Not a baby any more. Yes… He had been shocked by how much Ella had changed since he'd last seen her. It was mainly due to such an improvement in her condition but three months was a long time in a baby's life. She had more teeth and her smile looked different. Her hands were so much cleverer and her baby babble was beginning to have the inflections of real speech. She could stand up and even walk if someone held her hands. She'd barely been able to sit unaided when he'd last seen her.

He'd missed so much and that added another painful layer to the guilt he already felt at having left Abbie to cope alone in New York.

Rafael tried to shake his swift train of thought. 'Order the taxi for four-thirty,' he instructed Nicole, picking up the bear and depositing it in a corner of the office. 'I don't want to get stuck in rush-hour traffic. Anything else urgent I should know about?'

'No.'

'Good. I'll get on with my clinic notes, then.'

Except that the pink bear sitting in the corner kept catching his peripheral vision. Making him think of Ella.

And of Abbie.

Would she forgive him for leaving her to cope alone in New York like that? For sending her away with the threat that their marriage was finished? It wasn't the time to push too hard right now. Not when she was exhausted and trying to get settled back into being in London. When she not only had Ella to care for but she was starting work again as well. He wanted to help but between Abbie and the wonderful staff on the paediatric oncology ward there was nothing he could do there. It hadn't gone down very well when he'd tried to lighten Abbie's workload at the outpatient clinic this morning either.

And she didn't seem to be making any effort to close the distance between them. She hadn't even followed him into the room when he'd rushed in to see Ella yesterday, and ever since then it had felt like she was enclosed in a bubble. There but not there.

It was frustrating.

So was fighting London traffic to get to the Hunter Clinic by 5:00 p.m. It wouldn't have been so bad if he could have gone home after this meeting because home was in Primrose Hill, about halfway between the Lighthouse and Harley Street, where the Hunter Clinic was located. But he had to get back to the Lighthouse as soon as he could because he still had patients to see, including Anoosheh. Apparently she was running a slight temperature and there was concern about potential infection. His entire day had run a little behind schedule thanks to taking on extra outpatients to ease the load on Abbie this morning.

Rafael desperately wanted to spend time with Ella, too. As long as possible. He wanted to give her the bear and see if it made her smile. If it didn't, he would have to go looking for something else. What *did* make her smile these days? What did she like best of all to eat? What songs did she like to have sung to her?

There was so much he needed to find out.

And home wasn't really home any more, anyway, was it? It hadn't been, from the moment Abbie had walked away from that final, dreadful row, when he'd told her that if she took Ella to New York, their marriage was over.

Oh, her clothes still hung in the wardrobe and her books were still in the bookshelves. It was still the same gorgeous period-conversion apartment that they'd both fallen in love with and purchased in the week before their wedding. It still had the same fabulous view towards the Regent's Canal and the bonus of the private courtyard garden that boasted a tree.

A tree they'd put a baby's swing in to celebrate the six-month mark of Abbie's pregnancy. A swing that had never been used. It had collected leaves in autumn and been filled with snow in the winter. Now it just hung there, too bright for a garden that had yet to blossom for spring. A cruel reminder of what could have been.

All these things taunted Rafael now so he spent as little time as possible in the apartment. He couldn't stay there if their marriage was truly over. Maybe Abbie would want to live there with Ella. So that she could use the swing…

'This is fine.' Rafael rapped on the glass partition to alert the cab driver. 'I can walk from here.'

Giving the driver a generous tip, Rafael took his briefcase and umbrella and strode down Harley Street, his long coat flapping. He should button it up to protect his suit because the leaden sky looked as if it could open at any moment but he was in too much of a hurry. The usual reverence the old buildings in this street instilled was gone, too. He didn't even glance at any of the brass plaques that advertised the famous medical people who had once worked in these fabulous old buildings.

The facade of the Hunter Clinic, at 200 Harley Street, blended seamlessly with its historic neighbours but the interior made it look more like an exclusive hotel than a clinic. The heels of his Italian shoes tapped on a polished marble floor as Rafael marched through the huge reception area, past the inviting white sofas bathed in soft light from the table lamps beside them.

Only Helen, the senior receptionist, was on duty at the moment. In her late forties, Helen was always immaculately groomed and conveyed just the sort of welcome the clinic wanted. Capable, calm and compassionate. Weren't those words in the clinic's mission statement somewhere?

'Mr de Luca.' Helen's smile held no disapproval of the fact that he was nearly ten minutes late. 'How lovely that you could make it. They're all ready for you in Leo's office.'

Leo's office? They were *all* ready for him?

What the hell was going on here?

Leo was the older of the two brothers—sons of the celebrated plastic surgeon, James Hunter. Rafael had never delved too deeply into the scandal that had surrounded James's death. He only knew that it was through the tireless efforts of Leo that the clinic had survived and the cloud had been lifted from the Hunter name. He also knew that a huge rift had appeared between the brothers when Ethan had joined the army and left Leo to fight alone to save the clinic, but that was in the past, wasn't it?

Ethan was back. And Leo had finally settled for one woman.

These were happier times for the Hunter brothers. So why weren't they looking happy right now?

And what, *in nome di dio*, was *Abbie* doing here?

She looked pale. Frightened, almost. Rafael hadn't seen her look like this since that terrible time when they had been waiting for the first results to find out what was wrong with their tiny baby. What had Leo and Ethan said or done to make her look like this now?

How *dared* they?

The need to protect Abbie was sudden and fierce. Rafael dropped his briefcase and umbrella on the nearest chair but he didn't sit down. He didn't take his coat off. Instead, he stepped behind Abbie's chair and gripped the back of the seat.

'What's going on?' he snapped.

Had they fired her? Because she couldn't give the kind of focussed dedication to her job that she'd been known for before she'd become a mother?

Before she'd become his wife?

Surely not. Everyone here at the clinic, especially these brothers, had done all they could to support the de Luca family through the crisis. They'd given Abbie unlimited paid leave. Helped enormously with the logistical details and appalling expenses that Ella's treatment in the States had engendered.

He shouldn't have let them be so involved. This was *his* family.

He would look after them.

No matter if Abbie had been fired. He could support them. *All* of them. He would protect them. With his life, if necessary.

The Hunter brothers exchanged a glance. It was Leo who spoke.

'Sit down, Rafael. Take your coat off for a minute. This won't take long.'

'I do not *want* to sit down.' The anger was building rapidly. 'I want to know what you've said to my *wife* to make her look so upset.'

He heard Abbie's sharp intake of breath at his tone. Or was it the way he'd referred to her as his 'wife'—as if she were some kind of possession?

Rafael closed his eyes and took a deep, inward breath as he deliberately dialled down his anger. Whatever was going on, becoming too passionate about it would only make things worse. Hadn't he learned that lesson already?

Towering over everybody else in this room wasn't going to help anything either.

Opening his eyes again, Rafael inclined his head in acquiescence that something clearly needed to be dealt with and he moved to lower his body into the empty seat beside Abbie.

He took a sideways glance at her, still concerned by how pale she looked, but Abbie was staring down at her hands. He wanted her to look at *him* so that he could send her a silent message that everything would be all right. *He* would deal with whatever it was that had prompted their summons into this office.

There was a beat of silence in the room and then Ethan cleared his throat.

'We asked you both to come in this afternoon,' he said into the silence, 'because an issue has been brought to our attention that we thought needed urgent resolution. A complaint has been made—'

'Che cosa?' Rafael's gaze jerked to meet Ethan's. 'What are you talking about?'

'It's not a complaint, exactly.' Leo flicked an unreadable glance at his brother. 'I would phrase it more as an expression of disappointment that a client feels strongly enough about to bring it to our attention.'

'I have no idea what you're talking about,' Rafael snapped. 'Is someone unhappy with my work? And why is Abbie here?' The speed of his speech was increasing. So was the volume. 'Nobody could have complained about her work because she hasn't even been in the country for three months.' Rafael shook his head in frustration and tried to calm down again. 'Or is that what this "disappointment" is about? The fact that we have had to deal with a family crisis that has disrupted our ability to work?'

Again the brothers exchanged a meaningful glance.

'You could say that,' Leo said. 'Sort of.'

'Spit it out, man,' Rafael growled. 'I'm hoping to have enough time after my *work* to visit my daughter before she's asleep for the night.'

'Of course.' Leo turned to smile at Abbie. 'And can I just say again how wonderful it is to have you and Ella back? Especially when you've come back with such a great result.'

'Thanks, Leo.' Abbie's nod was stiff. She caught Rafael's gaze briefly then and he could see that she was just as mystified as he was by the reason for this meeting.

Ethan took his cue from Leo's nod. He looked directly at Rafael, who had the strange impression that a game of 'good cop, bad cop' was going on here. And Ethan had been designated 'bad cop.'

'I believe you saw the MacDonald family at your outpatient clinic this morning? With their seven-month-old son, Angus, who's now ready for admission for repair of his bilateral cleft lip and palate?'

'That is correct.' Rafael frowned. What on earth had the MacDonalds found to complain about? 'They seemed perfectly happy to know how well the stretching and reshaping of the tissues has been with the taping and use of the retainer. He's a good candidate for a single initial surgery to repair the defects in both his lip and palate.'

'He'll still need further surgery for cosmetic improvements, though.' It was Abbie who spoke.

It was Abbie who'd first seen Angus back when the newborn had been brought down from Scotland by his distressed parents. She'd immediately called Rafael to share the consultation and reassure them that they would be able to achieve an almost perfect result for their son.

He nodded. 'You can deal with that further down the track. And I'll do the gum repair later. When Angus is around seven years old.'

Ethan had listened to the exchange and was shaking his head. Rafael glared at him. 'The MacDonalds were delighted to know that their son can be admitted for the surgery as early as the end of the week. What *is* the problem here?'

'The MacDonalds came to the Hunter Clinic for a private consultation within weeks of Angus being born,' Ethan said. 'Do you know why they chose us out of all the places they could have taken their baby for surgery after they'd decided they didn't want to go on a National Health waiting list?'

'We treat a lot of these types of cases,' Rafael responded. 'Our reputation is very good.'

'No.' It was Leo who was shaking his head this time. 'Our reputation for dealing with this particular birth defect is the *best*. And you know why?'

Rafael met his gaze squarely. 'My background in craniofacial surgery for paediatric oncology patients gave me a very good training that has easily transferred to birth defects.' He shrugged, still puzzled. 'I'm good at what I do.'

Repair of this kind of deformity that was so distressing to parents wasn't just about the reshaping of bones and tissues, though, was it? How good the final result was was largely dependent on the skill of the plastic surgeon involved in the finer, external work.

'And Abbie's very good at what *she* does,' he added. 'The best, in fact.'

'Exactly.' Leo and Ethan exchanged a satisfied glance this time. 'And therein lies our issue.'

Rafael raised an eyebrow.

'You saw the MacDonalds this morning.'

'Yes. You know this already.'

'But Abbie didn't see them. We understand that the case had been on her list, with a note to share the consultation with you. But you...ah...rearranged the lists this morning.'

'Only so that Abbie wasn't overwhelmed with work on her first day back.'

'You also told the MacDonalds that you would be performing the whole surgery. Alone. That Abbie would not be available to work with you on the case.'

'Ah...' Rafael could feel Abbie's stare. She wasn't happy. But it had been her choice to let him shift the case onto his list this morning. Women! *Dio*... The way their minds worked was an unfathomable mystery sometimes.

'The MacDonalds came to the Hunter Clinic because of the reputation that both of you have in dealing with a case like theirs. The emphasis here is on *both* of you. They'd heard about the Hunter Clinic's "dream team." Now they're feeling...cheated.'

'Look...' Leo sounded uncomfortable. 'We're well aware of your personal issues but whatever problems you have need to be put aside in working hours for the benefit of the clinic, not to mention the benefit of our clients.'

'There's a waiting list of elective cases like this,' Ethan added swiftly. 'And an even longer list of potential charity cases. This is an incredibly common birth defect.'

'We can't support this separation at a professional level,' Leo put in. 'You have to be able to work together.'

'We were working together,' Abbie said. 'This morning. And, yes, Rafe did take the MacDonald case off my list but I had the choice. I *could* have kept it.'

'You're missing the point,' said Ethan. 'It's not a case

of who gets who. Even a few minutes ago you were both talking about future surgery that Angus would need like it was some kind of "pass the parcel" game. That might be all very well with elective cases but what's going to happen with an acute case? An emergency? Are you two going to be squabbling in a corner because you're not professional enough to work on the same case? In the same theatre? *Together*?'

'No.' Abbie's voice sounded strangled.

'Of course not.' Rafael was insulted. 'That suggestion is *ridicolo…*'

'You were a tight team,' Leo said quietly. 'The best. We want that back.'

'Everybody knows how tough it's been,' Ethan said. 'And we've all done our best to help but the worst is over now and the kind of disruption we've seen today can't be allowed to happen again.' He shook his head. 'If word gets out that you two are not happy working together, it will cause untold damage to our reputation and we're not going to allow that to happen.'

Leo sighed. 'If it continues, we might all have to re-think whether you can continue in your current employment.' He eyed Abbie. 'You've been a full-time mother for months now. If that's more important to you than your career then we'll find a way to work around it, but you need to be up front with us.'

'I am being up front with you.' Abbie's voice was shaky. 'And I've never considered choosing to give up my work. My daughter is the most important person in the world to me but I know how brilliant the childcare system at the Lighthouse is. We'd always planned to juggle our careers and family life to allow us to both continue working.'

Rafael felt something tighten inside his chest. He remembered those planning sessions. Lying on the bed beside Abbie, admiring the increasing size of her belly. Keeping his hand resting lightly on her skin so that he could marvel at the movement he could feel beneath it. Imagining them both collecting their baby from the crèche and taking her home for family time.

Life had been so perfect back then. So full of exciting dreams for the future.

How had it all turned to dust? He wanted it back. All of it.

But Abbie wasn't even looking in his direction again now. She was facing her employers here at the clinic. Fighting for her *career*.

'Then the issue is simply whether you can continue working together.' Both Ethan and Leo shifted their gaze from Abbie to Rafael. Abbie also turned to look at him.

'I can,' she said.

There was determination in her eyes. And something more.

Hope that this could be a way through the enormous barrier that still lay between them?

Or was that wishful thinking on his part?

Whatever. It was a first step.

Rafael smiled. 'So can I,' he said. 'I look forward to the privilege of working with you again, Abbie.'

CHAPTER FOUR

SHE HADN'T EXPECTED THIS.

She'd been in perfect agreement with Leo and Ethan during that meeting this afternoon. Okay, she was partly to blame because she'd consciously chosen to let Rafael see the MacDonalds as part of his outpatient list but he'd had no right to push her out of being involved with Angus MacDonald's first surgery. He'd actually told them she was *unavailable*?

Abbie scrubbed harder. It had been a long time since she'd been through this routine and her skin wasn't liking the stiff bristles of the soap-impregnated brush. It stung as she spread her fingers and scrubbed between them and then moved on to the backs of her hands and the insides of her wrists but she didn't lighten the pressure. The physical pain was an echo of the simmering anger she was prodding.

Rafael had been unprofessional. What had stopped him from popping his head into her office and just asking whether she *wanted* to be involved? He hadn't needed to, though, had he? She'd already told him that it was another case she'd love to do.

Being pushed out like that was also confusing. And hurtful.

Wasn't he the one who was so good at maintaining a professional distance that he could put his own emotions aside to make life and death decisions for his own daughter?

Why didn't that automatically apply to his wife?

Because he hated her *that* much now? So much that his desire to avoid working closely with her was enough to make cracks appear in that ability to distance himself?

So much for thinking that they might be able to repair their marriage.

It was proving difficult enough to repair a professional relationship.

Not that others seemed to see that. The nurse who was waiting with a sterile towel held in a pair of tongs was smiling.

'It's so good that you and Mr de Luca are going to be working together again. Everybody's really excited about it.'

Not everybody, Abbie thought grimly. But she smiled back as she took the towel to dry her hands.

'It's been a long time, hasn't it?'

'It's never quite the same without you. Nobody else can work with Mr de Luca like you can. He gets quite cross sometimes.'

Abbie's eyebrows rose as she pulled on her gown and then turned so that the nurse could tie it.

It made her feel a little better to know that no one else could partner Rafael in Theatre as well as she could but it wasn't really a surprise, was it?

Their professional relationship had been astonishingly good from the moment they'd first shared an operating theatre together nearly two years ago.

Had any two surgeons ever clicked like that from the get-go? Complemented each other so perfectly it was as if one surgeon had suddenly doubled their skill set. And not only that. They worked in such a similar way that they could anticipate what the other was thinking or about to do. A silent form of communication and co-operation that had quickly become a talking point in their professional circle.

They'd been dubbed the 'dream team.'

And they'd loved that.

But that had been then. The nurse's comment had been a boost but she'd disappeared with an armful of dirty linen back into the changing rooms, and without her enthusiastic support the thought of working side by side with Rafael in Theatre was enough to make Abbie's heart race and her mouth feel dry.

'Get a grip,' she ordered herself sternly, as she pulled on a pair of gloves.

She'd faced far harder things than this in the last few months. She'd had to make decisions and take actions with nothing more than her instinct to guide her at some points. And she'd had to do it firmly and swiftly. Because she'd had to do it alone.

So she could handle this.

Even if she hadn't expected a challenge like this to appear so fast after Ethan's edict that they work together—or face the consequences.

It was only 11:00 p.m. on the same day, for heaven's sake.

A child had been brought in by helicopter for emergency surgery. Unrestrained, the six-year-old had been ejected from a car in a smash. She had multiple injuries, including two broken arms and major facial trauma.

She needed the best surgeons the Lighthouse had to offer.

Abbie was one of them, so that she could deal with the initial repair of the facial tissues and skin in the hope of a result that wouldn't be too disfiguring in the future.

Rafael was the other surgeon and he would be able to handle anything that Abbie couldn't. Thanks to his experience as a general paediatric surgeon before he'd specialised first in oncology and then in reconstructive surgery, there was nothing that could happen in an operating theatre that he couldn't manage, at least in an emergency situation.

Knowing that had always made her feel safe.

Confident.

All she needed to do now was to tap back into that background confidence. And remind herself of just what she'd achieved with Ella's treatment without that umbrella Rafael could provide.

She could do this. Even if Rafael *didn't* really want her in there.

Taking a deep breath and pressing her lips together in a grimly determined line, Abbie crossed her arms in front of her body and turned so that she could use her back to bump open the swinging doors that led into the brightly lit operating room.

Rafael saw Abbie enter the theatre from the scrub room, holding her gloved hands crossed in front of her body, with only her eyes visible between the bottom of her hat and the top of her mask. He watched only until her gaze met his. He held the eye contact for a heartbeat and then nodded once, turning back to the task ahead. It was a simple gesture but one that had become significant to them both in the past. It conveyed satisfaction. Gratitude. Confidence. There was a difficult job to be done. He needed her to be here. She had arrived.

Things were as good as they could be for the moment.

Had he really thought it would be better if they tried to keep their professional lives as separate as their personal lives had become? At least until things had settled down? Thank goodness Ethan and Leo had taken them both to task and made it a professional duty to start working closely together again or it could have been a very long time before he'd had the bonus of having Abbie by his side like this again.

And he did need her. Rafael had been shocked when he'd met the helicopter crew in the emergency department as they'd transferred the care of little Lucy to his team. She'd been stabilised as far as possible in the rural area where the accident had occurred but there were bigger challenges ahead. The first had been dealt with in the emergency department with the help of a specialist paediatric anaesthetist. Securing a definitive airway had been extremely difficult due to the level of facial trauma but at least it had given him time to get used to the horrific injuries. He just wished he'd had more time to warn Abbie before she arrived in Theatre.

'Oh, my God...' He could hear the way Abbie's

breath caught in her throat as she whispered her first reaction.

'It's actually not as bad as it looks,' he told her quietly. 'The jaw's broken in three places and she's lost several teeth. Cheekbones are both fractured and displaced. As is the nose. One ear has been partially amputated but there's no skull fracture or brain haemorrhage. And I think her eyes are okay. It will be easier to see what other damage there is when we get these parts of her face back where they should be. It's the soft-tissue damage that's making things look so bad. The scans are up over there if you want to have a look.'

'Is there a photograph available?' Abbie's initial shock had worn off commendably fast. 'Of what she used to look like?'

'Yes. The grandmother emailed one through. It's been printed out and is beside the viewing screens.'

'Thanks.' Still holding her crossed arms carefully in front of her to avoid any potential contamination and need to rescrub, Abbie moved to examine the images of both the damage and what the little girl's face should look like. It was several minutes before she came back to the table but that was fine. Rafael had a lot of work to do before there would be an area ready for Abbie's delicate touch in repairing delicate vessels and skin tears.

And he needed to concentrate. It wasn't easy, trying to manoeuvre tiny titanium rings into position to try and fix fractured bones back together.

'What's been said about her arms?'

'Colles' fracture on the left. Spiral fracture of the radius and ulna on the right. Looks like she put her arms out to break the fall and then hit the ground face first.

Not pretty but it may have saved her from a bad head injury or internal damage.'

'What's been done for them?'

'The arms?' Rafael didn't need this distraction. 'Just support with back slabs until orthopaedics can come in. It's well down the list of priorities.'

'Do we have the X-rays?'

'They're on digital file. Why?' Rafael needed Abbie to focus on what was more of a concern right now—putting this little's girl's face back together.

'Look at this.'

'I can't.' Rafael was waiting for his senior theatre nurse to suck blood away so that he could see where to place the ring he was holding in his forceps. 'I could use some help here, Abbie.'

But Abbie ignored him. 'Scalpel, thanks,' she ordered a registrar. 'And someone throw some antiseptic on this arm.'

Rafael gave up on the ring and looked up, incredulous. 'What are you *doing*?'

'Opening this arm.' Sure enough, Abbie waited only until a nurse had hurriedly swabbed the skin of a small forearm and then she was slicing into it with her scalpel. Rafael's jaw dropped. He'd never seen her act like this.

Ever.

Seconds later, Abbie dropped the scalpel, having left a long, deep incision in the small arm. She reached for the hand still lying on the table and pressed one of the small fingernails.

'Capillary refill's slow but at least it's there now.'

'It wasn't there before?' Rafael was frowning now. This was the child's right hand, which many might consider even more important to her future quality of life than how her face looked. Had there been a major problem with circulation that had been missed due to his focus on her face? Yes. He could see the unhealthy dark colour the fingers still had. How puffy they were.

'You can still see the swelling in her arm. The fingers were cold and blue. There was no radial pulse.'

'Compartment syndrome...' Rafael took a deep breath. That was why Abbie had incised the muscle casing so decisively. If she hadn't, the result could have been catastrophic. Lucy might have lost her whole hand, let alone the efficient use of it. 'Thank goodness you noticed.'

'If it had started when she was conscious, the pain level would have alerted someone.' Abbie's gaze was in no way accusing. 'It's just lucky I came in late and wanted an overall picture before getting focussed.'

Rafael could only nod. This was not the time or place to tell Abbie that he was proud of her picking up on the complication. And taking control without waiting for his opinion.

Getting that overall impression was a characteristic that Abbie had much more noticeably than he did these days. She was always fastidious in gathering every piece of information she could about a case. Looking at a bigger picture that included things like family circumstances and relationships. A way of looking at a case that invariably led to the kind of emotional involvement in a patient that he preferred to avoid when possible. That was why they'd always made such a good team. Two halves of an amazing whole. The 'dream team,' as Ethan had reminded them only today.

But hadn't he always been the unspoken leader of that team?

No longer, by the look of things. Abbie had changed since the last time they'd worked like this together. She'd become more decisive. More authoritative. More…independent? In here, that was a good thing. It would give him a partner he would enjoy working with even more. Out of here? That was another matter entirely. Persuading Abbie to forgive him and give their marriage another chance might be an uphill battle.

'Call Orthopaedics,' she was instructing a nurse. 'We'll need them here sooner rather than later. And someone find a dressing to cover this wound in the meantime, please.' She stepped around the table to stand beside Rafael.

So close that their shoulders were touching.

'Now…' Abbie was peering into the area Rafael was working on to align the small jaw again. 'Can I start debriding the cheek tissue? I'd like to get an idea of how much skin we've got left to work with. I suspect we're going to need some grafts.'

Rafael absorbed the feeling of having her this close. He could hear the calm confidence with which she was now assessing the work she had come here to do. Suddenly it was easy to push anything personal and negative into a space that had no relevance in here. He knew without any doubt that within minutes he and Abbie would be working together seamlessly. The way they always had. His own confidence soared. They could do this. Between them they would get the foundation work done that would end up with little Lucy looking as close to the way she'd looked before the accident as was humanly possible.

He hadn't felt this inspired—this *happy* in his work—since...well, since Abbie had left.

How had he not realised how much he'd missed this?

Because he had isolated himself emotionally from his work so effectively?

The way he'd isolated himself from his wife and daughter?

That was in the past. He'd learned his lesson. With the resolution that things were going to change from now on, Rafael didn't dismiss the pleasure of having Abbie working beside him. Instead, he channelled it into making sure he did the best work he was capable of.

Talk about diving into the deep end.

Six hours later, Abbie all but staggered into the changing room where she'd stored her clothes in her old locker. The one beside Rafe's.

She headed for the closest shower, which offered a private area that included a slatted wooden bench seat beneath a hook on which to hang her dry clothes. Having hung what she would change back into on the hook, however, Abbie didn't immediately close the door or turn on the shower to let the water get hot. Instead, she sank down on the wooden seat and closed her eyes for a moment.

Everything ached. Her back and feet seemed to have totally forgotten their ability to stand in one spot for so long without major discomfort. She had cramp in her fingers from the fierce control she had exerted to make every one of the countless sutures she'd made as perfect as possible. Her eyes felt gritty, with a fatigue that was numbing her mind and making it impossible to think of anything but finding the energy to get up and turn on that shower.

And yet Abbie was smiling as she rolled her head in a slow circle, trying to get the painful kinks out of her neck.

How *good* had that been?

Challenging. Intense. But *so* satisfying. She hadn't hidden her skills beneath a deep layer of rust like she'd feared. Even better, she and Rafael had worked together just as they always had. There'd even been at least one of those magic moments when that complete harmony had kicked in and it had felt like it was one surgeon who happened to have four hands.

Finally, Abbie found the strength to stand up and turn on the hot water. She knew it would take at least a minute to heat up, unless they'd made some big improvements in the plumbing while she'd been away, so she stood there waiting and tried rolling her head again because there was one particularly painful spot between her shoulder blades.

'Sore neck?'

The query was accompanied by the metallic scrape of a locker door opening. Rafael must be feeling every bit as exhausted as she was. They'd both gone to Recovery with their small patient to watch over her as her level of consciousness lifted but Rafe had stayed longer, wanting to adjust the level of sedation they would keep her under.

Something stopped Abbie turning around. They had just spent a considerable period of time working so well

together. Was it that she didn't want to spoil that by
finding that he was avoiding eye contact, perhaps? Or
that she might see resentment that would confirm he'd
only sent for her because Leo and Ethan had hauled
them over the coals about *not* working together?

She put her hand under the stream of water to check
the temperature and to excuse her not turning around.
'How's Lucy doing?'

'Very well. When I've had a quick shower, I'll find
her grandmother and take her to visit Lucy in Recovery.'

His voice was getting louder with every word. Good
grief, had he stepped into this shower cubicle with her?
Abbie tensed, ready to turn, but then froze. Apart from
the sound of the running water, there was an odd stillness. Maybe Rafe had just gone past the open door to
get a towel or something. She might turn and he would
be nowhere to be seen and even in the split second
when she imagined that possibility, she could also feel
the thud of disappointment it would create. But, even
as that flitted through her brain, she felt the touch of
his hands on her shoulders. His thumbs digging into
her spine as they made small circles over her knotted
muscles. He knew *exactly* where that sharp ache tended
to settle, didn't he?

'Oh…' Abbie let her head droop. 'That feels *amazing…*'

It was by no means the first time she'd been treated
to a neck massage after a tough stint in Theatre so it
was no surprise he could do it so well. It was, however,
the last thing Abbie had expected right now.

What was happening here? The magic she'd wanted
when she'd first seen Rafael again and had imagined

an embrace that could wipe all out all the grief they'd given each other?

Certainly the sensations Rafael's fingers were conjuring up were enough to wipe out rational thought. Like worrying about any hot water that was being wasted. Tendrils of a pleasure-pain mix were shooting down her spine and arcing right through her body.

But it was just a neck massage. If they hadn't happened to be standing in a shower cubicle it was something that could be perfectly acceptable between any colleagues who were friends and understood the aftermath of the physical challenge they'd just shared. If she started thinking it was intended to be intimate she could well be lining herself up for disappointment.

'Thanks.' Abbie's movement was subtle but the touch of Rafael's hand vanished instantly. She could feel him taking a step back even as she turned her head to smile at him.

'We did it,' she said.

'Indeed.' Rafael had one hand on the door. He raised his other hand to rub his own neck. 'I'm sure Ethan and Leo will be delighted to hear how well we managed to work together.'

Oh, yes...that disappointment had only been waiting to hit Abbie hard enough to make her lose her emotional footing.

'That wasn't what I meant,' she muttered.

Rafael leaned closer to hear her. Was it intentional that the movement pushed the door closed behind him? 'What *did* you mean?'

'That we put Lucy back together. I...I think she's going to get a good result.' Sudden, unwelcome tears stung the back of her eyes. Abbie turned them towards the shower so that Rafael wouldn't see. There was steam billowing out over the top of the curtain now. At least she'd be able to have a good cry when she was under that stream of water. She needed Rafe to go away. Now.

But he didn't. 'We certainly did,' he said. 'And what's more, you probably saved her hand, Abbie. Well done, you.'

The praise was sweet. So sweet that Abbie couldn't hold back the tears now. She had to swipe at them with her hand.

'Oh…Abbie…*cara*…'

Rafe was turning her to face him. Tilting her face up with gentle pressure under her chin. The warmth of the steam around them had nothing on what was sparking between them and had it dampened the oxygen level as well? Abbie's lips parted as she tried to find a new breath.

The caring tone of the endearment Rafael had used still hung between them and it made the flicker of desire in his eyes totally irresistible. Abbie couldn't look away. Her fatigue was forgotten as her body strained towards his, her mind willing him to touch her. To *kiss* her.

She had no idea who moved first, and what did it matter?

This was no gentle reunion kind of kiss. It was how Abbie had dreamed it might be. An incandescent moment that would burn everything else into oblivion. A leap straight back into the fierce passion they had discovered the first time they'd touched each other. A passion that had only grown more powerful the more they'd learned about each other's bodies.

He knew exactly what took her over the edge. The slide of his tongue against the inside of her lip and the way it tangled with the very tip of hers. The slide of his hands inside her clothing and the way those strong hands cupped her buttocks and pulled her against that hardness she knew so well. Wanted so badly...

But somehow it didn't feel right. Maybe it was becoming aware of the splash of water beside them and remembering where they were and how inappropriate this was.

Or...maybe it was something much bigger than that.

In the same way that she had seen the massage as being nothing more than a physical action, a part of Abbie's brain could see that this was only sex.

Passionate, exciting, mind-blowing sex certainly. The kind that had sealed their initial relationship and had led to Ella's conception and had had them rushing headlong into marriage and a lifetime commitment, in fact. A kind that had been enough to keep them sane during the terrible times they'd been through in the course of Ella's illness but, at the end of the day, it was just that. Sex.

And perhaps that wasn't enough any more and that was what didn't feel right.

It was Abbie whose hands stopped moving and touching. Whose lips stilled. Who wriggled free of the intimate contact of their lower bodies.

'We can't do this,' she gasped.

Rafael's gaze slid towards the shower and he sighed. 'Come home with me, then.'

'No.' Abbie shook her head. 'I don't just mean we can't do it *here*.'

There was bewilderment in his gaze now. He had no idea why Abbie had pulled away.

'Can't you see? It's not going to solve anything, Rafe.'

He still didn't understand. And he didn't believe her. He thought he was being rejected and at the flicker of pain—anger, even—Abbie's heart sank. She was doing it again, wasn't she? Attacking his pride. The surest route to strengthening the barrier between them instead of starting to dismantle it.

But she could also see the internal struggle going on. The effort he was making.

His voice was raw. 'Then what is going to solve it, Abbie? *Tell* me.'

There was nothing Abbie wanted more than to tell him.

If only she *knew*.

Rafael waited for a heartbeat. And then another. And then, muttering something in Italian that was probably a curse, he turned and left.

A second later, Abbie heard the bang of a locker door. And then the thump of the changing-room doors being pushed open. Rafael was going somewhere else to shower and who could blame him?

What had she done?

Blown the best chance she could have had to reconnect with the man she loved?

The fatigue came back in a wave that made it unbelievably hard to get on with what she had to do. The feel of her own hands on her skin as she pulled off the scrubs only reminded Abbie of the touch of Rafael's hands and made her feel worse.

What *had* she been thinking?

* * *

There was very little traffic around at this time of day, which was just as well because Rafael wasn't paying much attention as he gunned his car in the direction of the only safe place he could think of. His home.

Abbie didn't want him.

Her body did, that much had been obvious, but her heart didn't and that was what mattered.

How the hell could he let her know how much he still loved her if he wasn't allowed to touch her? To let his *body* say the things that were too hard to put into words?

She was being unfair. Shutting them both out of the one area of their relationship they'd never had any problems with. Making sure the spotlight was shining onto the battleground that the rest of their relationship had become.

Why?

The slap of his open hand on the steering-wheel was hard enough to be painful but it didn't shut up the annoying voice in the back of his head. Beneath the burning frustration and the simmering anger it was still there—the faint but insistent message that suggested Abbie was right. That reconnecting sexually would only push the destructive differences under a carpet. That it wouldn't *solve* anything.

But she couldn't even tell him what would.

The way he slammed the car door shut probably woke up several neighbours but Rafael didn't care.

Maybe neither of them knew.

Because the solution didn't exist.

CHAPTER FIVE

'Mum-mum-mum...'

Ella was standing in her cot and she flung her arms into the air when her mother entered the room.

'Hey, baby girl...' Abbie reached into the cot and gathered Ella into her arms, careful as always not to tangle the IV line. 'How are you? I've hardly seen you *all* day and I've missed you *so* much.'

'Mum-mum-mum...' Ella's tiny hands were busy, touching Abbie's hair and then her face. And then she rubbed her nose on Abbie's collarbone and made a grizzling sound. Abbie's gaze flew to Melanie, the nurse who was moving to straighten the cot.

'She's just hungry. I was waiting to give her her bottle in case you made it back in time. I'll go and heat it up now.'

'Thanks, Mel. So she's been okay today?'

'Good as gold. They had a good chat about her on ward rounds. Everybody's very excited about her being such a success story. I think there's a bit of competition over who's going to write up the case history and get it published in a journal.'

'They might have to compete with the guys in New York for that.'

Melanie smiled. 'I'm staying out of it. Bottom line was they only came in to brighten their day, I think. Nothing like a wee miracle like our Ella to make everybody feel better about life in general and work in particular.'

'Mmm.' Abbie cuddled her daughter, rocking her gently. Ella had put her thumb into her mouth and the vigorous sucking noises made both women smile.

'She's starving.' Melanie had picked up the huge teddy bear taking up half the cot, obviously planning to move it out of the way for the night.

The thumb came out of Ella's mouth with a popping noise. *'No-o-o-o...'*

Abbie could feel the small body tensing in her arms. Small lungs expanding to let rip with an uncharacteristic wail.

'Don't take it away,' she told Melanie. 'She's in love.'

'But it's so massive. It takes up most of the cot.'

Abbie's smile was rueful. 'It's pink. And it sparkles. And it was a present from Daddy.'

A somewhat loaded silence fell as Melanie put the tutu-clad bear back into the cot.

'Has...has Rafe been in today?'

'Twice.' Melanie nodded. 'You were visiting Lucy the first time and he was here for a bit this afternoon when you were in Theatre. He asked what time she got her bedtime bottle and said he'd try and get back.' She chewed her lip and the glance at Abbie suggested there was something she was debating whether to say.

Abbie could guess what it was. Rafael wanted to be the one to give Ella her bottle and put her to bed.

And that was something she wasn't prepared to give up.

Melanie said nothing as she went away to heat the bottle. Abbie settled herself in the armchair with Ella, trying to ignore the prickle of guilt at her determination not to willingly share the next half hour or so of her life. When Melanie returned Abbie asked the nurse to dim the lights in the room and then suggested that she take a break. She'd call if she needed any assistance getting Ella tucked up for the night later.

Bliss. Abbie adjusted the tilt of the bottle as Ella clutched it with both hands and smiled as her daughter relaxed into her sucking and lifted her gaze to meet her mother's. The pure joy of that eye contact with her precious baby as she sucked on the only bottle she had now was the highlight of her day. Just as good as the early days when she'd been able to breastfeed Ella. It was a time when the love she had for this little person was the only thing that mattered and it was huge enough to push everything else to one side.

During the dark days of being alone with such a sick child, it had been the one thing that had kept Abbie sane and offered hope. On the worst nights, it had only been cuddling her to sleep and now that she was well enough to enjoy her warm milk, the hope was even stronger and this time together something to look forward to even more.

It was *their* time. Surely a reward that she had earned?

Her breath escaped in a long, contented sigh as Ella's eyes flickered shut and then snapped open again in determination to stay awake. She wasn't the only one who treasured this time together. She wished she'd been there for the consultants' ward round today but she could imagine the looks and smiles that had been exchanged. Being with Ella did brighten everyone's day. The heaviness around her own heart was finally lifting, too.

The bottle was almost finished and the dead weight of the baby in her arms suggested that sleep had arrived when the door opened softly. Had the sudden tension of seeing Rafael transferred itself to Ella? The baby stirred and whimpered but then settled again, her mouth now slack around the teat of the bottle.

'Ohh…' Rafael quietly shifted the small upright chair and seated himself by Ella's head. 'I'm too late.'

'She was hungry.' The prickle of guilt came back again and this time it was intensified by the emotional turmoil Abbie had been in ever since she'd rejected Rafael sexually in the changing room yesterday. 'Would you like to hold her for a bit before she goes to bed?'

The question was clearly redundant. Big hands slid over her arms and beneath Ella to transfer the weight. Again, Ella stirred and whimpered but soft Italian words of love soothed her within seconds and then Rafael just sat, his head bowed over his daughter, his arms cradling her as if she were the most precious thing on earth.

Abbie was caught. Half lying in the reclining chair, it would take a huge effort to get up and leave father and daughter alone and it would only disturb the moment. Or maybe that was just an excuse. Maybe what had really captured her was the acute awareness of this man beside her.

The...*longing*.

He must have come straight from a shower because his dark curls were damp and she could actually *feel* the warmth coming from his skin. Could smell the fresh scent of soap and maleness. Abbie's gaze was locked on Rafael's hands as he held Ella. Such strong hands with those long, long fingers and the dusting of dark hair on the top. It had been his hands that had first stirred her attraction to him, hadn't it? When he'd been waving them in the air to illustrate something he had been telling her about a case. Or had it been his eyes? The way they could hold her like a physical caress?

What would happen if she reached out and touched one of those hands now? If, when he looked up at her, she gave him the silent message that she'd been wrong. That being together again in the most intimate way possible *could* be the answer to dissolving the barrier between them?

It had always worked in the past to solve an argument, hadn't it?

'Do you remember the couch?' The soft words seemed to come from nowhere and Abbie was as surprised as Rafael as his head jerked up.

'*Scusi?*'

'The couch. The white one.'

The supremely comfortable, feather-stuffed, totally impractical and ridiculously expensive white couch. It had been the week before their wedding and they'd been out shopping for furniture in the euphoria that had followed a successful offer on their new apartment. The same euphoria that had made them view Abbie's unexpected pregnancy as nothing more than a sign that they were meant to be together. For ever.

'Of course I remember. I sit on it every day.'

'Do you remember what happened when we found it in the shop?'

Rafael seemed to be ignoring her. He rocked Ella and pressed a gentle kiss to her head. And then he sighed and gave one of those eloquent shrugs.

'So it was our first fight. What of it? What is the point of remembering it now?

'Because…'

Because it was important, even though Abbie wasn't quite sure why.

'Do you remember what you told me? About your parents? About them never arguing?'

'It was true. They didn't.'

'Because your mother did whatever your father ordered to keep the peace. You said it was the Italian way and the husband was the head of the household and his word was law and arguing was a sign of disrespect. And I said it was the Victorian way and it wasn't going to work for us because I deserved just as much respect, and if it dented your Italian pride then you'd have to suck it up and get over it.'

A snort escaped Rafael. 'I remember. How could I forget?'

'And what did you do then?'

Something rueful tugged at one corner of his mouth. 'I gave you an order.'

'Mmm.'

He had 'ordered' her into bed. It had been a joke, accompanied by a kiss that had demonstrated the kind of passion Abbie knew would take her straight to paradise. The argument about the couch had suddenly become irrelevant and Rafael's pride had been soothed.

And they'd bought the damned couch. A week after it had been installed in the apartment Rafael had spilt a glass of red wine on it and the ugly stain was irreparable. Abbie had gone out and purchased a large, blue throw to cover it. A throw in the colour of the couch *she* had wanted to buy in the first place.

'It was a couch,' Rafael growled. 'A stupid piece of furniture. We could buy another one tomorrow if it mattered.'

'It's not the couch that matters.'

Abbie suddenly realised why she'd dredged up such an ancient disagreement. The reason they'd fought in the first place had just been a practice run for the fight they would have over Ella's treatment. Rafael's pride getting in the way of any kind of compromise had led to the awful ultimatum about the future of their marriage. 'It's the way we resolved the fight we had *about* the couch.'

Rafael's glare told Abbie just how much she *had* hurt him yesterday. But there was something else there, too. Confusion? That was understandable.

'The stain's still there, Rafe,' Abbie said softly. 'It just got covered up.'

He shook his head and muttered something incomprehensible in Italian.

'The reason we fought is still there, too. We never talked about it again, did we? We never tried to resolve anything by talking about it. We just…went to bed.'

'And it *worked*,' Rafael said fiercely. 'It was where

we could show each other how much we loved each other.'

'It didn't work when it was really important. When it was about Ella.'

Rafael was silent. He looked down at the sleeping baby in his arms. Abbie could only watch and wait. And hope, desperately, that she had managed to convey at least a part of how important this seemed to her.

But maybe she hadn't.

'It's time Fiorella was in her bed.' Rafael stood up, careful not to disturb Ella. He carried her to the cot and put her down, checking that her IV line and the pump attached to it was still intact and functioning. He tucked Ears in the crook of one arm and then drew the blanket over the small body. Then he reached to pick up the oversized bear at the foot of the cot.

'Don't take it out,' Abbie said. 'She'll cry if it's not there when she wakes up.'

Rafael looked over at her, his eyebrows raised.

'She adores it. Especially the sparkles.'

Abbie smiled. Rafael smiled back at her.

'Thank you,' she said then.

'What for?'

'Talking to me.' If nothing else, Abbie was beginning to see what the real barrier between them was. It had been there all along, hadn't it? They just hadn't paid any attention to it until it had been too late.

She saw Rafael taking a slow, inward breath. He held her gaze. 'Maybe,' he said slowly, 'we should talk some more.' A corner of his mouth twitched. 'Instead of going to bed?'

Abbie tried to smile but her lips wobbled. 'I'd like that.'

Rafael stepped closer. 'I could take you out. For dinner…or a coffee. We…we could go to that place you love in the park. The…what's it called? The Moo Cow?'

They'd been around a baby for long enough to change the way they thought and spoke, hadn't they? Abbie smiled again. 'The Cow and Coffee Bean.'

In Regent's Park. The buffer between their home and the clinic, it had always been perfect as an escape for some exercise and fresh air.

'Like…like a date?'

He inclined his head. '*Si*. Like a date.'

Like starting again, even? Maybe this was exactly what they needed. Swept along in the whirlwind of passion that had defined their early relationship and both so committed to their careers, had they ever stayed out of bed long enough when they'd been together to really get to know each other?

She could smile now. 'I'd love that, Rafe. Coffee. And a walk. It would be perfect.'

Perfect for what? A first date? A new beginning?

'It's Saturday tomorrow. I'm sure we can both find a suitable time to be together.'

Abbie held his gaze. Was it too much to hope that that was what they both wanted out of this? To be really *together* again?

'I'm sure we can.'

His nod was satisfied. Rafael touched his fingers to the top of Ella's head in farewell and then stepped away from the cot. For a heartbeat he looked as if he was going to step towards Abbie's chair. As if he wanted to kiss her goodnight. But she could see the way he paused just long enough to think about it and then controlled himself. How hard he was trying when he simply smiled and left.

Fickle spring weather decided to turn on a stunning April day on Saturday.

It felt as though fate was on his side as Rafael waited at the agreed meeting point at the start of the Broad Walk, just beside the zoo. The shriek of overexcited monkeys somewhere was having the opposite effect, however. Almost like maniacal laughter that was taunting him and setting his nerves on edge.

Did he really think that a pleasant walk on a sunny day was going to be enough to win Abbie back?

And what were they going to talk about? *Dio*...but women loved to talk, didn't they? To pick things apart and give them far more importance than they deserved to have. Far more power that could be so destructive.

Even a few words could destroy things. And once they were uttered there was no way you could ever take them back.

If you take Ella away to do this then our marriage is over.

Rafael pushed his fingers through his hair. He wished he had never uttered those fateful words. He wished Abbie had just let him take her to bed where he knew he could have put things right. He wished those damned monkeys would just shut *up* for a minute. Why wasn't Abbie here yet? Had she changed her mind about this date?

His breath came out in a whoosh of relief as a black

cab swooped into the kerb and Abbie climbed out. She was wearing a blue dress he'd never seen before, with no sleeves and a tight bodice and a swirling skirt that reached almost to her ankles above sandal-clad feet. Her hair was loose and shone like a halo in the sunshine and she had a cardigan draped over the arm that held a straw bag and made it look as if she was off to a picnic.

She looked...like the woman he loved. A beautiful, English rose. With that illusion of fragility that was so sexy when you discovered the steely determination and passion that lay beneath.

'Abbie...*salve, cara*. You look *cosi bella*.'

'Thanks.'

Abbie felt strangely shy. As if this really was a 'date.' A time to meet someone who was virtually a stranger to explore what you had in common with them and whether it might be enough to build a future on together. The mix of hope, excitement and physical attraction felt like a flock of butterflies in her stomach. She hadn't felt like this since...well, since her first date with Rafael.

'You...look pretty good yourself, Rafe.'

What an understatement. Old, soft, faded jeans and a black T-shirt. That leather jacket that was also so old it was nearly as soft as the jeans. Rafael pushed the sleeves up a little further, which made his look more casual. And definitely sexier. But his expression dismissed the compliment.

'In these old jeans? I think not.'

Rafael suppressed the urge to take Abbie's hand but couldn't identify what it was that held him back. A sense of Abbie being as tense as he was perhaps?

'Let's get away from here,' he said. 'These monkeys are driving me *pazzo*.'

Abbie's laugh sounded a little forced to her own ears but some of the tension evaporated. 'They are noisy today, aren't they? Can you still hear them from home sometimes?'

She could remember the first time they'd heard unusual sounds coming from the direction of the zoo. Guessing what could be making the sound had become a game as they'd stood in their garden or taken an evening walk down by the canal. Was that an elephant? Or a lion?

Sometimes Rafael would try and imitate the sound until Abbie laughed so hard he would pretend to take great offence and she'd have to soothe his pride. And that had never been difficult. She only had to tell him how wonderful she thought he was, even if he couldn't make an elephant noise to save himself. She only had to distract him with a kiss or two.

Happy times.

For a moment, Abbie was sure Rafael was thinking about the same thing. But then a shadow passed over his face and he shrugged.

'I wouldn't know. I don't seem to spend that much time there these days.' Rafael could see the flash of disappointment in Abbie's eyes. Had he made it sound like he didn't want to be in their home any more? 'Work's been so busy, you know?'

'Mmm. Ethan told me how hard you've been working while I was away.'

While she'd been away. There it was again. The huge thing that lay between them that Rafael had no idea how to make go away. Was talking about it really going to help?

They weren't even talking now. Just walking side by side in silence amongst the throng of Londoners out to enjoy a Saturday afternoon in the sunshine. Trees were vibrant with the fresh, new green of leaves just beginning to unfurl for the new season. Ancient trunks had skirts of bluebells and daffodils. There were young mothers pushing prams, a father giving a toddler a ride on his shoulders, small children on bicycles and tricycles, teenagers weaving with dangerous speed through the pedestrians on their skateboards...

'Mind out!' Rafael's arm was around Abbie's shoulders in a flash, guiding her out of the path of a speeding youth. The feel of the bare skin of her shoulder beneath his hand was a jolt of sensation that arrowed through his entire body. Hastily, he dropped the contact. Abbie didn't want this, did she?

Oddly, the touch of Rafael's hand on her bare shoulder had felt less intimate than his automatic instinct to protect her. And it had felt...wonderful. She might have had to stand completely on her own feet for the last few months and become stronger because of it but it didn't mean that she didn't want to feel cherished.

Loved.

The speed with which he dropped the contact was disappointing. Abbie bit her lip, trying to think of something to say.

'Do you think it will be this crowded in the coffee shop?'

'I expect so.' Rafael could feel himself scowling. If they couldn't talk to each other in the relative privacy of being outside, what was it going to be like in the café? Would they sit in silence and sip their lattes amidst the buzz of the conversation of others? With the tension between them steadily increasing?

'I know.' Abbie tilted her head, peering past people to see where they were exactly. 'Let's get coffee to go from the cart over there and take it to the Secret Garden. That's always quieter.'

It didn't take long because they knew the route so well. Off the Inner Circle and through the large circular garden with the statue of Hylas in the pond. You could see the imposing structure of St John's Lodge from here, reputedly owned by the Sultan of Brunei these days. But they weren't after an imposing view.

Rafael led the way on a wide grass path, past the blossoms of the dog roses and the twisted trees of white wisteria. Beneath a leafy arbour to the circle of lime trees around a stone urn. And...*yes*...the covered seat at one end of the garden was unoccupied at the moment.

For a moment, Abbie lost all sense of time. She wasn't here with her estranged husband, trying to find a way to reconnect. She was here with the man she was head over heels in love with. Wondering why he was leading to her such a secluded, *romantic* spot. Why the destination seemed so important, the mission so urgent.

And then the reality of the difference this time kicked in and Abbie's step faltered. It was an audible effort to catch her breath.

Rafael almost groaned aloud when he sensed Abbie's step faltering. What had he been thinking in following this particular route? He had led Abbie back to the exact spot he'd proposed to her.

Closing his eyes for a heartbeat, Rafael cursed himself for his insensitivity and wondered how he could rescue the situation, but then he heard Abbie take a deep breath.

'Perfect,' she murmured.

Rafael's eyes flew open. 'It is?'

'Mmm.' Abbie offered him a smile that was almost shy. 'If we're going to start again, what better place than back where it all started?'

They were going to start again? There was *hope*? And he'd chosen the perfect place? Rafael could feel his chest expand just a little. This time he didn't suppress the urge to take Abbie's hand and he didn't let go until they were seated side by side on the small bench. They could see people through the arbour but, for the moment, they had this small patch of the park to themselves.

'So…' Rafael cleared his throat. He was ready to face whatever was coming even if his heart did seem to be beating faster than usual. 'What shall we talk about?'

Abbie closed her eyes for a moment. What did he think they needed to talk about? The weather? The thought almost made her smile because that was exactly what they'd talked about the last time they'd sat on this bench. They'd actually had to brush snow away before they'd sat down and she'd been freezing and Rafael had opened his coat and tucked her in beside him. He wanted to keep her warm, he'd said. To look after her. For ever.

She opened her eyes but didn't look up at Rafael.

'Us,' she said quietly. 'That's what we need to talk about.'

Oh, no… Rafael drained the last of his coffee. This was worse than he'd feared. Abbie wanted to analyse their relationship and pick it apart. His voice came out more harshly than he had intended. 'What about us?'

Abbie met his gaze. There was a tiny frown line above her eyes. 'Well…we don't really know each other, do we?'

'*Pfff…*' Rafael couldn't help the incredulous sound. Or the movement of his hands, one of which slashed through the air while the other crushed the empty paper cup it was holding and dropped it on the bench beside him. It was an effort not to jump to his feet as the words tried to rush past each other to get out.

'Of course we know each other. We're *married*. We…' *Love each other?* No. He couldn't speak for Abbie. He changed tack. 'I know you, Abbie. I know that you like two sugars in your coffee. That you hate lacy knickers because they make you itch. That people who hurt their children make you very, very angry.' He was counting off his list on his fingers. 'That one of your favourite surgeries is making new little ears for children. That—'

But Abbie was shaking her head as she set her own cup carefully aside. 'I mean something that goes deeper than that. You don't know *why* I did what I did. Why I had to take Ella to New York even if it was going to mean the end of the marriage that meant so much to me.'

'But I do…' Rafael swallowed hard. 'I know that your little sister, Sophie, died when you were only twelve. That you felt your parents had failed her because they refused to try any treatment that might have added to her suffering when they knew it would gain nothing but a little more time. But that was different. It wasn't leukaemia and *we* tried everything we could even it *was* only going to give us a little more time. The idea that the treatment in New York could really work was...'

Way too much of a miracle to hope for. Rafael's words trailed into silence. It had worked, hadn't it? He'd been wrong.

'You knew the reason,' Abbie agreed quietly. 'But you didn't understand how I *felt* about it because if you had you would have been there with me, Rafe. By my side. And it really hurt that you weren't.'

It hurt thinking about Sophie, too. The little sister she'd lost. The way her family had fallen apart. Sophie had been ill for so long that family life had centred exclusively on her and Abbie had felt almost invisible. The feeling had only strengthened after her sister's death. Had her parents been too afraid to love her too much in case they lost her, too? Did they come to blame each other—the way she secretly did—for not having tried hard enough to save Sophie?

Or did all the love just die because it got smothered under the grief?

She'd tried so hard....

She'd been driven to fight for Ella instead of standing back and watching her die. But her new family had still fallen apart, hadn't it? Was it impossible to win in a dreadful situation like that?

Rafael could see the pain he'd caused by reminding Abbie of what she'd lost as a child. And by not being there for her in New York when she'd needed him. What could he say?

'I'm sorry.' The words were raw. 'I was wrong.'

This time it was Abbie who took hold of his hand. 'It's not just your fault, Rafe. Don't you see? I couldn't understand why you were so opposed to it, any more than you could understand me. Oh, I knew how much you hated to see children suffering when there couldn't be a positive outcome, and that's why you changed specialties to get away from oncology, but this was your own daughter. I just didn't get it.' She bit her lip. 'We don't get each other.'

'Get?' Sometimes, if he was really fired up about something, his languages could tangle in his head and make him miss subtleties.

'Understand. No…it's more than that, I think. If you really love someone and you can understand *why* they feel the way they do, then you'll support them, even if you might not agree with whatever it is.'

Rafael turned the words over in his head. 'You're right,' he said into the quietness. 'I should have supported you.'

'And maybe I should have supported *you*.'

'*Che cosa*? But I was wrong. You only have to look at Ella to see that I was wrong.'

'But if I'd understood *why*, maybe we could have changed things. All I could see was someone who was being a doctor, not a father. Or a husband. Someone who couldn't *feel* what I was feeling.'

It was true. He had isolated himself emotionally. Circumstances had then isolated him physically.

But they were closer now, surely? They were talking about things they'd never talked about before.

'It won't happen again,' he told Abbie. 'I love you. I love Ella. I want to be a good father and husband.'

He touched her face. Cupping it gently the way he always had before trying to convey his sincerity with a tender kiss.

But Abbie pulled away from his touch. 'Don't,' she whispered. 'Please, don't.'

It was too bittersweet, that touch. She could give in to it so easily but it still wouldn't solve anything. It would still be a throw covering a stain.

Rafael dropped his hand. He turned to stare straight ahead and Abbie followed his line of vision. Through the arbour she could see a young couple, wrapped in each other's arms, sharing a passionate kiss. As intent on each other as Abbie and Rafael had been when they'd first come here together. As oblivious to the twists of fate that might pull them apart in the future.

Rafael had to turn away from the sight of the young lovers. He and Abbie had been that close once. He'd hoped that they might get that close again today but they were as far apart as they had been before they had come here, weren't they? Talking had solved nothing.

'I'm still hurting, Rafe.' Abbie spoke so quietly he had to strain to hear the words. 'And I can't go through anything like this again. I know Ella needs her father as much as she needs her mother right now but...I need time. I need to be sure.'

Rafael closed his eyes. She wasn't the only one who was still hurting. 'And how did you think it made me feel, Abbie? When you wouldn't listen to anything I had to say? When you took Ella away and I was so sure I would never see her again? Never hold her? You're not the only one who was hurt.'

'I know. And I'm sorry.'

Rafael's fingers found a tangled part of his hair but he shoved them through the obstruction, welcoming the pain. 'Can we ever get past this? What do we do now?'

'I hope we can get past this.' But Abbie's smile was shaky. Unsure? 'And now? I think we should go and spend some time with our daughter.'

It was Abbie who picked up the empty coffee cups and found a rubbish bin to put them in. She put on the soft cardigan she'd been carrying because there were a few clouds in the sky now and when the sunlight dimmed, the temperature dropped noticeably. The picnic feel to the day was gone. The date was over. They walked out of the Secret Garden and back through the main park in silence but it was a different kind of silence from the one when they'd first entered the park together.

Things were out in the open. Yes, their marriage was still on the line but it seemed that they both *wanted* to repair it, at least. Surely that was a good thing?

'Maybe, one day soon,' he said, 'we'll be able to bring Ella to the park. To show her the Secret Garden.'

'I hope so,' Abbie responded. 'And we could take her to the zoo.'

'To see the monkeys.' The unenthusiastic tone made them both look at each other. And then they both smiled.

She understood. And if they did go to the zoo, she would know that it was a generous act on his part because those monkeys drove him *pazzo*.

He could feel his heart lift. The connection was there. And the love. Surely it was going to be possible to build a bridge over the troubled waters that still lay between them?

It had to be possible, Rafael decided as they went

through the ornate iron gates and he raised his arm to flag down a taxi.

It was as simple as that, really.

CHAPTER SIX

GIFTS WERE STARTING to pile up in Ella's room.

While the big pink bear was the frontrunner in the popularity stakes, everybody who looked after Ella was enjoying the growing stack of bright picture books and the toys, especially the board with the animal pictures and the buttons that made the appropriate noise for the animal when Ella pushed it. Her attempts to imitate the noises made them all laugh.

And Rafael had a new audience on which to try out his own animal noises.

'This is a lion, Ella. *Rrrroahhh…* You'll hear them when we take you to the zoo one day. You might even hear them at home. And this is a monkey. *Eeek, eeek, eeek.*'

The noises made both Ella and Abbie grin but they had yet to hear their little girl giggle again. What would it take?

'You don't have to bring a present every time you come, Rafe. You're spoiling her.'

'I want her to look forward to seeing me.' But Rafael put the bag he was carrying today on the floor and leaned on the edge of the cot, watching as Abbie caught the small, waving arms and pushed them gently into the sleeves of her sleep suit.

'Mum-mum-mum,' Ella crowed.

'That's me.' Abbie snapped some fastenings closed. 'Mama. Can you say papa?'

Ella stared up at her, her eyes round.

'Papa?' she repeated encouragingly.

Ella grinned. 'Mum-mum-mum.'

'I think that's the only word she knows.' Rafael was also smiling but Abbie could sense his disappointment. She tried to distract him.

'She's pretty good at "no." You should have heard her at lunchtime when I tried to persuade her to eat some carrots.'

'She doesn't like carrots?'

'Not yet. Same with pumpkin.'

'Maybe it's the colour she doesn't like.'

'Hmm… You could be right.' Abbie smiled and caught Rafael's gaze. 'It does clash with pink, doesn't it?'

His answering smile was swift and, for a heartbeat, things felt good. There were more of these moments now, when it felt like there was a real connection between them again. The time they'd spent in the park together had been a good starting point but, even with more time with both of them here with Ella and more moments when they were in tune with each other, that distance between them didn't appear to be shrinking.

Ella was the driving force behind Abbie's motivation for trying to repair her marriage. She desperately wanted her daughter to grow up with a loving father in her life. For them all to make a *real* family. But the connection had to there between her parents, too. It had to be more than physical and it had to be strong enough to last the distance. While they were reaching out tentatively to see if they could find and build on that kind of connection, sadly it was Ella who was making things harder.

Oh, she loved the presents. And she loved seeing her daddy and having a cuddle. As long as she wasn't tired. Or sore. Or hungry. Or had a dirty nappy or anything else that was making life a little less joyful. At those times, she only wanted Abbie.

Mum-mum-mum.

As the days passed it was obvious that Rafael was feeling excluded. It wasn't just an Italian's pride that was being dented. Any father would feel disheartened by the preference that Ella made crystal clear when it was needed. And it wasn't something that Abbie could fix, was it? Rafael hadn't been there for such a long time. A quarter of Ella's life. Was it any wonder that the baby saw him as a visitor in her life? That she expected her mother to provide everything from food to comfort?

Abbie glanced at her watch. Any minute now and the nurse would arrive with Ella's night-time bottle. And Rafael was here. She should let him feed her.

Maybe it was the biggest olive branch she could offer?

She couldn't put it into words but when she picked Ella up and offered her to Rafe as the nurse came in with the bottle of warm milk, she could see that he understood how significant this was. The way his gaze held hers with a flash of surprise and then gratitude and then a flood of warmth that felt like pure love was enough to bring a huge lump to her throat.

Rafael sat down in the armchair with Ella in his arms. She was happy enough to lie there until she caught sight of the bottle. The hungry whimper was followed by her head craning so far sideways Abbie feared for her neck.

'Mum-mum-mum...' Small arms were reaching out for her.

Rafael chased her mouth with the teat of the bottle but Ella was having none of it. She arched her body into a stiff bow and her face went an alarming shade of red.

Abbie had to force herself not to scoop Ella out of her father's arms. 'Try again,' she said above the noise Ella was starting to make. 'She'll get used to the idea of you feeding her in a minute.'

But Rafael shook his head. 'I can't bear to hear her this unhappy. You do it, Abbie.' He stood up and all but shoved Ella into her arms.

It felt like defeat. Worse, even when Ella settled and started sucking hungrily, the joy of doing this was somehow diminished. Abbie could feel Rafael's gaze on her, and she could feel his despair. And there seemed to be something accusing in the gaze Ella had fixed on her, too. She felt like the meat in a sandwich. All she was trying to do was stick the layers back together. Why was it so difficult?

'I'm sorry,' she said quietly to Rafael.

He gave one of those eloquent shrugs. 'It's not your fault. Fiorella is a baby. All she knows is what she wants to make her happy.'

But Abbie knew what she wanted to make *her* happy, too. And it seemed as far away as ever.

'I…um…thought I might come home tomorrow. After work.'

Rafael went very still. Oh, help…

'Just to see if I find a suitable dress and shoes and things or whether I'll need to go shopping. For the wedding on Saturday?'

'Ah… Of course.'

'I thought you might like to be here with Ella while I'm gone. If you're free about five o'clock, you could feed her her dinner.'

A faintly incredulous huff escaped Rafael but Abbie ignored it. 'If I'm not here, she might be happy to let you feed her. And food is different from a bottle. She lets nursing staff feed her sometimes. We can only keep trying, can't we?'

A sigh this time. *'Si…'* Rafael's expression was unreadable. 'This is true.'

'She's doing well, isn't she, Mr de Luca?'

'She certainly is.' Rafael stroked the hair of the little Afghan girl, Anoosheh, and smiled at her. It had been nearly two weeks since her massive surgery and the swelling was going down nicely.

'She's learning English fast,' his registrar put in. 'Can you say hello to Mr de Luca, Anoosheh?'

''Ello,' Anoosheh said obligingly. 'I am 'appy to see you, Dock-a-dor.' The words were an effort to produce and then her face twisted into an odd expression.

'She's trying to smile,' the nurse told them. 'It's still hard.'

'Keep trying,' Rafael told his small patient. 'Soon you will be lighting up the world with your smile.'

They all had to keep trying, didn't they?

Even when it didn't seem to be working.

The parts of his life were all there and, if you took each one on its own, there wasn't anything obvious that was broken.

Work was fine. Little Anoosheh was a triumph and one that was being followed closely enough by the media for Rafael's reputation to be growing rather too fast for his liking. Only this morning he'd had to pass a request to appear on a television talk show over to Ethan—who probably passed it to Declan. Far better that the charity projects of the Hunter Clinic got some good publicity than that he became the poster boy for reconstructive plastic surgery.

Ella was fine, too. Doing better each day. The three-month mark when her bone marrow could be checked again was rapidly approaching and if the results were good, her central line could be removed and she would be allowed home. Even better, his precious daughter was happy and she had no trouble lighting up the world with *her* smile.

There had been no objections when he'd been the one to feed her the other evening and he'd done it again last night because it seemed that Abbie did need a new dress for Leo and Lizzie's upcoming wedding and it had given her a chance to hit the high street.

Yes. The wheels of his life were turning perfectly well.

It was when Rafael's ward rounds took him to visit

Lucy, the little girl who'd been in the car crash, that he realised what was bothering him so much.

Lucy's grandmother was beside the bed, holding a drink that Lucy was sipping through a straw. She watched as Rafael checked the chart and then gently examined the little girl's face.

'Can you open your mouth a little for me, chicken? Does that still hurt?'

'Mmm.'

'It will get a little better each day. But only if you keep trying.' Rafael covered her right eye with one hand and then held up his other hand. 'How many fingers can you see?'

'Free.' The word had to come out without her mouth moving.

'Good girl.' Rafael smiled at the grandmother. 'The vision's improving.'

She nodded. 'Mrs de Luca had a specialist from the eye department come in this morning. They think it's going to be fine. And the orthopaedic surgeon is happy with her arms and the movement she's got in her fingers. Mrs de Luca took some of the stitches out of her face this morning, too. It's looking a bit better, isn't it?'

Rafael could hear the doubt in the woman's voice. 'If you'd seen Lucy when she came into Theatre, you would know that what Mrs de Luca did is just amazing. Lucy will need more surgery later but, eventually, I suspect you're going to have to look carefully to see any lasting damage.' His reassurance was sincere. The pride he felt in Abbie's work even more heartfelt.

'She's your wife, isn't she? Mrs de Luca?'

'She is.'

In name only, however. The taunting whisper stayed with Rafael as he finished his round of the surgical ward.

The wheels of his life might be turning perfectly well but the cogs weren't fitting together properly so the wheels weren't turning *together*. Was it only coincidence that working together to operate on Lucy had been the only time they'd been that close professionally since she'd returned?

She should be here now, sharing this ward round. Sharing the pleasure in the little girl's excellent progress. But she'd been here before him today and she was in Theatre this afternoon. Creating a new ear for the patient she'd seen on the morning of that first outpatient clinic together. The one that had led to Leo and Ethan ordering them to put their personal issues aside and work together properly again. But they weren't, were they? Even this patient they'd worked so hard on together was now being followed up on at different times.

His time with Ella was wonderful but she would only allow him to do things for her when Abbie wasn't there.

There was nothing wrong with his home either, except that the only time Abbie had gone there had been when he had been *here*, looking after Ella.

How could they possibly put things right when they were beginning to shape their lives into completely separate wheels? It wouldn't matter how smoothly they turned, it wouldn't be any kind of a marriage and he wouldn't blame Abbie for deciding it wasn't good enough.

Somehow he had to get the cogs to fit inside each other. To show Abbie that, by doing so, the 'machine' of them being together would be stronger. Able to do so much more. Could last for ever, like a beautifully crafted clock.

But marriage wasn't a machine, was it? He was thinking about this all the wrong way. And maybe it was that kind of thinking that had caused their problems right from the start.

Waiting by the lift when he'd left his junior staff to follow up on any new orders for his patients, Rafael couldn't shake off the disturbing undercurrent his analogy of timepieces had left him with.

You couldn't divorce emotion from things that happened to people. He was too good at standing back and seeing the big picture without the emotional layers. The way he had when it had come to making that decision about Ella's experimental treatment. Perhaps the way he had when he'd voiced that 'all or nothing' ultimatum about their marriage? When he looked at the big picture, he saw it in terms of benefit versus suffering for the individual involved from a clinical perspective.

Abbie was the opposite. She saw the same big picture, but her scales weighed the emotions of everybody involved and not just the patient at the centre of the decision to be made. And the results she came up with were very different sometimes.

But not *wrong*.

Rafael knew that. He also knew that he'd made things much worse while Abbie and Ella had been away in New York. He'd buried himself in his work and when he had thought about his family, the fear that he would never see his daughter again had been easily shrouded in anger and then resentment towards Abbie.

He'd been cool and clipped in any communication. No wonder it had trailed away into impersonal emails and text messages.

But how did you go about changing something that was a part of your personality? How could you learn to feel the things that someone like Abbie could feel?

By finding someone to teach you?

The lift doors slid open in front of him but, instead of stepping in, Rafael turned swiftly and headed for the stairs.

Abbie knew it was Rafael coming into the theatre without even having to turn her head.

What she didn't know was why he had come in. The surgery for the grade-three microtia on seven-year-old Annabelle was well under way. Rib cartilage had been harvested and Abbie was sculpting the new ear. She had to look up for a second as Rafael stepped closer, however. Had something happened to Ella?

The eye contact was reassuring. 'Don't let me interrupt,' Rafael said. 'I just had the urge to come and watch an artist at work.'

Abbie blinked. 'Really? What brought this on?'

'I was checking Lucy. Admiring your needlework. And then I remembered you were doing this today and it's been a long time since I've watched the procedure. Do you mind?'

'No, of course not.' Hardly. He had been admiring her work? Wanted to watch 'an artist'? How could anyone object to such a professional accolade?

It put the pressure on a little more, though. Not that

Abbie hadn't been doing her best before but now she was determined to make this *perfect*.

'This is Annabelle,' she told Rafael. 'She's been waiting a long time for this surgery but I needed her to be old enough to have sufficient rib cartilage to harvest.'

'She could have had the surgery much younger with a Medpor reconstruction, couldn't she?'

Was Rafael criticising her choice? Abbie couldn't help sounding a little defensive.

'Using an artificial framework means that the ear can't match the other one perfectly. It also doesn't grow with the child. This creates an ear that's alive. One that's going to last a lifetime.'

'But not many surgeons are gifted enough to do it well. Annabelle is lucky to have found you.'

There was a murmur of agreement from the rest of the team. Abbie shook off the praise. 'I think she chose me because I said I'd put an earring in to match her other ear so it'll be there when the bandage comes off for the first time next week.'

Happy with the shape of the outer ear she had carved from the cartilage, Abbie turned her attention to the peanut-shaped deformity that had been Annabelle's right ear until now. She could use the lower part for the ear lobe. The tiny gold stud earring was bathed in disinfectant and waiting in a kidney dish nearby.

Rafael was watching her examination of the deformed ear tissue.

'She must have been teased a lot at school.'

'Yes. She's kept it covered pretty well with her hair but she was very self-conscious about it. Her mother said they had all sorts of problems when she was expected to do swimming at school.'

'Has it affected her badly, do you think?'

'Well, she's very shy. Hard to say whether she would have been more outgoing without the deformity but I'm sure it's contributed. It would have become progressively more of an issue as she got older, of course.'

'*Si*... It would be torture for a teenage girl to look so different.'

'Mmm. That's why I favour the rib graft method. She'll need a bit more surgery to refine things down the track but by the time Annabelle's interested in boys, her ear will look and feel as if it's always been there.'

This was weird. She might have expected a keen interest from Rafael but Abbie would never have picked that it would focus on the emotional side of the surgery and its aftermath. Why wasn't he asking about the dimensions of the suture material she was using? Or the technique for elevating a skin flap to preserve all the hair follicles so that Annabelle wouldn't be left with a bald patch?

'She has conduction deafness, I assume?'

'Yes. There's no ear canal or eardrum on this side.' That was more like it. A clinical query.

'Is that causing problems for her? Or her family?'

'Doesn't seem to be.' He was doing it again. Looking past the clinical picture and considering the bigger, emotional picture. Something was going on in his head, Abbie realised. He was making a deliberate effort. To connect with her way of thinking about patients, perhaps?

Whatever it was, she liked it.

'They're under the care of an audiologist to make sure they look after the good side.' Abbie was peering through the magnifying lenses she wore to make tiny stitches that attached the ear lobe to the new part she had crafted. 'I think they're all more concerned about the cosmetic side of it all at the moment, though.'

She checked again that the lobe was at exactly the same level as Annabelle's other ear.

'Looking good.' Her registrar nodded. 'You ready for the earring?'

Abbie grinned. 'Let's do it.'

Even when the surgery was completed, the pressure dressing in place and protected with the plastic cup that was taped on, Rafael didn't seem inclined to talk about anything clinical.

'Were you happy with Lucy's progress?'

'She's doing well, isn't she?' Abbie stripped off her mask and gloves. 'I'll be happier when she can eat again, though. She's lost quite a lot of weight.'

'I've arranged for a physiotherapist who specialises in maxillofacial injuries to start working with her. Her grandmother's keen to help, too.'

'It's great that she's got the family support there.' But Abbie sighed as she pulled off her gown. 'Her mother's still in ICU. It's not looking hopeful.'

'And the father?'

'Not in the picture.' Abbie balled up the gown and threw it in the bin. 'Hasn't been since she was a baby.'

A broken family. The kind that Abbie didn't want for Ella. Or for herself or Rafael, for that matter. She forced a smile to her lips.

'On a more positive note, I found a gorgeous dress

and shoes for the wedding tomorrow. Did you get your suit cleaned?'

'I have to pick it up at the dry-cleaner's after work.'

'But you'll come and see Ella later?'

'Of course.'

The smile was genuine this time. 'We'll look forward to that.'

'Me also. And tomorrow…the wedding? It will be another date for us, perhaps?'

The hopeful expression in Rafael's eyes almost undid Abbie completely. If they weren't still standing in Theatre, with staff busy around them cleaning up after Annabelle had been taken to Recovery, she might have thrown her arms around his neck. Stood on tiptoe to provide reassurance with a kiss.

But all she could do was smile. And offer a quiet word that was only for Rafael.

'Absolutely.'

CHAPTER SEVEN

THE PHOTOGRAPHS OF this wedding would grace the pages of any magazine devoted to the lifestyles of the rich and famous.

As a venue, Claridge's was simply one of the best London could offer. Intimate tables for the wedding breakfast, which seated only three or four people each, could be seen in an adjoining area, draped in white cloth with centrepieces of trios of white roses in simple vases amidst sparkling crystal glasses and gleaming silverware. Larger arrangements of flowers, also white, were dotted everywhere amongst the pillars.

The area that Rafael and Abbie were ushered to be seated was also extremely elegant. There would be many more people arriving for the reception but the ceremony itself was more private and a semicircle of comfortably padded chairs for the guests was arranged beneath a spectacular chandelier, giving everybody a clear view of the sweeping staircase that the bride would come down to make her entrance. The seats were mostly filled by the time Abbie and Rafael edged into the back row. She said hello to Lexi Robbins, Head of PR at the Hunter Clinic. Lexi was holding hands with the man on her other side, surgeon Iain McKenzie, and it was almost palpable how much in love these two were. Neither of them was particularly aware of the existence of anybody else and their private, whispered communication was probably about a different wedding. One that they would be starring in themselves in the not-too-distant future.

It was a very different wedding that Abbie couldn't help thinking about, too. Sitting here, all dressed up, it felt like she and Rafael were in a silent little bubble amongst the other guests. A tense kind of silence. Was he also thinking about the last wedding he had attended?

Their wedding?

The memory of that day was blurry. If it wasn't for the photograph taken on the steps of the registry office and the ring she still wore on her finger, it would be easy to believe that it had never really happened. They'd done it all too fast, hadn't they? It was all rather a blur. Falling in love with Rafael, finding out she was pregnant and then buying the apartment and getting married within just a few weeks.

Would it have all been different if she hadn't been pregnant?

Of course it would.

Would Rafael have even proposed if things had been different?

Abbie stole a sideways glance at him but Rafael's line of vision was firmly fixed elsewhere. As the muted buzz of conversation faded around her, Abbie's head turned as well. Within moments of Lizzie appearing, the only sound around her was the soft classical music of the string quartet in the background. Leo stood near the foot of the staircase with Ethan beside him—Abbie had heard how Lizzie had convinced Ethan to be Leo's best man after he'd originally refused due to their strained relationship—and, like everyone else now, the groom's gaze was fixed on Lizzie as she came slowly down, her bridesmaid several steps behind her.

Her dress was gorgeous. Simple but striking with cap sleeves of the lace that overlaid the rest of the dress and a slim belt with a silver buckle above soft folds of fabric that flowed over the stairs and then grazed the black and white marble of the chequerboard floor. The bouquet she carried was simply a bunch of the same perfect white roses that were the centrepieces on the tables. Leo and Ethan had matching white rosebuds as buttonholes in their classic, dark morning suit jackets over pinstriped grey trousers.

The wedding vows exchanged were traditional. The same words that Rafael and Abbie had said to each other.

To have and to hold... For better or for worse... In sickness and in health...

To love and to cherish, from this day forward, until death us do part...

Maybe the memories of her own wedding day weren't that blurry after all. The words echoed in her head but something strange was happening in the rest of her body. Her heart was back in that registry office. Full to bursting with *so* much love.

So many hopes and dreams for her future with this wonderful man.

Her breath must have caught audibly. Not that anyone else would have noticed Rafael's attention being diverted but his body was suddenly closer. Touching hers. With no conscious thought on her part, Abbie found her hand stealing into Rafael's. Their fingers laced together and the grip was tight enough to know that she wasn't the only one being swamped by emotion.

They had vowed to love each other. In sickness and in health. Did it matter if it was Ella's health rather than either of theirs?

Of course it didn't.

Had they broken their vows? They were still married, weren't they?

Abbie was fighting tears as she watched the tender first kiss of the newlyweds in front of them.

Yes. She and Rafael had broken their vows because they hadn't cherished each other. And the fault was on both sides.

But how could they have given each other what they'd needed when they hadn't really known each other? They had both wanted the best for Ella. Rafael must be feeling so guilty now, thinking that he had been ready to give up, and here she was, defying the odds.

Abbie squeezed his hand more tightly and was grateful for the answering pressure. And then they both turned their heads as the clapping around them started and Abbie could have drowned in the depths she saw in Rafael's eyes. She couldn't pull her hand free to join in the congratulatory clapping. She couldn't look away from Rafael's gaze either.

This moment took her straight back to their own wedding. To the way Rafael had looked at her in the heartbeat after the celebrant had told him he could kiss his bride.

It was the most natural thing in the world for him to tilt his head towards her now and for Abbie to raise her face.

A soft kiss. Nothing like the explosive release of need that had happened in the changing room. This was tender. Too brief but long enough.

A cherishing kind of kiss…

'You're crying, *cara*.' Rafael studied her face as he raised his head again. He used the pad of his thumb to brush away a tear.

'It's a wedding.' Abbie sniffed and dipped her head, pressing her fingers against the bridge of her nose to force back any more tears. She looked up and tried to smile. 'You're allowed to cry.'

'*Si*…' Rafael was smiling back at her. 'You're lucky we didn't get married in Italy. The whole village might have been crying.'

Abbie snorted softly but the sound was poignant. The registry office had only been supposed to be a first wedding—getting the formal paperwork out of the way—because Abbie hadn't wanted to be a pregnant bride. Rafael had promised he would take her to Italy as soon as the baby could travel and they could do it all again in a village church on his beloved Amalfi Coast. She would have a beautiful dress and their families would be able to share the celebration not only of their union but the start of their family.

Was it another dream that was nothing but dust now? She had to clear her throat. 'Happy crying, I hope.'

'Of course. What else?' But Rafael's gaze had moved.

Somebody was turning from a chair in the next row to greet him and conversations were starting again around them as the newlyweds moved on to sign the register. They would disappear for photographs soon and Abbie knew that the gathering would become a glittering social occasion as the wider circle of guests arrived. There were rumours that royalty was expected, even, as some of the Hunter brothers' clients had been invited to share this celebration.

Suddenly Abbie didn't want to be part of it.

She wanted to be alone somewhere.

With her own husband.

Maybe he felt the same way. Maybe that was why Rafael kept hold of Abbie's hand when they were free to move around and mingle.

Abbie wasn't complaining.

It felt better than good. It felt right.

There was no shortage of people they knew to talk to and groups formed as champagne and canapés were served by an army of waiting staff. Friends and family of the bride and groom drifted into one group and the medical personnel from the Hunter Clinic, the Lighthouse Children's Hospital and Princess Catherine's made up another.

'Abbie...what a gorgeous dress.' The office manager from the clinic, Gwen, was balancing a glass in one hand and what looked like a tiny square of rye bread topped with caviar in the other.

Rafael nodded his approval of the compliment. The new rose-pink dress *was* gorgeous but, in his opinion, it only worked because it made Abbie's skin and hair look irresistibly beautiful. An elegant version of the picnic frock she had worn to the park the other day when she'd taken his breath away.

'Thanks, Gwen. I love your hat, too.' Abbie was eyeing the froth of flowers and feathers on Gwen's head. 'Though it's more of a fascinator, isn't it?'

'A hybrid.' Gwen smiled. 'I believe it's called a "hatinator." Whatever next?' She looked at the canapé her hand. 'This is my second one of these. They're simply delicious.' She glanced from Abbie to Rafael. 'You're not eating?'

'I wanted to hold my wife's hand,' Rafael said solemnly. 'But I couldn't refuse a glass of champagne. What is a man to do?'

He could feel an increase of pressure from the fingers entwined with his. Was Abbie privately expressing her approval of this contact?

He really didn't want to be here, being sociable, any more. He wanted to be alone somewhere.

With Abbie.

Gwen laughed. 'Now, there's an idea. A new kind of diet. You could write a book and become famous.'

'He's already famous.' Another figure joined their conversation. 'I hear that they want to make a movie about transforming the lives of Afghan children and Hollywood is demanding Mr Rafael de Luca as the star.'

The deadpan manner in which this information was delivered made it sound quite plausible. But this was Edward North who was speaking, a microsurgeon who was known for being slightly eccentric and a bit of a loner. He was awkward enough in social settings for it to be quite surprising to see him attend an event like this at all.

'Yeah, yeah...' Rafael's tone was mocking but he smiled to take any sting from the tone.

As if sensing a sudden tension in the air, Gwen moved away to talk to someone else and he could feel Abbie's fingers stiff and still in his hand now.

Rafael wasn't sure who released the contact first. Maybe it just didn't feel right to be standing here holding hands while they were talking to Edward. Because he'd been the cause of the trouble their marriage was in now?

Or perhaps Abbie had heard that his relationship with this particular colleague had not been the best recently. He *had* been angry with Edward and they'd barely spoken in the last few months, but he'd been justified, hadn't he?

Nobody could deny that Edward was a genius. Thanks to the endless nights he spent on his own reading and researching, he'd been the one to find the information on the experimental treatment that he thought Ella might be a candidate for.

He just wished that Edward had had some idea of the chaos his suggestion would have on his marriage. Had he even been aware of *his* misery in the last few months? Probably not. He wasn't a father himself. As far as Rafael was aware, he wasn't in a long-term relationship either.

Maybe, in his own way, the backhanded compliment disguised as the faux breaking news was his way of apologising. Edward was certainly aware of some undercurrents because he cleared his throat and ran a finger under his collar, as if it was uncomfortable, as he turned towards Abbie.

'How's Ella?' he enquired. 'I heard that she's back in the Lighthouse but…I haven't heard any details about the treatment.'

'It seems to have worked,' Abbie said quietly. 'For a while there, it didn't look like it would but—'

'Something went wrong?' Edward was frowning. 'Not graft versus host disease?' He shook his head. 'No, that wouldn't happen. It's the patient's own T cells that are being reengineered, isn't it? So that they'll recognise and attach to the CD19 protein that's on the surface of B cells.'

'There's another protein,' Abbie told him. 'I'll have to look up what it is for you but it's the same one that's involved with rheumatoid arthritis. Anyway, the levels got very elevated because of the new T cells and Ella became critically ill. She was in the intensive-care unit for weeks.'

Edward looked like he was making a mental note to investigate the unnamed protein himself. 'What did they use to treat her?'

'The same drugs they use for rheumatoid. With quite dramatic results. Her fever and temperature dropped rapidly and she was taken off the ventilator much sooner than any of us had hoped for.'

The atmosphere became even more strained. Edward looked vaguely appalled, as if how dangerous the treatment had been hadn't occurred to him when he'd suggested it.

'It did work in the end,' Abbie said. 'We wouldn't

have even known about it if it hadn't been for you. And we couldn't be more grateful.'

We.

They were both looking at him now. It was Rafael's turn to clear his throat. He tilted his head in acknowledgement of his own gratitude. Of course he was grateful for Ella's state of health but he still had the damage to his marriage undermining his happiness. Was it any wonder it was hard to make amends with Edward?

'Thank you,' he said aloud, finally. 'I'm sorry I haven't said so before.'

The apology seemed to be accepted but a new silence fell now and everybody was clearly trying to think of a way to break it. It was Abbie who turned her head and seemed to be looking for someone.

'They're taking a long time, aren't they?'

'Who?' Edward looked puzzled.

'Leo and Lizzie. I know they went for photographs but that was ages ago. They should be back by now. Look at all the new arrivals. The breakfast must be due to start.'

'Oh…didn't you hear? There was a helicopter waiting for them. Leo whisked Lizzie off to go and visit her parents in Brighton.'

'Good grief… *Really*?'

Edward nodded and then shook his head, looking bemused. 'I'd heard they were too sick to come to the wedding but it does seem a little over the top, doesn't it?'

Abbie's smile was tight. 'He loves her. And what a lovely thought, to let them see their daughter in her beautiful dress.'

It seemed that Abbie was uncomfortable talking

about the generous gesture. Defensive even. Did a man have to do something a little outrageous to prove how much he loved his bride?

Had he not done enough?

But the low-key service in the registry office hadn't been intended to be the only acknowledgement of their marriage, had it? Rafael had had all sorts of plans for a second wedding and honeymoon in Italy that would have been far more meaningful than a showy helicopter ride. If only Ella hadn't become sick so quickly...

If only...

Edward was looking around, clearly disinterested in discussing the bride's dress. Someone nodded at him and he moved away, looking somewhat relieved. Mitchell Cooper, the American plastic surgeon, and Declan Underwood, another plastic surgeon, who seemed to be here without dates but enjoying themselves, came past Rafael and Abbie, heading for the bar, and Mitchell winked.

'The game is to pick which of the guests has been a former client of the Hunter Clinic,' he murmured. 'I've spotted at least two.'

'And I've spotted the guests of honour returning,' Abbie said. 'I'm going to see if I can find where our table is.'

There was no chance of being alone with Abbie for quite some time, Rafael realised. Watching her disappear into the throng of guests, he had to wonder if she would even want that.

That moment of connection with Abbie during the wedding ceremony that had led to them holding hands was well and truly gone now. The conversation with

Edward had been a sobering reminder of how far they still had to go. He followed Mitchell towards the bar. His American colleague was probably searching for a Scotch instead of champagne and Rafael had a sudden desire for something a bit stronger himself.

The group of men at the bar was drawing the attention of every woman in attendance, including those who'd come with partners. And no wonder. Abbie watched them as they raised what looked like glasses of Scotch to toast each other. The dress suits they were all wearing made most men look more attractive but these were already exceptionally good-looking guys.

And Rafael was the best looking of the bunch, as far as she was concerned. His curly dark hair was a little too long, and his features a little sharper than some, but even from a distance she could feel the pull of his Italian passion, the warmth of the fire she knew ran in his blood.

Perhaps she had been too harsh in her reaction to that ultimatum he'd delivered when he'd been so frustrated at not being listened to. Maybe if she understood more about his heritage and the way his male Italian brain worked, she could learn to sort the wheat from the chaff and they could work through their differences, instead of pushing each other away.

Rafael was trying to understand how *her* brain worked. That had been obvious from his line of questioning during Annabelle's surgery. What could she do to let him know that she was just as willing to make an effort?

Ethan had joined the other men at the bar and he

downed a shot of spirits as though it was some kind of medicine. There were certainly undercurrents here for people other than Rafael and herself.

With a sigh, Abbie slipped into her allocated seat at one of the small tables. The chairs had been cleared from the chequerboard marble floor now and no doubt there would be dancing later. After the food and the speeches. Watching Ethan accept another drink from the bar staff, she had to hope that it wouldn't affect his ability to give the speech he was expected to make as best man.

There were choices to be made about the food as the courses came round, which Abbie found very difficult. Not because everything didn't sound absolutely delicious but her appetite seemed to have deserted her. She had to make an effort, though.

'I think I'll have the roast Portland scallops with the fresh pea velouté,' she decided. 'Whatever a velouté is.'

'I believe it's a French word.' Edward was sharing the table that had been allocated to the de Lucas. 'It means velvet. It's a sauce. Usually a white sauce, but I expect this one might be green.'

Abbie's lips twitched as she caught the twinkle in Edward's otherwise deadpan expression. There was more to this man than people appreciated, wasn't there?

'I'm going to have the Cornish lobster with hand-cut chips,' Rafael decided, when it came to the main course. 'Or perhaps the Aberdeen Angus filet steak with beetroot.'

Except he didn't seem to have any more of an appetite than Abbie did. There was just as much left on his plate as hers when it came time to be cleared away.

The dessert that Abbie chose was to die for. A chocolate fondant with a delectably oozy centre that came with a peach compote and a mascarpone sorbet. The speeches started before she'd taken more than a taste, however, and Abbie stopped and held her breath.

What would Ethan say?

He didn't seem to be showing any effect from the shots of Scotch he'd been throwing back, but then, his speech was so short it was hard to tell. He said something very complimentary about Lizzie and he wished the couple every happiness and that was it. Except that he finished by thanking his brother, saying that he appreciated the way Leo had always looked out for him.

As dessert plates were cleared away, Leo and Lizzie moved through the tables, stopping to talk to as many people as they could before they started the next part of the evening with their first dance. It was Leo who came to the table where Rafael and Abbie were now sitting alone. Edward had gone to talk to Declan.

'Thanks for coming.' Leo smiled. 'I hope you're all enjoying yourselves.'

'It's a beautiful wedding,' Abbie said. 'Lizzie looks stunning.'

'Great speeches, too.' Rafael grinned. 'Short. If we were in Italy they'd go on till midnight and nobody would get a chance to dance.'

Abbie hoped the length of the best man's speech hadn't been due to the lingering tension between the brothers. 'It was a nice thing that he said,' she offered. 'About you always looking out for him. You must have been an awesome big brother to have.'

Leo's smile looked wry. 'Whether he wanted it or not,' he murmured. 'It wasn't always appreciated.'

Abbie raised her eyebrows but Leo didn't get a chance to answer the silent query. A dramatically glamorous woman, dripping in diamonds, was sailing towards him as gracefully as only an aging prima ballerina could.

'Leo...*darling*... You must come with me. Tony and I are dying to talk to you.' With her arm firmly linked with his, Leo was hustled away.

Abbie had to smile. There would be no prizes for picking her as one of the clinic clients who'd scored an invitation. Everybody knew about Francesca, who had to be in her early seventies now, and had had her first plastic surgeries with Leo and Ethan's father, James.

And that thought led her back to Leo's cryptic comment. She turned to Rafael.

'Whether he wanted it or not? And it wasn't always appreciated? I wonder what that was about?'

Rafael shrugged. 'I've heard the father was a complete bastard. I suspect being the big brother made life pretty tough for Leo.'

'He looks happy now.'

'He just got married to a beautiful woman. Of course he's happy.'

'Where's Ethan?'

'I saw him heading for the restroom a while back.'

'So did I.' Abbie frowned. 'Was it my imagination or was he limping more than usual?'

Rafael mirrored her frown. 'Maybe I should go and check that he's all right.'

'I'll come with you.'

They slipped out of the crowd unnoticed because the music had started and Leo was leading Lizzie onto the dance floor.

They found Ethan in a hallway near the restrooms. Leaning against the wall, with his eyes closed, he didn't see them approach.

'Are you okay?' It was Abbie who asked.

Ethan's eyes snapped open. 'I'm fine,' he said.

He didn't look fine. There were deep lines around his eyes and his skin looked slightly grey. He looked like a man who was dealing with something physically painful.

'Great speech,' Rafael said. 'Well done.'

Ethan gave a noncommittal grunt. 'I didn't say much.'

'Sometimes it doesn't need much,' Abbie said. 'It just needs the right words.'

That brought the ghost of a smile to Ethan's face. 'What are you two doing out here, anyway?' he asked. 'You should be in there, having a good time.' His smile twisted a little. 'Or at least finding the right words.' He pushed himself off the wall and headed back towards the ballroom. 'I'm going to find another Scotch.'

Abbie and Rafael looked at each other.

'Shall we go back?' Rafael asked. 'Would you like to dance?'

Abbie shook her head. 'I think I might have had enough of so many glamorous people. And I've certainly had enough champagne.'

Rafael's face emptied of expression. Was he waiting for her to say that she needed to get back to the hospital? To Ella?

'You know what I'd really like to do right now?'

'No. What?'

Abbie reached out and took his hand. Her heart skipped a beat. This was how she could show Rafael how much she wanted to try and fix things.

'I'd like to go home,' she whispered. 'With you.'

CHAPTER EIGHT

STEPPING THROUGH THE door of the apartment in Gloucester Avenue was a bit like sitting with Rafael and waiting for Leo and Lizzie's wedding to begin.

Stepping back in time.

They'd been so excited when they'd found this place. It was perfect. A period conversion that had retained all the character of its origins but had been modernised enough to make it a joy to live in. Tall windows let in lots of light and the polished floorboards made it feel warm and homely. The kitchen and bathrooms had everything they could have wished for. There was central heating and the private garden was walled in and safe for young children. The location was ideal, pretty much halfway between the two places they both worked in—the Hunter Clinic and the Lighthouse Children's Hospital. Best of all, they had Regent's Park and all it had to offer within a few minutes' walk.

It was no surprise that their offer on the apartment was accepted because it was meant to be. So much in love, life just couldn't get any better. The stars were aligned and their perfect future together was just getting started.

So very, very different to the way things were now.

The furniture was all the same, right down to that controversial couch with its big blue throw, but the atmosphere was weird. Empty feeling. There was no excitement about the future lurking in any corners. This felt…awkward.

'There's wine in the fridge.' Rafael was turning on the gas fire to add to the background warmth of the central heating. Did he, too, feel the odd chill of the joy that had gone from these rooms? 'Can I get you a drink?'

'No.' Abbie took off her coat and draped it over one arm of the couch, dropping her handbag beside it. 'I had more than enough champagne at the reception. But you get something if you want to.'

'Maybe later.' Rafael stood with his back to the fire. The intensity of his gaze was unsettling.

It had been Abbie's suggestion to come home with him but now that they were here together for the first time in so many months she wasn't sure that it had been the best idea. What was she going to do now? Throw herself into his arms?

No. That would feel as unnatural as standing here feeling like a stranger in her own home.

Rafael was still staring at her. 'Would you rather go back to the hospital? Are you worried about Ella?'

'No.' Abbie shook her head quickly. 'I know she'll be fine. She won't even wake up until morning. And they'd ring me, anyway, if there was a problem. Oh…' She reached for the handbag she'd discarded. 'I forgot that I'd turned my phone off for the wedding ceremony. I'd better switch it back on.'

'I haven't had a call,' Rafael said. 'I had my phone

on silent. I never switch it off completely, just in case there's an emergency with a patient. If they hadn't been able to reach you, I'm sure they would have contacted me.'

'Of course.' But Abbie turned her phone on anyway and watched the spinning circle on the screen as it booted up. She put it down as she realised that her diverted attention was only making it feel more awkward for Rafael but almost as soon as the device was out of her hands it sounded a message alert.

Her gaze snagged on Rafael's and held there for a heartbeat. And then he turned away with a flash of something like defeat washing over his face.

She had given him hope, hadn't she, saying that she wanted to go home with him? Now it seemed like Ella was about to come between them again.

'It's probably just Melanie telling me that everything's fine.'

But she had to look.

And it wasn't about Ella at all.

Another heartbeat and all Abbie could do was close her eyes tightly as she clutched the phone against her chest with both hands.

Dio...

What the hell had been in that message?

Something devastating, by the look of her. Rafael was in front of Abbie in only a couple of steps. He gripped her arms.

'*Che cosa*? What has happened?'

Abbie struggled to take an inward breath. 'It's not about Ella,' she whispered.

'Then what? What has made you look like this? *Tell* me...'

'It's...it's...Toby.'

Rafael felt his heart stop for a split second and then thump painfully back into action. Who the hell was Toby? Had Abbie met someone else?'

'Toby?' His voice felt raw. 'He's someone in New York?'

Abbie nodded mutely. Her eyes were still tightly shut and she was clearly on the verge of tears.

Maybe it didn't matter who this Toby was. What mattered was that he could feel Abbie shaking under his hands. She needed support. Comfort.

Love...

He pulled Abbie right into the circle of his arms and held her against his heart. He didn't say anything because he had no idea what he *could* say. And he didn't need to say anything anyway because moments later words began to spill out of Abbie between wrenching sobs.

'He was only five...and he was such a brave little boy... He was getting the same treatment as Ella and his mum and I became good friends. Shelley was crying when we left...she said she'd miss us both so much but...but knowing that Ella had made it through was giving her strength...the suffering that poor little Toby was going through would all be worth it in the end because...because one day soon she'd be able to take him home to his daddy...the way...the way I was taking Ella home...to *you*...'

The words got strangled by the heartbroken sobs for some time after that. Rafael simply held Abbie and rocked her gently until the grief subsided. Clearly this little boy hadn't survived the treatment.

It could so easily have been Ella.

Rafael's throat tightened and he could feel an odd prickling sensation at the back of his eyes.

Tears?

No. Not possible. He hadn't cried since he'd been a very small boy. A man's pride didn't allow the showing of such weakness. He needed a distraction but there was none to be had at this moment. No work to be done. He couldn't even pick up a journal article and lose himself in that for a while. And then Abbie made it even worse.

'It could have been Ella,' she choked out, echoing his own terrible thought. 'I could have put her through all that suffering for nothing. Shelley must be feeling so *awful.*'

'She'll know that she tried everything she could to keep her little one alive. That it was the right thing to do.'

But Abbie was shaking her head as she tried to pull away from him. Rafael loosened his hold but still kept her within the circle of his arms.

'I just didn't think. I couldn't see your point of view at all. Ella could have died, just like Toby, and all that suffering would have been pointless and…and, worse… we would have been half a world away from you. You would never have been able to hold Ella again. It was wrong, Rafael…' Tears were streaming down Abbie's face. 'I'm *sorry.*'

Strangely, any threat of his own tears had evaporated. Rafael felt strong. He brushed tears from Abbie's face.

'*Si*, it could have been Ella but it *wasn't* so I was

wrong, too. We were both wrong. Isn't it time that we forgave each other?'

Abbie was nodding. Her sob became a hiccup and, instead of pushing out against the circle of his arms, she moved closer, lifting her own arms to wrap them around his neck.

This embrace wasn't about offering comfort or support. This was a new closeness. An affirmation of forgiveness.

It was Rafael who pulled back this time. So that he could cup Abbie's face with his hands as he kissed her forehead and then her closed eyelids. Slowly. Softly.

He felt her eyes open as he finished the third kiss. And then they were looking at each other, the way they had when Leo and Lizzie had been kissing at the end of their wedding ceremony and it had seemed the most natural thing in the world to kiss his own wife at that point.

Just like it did now.

Oh…*God*…

This was what she had been aching for. The tenderness of those gentle kisses in the wake of an emotional storm that had washed away anything irrelevant.

Was this what forgiveness felt like?

If so, it was incredibly sweet.

Healing.

And then Abbie became aware of more than the calm after the storm. She could feel the softness of Rafael's lips as they pressed so gently on her eyelids. She could feel the strength in his hands as he cradled her face. She had to open her eyes then and when she did, all she could see in his eyes was the caring.

The *love*.

She could feel herself rising to stand on tiptoe. To meet his lips with her own. They were so close right now. Closer than they'd been for a long time. Maybe closer than they'd ever been emotionally.

But it wasn't close enough.

Abbie wanted more. She wanted them to be skin to skin. To have Rafael touching her in a way that would affirm life, rather than provide comfort in the face of death.

'Take me to bed, Rafe,' she whispered. 'Please.'

Without a word, Rafael scooped her up into his arms and strode through the apartment without pausing to turn on any more lights. Their bedroom had French doors that opened into the private garden and there were lights beyond that. Enough to take the edge off the darkness in the room. And Abbie didn't need more than that. Her other senses were more than enough.

She could hear the slide of fabric as Rafael peeled off his shirt, the thump of shoes being heeled off and the scratch of the zip as he got rid of his trousers. She could feel her own fingers shaking as she tried to undo the fastenings of her dress and she could hear the catch of her breath that was almost a gasp as Rafael's hands closed over hers and took over the task.

It was colder in here, away from the fire. Rafael pulled the duvet from the bed and draped it over Abbie's shoulders as she sat there while he took off her shoes and tights. And then he somehow wrapped them both in the fluffy, light down of the cover and they were lying on the bed with Rafael half over her and he was holding her face again as he kissed her.

A kiss that started as gently as the one during the wedding service. There was almost wonder in it. He was treating her as something fragile and precious. But Abbie was kissing him back now. She knew the first slide of her tongue against his would ignite the same kind of passion that had been unleashed with that kiss in the changing room and that was what she needed. She pushed closer with her hips, too, to feel more of his body as she opened her mouth to him and deepened the kiss.

A rough sound came from deep within Rafael's chest and his hands were moving now. Swiftly tracing the outline of her body. Pausing to shape her breasts and bring her nipples to painful hardness, and then they were moving lower. Sliding over her hips and touching her exactly where it ached most.

It was Abbie's turn to cry out incoherently. She didn't want slow and tender. Not this time. She pushed against his hand and used her hand to reach for the hardness she knew she would find without breaking the rhythm as their tongues danced and passion spiralled to bright flames.

Rafael changed his position with the smoothness that could only come from the confidence of knowing someone so intimately. Her body welcomed him as if it had only been yesterday they had last made love and they were in total accord about the pace of this fiercely passionate coupling. They both knew it would be over too soon. But they also both knew that it would be very different next time. This was a release of tension that had become pent up enough to be destructive all by itself. And it was a statement, too. An underscoring of the forgiveness perhaps.

Whatever emotional currents ran beneath the physical communication, the hard, fast sex left a curiously calm aftermath. It took some time for their heart rates to drop and for both of them to catch their breath enough to be able to talk. Abbie was content to lie there in Rafael's arms, their heads on the same pillow and their noses almost touching.

'I've missed you so much,' she whispered. 'I've missed *this*.'

Rafael only had to tilt his face up a little to kiss the tip of her nose. And then her lips. The sound he made was one of absolute agreement.

'*Ti voglio molto bene,*' he murmured. '*Sei tutto per me. E…e ho bisogno di te.*'

A smile curled the corners of Abbie's mouth. She'd learned more Italian than she'd realised in her time with Rafael.

'I love you very much, too,' she said softly. 'You are everything to me as well. And…and I do need you, too. Very much.' But then she caught her bottom lip between her teeth. 'Is it enough, do you think? That we love each other?'

'*Si.*' The word was adamant. 'Of course it is.'

For a while they lay there in silence. Abbie hoped Rafael was right but they'd always loved each other like this, hadn't they? And it hadn't been enough when it had come to the crunch over Ella's treatment.

It was Rafael who broke the silence. 'You understand Italian very well now, *cara*. It's time I took you to see my birthplace. To meet my family. I've kept them shut away from this for too long already.'

'They'd been about to come, hadn't they? Your mother and your sister? Just after Ella was born.'

'And then she got sick and was in isolation and I told them nobody could come. I couldn't tell anybody about the...difficulties we were having after you'd gone to New York but my mother still called every week or two. She wants to know why she can't meet her *nipote*. Why I'm not allowing her to meet my bride. "What's so wrong with us?" she asks. "What's wrong with her?"'

'Oh, help...' Being estranged from her own parents had made Abbie focus on nothing more than the nuclear family she and Rafael had made with Ella. How selfish had she been, not realising the ripple effect this had all had on Rafael's relationship with his own family? He was Italian. Family was everything. 'I'm going to be very nervous about meeting my in-laws now.'

'It will be fine. They will all love you. And they will adore Fiorella. It will only get harder if we leave it too long so we should do this as soon as our little Fiorella is well enough to travel.'

'I'd love that. I've heard so much about how beautiful the Almafi Coast is.'

'It's beyond beauty. The ancient villages that cling to the rocky cliffs. The sparkling blue of the sea. The scent of lemon trees and sunshine...'

Abbie blinked. 'You sound...homesick, Rafe.'

She could feel his whole body move with the shrug that was automatic. 'Perhaps I am, a little. Not so much for the place but for the memories of childhood. The... the safety?'

Abbie understood. 'It was so much easier, wasn't it? Having other people make the big decisions. Knowing that, whatever happened, there would always be a place to call home. People to love you.'

'This is home now.' Rafael kissed her again. '*Our* home.'

'It won't really be home, though, will it? Until Ella is here.'

'Family,' Rafael agreed on a sigh. '*Si...*'

'I'm glad you had a happy childhood, Rafe. That's all I want for Ella.'

'I had brother and sisters. And cousins. Lots of family. She will be welcomed with open hearts.'

And maybe she would have some brothers or sisters of her own one day. But that was a dream Abbie wasn't ready to share aloud. This new space they were in felt too fragile to test the boundaries.

'Your parents are still together, aren't they?'

'*Si*. They probably still argue with each other all the time and complain that neither of them listens to the other but they will always be together, I think. For the sake of the family.'

'I don't want to be like that,' Abbie said. 'I don't want to be together just for Ella. Or to keep up an illusion of family. And...and I don't want us to argue all the time.'

'We will be together because we truly love each other.' She could see Rafael's smile. 'But...I am Italian...I can't promise there will never be a disagreement.'

'As long as we talk.' The words were urgent. 'And *listen* to each other. And try to understand.'

'We will. I promise you that.'

Would even that be enough? 'I look at my parents,' Abbie whispered. 'And the way things fell apart after

Sophie died. The way they backed out of our lives as
soon as they knew Ella was sick. Was it because they
didn't love each other enough that it destroyed them?
That they didn't love *me* enough?' Her words wobbled
this time.

'*I* love you enough,' Rafael said fiercely. 'You have
to believe that.'

His hands were moving over her body again now.
Slowly, this time, as he stopped any further conversation by covering her lips with his.

And once again they were in total accord. They
didn't need fierce, hot sex now. They needed the comfort of slow, tender lovemaking. An affirmation of love
rather than life. Healing for things that went a long way
further back than the troubles in their own relationship.

This certainly wasn't about pushing issues out of
sight by distracting themselves with physical passion.

This was new. Making love with the depth of a new
understanding about each other. A new resolution to
make things work.

A whole new dimension to the love they shared.

A long time later, for the first time ever, Abbie found
slow tears trickling down her face in the aftermath of
lovemaking.

Rafael was horrified. 'You're crying, *cara*.'

'It's okay,' she whispered. 'They're happy tears.'

'Like at a wedding?'

'*Si...*' Abbie's smile wobbled. 'Exactly like at a wedding.'

Happy tears.

That was all right, then.

Rafael could hear Abbie's breathing slowing a little. Feel her relax even more in his arms as she drifted into sleep. He would not sleep yet. Not until he was sure that she didn't need anything more from him in the way of comfort. Or love.

Everything was all right again. This was exactly what they had needed. Where they needed to be.

In their own home.

Their own bed. Where he could show Abbie how much he loved her. Apologies had been made and accepted. They had forgiven each other.

They had both been wrong but they had put it behind them. Admitting fault meant that honour could be restored. Forgiveness meant that pride could be smoothed.

Si…

They could move forward again now. All of them, including his little Fiorella.

Mia famiglia.

It was with a smile on his lips that Rafael finally allowed himself to sink into slumber.

CHAPTER NINE

'IT'S LOOKING GOOD.'

'Yes. The retainers have done a good job bringing the tissues closer together.'

'The parents need a lot of the credit. It can't be easy keeping those retainers in place when you've got a baby that needs feeding and washing.'

'And when he's miserable and doing his best to pull things off his face.'

'I guess you do what you have to do when it's your baby.'

'Mmm.'

A quick shared glance spoke volumes between the two surgeons. The theatre staff around them also exchanged similar glances. Who knew better than the de Lucas how hard it could be, doing what you had to do for your baby?

Baby Angus MacDonald looked tiny, lying on the operating table. His eyes were being held closed by wide pieces of tape. His mouth was held open by retractors that hooked over the top and bottom lips. A breathing tube was as far out of the way as it could be to one side. Rafael was putting the final stitches into closing both the baby's hard and soft palates.

Now it was Abbie's turn. She studied the tiny face, using callipers to measure the space between the nostrils and the lips. There were two clefts to repair here and she had to mark the skin carefully so that her final rows of neat stitching would make straight lines from the centre of the nostrils to the lips. She created a map of tiny dots of indelible ink.

'Local?'

'Please.' The less bleeding that occurred as she used the scalpel the better as far as making the cuts as accurate as possible.

The incisions were a Z shape. Excess muscle and fat was removed so that the surface tissue would fit together with absolute precision. Rafael was ready with the cautery to seal blood vessels. A theatre nurse held a pair of scissors to snip off the ends of the stitches as Abbie deftly looped and tied the thin suture material.

It was so satisfying to pull the tissue together and see it nestle into exactly the position that she had mapped out. Nobody would see the precise work Rafael had achieved inside Angus's mouth and Abbie hoped that, eventually, nobody would see what she had done here, on the outside. In a few years' time, these scars should be invisible.

It wasn't the end of this surgery, however. The baby's nostrils were an odd, flattened shape due to the birth deformity and that was something else they could fix in this operation. Not only could they pull the tissue inside the nostrils together to make them a normal shape, they could ensure that the passages inside were clear enough to improve breathing. She and Rafael worked together on this last task and thirty minutes later they stood back as a nurse gently wiped the little face clean.

'His parents are going to be thrilled when they see how he looks,' she said.

There was a murmur of agreement around the table. Apart from the two lines of visible stitching and the lips being more swollen than they should be, this was a normal-looking baby. A beautiful little boy.

This time, when Abbie looked up to the space between Rafael's mask and theatre cap she could see the crinkles at the corners of his eyes and she knew he was smiling.

'Good job, Mrs de Luca.'

'Likewise, Mr de Luca.'

Another murmur of general agreement was accompanied by a ripple of laughter this time. The atmosphere was relaxed and happy. Not only was this surgery a great success but the de Lucas were obviously working well together again.

The "dream team" was back in action.

And it wasn't just in Theatre that they were working well together again. After watching that Angus had no problem coming out from under the anaesthetic, Abbie hurried to catch up with Rafael in the changing room.

'I've got them,' she said.

'Got what, *cara*?'

'The colour charts. Melanie's boyfriend works in a paint shop and she says that if we choose the colour, they can deliver it for us any time. They can do all the brushes and rollers and everything, too.' She opened the door of her locker and shifted the clothes and shoes she had left in there. A moment later she held up some glossy brochures triumphantly.

'Are you sure you want to do this? We've never done any decorating ourselves. We might be better to get some experts to come and do it for us.'

'That would take ages. Mel says that good firms are booked up months in advance. And it's easy...'

Rafael didn't look convinced.

'Ella's due for her biopsy in a few days. If it's good news then we're going to be allowed to take her home soon. Don't you want us to have her room all ready for her?'

They were both assuming that the news would be good. How could it not be when Ella was looking so well? The time that Abbie and Rafael had spent with their daughter over the last few days since the wedding had been a joy.

The time they had found to be together at home had also been a joy. They had started talking properly about the immediate future. About wanting to get the garden sorted so that Ella could play out there and use her swing in the summer. About turning the room they'd never had the chance to really use as a nursery into a bedroom fit for a princess.

'You really want to do this, don't you?'

Abbie nodded. It wasn't just to have a pretty new room ready for their daughter. This was something they could do together. Another way to build on the foundations they were laying for their future together.

'I've already found a colour that would be perfect. Look...'

'*Dio.*' Rafael eyed the square Abbie was pointing to. 'It's very…pink, isn't it?'

'It's exactly the same shade as that ballerina bear you gave her. There's a catalogue here of friezes you can get and there's one with pink teddies on it.' Abbie shuffled through the handful of pamphlets she held. 'And I thought we could do silver stars on the ceiling. You get a template and you can spray paint them on and put glitter on while the paint's still wet.'

Rafael closed his eyes for a moment.

'We can do this, Rafe. Maybe it won't be perfect but does that really matter?'

She watched him take a deep breath. 'When do you want to start?'

'Tonight. After Ella's settled. We could get some take-aways from our favourite Italian restaurant to have after we've done some painting.'

By eleven that night, there was a deep-dish lasagne still in the oven that had probably dried out to the point of being inedible. Abbie had streaks of pink paint on her nose and in her hair and the one wall they had finished painting looked terrible, with splotches of its original colour showing through all over the place.

'It just needs another coat,' Abbie said. But she looked close to tears.

Rafael wanted to say that he knew it would have been a better idea to get the experts in but he bit his tongue and kept scrubbing at the drips of paint on the polished wooden floor.

In the silence that followed he glanced up to see Abbie just standing, looking dejectedly at the wall.

A roller dangled from one hand. Her shoulders were slumped. The pink stripe in her hair had come from pushing stray strands back towards her ponytail. The ancient T-shirt of his that she was wearing to cover her clothes might not be something she would ever wear in public but her stance reminded him of when he'd seen her again after her long absence.

When she'd been standing outside Ella's room and he'd realised how hard it had all been for her. He'd wanted to put his arms around her then and tell her how much he loved her. That everything would be all right. That he would never let life be this hard for her again.

He hadn't been able to bridge the gulf between them then.

But he could now.

What did it matter if there were pink marks left on these floorboards? Rafael got to his feet. He stood behind Abbie and wrapped his arms around her, loving the way she leaned back into him without hesitation.

'Paint always looks bad before it dries,' he said with conviction.

'How do you know that? Have you ever painted a wall before?'

'I just know,' Rafael said. 'And if it doesn't look good when it dries, then we'll just give it another coat. And another and another until it looks perfect.'

Abbie groaned. 'Why do rooms need to have *four* walls?'

Rafael laughed. 'We need to eat. And then we need to shower.' He held up the cloth he was still holding in one hand. 'I can get all that pink paint off your skin. I have been practising.'

'I'm too tired to eat. Couldn't we just go to bed?'

Tempting. But it would have to wait. Rafael shook his head. 'Food,' he said.

'Is that an order?' Abbie was smiling as she swivelled in his arms to look up at him but then her smile faltered. What had been intended as a joke had an undercurrent that had the potential to reopen old wounds. Her mouth twisted into a grimace. 'I'm too tired to think,' she sighed. 'I *hope* it's an order.' Her smile reappeared. 'Feed me. Please?'

The following evening Rafael made sure they ate before they started work on Ella's room. Thai food tonight, instead of Italian. Maybe they could do Turkish or good old English fish and chips next time.

There were parts of this project that were very enjoyable. Cleaning up afterwards, for example. Long, hot showers where they could soap each other's skin and linger in one spot.

'Pink paint,' he'd say. How Abbie might have got so much pink paint on her breasts was open to debate but she didn't seem to mind his ministrations.

He certainly hadn't dripped any pink paint inside his trousers but he wasn't going to complain about Abbie's attention to certain parts of *his* anatomy either.

It even worked when they were out of the shower. When he wanted to take his time to taste her skin.

'Must have missed a bit,' he would murmur as he licked. 'Pink paint.'

It made Abbie giggle and the code slipped into that special place that was the private language of people who loved each other. A way of saying so much with only a look or a word or two that would make no sense to anybody else.

Eating together was another very enjoyable part of these snatched hours together. Not just because they could share the food and the feeling of home but because it meant they could talk about their days the way they'd done when they'd first known each other.

'It's a giant mole.' Abbie had a new patient to tell him about on the night they finally finished the last coat of pink paint. 'Covering her whole lower leg. I'm going to insert saline pouches under the skin of her good leg and we'll inflate them gradually over the next few months until we get enough new skin.'

'And then you'll remove the mole?'

'Yes. And we'll keep the skin attached to its source until it's established a blood supply and got locked into its new location. Means we'll have to keep the legs splinted together for quite a while but it'll be worth it. Her mother's happy to do it.'

Rafael had news to share on the night they glued the teddy-bear frieze into position halfway up the walls.

'Anoosheh met her adoptive parents today. She's going to have brothers and sisters and they've got a pet rabbit. She's very excited.'

'That's fantastic. You must be so happy about that.'

'I am.' It had, in fact, been surprising how happy the news had made him feel. Even more so than the excellent result that was appearing from the first major surgery the little girl had needed.

Maybe he was changing. Learning to see things more like Abbie?

'Ooh...' Abbie paused in her task of trying to get the

air bubbles out from beneath the strip of frieze. 'Do you think Ella would like a pet rabbit?'

'She has Ears. I don't think we need to rush into getting a real one.'

'No...I guess not. I just thought it might be a nice birthday present.'

'She's had her birthday.'

'Yes, but we were in New York. And she was too sick to celebrate. I thought...maybe we could have another birthday party? When she gets home?'

'Coming home will be enough to celebrate all by itself, won't it?'

Abbie was standing very still now. Her eyes were huge. She opened her mouth to say something but nothing came out so she nodded instead.

Rafael couldn't find anything to say to fill the silence either. Perhaps it was because Ella was due to have her bone-marrow biopsy tomorrow. He stepped forward to take the sponge out of Abbie's hand. What did it matter if there were air bubbles under the frieze for ever? It was time they stopped working and went to bed. Time they held each other for a while and gathered strength for what would undoubtedly be a tense day.

This was the first major procedure that Rafael had seen Ella undergo since before they'd left for New York.

How would he handle it?

Would he even want to be present?

Apparently he wanted to be more than simply present. It was Rafael who held Ella in Theatre as the powerful sedative took hold and Abbie could sense his tension skyrocket as their baby lost consciousness.

Rafael was curled protectively over their daughter as her head lolled sideways, using the crook of his elbow to support her neck and his hand to catch the tiny arm that flopped like a rag doll's.

Abbie could remember the first time she'd held Ella under the same circumstances and that terrible moment when she'd gone so boneless and still in her arms. The awful thought that she couldn't hold back.

This is what it will feel like when she dies...

Was that what Rafael was thinking as he laid Ella down on the bed so gently? Abbie's throat tightened painfully. A nurse made sure that the little head was positioned well on the special pillow and the young registrar assisting the oncology consultant tilted Ella's head back to ensure that her airway was protected.

Rafael came to stand beside Abbie as they prepared Ella for aspirating the sample of her bone marrow that would tell them what was happening on a cellular level. A lab technician was arranging a series of slides on the top of a trolley that she would prepare as soon as the sample had been obtained. Another trolley was covered with the bone-marrow aspiration kit, which included intimidating items like long needles with handle-type attachments, along with the usual plastic syringes, needles and a scalpel.

Ella was moved carefully into a recovery-type position, with her knees flexed, and then the skin over the back of her hip was swabbed with disinfectant and covered with a sterile drape that had a small square window in it.

'So, it's the posterior iliac crest that's being used.'

Rafael's voice sounded tight. 'The last time I saw this, it was the tibia that was used.'

Was he trying to distance himself from what was going on by looking at it in a professional sense? Was it the only form of protection he thought he had?

'It's been the iliac crest for the last few times,' Abbie responded. 'The tibia's only a suitable site for very young babies. It's too hard to get the sample and there's the risk of causing a fracture.' Her voice was just as tight. She *hated* watching this.

Her tone must have carried because the consultant looked up from where she was infiltrating the area around Ella's hip with local anaesthetic.

'You don't have to stay,' she said, with a sympathetic smile. 'You could go for a walk maybe. Or get a coffee. We'll come and get you as soon as it's all over. Ella's sound asleep. She doesn't know if you're here or not.'

'*We* know.' The words were ground out of Rafael as if uttering them was painful.

There was no professional distance in insisting that they stay in the room. Abbie knew that there was nowhere for Rafael to hide in that moment. That he was vulnerable. She also knew that there was another way to protect yourself. One that she had yearned for so often when she'd been in New York.

Could she get over the resentment of not having it and offer it to Rafael right now?

Of course she could. She *loved* him, didn't she?

Abbie reached for his hand and squeezed it, offering some of her own strength. An acknowledgment that she understood exactly how he was feeling. That they were in this together.

She offered an encouraging smile, too, as her hand was squeezed back, hard enough to crush her fingers painfully. She was sure the results of this test were going to be good. That putting Ella through this procedure was worthwhile.

Impossible not to feel a little sick, though, watching that big needle around the stylet being twisted into their baby's hip bone. The top of the needle was unscrewed and the stylet removed and then a syringe was attached. You could almost feel the pain that the suction that was needed to try and aspirate the bone marrow would have caused if the patient had been conscious. That first attempt wasn't successful, so the stylet had to go back in and the needle advanced a little further.

And all the time Abbie could feel how tense Rafael was. Closing her eyes, she got a real sense of the struggle he must have gone through when Ella had been so tiny. How gut-wrenching it had been for him to see his baby undergoing this kind of procedure when the professional side of his brain must have been not only trying to protect him but arming him with the statistics of how remote the possibility of a cure was.

Whereas Abbie had focussed only on any tiny gleam of hope. When the only protection she'd had had been the comfort of Rafael's arms. Had she given as much comfort as she'd received?

Probably not. Rafael had taken on board the suffering of the woman he loved as well as their baby's suffering.

No wonder he'd reached breaking point. When it had all become too much.

Abbie tightened her grip on Rafael's hand. As gruelling as this was, she had never felt closer to him. She could only hope that he was feeling the same.

Rafael had to consciously control the pressure he was putting into holding Abbie's hand because he knew that if he squeezed as hard as he wanted to he would cause her physical pain.

And causing pain to someone he loved was simply abhorrent to him, whether that pain was physical or emotional.

He loved Abbie with all his heart and he'd never wanted to cause her pain by not being there to support her when she was watching things like this. But his love for Ella was different. She was an actual *part* of his heart. Of his soul. He could feel her pain as keenly as if this procedure and the countless others that had come before this one were being performed on him.

And how could anyone justify continuing to inflict pain like that when the likelihood of success was so remote?

The weight of that pain and the darkness hovering in the future had been all that Rafael had been able to see.

But Abbie had been able to see the glimmer of hope and, this time, Rafael could see it too. If these results were good, Ella's central line would be taken out tomorrow. They would be able to take her home very, very soon.

He turned his head and, as if sensing the subtle movement, Abbie looked up and caught his gaze.

The love he could see in her eyes made his throat tighten so much he couldn't take a new breath but he could feel his lips curl in a gentle smile as his gaze clung to hers.

I love you, too, was the silent message. *I think I understand now.*

The second attempt at aspiration was successful. The lab technician was dotting what looked like dark blood onto the slides and then using another slide to smear the sample over the glass. They would be ready for staining and microscopic examination of the cells in no time at all. The registrar was holding test tubes with additional small amounts of the bone marrow, tipping them end to end to mix the anticoagulant and make sure that these samples didn't clot and become useless.

They would have the results very quickly.

And it was all over. The needle was out and the nurse had a dressing she was using to apply pressure to the almost invisible wound. The registrar was drawing up the medication to reverse the sedation.

Ella was a little grizzly as she began waking up properly.

'You carry her back to the ward,' Abbie said to Rafael. 'She's probably hungry more than anything after being nil by mouth this morning. I'll bet she lets you give her a bottle when we get her settled back in her room.'

Rafael was more than happy to oblige. He carried Ella in his arms, jiggling her gently to try and comfort her. Even being back in her room with Ears and ballerina bear didn't seem to distract her and she made it very clear she wasn't interested in having a bottle, from either her father or her mother.

She was still unhappy half an hour later.

'Is she in pain, do you think?'

Abbie shook her head. 'They put lots more local in when they finish the procedure and she's got paracetamol on board. I've never seen her react like this after an aspiration before. Try her with the bottle again.'

'You try first this time.'

But Ella wouldn't drink her milk, even with Abbie holding the bottle and cuddling her in the chair. She pushed it away with her little fists and cried harder.

Rafael tried reading her a story and making animal noises but it couldn't provide a distraction and it only made him feel foolish so he gave up. Abbie tried singing songs but petered out just as quickly. Even her beloved toy Ears was roundly rejected time and again and he ended up abandoned on the floor.

Ella was exhausted but still whimpering when the oncology consultant came to visit.

'The news couldn't be better,' the consultant told them. 'There's no evidence of the cancer whatsoever and the new T cells are still there, ready to fight any recurrence.'

Abbie burst into tears at the news. Rafael had to swallow very hard before he could produce any words.

'Thank you,' was all he could manage. 'Thank you *so* much.'

But the consultant's smile was fading already. 'She's not sounding too happy, is she?'

'She's been like this ever since the aspiration,' Abbie said. 'I don't understand. She's never reacted like this before.'

'She's breathing fast.' The consultant stepped closer

to where Abbie was holding Ella, rocking her. 'And she's feeling rather warm, don't you think?'

'She's been crying for a long time.'

'She must still be in pain,' Rafael said. 'Can we not give her something more for it?'

'I don't think it's her hip that's bothering her.' The consultant was frowning as her fingers pressed against Ella's upper arm, taking her pulse. 'I want a full set of vital signs done and a blood count.' She looked from Abbie to Rafael. 'I don't want to worry you but I have a feeling she might have picked up a bug of some kind.'

The blood-test results came back almost as fast as the results on the bone marrow had, but this time the news was very different.

Thanks to the strain on her immune system for so long, Ella had been unable to fight off whatever infection had sneaked past all their precautions.

Her cancer might have been beaten but there was a new enemy to fight now and it looked like a fierce one.

Over the rest of that day Ella's condition deteriorated bit by bit. Her heart and breathing rate increased. Her oxygen saturation dropped. Her temperature climbed. Various specialists were called in to assess her and, by that evening, they were all looking concerned.

'I'm so sorry,' one of them said to Rafael and Abbie, 'but this is looking serious. I'm afraid we need to shift Ella to Intensive Care.'

CHAPTER TEN

THEY'D BEEN HERE before but this was different.

The end of the road?

Abbie was beyond exhausted.

Beyond hope?

Ella had been intubated shortly after arriving in the intensive-care unit and the breathing tube attached to the ventilator had quickly been joined by other invasive monitoring devices, including an arterial line to measure blood gases, a second venous line to administer fluids, a urinary catheter and a nasogastric tube. She was transferred to an isolation room, X-rays taken and antibiotics started.

Now all they could do was watch and wait. To try and offer life support until such time as Ella's tiny body could muster the resources to overcome whatever new enemy had made its unwelcome appearance. The decisions that might need to be made if the situation got any worse were just too awful to contemplate.

They'd been so close to victory.

So close to fitting all those pieces of the perfect life back together again where they could have made a picture that was stronger and brighter than it had ever been before.

But now the colours had been muted. Virtually erased. Everything looked clinical and white and frightening in here. The only hint of colour around Ella was the faded pink of the bedraggled old toy, Ears, which Abbie had insisted on bringing with them and which now sagged forlornly at the far end of her bed, well out of the way. The sparkly pink ballerina bear had been left behind in the ward, seemingly along with all the other bright colours and hopes. Even Ella's pretty pink pyjamas were gone. She wore nothing more than a nappy in this warm space because her chest had to be bare due to all the electrodes that were stuck to her skin and easy access was needed to all the tubes invading her small body.

The sparkle of that new closeness with Rafael had gone, too. Things felt brittle between them again. As tense as they had been when she'd returned with Ella from New York. Far too similar to what things had been like just before she'd left when huge decisions had had to be made and they had been on such different pages. Just before that terrible row that had ended the marriage they'd had until then.

They were both in this small space with their daughter but the gap between them had widened. For Abbie it was too close to where she'd been when Ella had been so sick in New York and she had been there by herself, watching every breath her baby had taken in case it had been her last. Feeling…betrayed, because Rafael hadn't been there beside her.

He *was* here physically now but he seemed to be distancing himself, just like he had in the past. Standing back emotionally and weighing up whether it was fair to put a tiny person through so much suffering when… when there was no hope?

He was sitting on a chair in the corner of the room at the moment, his head tipped back and his eyes closed. His face was grey but neither of them had had any sleep since Ella had been brought into this intense place where small lives hovered between life and death. She hoped he was actually asleep now and not just trying to shut himself further away but it seemed unlikely given that two of the PICU doctors and a nurse were in here, quietly reassessing their newest admission after her first twelve hours of intensive care.

There *had* to be hope. Surely Abbie would be able to find it again when the stunning effect of this new blow wore off? Or when a new blood-test result came in that showed that one of the raft of antibiotics and other drugs was already helping to get the infection under control.

Abbie stared at the bank of monitors around the bed as the doctors spoke quietly to each other.

'Have you got a blood-gas syringe there?'

'Yes. Here it is. Do you want venous samples as well?'

'Yes. Let's get a full blood count and electrolytes. We need to keep a close eye on renal function, too.'

'What's the central pressure at the moment?'

'Down to nine. Let's get some more fluids up. I don't want it dropping any further.'

'Happy with sedation levels?'

'Yes. We'll keep the fentanyl and midazolam infusion going.'

The tracing of Ella's heartbeat blipped across the screen. Too fast but at least it was steady. Even a single missed beat right now and it might be too much for Abbie. She stared at the screen, willing it to continue.

One of the doctors handed a tiny syringe of arterial blood to the nurse, who whisked it away to test the oxygen levels. He checked all the figures being displayed on the ventilator and then glanced sideways.

'How are you doing, Abbie?'

Abbie shrugged. Goodness...had she caught such an Italian gesture from Rafael? She tried to swallow the huge lump in her throat.

'Oh...you know. We...really weren't expecting this...'

'I know.' The tone was full of sympathy. The doctor turned to look at Rafael. 'Things are stable at the moment. You two look like you need some rest. You know there's a bed that you can use? The nurse can show you where it is. You could take it in turns to get a bit of sleep.'

Rafael's eyes opened slowly, revealing how aware he was of everything going on in the room. 'I'm not going anywhere,' he said. 'Not this time.'

For a short time, when the doctors had done all they could for the moment, Rafael and Abbie were left alone with their daughter.

'Are you going to call your parents?'

Abbie shook her head. Any hope of the birth of a grandchild ending the estrangement had evaporated when her parents had disappeared from contact after learning that Ella was so sick. Such an obvious lack of support was the last thing she needed to be reminded of right now.

She only had Rafael, didn't she?

She'd thought he would be all she ever needed in the

way of family but the way he was pulling into himself with this latest crisis was leaving her feeling horribly isolated.

Desperately frightened, in fact.

Abbie had believed she was over the grief of losing the closeness she should have had with her own parents but it wasn't buried that deeply, after all, was it?

'Are you going to call yours?'

'*Si.* Of course.' But Rafael rubbed at his forehead and pushed his fingers through his hair. 'Even if it will worry them, they need to know. They are *la mia famiglia.* Fiorella's family.'

It was much later in the day before Rafael took the time to call Italy, however, and when he came back he went straight to Ella's bedside, where he stood staring down at the unconscious baby, resting a hand lightly on the top of her head. He looked tense enough to explode into a million shards.

'What's wrong?' Abbie asked.

'My mother…I can't believe she didn't tell me. She said she didn't want to worry me and it was nothing. But it's *not* nothing… It's…' The hand that wasn't touching Ella curled into a fist.

Abbie's heart sank to a new low. The world was spinning out of control with increasing intensity. 'What's happened?'

'My father. Apparently he had a heart attack two days ago.'

'Oh, my God… How bad was it?'

'I don't know. I need to clear my head a little before I try and ring the hospital. My mother's version of events was somewhat garbled. She said he's fine. That my father was far too stubborn to let something like a heart attack kill him.'

'Is *she* all right?'

A huff of sound came from Rafael. 'She made it sound as if it's nothing more than a head cold. As if... as if she doesn't actually *care*.'

The shaft of pain in Abbie's chest made her wonder if it was physically possible for a little piece of heart to break off.

Rafael was a passionate man who cared very deeply about the people he loved but had he been taught at an early age to step back from the worst of the pain that that sort of caring brought with it? To use *dis*passion as protection?

That would explain so much.

'You know that's not true,' she said softly. 'You know she cares very much. She's trying to protect you. Protect *herself*...'

Rafael stood there motionless for a long moment and then gave a terse nod. 'I'm sure you're right. They might have always fought a lot but they'd be lost without each other. She must be very afraid at the moment.'

'Why don't you go and ring the hospital? Ella's good. There's been no change.'

Good was hardly the word to describe Ella's condition, but while there'd been no improvement neither had there been any further deterioration, and maybe that was enough to qualify as 'good' for now.

It was nearly an hour later that Rafael returned again and this time some of the tension had gone.

'He *is* all right,' he told Abbie. 'I spoke to him and I spoke with his doctors. It was a small heart attack and he got to the hospital in good time. He's had several stents put in, which has probably saved him from having a much worse attack. Saved his life even…'

As before, Rafael had gone straight to Ella's bedside and was touching her again. A soft touch. And this time it was accompanied by the hint of a smile. Was he trying to transfer the hope from the news about his father to his daughter? Hoping against hope that another life was about to be saved?

Oddly, it made Abbie feel more isolated. She was relieved for Rafael and his family, of course she was, but did this end justify the means? Make it acceptable to put up those emotional barriers when things got tough?

'I…might go and have a shower,' she said. 'And see if I can get a couple of hours' sleep. If you're okay to stay with Ella?'

'Of course.' This time it was Abbie who received that gentle touch. 'I'm here. You do whatever it is you need to do.'

They couldn't spend every minute of every day in that small isolation room with Ella, no matter how hard it was to be away from her.

They had to eat. They had to use the bathroom. They had professional obligations that became more of an issue as the hours ticked into the third day of this crisis, even though their colleagues were only too happy to be covering for them.

'The MacDonalds want to speak to us before Angus is discharged,' Rafael said after a phone call. 'Maybe I should go and see them. It would be bad if they caused trouble for the clinic by making another complaint.'

'I'm sure Ethan could handle it.' But Abbie glanced at a message on her own pager. 'Annabelle's due to have the dressing taken off her new ear today. I do feel bad about missing that.' She tilted her head back to rest on the chair, covering her eyes with her hand. How long could you go on like this? Was there a point where physical and emotional exhaustion simply became too much? What happened then? A numbness that never left? Did you have to go through life like a robot? Going through the motions but incapable of feeling anything, good *or* bad?

'Ella's stable. Maybe it would be a good idea if we had more of a break than we've been getting. As long as one of us is here with her. We don't know how long this is going to go on for.'

Or how it was going to end. Ella was clearly fighting hard for life because the holding pattern was continuing and she wasn't getting any worse. But they all knew that she could reach the limit of her physical resources at any time. That she could crash and there would be nothing that any of them could do to keep supporting her.

Abbie took her hand from her eyes to find Rafael's concerned gaze resting on her. He wanted to help, didn't he? He just didn't know how because he was too far away. Emotionally distant. Protecting himself.

This was no time to attack him for something he probably couldn't help. Or change. And yet this was the kernel of why their marriage had got into trouble. The part of each other that they didn't get. Abbie thought she could understand why Rafael was like he was now but the real question still remained. Was he capable of giving her what she needed for the rest of her life?

Maybe nobody could. Maybe her expectations were simply too high.

The whole issue of their relationship was too much for her exhausted mind and body. Yes. Maybe they did need a break from being in here with Ella.

Maybe they needed a break from being with each other.

'You go and see the MacDonalds.' It wasn't as though it would be a new experience to be keeping this kind of a vigil by herself. 'I'll decide later about Annabelle.'

But Rafael was reluctant to go. 'Are you sure? I want to be here for you this time. For every minute.'

Didn't he want to be here for *Ella*? Had he given up hope on her again? Abbie had to blink back tears. She was being irrational but it was hard not to be when you felt this fragile. She had to get a grip. For Ella's sake as well as her own. She couldn't help her precious child if she fell apart herself.

'Go,' she said. 'You'll be back here soon enough. I'll be okay.'

Except she wasn't. Even if Rafael was holding himself distant emotionally, his presence had been more comforting than she'd realised. Being the only parent with nothing to do but watch and hold the tiny hand that emerged from the bandages covering the tubes was so lonely. So heartbreaking.

Maybe that was why Abbie allowed herself to be persuaded to take a break herself when Rafael came back with the news that a very happy MacDonald family was on its way home.

Her registrar and the ward nurse were surprised to see her appear in the treatment room.

'We weren't expecting you.'

'I needed a break,' Abbie told her colleagues quietly. There was no need for her patient's family to know that she had personal issues that outweighed any professional responsibilities. They were here with *their* precious child. The world outside Ella's room was continuing to revolve and maybe it was a good thing to be reminded of that.

'How's it going?' her registrar asked.

'As well as it can. No change yet.' Abbie raised her voice, turning to the nurse, who was carefully melting the sticky side of tape with an alcohol-dampened cotton bud. 'How's it going *here*?'

It was a fiddly business, removing the elaborate dressing that had been protecting Annabelle's new ear since her surgery. The plastic cup had been taped to her face and bandaged in place. Inside the cup were layers of soft dressings around and inside the ear.

'You're being very brave,' Abbie told her small patient. 'I know it's a bit sore when things stick like this.'

'Can I see it?' Annabelle asked. 'Can I see my new ear?'

'You sure can. It's going to look a bit pink and funny for a while, though. It takes time for the swelling to go down.'

'I want to see it.'

Abbie took a hand mirror from the nurse and held it for Annabelle, who tilted her head and stared intently at her image. The smile that lit up her face moments later was heart-warming.

'Do you like it?'

Annabelle nodded happily. 'I've got *two* earrings.'

'We'll have to put a new big dressing on it and hide it away for another couple of weeks but it's looking great.' Abbie smiled at Annabelle's mother. 'I'm really happy with the result.'

'Oh, so are we, Mrs de Luca. Thank you *so* much.'

It had been a good idea to take the short break. To connect with the world beyond what was happening to Ella. The warmth of Annabelle's smile stayed with Abbie as she hurried back, feeling stronger than she had when she'd left.

The smile with which Rafael greeted her return was also heart-warming. He was beside Ella, stroking her wispy, dark curls and talking to her quietly as a nurse took a set of vital-sign recordings. Abbie waited until the nurse was finished before going close enough to press a kiss to Ella's forehead.

'Hey, baby girl. How are you doing?'

'Still no better,' Rafael said quietly. 'But no worse either. We can only wait. How was Annabelle? Are you happy with the ear?'

Abbie nodded but she didn't want to talk about it. Already, the outside world had vanished again and the only thing that mattered was here in this room. She watched Ella breathing for a minute. Touched her hand that lay upturned, with the fingers curled in complete relaxation, as though she was having a natural sleep.

But this was anything but natural. This was state-of-the-art technology and a battery of medication that was keeping her baby alive. Needing comfort, Abbie picked up Ears. She turned away as she cuddled the toy under her chin. She could smell Ella on the toy and it made her want to cry.

'What's that?'

The fat file open on the chair Rafael had been sitting on distracted her.

'I've been reading Ella's story,' he told Abbie. 'From the first admission. I'd forgotten that we thought she'd just had a cold.'

Abbie sat down and picked up the file. The paediatrician had made meticulous notes.

'"Presenting symptoms,"' she read aloud, '"pale skin, unexplained fever, refusing feeds, crying a lot, irritable..."' Her voice caught. '"Query persistent pain."'

'She was only a few weeks old. Life is so unfair sometimes.'

Abbie was looking at the first sheaf of blood-test results that had come back on Ella. At notes from the new specialists that had been called in. At the plans for chemotherapy, steroid treatment and blood transfusions. The words blurred in front of her.

'It was unbelievable, wasn't it?'

'I thought it was my fault.' Rafael's soft words were shocking.

'What?' Abbie's jaw dropped. 'How could you possibly think that?'

'Because of Freddie.'

'Who's Freddie?' Abbie was bewildered. She'd said that they didn't really know each other but it had never smacked her in the face quite like this. She could see now that Rafael distanced himself as a form of protection but was it so effective she'd never even guessed at something so dark?

Rafael thought that Ella's illness was *his* fault?

'Freddie was a little boy who had ALL.' Rafael was still stroking Ella's head as he spoke softly. A slow, gentle movement of his hand that was probably comforting him as much as Ella, if she was aware of it. 'I got involved in his case just before I left oncology. He was the grandson of some of my parents' closest friends and they insisted that they brought Freddie to me. That, if anyone could save him, I could.' He glanced up at Abbie, one corner of his mouth lifting in a lopsided smile. And then he moved away from Ella, coming to perch one hip on the arm of the chair Abbie was sitting in. 'He was such a sunny child. His parents adored him and would have gone to the ends of the earth to save him.'

As they themselves would have for Ella. As they still would. Abbie swallowed hard.

'The initial treatment went well. He was a good candidate for bone-marrow transplant and, being Italian, of course there were any number of family members who were desperate to get tested. Unfortunately the only match was his little sister, who was only two and she couldn't understand why people wanted to hurt her. It was very tough on the whole family.'

There was more to this story. The absolute faith everybody had in him must have created an unprecedented pressure on Rafael to save this child. Abbie touched Rafael's hand to encourage him to continue.

'The early results after the transplant looked good but Freddie developed graft-versus-host disease. We tried everything we could. I pushed for us to try anything new that had even the slightest hope of success. I persuaded his parents to sign consent forms and told them that the extra suffering would be worth it when we succeeded. I was so determined to save him. And they were desperate to believe in me. I think we all believed that it would work in the end but he was admitted to Intensive Care a few weeks later. He was in there for four weeks. One by one, his vital organs gave up the struggle until there was nothing keeping him alive except for the machines, so there was a meeting and…and they decided it was time to stop. To turn the machines off.'

Abbie felt an icy chill run down her spine. 'You were *there*?'

'No. I was in my office later that day when Freddie's father came to see me. He was distraught. They'd all been through so much. He couldn't believe it hadn't worked. He kept asking me, *"Why…?"* And he was crying. I've never seen a man cry like that. And the way he was looking at me. They had believed in me. They had put their precious little boy through so much pain and suffering because I had persuaded them. And I'd let them down. Failed them all. It ripped me to pieces.'

Abbie squeezed his hand. 'Of course it did.'

'And that was when I decided I couldn't stay in oncology. That it would destroy me in the end. I was a coward and that was why I thought that maybe it was my fault that Ella became ill with cancer. A fitting punishment for my cowardice.'

For a man as proud as Rafael the admission was so huge it took Abbie's breath away.

'I wish you'd told me.'

'And shown my weakness? At a point when you needed me to be strong? What difference could it have made?'

'All the difference in the world,' Abbie whispered. 'That's what I meant by not understanding each other. If I'd known, I would have understood why you were so against the treatment in New York. That you couldn't bear to see Ella continuing to suffer. You'd been through it all before, with Freddie. You knew that the extra pain and suffering might be just that. Extra pain that Ella didn't have to endure. That it wasn't because you didn't care enough.'

Rafael swore softly in Italian. 'How could you ever have thought that I didn't care enough?' The words were fierce enough to sound angry.

'You thought your mother didn't care,' she reminded him quietly. 'She didn't let you in, did she? She couldn't show you how she felt after your father's heart attack. Maybe she was blaming herself. Maybe she was remembering all the arguments they'd ever had and decided that was what had caused it all.'

Rafael was silent. Was he seeing the connection? Understanding something of how *she* had felt when he hadn't been able to listen to how she'd felt about Ella's treatment?

Her breath escaped in a half sob. 'You know what the funny thing is?'

'Funny?'

'Funny sad, I mean. Because there was something I didn't tell you then either.' Maybe the inability to share the important things wasn't completely one-sided. Perhaps she had been trying to protect herself as well by holding back. She couldn't do it any more. She *shouldn't* have done it at all.

'What?'

'That I thought it was *my* fault.'

'*Che cosa*? Why?'

Abbie's voice was choked. 'I've always felt guilty, you know? That I survived when Sophie didn't. My parents loved her so much.'

'I'm sure they loved you too.'

'But it was Sophie who was hurting. Her pain that they couldn't bear. I don't think they even saw *my* pain. I was alive, wasn't I? I was the lucky one.'

'Oh…*cara*…' Somehow Rafael had gathered her into his arms and he was holding her.

'I felt like they couldn't stand seeing me still alive because it reminded them of what they'd lost. And I hated it. I must have made life so much harder for them and I wondered later if that was why they broke up. And… and I thought, maybe Ella getting sick was *my* punishment…to show me how hard it had been for them.'

Rafael held her shoulders firmly, pushing her back far enough to see his face clearly.

'It was not your fault that Ella got sick.'

Abbie held his intense gaze. 'It wasn't your fault either. Don't *ever* think that.'

'I couldn't care more. For Ella *or* you. I would give my life to keep either of you safe.'

'I know that now.' There was a new pain in Abbie's chest. Her heart felt like it might break again but for a different reason this time. Because it felt so full of love it was in danger of bursting at the seams. Maybe the pain came from stretching rather than breaking. Hearts could do that, couldn't they?

Maybe there was even room in there for her own parents, too. Maybe, with her new depth of understanding, she would be able to forgive and old wounds could begin to heal. For all of them.

The beeping of the machinery surrounding Ella was the only sound in the room for a long moment. Somebody from the team caring for their daughter would no doubt be coming into the room at any time to check on things but just for now, they were in a little bubble of time that was just for them.

A moment that had brought them closer than ever.

A louder beeping was issuing some kind of warning. A dropping level of oxygen saturation, perhaps, or an indication that blood pressure was getting too low.

It made Abbie flinch.

'I can't do this, Rafe,' she whispered fiercely. 'Ella might die and I don't think I can live with that.'

'Yes, you can. If you have to, you can… You must.'

The words sounded oddly strangled. Abbie raised her gaze to see tears on Rafael's face. Tears that chased each other in rapid succession to trickle down the sides of that proud nose and follow the deep grooves to collect at the corners of lips that were trembling.

Tears. From the man who never cried. From the man she'd thought was keeping a safe emotional distance from what was happening to their daughter. A safe distance from her.

Tears from the man she loved so much.

'You can feel that pain and you *can* survive,' Rafael told her brokenly. 'And you know how?'

Abbie shook her head.

'Because you're loved. I'm not like your parents, Abbie. I see your pain. I understand. And...and I *love* you.'

'I love you, too.'

Rafael nodded. 'I know this. And that's how I know I would survive, too. But only if I have you. You only feel afraid if you're not safe and...and maybe I've never been brave enough to let myself feel it, but—'

'We can love each other,' Abbie finished for him. 'We can keep each other safe.'

And, with Rafael's arms tightly around her, Abbie buried her face against his shoulder for a moment, to gather her strength as people rushed into the room to find out what had tripped the alarm they'd seen from the central station.

'She's fighting the ventilation,' one of them decided. 'Trying to breathe for herself.'

'Maybe it's time we lightened the sedation. How's everything else looking?'

Abbie stood there in the circle of Rafael's arms as the medical team did a thorough assessment on Ella and debated the juggling of her medications and interventions.

She was a fighter, all right, their little daughter.

And they would be here, together. By her side for every minute of this fight.

And whether it ended in victory or not, they would still be together. Abbie knew that now with absolute certainty.

Their marriage had been put through a trial by fire because of Ella's illness. The battle for their little girl's survival wasn't over yet but the reason they'd been pushed apart was.

There was nothing they couldn't survive from now on.

As long as they were together.

Loving each other.

Keeping each other safe.

EPILOGUE

Six months later...

IT WAS EARLY autumn but it still felt like summer here on the Amalfi Coast.

Abbie thought the small Italian town of Amalfi was every bit as beautiful as Rafael had hoped she would.

The perfect place for a wedding.

A place that filled such a special part of his heart. The ancient, sun-baked buildings in soft pastels and terracotta that clung to the foothills of the dramatic cliffs and jostled for space all the way down to the shoreline, where the beach umbrellas took over. The somnolent serenity of the lemon groves high on the hillsides that surrounded his family estate. Rafael was enjoying the view of the lemon groves at the moment, leaning on the warm stone balustrade of the terrace. Taking a moment from a busy day to count his blessings.

Like the warmth and generosity of his family as they were finally able to welcome Abbie and Ella into their midst.

They had been puzzled by the news that Abbie's parents weren't coming to the wedding.

'But why not?'

'It was too far for them to come.'

Abbie hadn't been talking about physical distance. The emotional gap was still too big to bridge but at least the invitation had been offered. Contact had been reestablished and the door was open again. Abbie was quietly confident that, one day, those old wounds would be healed.

'We're going to visit them when we get back to England. They want to see all the photographs.'

The planned visit might have been tentatively suggested and warily accepted but it would be a huge step forward and, in the meantime, Rafael's family was more than prepared to step forward.

'We are your family now, too,' Rafael's father, Georgio, declared, 'and if you will permit me the honour, I will be the one to give this beautiful bride's hand in marriage to my son.'

'It's me who would be honoured,' Abbie had responded. *'Grazie mille, Papa.'*

Oh, they'd loved hearing her not only try out her Italian but take her place in the family. Rafael could understand the tears of joy in his father's eyes because he'd had that reaction himself the first time Ella had called him *Papa*.

She could do more than that now. She could say, *'Ti amo, Papy.'*

I love you, Daddy.

There had been many tears of joy being shed in this part of Salerno over these last few days. His mother and his sister, Marcella, who was going to be Abbie's bridesmaid, were probably encountering a fair few of them today as they took Abbie and Ella out for some last-minute, pre-wedding shopping and probably a gelato down at the beach.

Everyone they met would know the de Luca family and would have heard their story. They would know instantly who the beautiful little toddler was and Mama would no doubt be only too happy to stop and let them marvel.

'Isn't she the *bambina* who has been so terribly ill?'

'But she looks so *sana* now. So healthy…so happy…'

'It's surely *un miracolo*.'

It was indeed *un miracolo*.

The road hadn't been easy but Ella had kept fighting after the life support of the ventilator had been deemed unnecessary and she had gone from strength to strength since then. They'd had another visit back to the hospital when she'd been due for another bone-marrow biopsy at the six-month mark after her ground-breaking treatment and that had gone without any complications. And they'd been rewarded with the same astonishingly good news that they'd had after her last biopsy.

There was no sign of the cancer that had threatened to take this joy from their lives and the new cells were still there, ready to fight any attempted recurrence. It wasn't just the exuberant Italians who were labelling it a miracle. Ella's case was being written up in many journals. Being held up as an example of why all the time and effort and money spent on medical research was worthwhile.

She'd been able to go home the same day that time. Back to their home that was finally a *real* home. One that had a sparkly pink bedroom that Ella adored. He and Abbie had finally managed to paint the silver stars on the ceiling. They'd even managed to stick the glitter on so that they sparkled as much as dancing bear's tutu did. Seeing those stars for the first time had been when they'd heard something they'd never thought they'd hear again.

Ella gurgling with happiness as she'd stretched her arms and tried to reach the new sparkles in her life.

He and Abbie had looked at each other. They'd both opened their mouths to say it…

Ella's being a plughole…

But neither of them had been able to utter a word because the moment had been so choked by joy.

Just the memory of that moment, the echo of the sound of childish delight, would always melt his heart.

And beneath those stars Ella had a real bed now. There was room for dancing bear and Ears and all sorts of other beloved toys to share her sleeping space.

Her hair had grown back into a soft cluster of dark curls. She was still a little too thin for her age, which made her eyes look even bigger, but she was, without doubt, the most beautiful child that had ever existed.

Being healthy was what really mattered, though.

And his father, busy at the moment searching for the tie that matched his best suit, was also healthy again. Healthier than he had been for many years.

The heart attack had been a blessing in disguise.

Not just because his father had had his damaged arteries repaired and had now modified his lifestyle to exclude smoking and include exercise and would probably live to be Ella's *nonno* for many years to come.

No. The blessing had also come from how shocking

his mother's apparent lack of concern had been. How he could see so clearly the damage that emotional distance could inflict on others.

He would never be like that again. Or if it happened even a little before he noticed it, Abbie would remind him. She would only need to look at him with that special look she had for him alone and he would remember how safe he was.

How safe he would always be.

Because Abbie loved him so much.

Rafael de Luca took a deep, deep breath of the warm, lemon-scented air and then straightened and turned to go back inside. Not that he really needed to help with the preparations for the big day tomorrow because it seemed like the whole town had been given a part to play, but he wanted to be part of it. He wanted to revel in every single moment of this special trip home.

He paused for just a heartbeat longer, however, as he let his breath out in a long, contented sigh.

He really was the luckiest man on earth.

Abbie took a deep, deep breath as she got out of the car.

This was it. The long-awaited dream wedding that had been put on hold for so long.

She had known it would be special, coming to Rafael's home town to pledge their commitment to each other in public, but she'd had no idea that she would be so unquestioningly adopted by an entire family.

By a whole town, it seemed.

There were people clapping and cheering already, as Georgio de Luca came to open the door of the car, even though they had a short walk before they got anywhere near the intimidating flight of stone steps that led up to Amalfi's famous ninth-century cathedral. Cars couldn't get into the narrow streets that led to the *piazzo*.

The soft fabric of her wedding dress rippled around her as she got out of the car into the warmth of an endless Italian summer afternoon. Abbie had wanted traditional but not over the top and her classic lace dress had a fitted, beaded bodice, a tiny waist and a deliciously swirly, feminine skirt that brushed the ground and had just a small train.

She'd chosen a natural style for her hair, too, because she knew Rafael loved it best when it was loose and flowing. The hairdresser had tamed the waves into shapely, soft curls, clipped some of the hair back to keep it out of her face and then cleverly looped some of the tresses to create a casually elegant look that was perfect for the tiny white flowers that would be her only accessories. It had seemed too much to hope for that lemon blossoms would be available so early in the season but somehow it had been made possible.

Abbie hadn't wanted a veil and as she stepped out to see the blue sparkle of the sea and the happy faces of people lining the route she was about to take into the Piazzo del Duomo, she knew she'd made the right decision. She didn't want anything that would put even a flimsy barrier in front of any part of this day.

Smiling her thanks at Georgio, Abbie turned and bent down to peer into the car.

'You ready, baby girl?'

A mop of shiny, dark curls adorned with a clip that held a tiny lemon blossom flower to match the ones in Abbie's hair nodded agreement but Ella didn't wait for her mother's help. She wriggled across the seat, turned onto her tummy and slid out of the car.

Her dress was pink, of course. A version of the same tutu that her ballerina bear still wore, and Ella adored it. She loved her lacy white socks too and the sheer cuteness of the pink ballet pumps on her small feet would always make her parents smile.

Marcella was hurrying to catch up from the other side of the car.

'Ella. Come here, *cara*. *Zia* Marcella will carry you to the church.'

'No. Ella *walk*.'

'It's a long way, *cara*.'

Abbie smiled at the new sister she already loved. 'Let her walk, Marcella. Her little legs will get tired before we get halfway up those steps and then we can pick her up.'

It wasn't Ella's legs getting tired so much as the press of people wanting to see the arrival of the bride that made her want to be carried. And it wasn't her new aunty that she wanted.

'Mum-mum-mum…'

Abbie handed her bouquet to Marcella to carry and scooped Ella into her arms.

'It's a long way,' Marcella said anxiously. 'Maybe Papa should carry her?'

Abbie looked at the huge set of steps she needed to carry her daughter up. It would be a challenge but nothing compared to the challenges they had already faced and won. Smiling, she declined the offer.

Somewhere, at the top of all those stairs, Rafael was waiting for them. The love of her life.

Ella's papa.

How perfect was it that she would carry their daughter into the ceremony that would show the world their commitment to each other as a family?

She shifted Ella into a slightly more secure position on one hip as Marcella arranged her train so that it would flow beautifully up the steps.

A quick glance down at her dress showed her that nothing was out of place.

Abbie pressed a quick kiss to Ella's curls to hide her smile.

She'd always said she didn't want to be a pregnant bride but this was okay because it was early days.

Still a secret between her and Rafael.

She couldn't wait any longer. Abbie began to climb the steps.

It wasn't really okay, was it?

It was more like *perfect*.

* * * * *

200 HARLEY STREET: AMERICAN SURGEON IN LONDON

LYNNE MARSHALL

For my husband of thirty-one years.
I'm so glad I found you.

And special thanks to Flo for inviting me into
this continuity.

CHAPTER ONE

GRACE TURNER GLANCED around the perfectly appointed guest apartment—cream-colored walls, beige couch and a matching club chair, with half a dozen colorful pillows strategically placed, red accent chair on the opposite side, fresh-cut white calla lilies in a tall vase on the glass-topped coffee table. There was even a small cherrywood desk pushed into the corner with internet hookup. Her laptop fit perfectly there.

Everything was in place for her convenience, and she was definitely thankful to the Hunter Clinic for the comfort in her new home away from home. The apartment was also supposed to be a mere ten-minute walk around the corner to 200 Harley Street and her new job.

Her gaze drifted into the single bedroom with the extra-large bed. *That's not going to see any action. A single wide would have been more than adequate.* Surrounded by luxury and taste to the hilt, the guest apartment was already closing in on her and she needed to get out. Desperately.

The extended-stay hotel was fully serviced, and though she hadn't had a chance to shop for food yet, she didn't feel like ordering room service. She'd heard of a tiny car-free street somewhere nearby, also within walking distance, where she could window-shop and dine alfresco, but she was sick of being alone. And why bother to buy new clothes when she didn't have anyone to wear them for?

She paced the length of the living room, noticed the invitation placed carefully on her mantelpiece before her arrival from the States yesterday, and picked it up. It was a duplicate of the one sent to her a couple of months back. Frankly, she'd forgotten all about the fundraising event at the London Eye tonight. Leo Hunter, the man who'd personally asked her to join his clinic, had said he'd be attending. The combination of meeting her new boss a day early and in a more casual setting at a charity event, and a bit of fun on the London Eye sounded like the perfect antidote for her early-onset cabin fever.

Grace strode to the eye-popping white kitchen and put on some water for tea. Even though she was tired, she felt too restless to sleep. She needed a little caffeine to ward off the quickly approaching fatigue from the long flight. Then she headed for the bedroom to find the perfect outfit.

Never an easy chore, finding fashionable clothes that covered her scars, Grace burrowed through her two suitcases, tossing tops, dresses, slacks, and underwear every which way. Making a mental note to put things in the drawers and closet at her earliest convenience, she continued to dig through the luggage. Ah, there was the black lace bodysuit, the one with a mock turtleneck and wrist-length sleeves. It would go perfectly under that low-cut black evening dress with the puffy shoulders and cap sleeves, and the above the knee-length dress would showcase her best attribute—her legs.

It being May in London, she could definitely get away with bundling up for the clear but chilly evening. No one would raise an eyebrow about the extra layer of underclothing, especially as it was sexy. She'd discovered over the years that there was nothing quite like fine black lace to cover up the scars.

An hour later, invitation in hand, a new layer of makeup carefully applied, and with a glittery fake jeweled barrette in her hair just for fun, she made her way toward the apartment door.

Grace felt like a kid again. Getting out of the taxi near Westminster Bridge, her eyes went to the huge, brightly lit, famous Ferris wheel. The cabbie instructed her toward the entrance, and off she went, entranced by the huge ride, following the spectacle that filled up this part of the London skyline. Showing her invitation to the official-looking security guard, she was let inside the gate. A fairly large crowd of impeccably dressed people of all shapes and ages milled around, chatting, sipping drinks and eating tidbits provided by tuxedo-dressed helpers with flashy silver trays.

Though she was considered wealthy back home by Scottsdale, Arizona standards, they paled in comparison with tonight's larger-than-life festivities. She ate a salmon puff, sipped some champagne and looked for a familiar face. The only face she knew, actually, and that was from an interview on world-renowned plastic surgery clinics she'd seen on TV, was Leo Hunter's.

A half hour later, still circulating through the crowd,

a gaze here, a nod there, a smile every once in a while, she noticed one particularly grandly dressed couple get off the Eye. She'd seen them get on—she checked her watch—about half an hour ago. Still unsuccessful in finding Leo Hunter, she decided to quit looking for him and take the ride.

She might not be able to meet Leo tonight, but she could at least grab a few quiet moments and take in the amazing sights of London all lit up. She read a sign with a few facts about the Eye. After doing some quick mental math, converting meters to feet, she took a deep breath, realizing she'd soon be more than four hundred feet in the air. Her phobia wasn't fear of heights so much as fear of falling. She glanced at the sturdy-looking steel-and-glass pods, convincing herself they'd hold. But she'd keep safely away from the windows. So she walked up the ramp and, with the Eye closed to the public for the charity event, was able to follow a handful of people onto the next pod.

One man already on board didn't bother to get off.

Two middle-aged couples talked quietly on one side of the egg-shaped pod. She nodded at them and they smiled, but clearly their circle of friends was closed to outsiders. She considered sitting on the wooden bench in the middle to help lessen her fear of falling, but changed her mind.

On the other side of the pod, that single figure taking a second trip gazed outside. Something about him drew her to his side of the pod. From behind, he had broad shoulders that filled out his tuxedo perfectly, and rich brown hair that kissed the collar on his shirt. He seemed closer to her age than the others, too. He leaned against the rail, shoulder to the glass, arms folded, deep in thought. She took a tentative step closer, not invading his privacy but close enough to see his profile.

Wow. The man was nothing short of gorgeous, with a high forehead, strong brows and jaw, a nose that could be claimed perfect if it wasn't for the attractive bump on the bridge. The decisive cleft in his chin was almost overkill. Speaking strictly as a reconstructive surgeon, this guy was a natural work of art. Even the shell of his ear was attractive.

She'd never been one to swoon over looks, especially in her line of work, when she knew people could alter their appearances to be more perfect looking, but this man in all his glory elicited chill bumps. Tingles danced along the skin of her arms and up the back of her neck as he awakened something inside her, long forgotten.

She took in a slow breath to steady herself. Perhaps it was the fact the pod had reached a point where she realized she'd soon be dangling from a height almost twice that of the Statue of Liberty that made her knees weaken. She snuck another glance at him and reached for the rail.

There was something more than pure handsomeness in this man. Something about his brooding, the tight upper lip and mildly pouting lower lip, how lost in his thoughts he seemed. There was something about his dissatisfaction about God only knew what that drew her in. Unfortunately, she'd always been a sucker for brooders. And she was definitely drawn to his contemplation, against her will maybe, but will seemed to have nothing to do with it. She couldn't stop herself from staring.

He was a perfectly made man who, from the expression on his face, seemed perfectly miserable, and that was the part that touched her most—it made him someone she could relate to.

"Hi," she said to him, surprising herself, but what the hell, if she was going to spend the next half hour dangling above the Thames, she may as well be talking to the handsomest man she'd ever laid her eyes on. Who knew? Regardless of the millions of people who'd already ridden it safely, something could go wrong on the Eye tonight. For all she knew, this might be the last thirty minutes of her life.

Wouldn't it be smart to spend those last minutes staring into the most intense eyes she'd ever seen?

Grace smiled to herself, thinking she'd officially turned into a fatalistic drama queen. Apparently the handsome stranger's doom and gloom had rubbed off on her.

This was the last place Mitch Cooper wanted to be tonight, but Leo had needed someone to cover for him while he and Lizzie were seeing a travel agent about their upcoming honeymoon in Paris. Between Leo and this highly sought-after travel agent's schedules, the appointment landed at eight o'clock on a Sunday night.

The black-tie affair had been on the calendar long before Leo had finally seen the light and popped the question to the head nurse at the Hunter Clinic. Though the newly marrieds had put off their honeymoon until the summer, he understood the guy needed an extra night off duty every now and again.

Mitch would rather be home, reading a good-night

book to Mia. Sure, Roberta was there, but no nanny could replace a father's love—or a mother's.

He braced himself for more nights like these, since Leo had asked his surgeons to step in and help with the multiple and necessary social functions and fund-raisers related to the Hunter Clinic. Especially now that Leo had gotten married, he'd want a life away from the clinic and that meant the rest of them attending more events. And as a team player, Mitch would do his share.

After all, the clinic with the wealthy donors who kept things running for the sake of those in need, not to mention the eternally nipping-and-tucking plastics patients, was everyone's bread and butter. If he wanted to stake out a new life for himself in London, and provide the kind of life he dreamed of for his daughter, this small price to pay wasn't so bad.

Tonight he'd rubbed elbows with as many guests as humanly possible. He'd made the rounds, done his duty and had now decided to sneak off and take in the view one more time before heading home. He'd have to bring Mia here one day. She'd love it.

He really did love London, especially after dark, and most especially after leaving Hollywood and all the bad memories behind.

Someone spoke—a woman. He dragged himself out of his dark thoughts, which always managed at quiet times like these to circle back to his ex-wife and best friend.

"Hi," he said robotically, looking straight ahead. "En-joying yourself?" Then, back on duty and clicking into host mode, he actually glanced at the person to his left.

Time slowed as he took in the strikingly beautiful

woman. Large and inquisitive pale eyes, enhanced by dark eyeliner and curtained by thick bangs, stared expectantly at him. Having never seen her before, because he'd definitely remember this face if he had, he assumed she was a wealthy donor.

With no sign of plastic surgery or Botox injections, she smiled naturally, with fine crinkles beside her eyes and mouth. Her cheeks grew more prominent, and that sweet little mouth with meticulously applied pink lipstick stretched into a serene smile. The sight of such a lovely face buoyed his spirits nearly to the height of the pod.

Could he be so superficial, letting natural beauty grab him like this? Yes, and his broken marriage proved it. Hadn't he learned his lesson? "Have you been to the London Eye before?"

She shook her head of dark hair—half of it piled high on her crown and with a shiny barrette meant for nothing more than show, something his daughter might wear—the rest of the hair dropping in waves around her neck. "I'm new in town."

Probably here for some plastic-surgery work since tonight's guests were by invitation only. All the beautiful women he'd ever known thought of plastic surgery as their little beauty secret. Maybe he could talk her out of whatever procedure she'd come to have. Why mess with genuine perfection? God, he hoped she didn't plan to change her lips. They were just fine as they were, with the classically shaped Cupid's-bow upper lip and the plump lower mate. Bigger was not always better, and lip jobs never looked completely natural, in his opinion. Even under his skilled hands.

"If you're new in town, then I guess I need to be a gentleman and point out a few landmarks, don't I?"

She continued to smile and her expression changed to one of playfulness. "Definitely. By the way, I notice you're American, too."

He nodded. "I'm from California originally. How about you?"

"Arizona."

Didn't they have highly acclaimed plastic surgery clinics in Scottsdale? Maybe, as Scottsdale could be a tight-knit small town, she didn't want anyone to know she was undergoing a procedure. Maybe she'd told everyone she was going on vacation, and when she went home she'd look amazingly well rested. Who knew? Who cared? Maybe he should quit reading so many sleuth novels and stop assuming the worst about women.

Right now, he'd grab a moment for himself and enjoy it with…what was her name?

"I'm Mitchell, by the way, and you are?"

"Grace. Nice to meet you."

Yes, of course her name would be Grace, she almost shimmered with it.

"So, Grace, across the Thames there you'll notice Big Ben, and the Gothic-style building with all of those lights right on the river are the Houses of Parliament."

She followed wherever he pointed, smiled and nodded. He liked it that she'd stepped a little closer and a refreshing, brisk, fruity scent floated up his nose. She wore a sexy black dress with a diving neckline, but instead of flaunting everything God had given her—there he went assuming again, but her breasts were probably real as they were shapely but not overly large—

she'd covered up with amazingly alluring thin black lace. Sexy. And not fair. The subtle holding back made him all the more curious about what lay beneath. Some women knew how to make a man take notice and beg for more. Hats off to the beautiful Grace from Arizona.

He cleared his throat, forcing his thoughts back on task. "Oh, and over there is Westminster Abbey. Look down just a bit more. There."

She inched forward and grimaced when she glanced downward.

"Fear of heights?"

"Fear of falling."

"Ah. I promise I won't push you or swing the pod." She smiled and another moment stopped in time. He grasped for something to say. "Remember trying to make the Ferris-wheel gondolas swing when you were a kid?"

She gave him an incredulous and funny look.

He grinned. "Maybe that was just a guy thing. Anyway, I'll point out a few more places...."

She oohed and ahhed over everything, giving him the impression he was doing a fantastic job as a tour guide. Maybe he could start a second career? But then again, maybe she was easily pleased.

"The lights make everything so much more beautiful, don't they?" she said, her sweet, husky voice soothing every wrinkle in his mind.

The sparkling city lights reflected off the pod window and dappled her face in shimmering whites and muted colors. He dipped his head in agreement with her statement—the lights did make everything look more beautiful, especially her.

They continued the rest of the ride in casual conversation, just two Americans in London sharing a fun moment together. It was a hell of a lot better than what he'd been doing before she'd spoken to him.

She laughed easily when he tried to be charming and he liked that—made him want to keep talking. He also liked it that her fashionable shoes made her only a couple of inches shy of his six feet—all the better to stare into those amazingly vibrant blue eyes.

Suddenly energized, as the pod ended its full circle journey, and not wanting to say goodbye to the lovely lady, he got a crazy idea. Ask her out. Why not?

But he was so out of practice at spending time with women. Didn't have a clue what she might like to do. Where did the only female that mattered in his life like to go best? "Do you enjoy swinging?"

A shocked and offended expression replaced Grace's prior childlike enjoyment. She really had a way with giving "looks" that said it all.

Realizing his unintentional allusion to carefree sex—*swinging*—he raced to make things right. "On swings, I mean. Actual swings. Uh, the kind you sit on. Swinging?"

She blurted out a laugh, relief softening her eyes. "Oh. Well, in that case…I haven't been on a swing in ages."

The pod door opened. The other couples exited. He took her by the arm and led her out. "I know a place nearby—that is, if you're up for it. We could walk over. Maybe have a drink afterwards?" He let go of her arm, not wanting to seem overbearing. "No strings."

He gazed earnestly into her blue—yes, they were definitely blue—eyes. "What do you say?"

He'd laid it on the line, stuck out his neck and set himself up to be humiliated with a firm no, but he couldn't help it. Something about her had made him ask. Suddenly, his only desire was to spend more time with this woman.

But for all she knew, he could be a London serial killer. He, on the other hand, had known immediately that she definitely wasn't a serial killer, just a lovely lady biding her time before "donating" to the Hunter Clinic.

"I'm still on Arizona time, everything's all mixed up, but I'm not ready to turn in yet. Sure. Why not?"

Apparently as good at reading people as he was, she, and their mutual trust of strangers at charity events, overcame all her doubts. And he couldn't have been happier with her decision.

The man named Mitch—and she was perfectly happy not knowing his full name, because once she began her new job she wouldn't have a spare moment to get to know anyone outside work anyway—grabbed each of them some champagne in a plastic flute and directed her out of the gate. Facing away from the Thames, they turned left and soon came upon a few straggling street artists, no doubt holding out for the last of the tourists of the day. Or night. She checked her watch, it was almost ten.

One street artist was completely silver and stood on a small box with a large jar for tips at his feet. His head was shaved, he wore a suit and was reading a book. Perfectly still. Another fellow wore a fedora and a raincoat, all bronze from head to toe, arms folded, one foot forward looking like something from out of the forties or fifties.

"What if their nose itches?" she said, taking a long sip of her bubbly, admiring the live art.

Mitch laughed. "I'll ask." He stepped forward, dug into his pocket and put a bill into the tip jar. "What do you do if your nose itches?"

The pavement artist slowly and believably came to life. First his eyes moved, then he twitched his nose. He unfolded his arms and robotically took his index finger and ran it up and down the bridge of his nose. Then, just as methodically, as if he were a machine or wind-up toy, he returned to his original stance.

Grace clapped. "Love it."

Mitch gave her an odd look as he took the crook of her elbow and pulled her down the path. She followed willingly. Halfway down the wide walkway they came upon a huge fenced-off playground on the right.

"This is, bar none, my favorite playground," he said.

Why would he have a favorite playground? Was he married with children? Could her innocent desire to forget and enjoy the night damage someone else's relationship? She slowed. He noticed her hesitation, raising an eyebrow over it.

"I'm just a big kid, I guess."

He said it so matter-of-factly that she didn't pursue the rest of the story. He'd told her everything she needed to know. He was a big kid who happened to know about children's playgrounds.

Yeah, he was probably a dad. A single dad? One could only hope.

But tonight wasn't about making a new friend, learning about family trees, personal baggage, regrets, or joys. Tonight was about letting go and having a little adventure with a complete, and totally handsome, stranger. The less she knew the better. Just to be on the safe side, though, she'd memorized the walk back to the Eye and could get herself there in a flash.

She nodded. He took the cue and they walked to the entrance of the Jubilee Playground, which had a large green sign on the gate.

"'Young adventurers this way,'" he read, glanced at her and winked. "That would be us."

Grace saw the shoulder-high fence railings and closed gate and wondered how they'd manage to get inside, just as two hands took her by the waist and hoisted her upward. He lifted her as if she weighed nothing. "You want to go first? Or should I?"

She suppressed her need to squeal, sucking in a breath instead. "Let me take off my shoes at least."

He put her down and moved a few feet over to an embankment where the fence was much lower. He jumped up on the cement ledge and offered down his hand. She threw her shoes onto the grass and climbed up with his help. To hell with the sexy dress, and thank God she had on the body suit!

His eyes sparkled when he glanced at her just before he jumped the fence. How the hell was she supposed to do that? Realizing his mistake, he jumped back over and helped her up, giving her time to get her footing and gain confidence, and soon, with the help of his cupped hands for her foot, she'd also scaled the fence.

Everything in the playground was made of sturdy logs and wood, encouraging the "young adventurers" to climb and play. Like a man who'd been here a number of times, Mitch led her to the swings and helped her on, then gave her a big push.

He had to be a father. And husband? Oh, no, she hoped not.

She curved into the night, feeling like a kid again. Soon he joined her on another swing and they quietly went about the business of letting down their hair in the cool evening breeze.

"This is great," she said, having pumped her feet enough to take her to the hilt on the swing. "Haven't done this since I don't know when."

"Then I'd say you're overdue. Hey, for someone with a fear of heights, you're awfully high."

"That's 'cause I'm in control."

"Ah, a lady who likes to be in control. How refreshing."

She'd play along with his teasing jab about pushy women. "Watch it, buddy." With that she jumped out of her swing in midair, feeling daring, and more like a kid trying to impress an older boy than a thirty-two-year-old reconstructive surgeon.

He applauded then used his feet to stop his swing the old-fashioned way. "Want to go down the slide?" He looked directly at her in the darkness of the playground, daring her to take his challenge.

She sputtered a laugh. "In this dress?"

"You climbed the fence and dove out of the swing, didn't you?"

"True," she said, dusting off her hands. "But I really don't want to ruin my dress on a slide." She ignored his dare and walked farther on. "You're probably renting that tuxedo, and don't care what happens to it," she said, one last attempt to save face.

"How about the monkey bars, then?"

"Who's there?" came a gruff voice from over the fence. A high-beamed flashlight danced around the vicinity of the swings. She fought the urge to hide sideways behind a pole. "No trespassing."

"We were just leaving, Officer." Mitch stepped up and offered a hand to Grace. Her heart pounded from the swinging, and now for getting into trouble for it.

She grinned to make up for her nerves and decided to go the teasing route. "That's what I get for going off with a strange man on an adventure. Next I'll be thrown in jail and I've barely been in town twenty-four hours."

The security officer noticed the fact that Mitch wore a tuxedo and she was in an evening dress, and he beetled his brows and tugged his earlobe. "You're not dressed for the playground, are you?"

"No, sir, we're escapees from the Hunter Clinic charity function at London Eye tonight," Mitch said.

The man's expression brightened. "The Hunter Clinic helped my niece when she'd burned her face on a campfire. Wonderful place, that clinic on Harley Street. Now if you'll just run along, I'll let you off with a stern warning."

"Thank you!" Grace called out, walking briskly toward the exit.

The officer stood by and watched with one brow raised as they jumped back over the fence, Mitch helping Grace up and over. Then Mitch shook the man's hand and the officer bid them good-night. They all walked away, the officer one direction, they in another.

"I'm starving. How about you?" Mitch asked, grinning like a kid who'd just gotten away with mischief.

Besides the salmon puff she really hadn't eaten anything today, not yet having had time to stock food in her new kitchen. "Come to think of it, I am, too."

"I know a great place about ten minutes away. You okay to walk in those shoes?" He nodded toward the shoes dangling from her fingers.

"I made it here, didn't I?" She brushed off her skirt with the palm of her free hand and worried about how messed up her hair must look.

He smiled and his white teeth gleamed in the night. It wasn't fair he was that gorgeous. "That's the spirit."

Fifteen minutes later they wound up past the Hungerford Bridge on the third floor of the Royal Festival Hall in an upscale restaurant overlooking the South Bank. They sat at the huge modern wraparound bar with a distinct 1950s-influenced design. The view was gorgeous, and Grace ordered a Cabernet Sauvignon and gnocchi. Mitch ordered a mixed drink and steak.

Up close, in the brighter-than-average lit bar, his eyes were green, more sea-green blue, and she realized she'd gotten lost gazing into them. He must have noticed and lifted the corner of his mouth in an angled smile.

"For someone from the sunny state of Arizona, you have a really creamy complexion," he said.

"I own stock in sunscreen." Feeling flattered he'd noticed something about her, she smiled.

He smiled back, and added a light laugh. Maybe she hadn't lost her touch with social conversation after all, or he was going out of his way to be polite.

It was easy to make him chuckle, and their evening went on in free-flowing banter. No topic scratched below the surface. Somehow they'd made a pact not to really get to know each other. Yet she picked things up, like the fact he hated onions and separated them out of his dinner salad, and even after cavorting in the park he smelled fresh and trendy. The scent probably cost an arm and leg from some designer store. He owned his own tux and he knew where to take children to play.

The nagging question returned. Did he have a wife and family? And if so, who looked after them while he gallivanted around at charity events with strange women? Maybe he was one of the wealthy Hunter donors and could afford to live a double life.

She really needed to quit trying to figure him out and just enjoy his company. After tonight she'd never see him again anyway.

Her gnocchi was delicious and she forced herself to eat slowly. The cabernet warmed her brain and for her first night in London she had to admit she would never have come up with this scenario in her wildest dreams. *Thank you, Leo, for inviting me to the Eye.*

By half past midnight, rather than get to know each other, they'd discussed half a dozen couples from the bar, sizing them up and guessing their circumstances. Then, after making up far-fetched stories about secret agents and international spies along with who the couples must be, they pondered what other people might surmise about them.

"Maybe they think we're two famous doctors out to save the world," Mitch said, hitting very close to home in Grace's situation.

"How about a rich American actress and her best friend's husband," said Grace, raising her brows, wanting to throw him off track. She must have done a good job as his expression faltered for a millisecond. Oh, no, she'd pushed the game too far. Had she hit a nerve?

The next few moments ticked by in silence, and he seemed to have lost interest in playing the game.

Mitch finished his drink and looked at his watch. "I should get you home."

Okay, she'd definitely hit a nerve, and now she'd ruined their evening. "Yes," she said, suddenly feeling awkward for the first time that night. "I imagine you've got to get home, too." *To your wife and family.*

"I'm divorced, in case you're wondering." His mood had shifted toward all business and she suspected it was because of what she'd hinted at. Or could he read her mind?

He reached for his wallet when the bill came.

"Let me pay for mine, okay?"

He scowled at her, but quickly turned the look playful. "Not on your life. I almost got you into trouble back there. It's the least I can do."

She glanced at the huge run in her hose. "True. And I've ruined my stockings."

"Sorry about that. Maybe I should buy you another drink?"

"No, thanks." She sat straighter. "It was fun. Well worth the cost of new stockings."

"It was, wasn't it?" He left the right amount of cash plus a generous tip and got off the barstool. "We're pod people," he said, offering his hand. "Pod people and young adventurers, and we must stick together."

And total strangers, don't forget.

Grace grinned and accepted his hand to help her down then followed Mitch out of the bar. They took the elevator, more subdued than earlier, though he made eye contact with her several different times. She wondered if he'd ask for her phone number, but he didn't. When they hit the street, he hailed a cab, opened the door and helped her to get in.

"Look," he said, sticking his head inside but not getting into the taxi, "I've had a great time tonight. You're a beautiful woman, and I thank you for spending these past few hours with me." He sucked in a breath and Grace waited for the "but".

"But I have a demanding job and what extra time I have...well...I don't have time to date." He glanced into her eyes, as if looking for understanding. She held his gaze, not saying a word. She wasn't his type, or... Was this how men who were involved handled things? "If it was a different time in my life. If circumstances were different. The thing is, I just don't have...well... it just wouldn't be fair."

"Shh," she stopped him. She'd heard enough.

He'd made his point quite clear. There was no room for anyone else in his life. He was probably living with someone and had needed a night to himself, that was all. He was an honorable guy who didn't fool around on the side, just hung out with strange ladies.

He'd been the one to say no strings immediately after inviting her to walk with him. What had she expected?

Silly thoughts invaded her mind but nothing could stop the disappointment that came crashing down around her. Though in her heart she knew exactly what he'd meant about not having any time beyond work. Hell, she'd been thinking those very thoughts earlier. She was in London to start a new job as a reconstructive surgeon at the Hunter Clinic on Harley Street, she planned to put her heart and soul into her job, and where did that leave her? Exactly in Mitch's shoes.

There was simply not enough time to have a well-balanced life in her line of work.

Grace reached for his hand and squeezed it. "Thank you so much for this superspecial introduction to London. Every time I look at that overgrown Ferris wheel I'll think of my adventurous pod man and smile."

He grinned, moved in closer and pecked her cheek. "Thank you for understanding."

She lowered her eyelids and nodded. "More than you know."

He connected with her eyes once more; there was that pang of remorse again as they shared a silent agreement—this had only been for tonight. The poignant moment stretched on until the cabbie cleared his throat.

From the mood she'd slipped into, she'd probably only projected what she thought had been a look of regret in his eyes. She knew for a fact he could detect it in her gaze.

Soon the door shut, he gave the cabbie some money and instructions. "Take the lovely lady home."

As the car pulled away from the curb, and Mitch's scent lingered on, Grace looked out the back window at the most amazing man she'd ever met. He stood there, posed with one hand in his pocket and his head cocked slightly to the side, as if he was a suave street artist, watching her leave.

Whatever or whoever he was, he would forever be etched in her mind as her pod man—quite possibly a figment of her imagination.

But then she glanced down at her legs and saw the gaping rip in her stockings.

No. Adventurous pod man was real. She sighed.

Life sure had a sucky way of rubbing bad timing into her scarred skin, and reminding her she was completely alone and without prospects beyond her new job.

CHAPTER TWO

Grace walked up the four steps to the classic white building on Harley Street. The twin black doors on either side of a window with a colorful blooming flower box, separating entrance and exit, looked sedate and simple. But when she opened the door to the most sparkling, modern, opulent waiting room she'd ever seen, she blinked. Gray-and-black marble floors, white leather chairs, a crystal pedestal beneath a glass table in the center with a fuchsia-colored chandelier above it, nearly took her breath away.

A young and attractive blonde woman sat in one of the seats, quietly thumbing through a fashion magazine. Next to her, a middle-aged redhead, showing the results of some recent facial surgery, watched Grace's every move.

She walked to the front desk, where another middle-aged, beautifully coiffed woman, with a name badge that said Helen, Senior Receptionist waited with a smile. Grace gave her name and her reason for being there, then turned to take a seat. She barely had time to sit in one of those amazing chairs or read the long list of surgeons' names on the wall when the dashing Leo Hunter himself opened a door and invited her inside. Where had he been last night?

Tall, with longish black hair that flipped out a little under his ear lobes, sparkling, ocean-blue eyes, and a totally fit-looking frame, he was a man who obviously turned a lot of heads when he walked down the street. At least, he'd already turned hers, plus those of the two other ladies sharing the waiting room, though she hoped her obvious appreciation of his great looks wasn't as obvious as theirs.

The dashing surgeon offered a welcoming smile. Great teeth, too! "Grace, it's a pleasure to meet you."

"Thank you. Nice to meet you, too. Sorry I missed you last night. I had a good time, though."

He took a beat to think before those gorgeous eyes lit up. "Oh, the fund-raiser. Glad you enjoyed it. Yes, well, I had a great excuse—making honeymoon plans with the busiest travel agent in London."

"How wonderful. Congratulations."

They shook hands and he showed her into his office, gesturing for her to sit as he rounded his huge walnut desk and took his seat. "You're going to love it here, and I've been eagerly awaiting your arrival." He shuffled papers around while she sat.

"Thank you. I'm very excited about getting started myself."

Leo settled down and rested one hand on top of the other at his desk. "You've come highly recommended, you know. And what you did for those childhood cancer survivors in Arizona—reconstructing their faces, noses and jaws—well, I was blown away by your talent. That's when I knew I wanted, no, needed someone of your caliber here at our clinic."

Overcome with his compliments, she felt a blush coming on. She'd worn a thin white turtleneck under her spring-blue blazer. Maybe she'd have a fighting chance to cover up the warmth as it started on her chest and worked its way up her neck and cheeks before blossoming into pink. "You're too kind, Mr. Hunter."

"Call me Leo, please."

"Leo," she practiced, knowing that out of respect for him and his world-renowned clinic, it would probably never come easily to her.

"We have weekly staff meetings to discuss our various cases, and we share notes from both our successes and challenges. The point is to keep growing and learning. Don't you agree?"

"Wholeheartedly. That's why I accepted your generous offer to work here." She wouldn't go into the fact about needing to get away from her stuck-in-first-gear life.

He flashed that charming smile again and stood. "What do you say I give you a tour of our clinic? You'll have an office here as well, of course, plus scheduled procedures, but you'll be doing your more complicated surgeries at Princess Catherine's or the Lighthouse Children's hospitals, like everyone else."

She nodded as he came round the desk again and directed her out of his office door.

"I'll introduce you to some of the staff. Unfortunately, a lot of them are in Theater this morning."

He walked her further down the long, pristine hall, with original artwork hanging on the walls, stunning her with color and beauty. Not a single comfort had been spared in this clinic.

He popped his head inside an office. It was empty. He respected the privacy of all occupied procedure rooms, but announced himself then tugged her inside the staff lounge. A half dozen nurses greeted her with genuine smiles, and she felt warmly welcomed and thought maybe she'd finally found a place where she could belong.

Though most of the office doors were closed, she saw the nameplates on them: Iain McKenzie, Rafael de Luca, Edward North, Abbie de Luca, Declan Underwood, Kara Stephens. The hallway forked in another direction, with more names on the office doors. All closed. Then around the corner, at the far end, was another closed door. The plaque read Ethan Hunter, his office as far away from his brother's office as possible in this building.

"Sorry things look a bit like a ghost town today, but we keep a heavy schedule. Mondays are always busy and everyone is either in Theater or preparing to do surgery."

"I understand."

A chirpy female voice came from another office as they doubled back.

"Oh, at least I can introduce you to Alexia Robbins. Lexi, as we call her. She's our head of public relations." He tapped on the partially open door. "Lexi?"

She was on the phone, but immediately waved them in while she quickly finished up her conversation. "Great, I'll have all the information to you by this afternoon. Thanks!"

She hung up and looked excitedly at Leo. "Just

scored a two-minute promo on the local news station about yesterday's charity event at the Eye." She stopped talking when she realized Leo wasn't alone.

"Fantastic," he said. "Tell me all about it later."

"Will do."

"Lexi, this is Grace Turner, our newest reconstructive surgeon."

"Oh, lovely to meet you." Lexi jumped to her feet and offered her hand. They shook lightly. Grace immediately liked the tall, bubbly lady with blonde hair and an hourglass figure, wearing a bright pink dress. Her flashing blue eyes gave off a mischievous glint. "If there's anything I can do to help in any way…"

"As a matter of fact," Leo said, "I was hoping you'd give her a tour of the hospitals this afternoon."

"Love to."

"Grand. Talk later." Leo moved toward the door.

"Hold on, mister," Lexi said playfully. "How is the honeymoon planning going?"

Leo gave her a look. She wouldn't back down. "Well?"

"What do you think, Lexi? I've married the most wonderful girl in the world. Paris in June will be perfect."

Lexi's cheeks pinkened with pleasure. She nearly sighed, like a woman in love. Leo glanced at Grace, who was feeling very out of the loop.

"Lexi recently got engaged herself, so she's being a busybody."

"It's my job, being in PR and all," she teased back, playing with the ring band…which held a huge rock. Wow.

Grace had never seen anything like it. Whatever the

stone, it was humongous and pink, and all the little surrounding diamonds sparkled around it.

"So what do you say, Grace, is noon good for you?" Lexi tore Grace away from her thoughts. "We can grab lunch at the clinic buffet before we head over to the hospitals."

"Sounds good. Thank you."

Off Leo and Grace went, retracing their steps along the row of closed doors. "We do a lot of our plastics on-site. Down there is the recovery room. Plus we make arrangements for many of our patients to spend the night in nearby luxury recovery apartments," he said.

She'd gotten the impression many of the first-floor apartments in her building were there for that very reason.

"I've put you next to another American. Wanted to make you feel at home."

He opened the door and showed her the beautifully decorated office that would be hers. It was small but comfortable with a lovely window that let in daylight. She turned in a circle looking at everything, thinking how she'd utilize the space, cabinets and amazing medical library. She went behind her chrome-and-glass desk and tested out the white leather chair. "I love it."

"Wonderful." Leo leaned against the doorframe. "Cooper! Come out and meet your new neighbor," Leo called into the hallway, then looked back at her. "I'm glad you like it. You'll get along swimmingly with Mitchell Cooper. He's one of our top plastic surgeons. Been with us four years now." Leo smiled at someone outside in the hallway. "Come and meet Grace Turner. She's American, too."

Popping into the doorway, sporting a wide grin, adventurous pod man appeared. And Grace nearly fell out of her custom comfort chair.

She looked at him. He stared back. Both of them were wide-eyed and unbelieving. A silent message jumped between them, followed by a quick bargain. Leo wouldn't find out that they'd already met. Agreed.

"Grace, meet Mitchell Cooper."

Mustering every ounce of poise she owned, Grace stood and stretched out her hand. "It's a pleasure to meet you, Mitchell."

He accepted her proffered hand and shook it. "The pleasure's all mine. Welcome to Harley Street." Quick memories of how she'd squeezed his hand in the cab, just before he'd bussed her cheek, caught her off guard.

A large cat must have hovered over the office, taking their tongues as heavy silence overtook the room. Leo glanced between the two of them, as if trying to figure out what had just happened. "Do you two already know each other?"

"No!" they said in unison, exchanging surreptitious glances.

Leo didn't look convinced, but didn't press it. "Well, I'll leave you alone to get acquainted, then. You can talk Dodger dogs and touchdowns, or whatever it is Americans..." His voice trailed off as he headed for the door then turned on his heel. "We've got some major cases coming in and we'll be utilizing your skills and talents right off, Grace. I've left the first one on your desk." He glanced at Mitchell. "And I think you'll make a great team on the Cumberbatch case, too." Then he was off.

The silence grew nearly deafening as Grace stared at

Mitch in disbelief, not knowing whether to be happy or regretful that she'd seen him again. What if he was in a serious relationship with someone, and he'd strayed a little last night? How awkward. From the caution in his eyes, Grace settled on the regretful side of the scale.

"Look," he said, "I had no idea you were our new surgeon." He grabbed his head. "Stupid, stupid, stupid. I should have put things together."

"I didn't offer any information either."

"I should have asked, but I got this crazy idea about having a minivacation with Madam X." He made air quotes with his fingers around the name. "For crying out loud, I apologize." He looked seriously sorry, too.

"There's nothing to apologize for. I had fun. I don't know about you, but I did, anyway." She leaned against the edge of her desk.

"Yes. Of course it was fun. But the thing is, I never would have treated you that way if I'd known you were the new team member."

"Then I'm glad you didn't know."

"It's just bad business on my part. Bad form." His hands rested on his trim hips. She couldn't help but notice.

He wore a starched white shirt and blue Paisley-patterned tie to complement his navy slacks. His knee-length doctor's coat covered all of his best parts, as she recalled—the wide shoulders and strong arms—arms that had lifted her nearly over the fence without effort.

"Stop it," she said. "We did what we did. Now we forget about it and get professional. That's all. It's not like we had sex or anything."

An impish gleam entered his wonderfully green eyes.

Thank goodness he remembered the fun they'd had. "But we're pod people. Young adventurers. How do we forget that?"

She couldn't help it. He'd tried to lighten the mood and successfully made her laugh. Were all women like putty in his hands? "Stop it."

She searched for something and ineptly threw a piece of paper from her desk at him. A sorry weapon, it floated nowhere near where he stood. He pretended to dodge it anyway. "But I suppose we'll always have that." She fought back the urge to laugh more, liking him for bringing it up.

He raised and dropped his brows. "Just two peas in a pod."

That did it. She sputtered a laugh, and he joined her. "Stop it, I said."

He shook his head, looking chagrined. "I broke up with you." He pinched the bridge of his nose and grimaced. "Do you realize I had the audacity to pick you up in a pod, nearly get you arrested in a public playground, buy you dinner on a barstool, then send you home in a cab, hardly explaining why I could never see you again? I'm an idiot. What in the hell must you think of me?"

She wanted to say she'd thought about him the rest of the night. She'd thought about him as she'd showered and dressed for work today, too, and the word *idiot* had never come into the mix. But she knew better.

They needed to forget their extraordinary night out and move on to reality. They were colleagues now. They'd have to see each other every day, and it was never a good idea to get involved with a coworker, especially in such a small clinic like this. They needed to keep their distance from each other, leave well enough alone. It was so obvious.

Just because he'd said he was divorced last night, it didn't mean he was a free man. He probably had half a dozen kids he needed to divide all of his spare time among. But look at that, he was staring at her legs, and since she'd worn a high-waisted pencil skirt, there was plenty of leg to stare at. She crossed her ankles and pretended not to notice.

He'd sent her home in that cab for a good reason, and there was no point in dredging it up now. "What I think of you doesn't matter any more because we're colleagues and I've already had my first case assigned to me. From now on we're strictly business. Okay?"

It was safe, too, since she'd never shown her scars to a man who wasn't one of her doctors. Except for her ex-fiancé, and what a disaster that had turned out to be. How could she possibly venture into a relationship with anyone, no matter how well and easily they got along, when no man would ever want her. Boy, she'd certainly jumped ahead.... What was it about Mitchell Cooper that made her want to?

His tentative expression turned thoughtful. He was obviously working through the steps on how to undo a perfectly wonderful evening with a woman he'd never expected to see again but who was now his office mate, too. "Okay. Makes sense. Strictly business partners. Got it. Probably for the best anyway."

She spotted that same look he'd left her with last night, and she'd interpreted it—projected her own feelings into it—as regret. That truly was how she felt, and that's how life was sometimes—loaded with regret. And secrets best not shared.

He took her hand and shook again. "Nice to meet you, Grace Turner. If you need any 'strictly professional' help, I'll be right next door." With that, he turned and left.

Mitch wanted to kick the hallway wall. He'd botched up a perfectly good partnership, making his new colleague feel uncomfortable and regretting ever having laid eyes on him. The thing was, he'd really, really liked her, and it had taken every last kernel of restraint not to ask for her phone number last night, even though on the surface she wasn't the kind of mommy material he had in mind.

But as always, before he'd been able to get the words out, the pain he'd endured from his wife choosing his best friend over him had strangled the thought out of him. He needed to forget about women for a while, especially beautiful women, and focus on what mattered most in his life—his daughter, Mia, and his job.

Some flaw in his ex's self-esteem had turned her into a plastic-surgery addict, even though she'd been beautiful to begin with. Now he hardly recognized her doll-like appearance. And he was damned if he'd let that weakness be a constant example for his Mia. He'd moved as far away as possible four years ago, once they'd divorced and Christie had given him full custody of their daughter.

Those were the things he needed to focus on—his reason for being at this clinic, and for moving to London. A better life for Mia. Not the beautiful and fun-loving Grace Turner next door. A man was an idiot if he didn't learn from his mistakes.

He plopped into his desk chair and tried desperately to get her crystal-blue eyes and especially her gorgeous mouth out of his mind. Damn. And after several moments of wrestling with his thoughts, he resolved to keep Grace at arm's length. For his own good.

He'd given up beautiful women, had only dated stable potential-mother material after his first failed relationship on moving to London four years ago. He'd gotten himself involved too soon with one of the Hunter Clinic nurses right off. That had turned into a disaster with the nurse leaving the clinic rather than work with him once they'd broken up. So far the process of sticking with mommy material had been a huge failure, but he'd keep on. It was the only way. Nothing would stop him from finding a proper mother for Mia.

But knowing Grace was on the other side of their adjoining office wall would make deleting her from his personal life as difficult as—he fished around on his desk for the surgical referral of his next patient—making Mrs. Evermore look twenty years younger, which was her surgical goal on the application for a face-lift.

Grace spent the afternoon with Lexi on a tour of the two state-of-the-art hospitals where she'd be authorized to perform surgery. The Lighthouse Children's Hospital was merely ten minutes away, and Princess Catherine's was beautifully placed alongside the Thames with magnificent views from most patients' rooms.

Lexi was a natural conversationalist so Grace didn't feel pressured to talk much.

"If you'd like, we're meeting for drinks at Drake's wine bar after work tonight," she said. "I'm bringing pictures of my dream dress for my wedding day. Now all I have to do is find a way to pay for it!" She laughed.

"Well, I can't miss that, now, can I?" Thinking about the pristine and lonely apartment, Grace agreed to meet at the wine bar, as Lexi had described it.

"Great. We'll go together." They got into an elevator with a glass wall to allow the full view of the river Thames all the way down. "Oh, and the shoes I've got in mind are to die for. Of course, I might have to pawn the ring to buy both." She beamed and poofed her hair.

Grace smiled, adoring the lady's spirit.

Before she left the hospital, Grace met the man who'd be the lead surgical nurse on her team, Ron Whidbey, a middle-aged man of African descent who'd been born and raised in England.

Her first case—reconstructing a face, status post-cancer resection—was one that Mitchell would be involved in as well, as the twenty-five-year-old woman would need new lips. Apparently, that was his specialty. As for herself, she'd concentrate on reconstructing the nose and cheeks and recreating a philtrum in preparation for Mitchell's side of the operation.

Tomorrow, during surgery, she'd be so focused on her patient she'd probably not even notice Mitchell was there. A girl could hope anyway.

After a long discussion with Ron about what instruments and setup she preferred and how she liked to approach reconstructive surgery, she felt they were both on the same page and had a firm understanding of how it would be working together. He promised to meet her in O.R. Six at Kate's, as the locals liked to call Princess Catherine's, at 6:00 a.m. sharp with the room set up and ready to go per her orders. Then off he went to have a meeting with his nursing team.

At 6:00 p.m., having not seen hide nor hair of Mitchell for the rest of the day, Grace heard a tap at her door. It was Lexi, keeping her promise to take her to Drake's wine bar, at the Regent's Park end of Harley Street. Within fifteen minutes she was sitting in what resembled a classic Victorian chamber with crystal chandeliers and overstuffed benches and booths, amidst dark colors and dim lights.

Surrounded by several of her new colleagues, she'd been served a glass of crisp, unoaked Chardonnay, and as happy as a lark she munched on crackers, cheese puffs, veggies with hummus dip and mixed nuts.

Across from her, Lexi's fiancé, Iain, a fellow reconstructive surgeon who'd been working at the Hunter Clinic for the last few years, draped his long, muscular arm about Lexi's hip and the woman seemed to no longer need a drink. Several of the nursing staff were also there. A chestnut-haired woman sidled her way between Edward North, the stiff but gifted microsurgeon, and another nursing colleague, then introduced herself to Grace as Charlotte. They chatted about the weather and the surgeries the clinic undertook. Since Grace had been watching and waiting for Mitchell to show up, she said a little prayer of thanks for the welcome distraction with Charlotte.

Next, Lexi gathered all the ladies at one end of the bar. Grace joined them.

"Look what I've got." Lexi whipped out a picture of

a divine designer dress torn from a fashion magazine. "Isn't it gorgeous? This is what I intend to wear the day I get married."

A couple of nurses squealed over the dress. Charlotte was one of them. Grace had to admit the pink chiffon with ribbon waistband and decorative sequins was a sight to behold. She glanced at Lexi, who was transfixed, along with the nurses. She obviously liked pink, judging by the dress she'd worn today, and pink was certainly her color.

"Now the only problem is hunting down a good knockoff because there's no way on earth I can afford this one."

"If anyone can do it, you can, Lexi," Charlotte said.

Grace smiled. "Good luck. Something tells me you'll find your dream dress at the right price."

"From your lips to the shopping goddess's ears," Lexi said. Once she'd put the picture away, the nurses went off to the ladies room, and Grace followed Lexi back to the Hunter Clinic corner of the bar.

Glancing around the extremely attractive group of people, Grace thought good looks might be part of the job requirement to be employed at Hunter Clinic, but then wondered why she'd been hired.

Though the clinic group seemed tight knit, they went out of their way to make her feel a part of things. She'd just about finished her drink and was feeling relaxed, and as she was performing surgery in the morning decided she wouldn't have another. She asked the server to bring her a glass of water and just as she looked up, in walked Mitchell. Their eyes locked briefly, long enough to set off flutters in her chest, and he went straightaway to the bar to order a drink.

Every time she saw him her heart stumbled over beats. How could a guy like that not be involved with anyone? She watched the door for a lady to follow him inside, but no one came. Just about the time her water arrived, and another Hunter Clinic surgeon named Declan Underwood was deep into explaining rugby to her, Mitch swaggered up with a beer in hand.

"Evening, all," he said.

Everyone called out some greeting or other.

"Lips!" Iain said, and Grace wondered if it bothered Mitch to have such a nickname, though she did understand men loved to gibe each other like that. In fact, in her psychology classes in med school she'd learned that kind of behavior was a sign of affection—something most men would never be caught dead admitting.

She found it hard to concentrate and simply nodded hello when Mitch approached.

"May I sit here?" he asked, pointing to the barely six inches of padded bench next to her.

"Of course," she said, scooting closer to Lexi. Avoiding Mitchell Cooper was out of the question now, so she decided to get used to it right off. Crammed in next to her, she felt the warmth radiate from his body, and caught the scent of the same tangy, expensive aftershave that had lingered in the cab the other night. What should she do now?

"How was your first day?" he said.

"Fine. After the shock wore off."

He caught his lower lip with his teeth and nodded. "There's a lot of names and faces to put together," he said, not letting on he'd understood her true meaning of "shock," which had nothing to do with meeting the staff.

"Yes. That's for sure." How inane could their conversation get? It had flowed so easily last night, when they'd been strangers. She longed for the clock to turn back twenty-four hours.

He reached for a handful of nuts and crammed them in his mouth. So much for continuing the conversation.

Lexi appeared in front of them. "Iain and I are leaving early," she said to Grace.

From the way the couple had had their hands all over each other, Grace didn't need to be told the reason why they wanted to leave early. She smiled.

"Can we drop you off?" Iain asked.

Grace waited for Mitchell to offer to take her home, but after half a beat, when he hadn't volunteered, she stood.

"Thanks, I'd love that," she said. "Good night, everybody. It was great to meet all of you."

"You'll see everyone else at Friday's staff meeting," someone called out, but she was so distracted by Mitch and now her leaving that she wasn't even sure who'd said it.

"See you in surgery tomorrow, Mitchell."

He nodded.

Everyone else smiled and cheered her off, while Mitchell still chomped on his mouthful of mixed nuts, watching, looking clueless and disinterested, and nothing like the adventurous pod person she'd met last night. At least he'd kept his word—from now on theirs would be a strictly business relationship.

* * *

The next morning, at a quarter to six, Grace scrubbed in. It was a process she preferred to do by herself, since the short-sleeved scrub top revealed a large portion of her scars. But gowning was different. She needed help to do it properly. Grace caught the quick, surprised glimpse in the scrub nurse's eyes as she helped her don the sterile gown and gloves, and tried to act as if nothing was unusual.

Once her mask was in place, she used her shoulder to push the plate for the automatic door opener to the surgical suite. Happy to make eye contact with Ron right off, she saw him nod, and from the squint of his dark eyes above the mask, she knew he smiled beneath.

She assessed her O.R. A quick check of the instruments satisfied her strict stipulations. The anesthesiologist began to put the mildly sedated patient completely under right after Grace had introduced herself. Two nurses were on hand to assist with the operation, and once she'd done the lion's share of the surgery, Mitchell would step in to create the actual lips for the young woman. She hadn't seen him this morning, but had been told he was on the premises and would wait to enter the O.R. until needed. It relieved Grace, knowing he wouldn't be looking over her shoulder. She couldn't allow a single distraction in her O.R.

Cancer had claimed most of the patient's face, and after the dermatologist had made wide resections of the mass, very little was left of her nose or upper lip. It broke Grace's heart, suspecting the twenty-five-year-old patient felt more like a monster than human with a hole for her nose, and gums showing where her upper lip should have been. When Grace had first been burned, before the multiple skin grafts, she'd felt like a monster, too. Her job today was to put the woman back together again. The young woman's face would never look as it once had, but at least she'd have a face she wouldn't be ashamed to show in public.

Grace would have to borrow cartilage from her ears to rebuild portions of the bridge and nose tip, and take bilateral transpositional flaps from her cheeks to cover the nose, reconstruct the natural curvature of the nasal rim, and create the missing upper lip. After she'd finished the general rebuilding, Mitchell would make a more natural-looking mouth by using treated fat transfer from the patient's abdomen.

"Let's give Julie Treadwell a beautiful new face, shall we?" she said. Everyone present nodded. "Scalpel," she said, then made her first incision.

An hour and a half later, up to her elbows in blood, cartilage and skin flaps, one lone straggler entered the O.R. She knew it wasn't the circulating nurse, because she hadn't requested anything. She'd just made two small labial folds on either side of the nose flap, and had asked for the small curved needle and sutures to stitch everything in place.

She glanced up. It was him.

Knowing Mitch Cooper was there made her hand tense slightly, but only for a brief second. The patient deserved one hundred percent of her attention. She waited until she'd recovered her concentration to put the finishing touches on her portion of this two-stage surgery.

When she'd finished, she handed the patient over to

Mitch then prepared to step outside to watch him work his wonders.

"Stick around," he said. "You might learn something."

She smiled at his teasing—now, that was more like the guy she remembered. "Wouldn't want to get in the way."

"You won't. Besides, I might need to pick your brain on some of the trickier parts. From the looks of Ms. Treadwell, you've done a fantastic job, Miss Turner."

Why his compliment meant so much, she couldn't fathom, but it did. Going against her instinct to leave the good surgeon to his work, she accepted his invitation and stuck around.

Mitch took his time making sure everything was exactly as he needed it to be. Grace had already laid down the framework preserving the intraoral mucosal lining. Now he worked to maintain the oral aperture. The entire procedure would require a three-layer closure of mucosa, muscle and skin with tiny drains inserted. It couldn't be rushed.

He'd originally planned on making a traditional mouth—a serviceable mouth. Anything would be better than the completely missing lips that the patient currently had. But since Grace had blown into town, he couldn't get a certain styled mouth out of his mind, and he thought he'd give that style a go. The classic and beautiful Grace Turner mouth. If all went well, he'd duplicate it on Julie Treadwell.

Mitch worked his wonders, creating a cupid's bow for the upper lip, then using the autograft flap from the donor site—the delicate radial forearm epidermis—for best match to the facial skin. If the patient desired more color to her lips, he'd suggest she have them tinted once everything was healed. But that was down the line. His job today was to create the size and shape of the lips.

He glanced up over his surgical magnifying glasses at Grace, but realized he'd have to work completely from memory as she wore her O.R. mask.

"Pass the syringe," he said, once everything had been accomplished as planned. His surgical nurse knew exactly what he wanted and handed him the syringe with the treated fat from Julie's abdomen. Meticulously, he injected the material along the path he'd just created with the tender fasciocutaneous flap, and carefully manipulated it into place. Everything had to be just so to form the perfect amount of plumpness, and he couldn't waste any of the prepared fat. He would continue until every last bit of it had been used.

If all went well, tomorrow morning Julie Treadwell would be the proud owner of a replica of Grace Turner's luscious lips.

Over the last hour, Grace had developed new respect for, and maybe a tiny crush on, Mitch Cooper and his skills as a cosmetic plastic surgeon.

When the surgery was complete, she complimented him then rushed off to dispose of her surgical gown and headed for the women doctors' lounge. Pride made her do it before Mitch had a chance to see the angry scars on her arms, chest and neck.

They met up later at the patient's bedside, after she'd left Recovery and was back in her room. Grace was dressed in a pale blue long-sleeved turtleneck underneath a gray pinstriped vest and matching slacks—scars safely covered, so no one would know. "How's our patient doing?" she asked Mitch, who'd beat her there.

"Really well." He finished rebandaging Julie's face. "No excess bleeding. No early signs of infection. Minimal edema. All drains intact." He glanced up at her. "The reconstruction is really superb."

There was admiration in those intense green eyes, and Grace fought off the urge to puff up her feathers. "That's great. I'd hate to make you unwrap her again, so I'll take your word for it. But tomorrow I get first dibs at the bandages."

"Roger that." He casually saluted above the sleeping patient. "Now, if you'd like, follow me, and I'll show you the staff cafeteria."

Did she want to spend time alone with him again? Her first reaction was no, it would just make her wish things were different. But Mitch was already heading toward the door, and truth was her stomach had grumbled just before she'd entered the patient's room. She was hungry. He knew where the food was. She'd be stupid not to follow him.

Before she left Julie's bedside, she took the young woman's hand in hers and squeezed it. "You were a great patient today, Julie. I'm so happy how things turned out." She spoke knowing that, even though the patient looked asleep, hearing was the last of the senses to go under and the first to wake up. Julie lightly squeezed Grace's hand back and it made Grace smile. Julie had heard every word she'd just said.

Grace gently brushed a few errant tendrils of hair

away from the bandages and looked hard into her covered face. She imagined how much better Julie would look when next she gazed into the mirror, and smiled. "Get some rest, Julie. It's been a long day and the worst is over."

Julie mumbled something but was already pushing through to the other side of consciousness.

Grace glanced up and noticed an odd expression on Mitchell's face. She smiled, and he gave a reverent nod.

The ride down in the elevator was awkward. After running out of compliments to give each other for the successful surgery, there wasn't much else to talk about as she chose to keep things strictly professional with Mitchell. As had he, which was obvious from his actions last night.

She saw him start to say something, or at least she thought that was what he'd meant by taking a quick breath and opening his mouth. But he bit his lips closed, as if thinking better of starting any kind of casual conversation. Again, they were on the same page. Two adventurous pod people long forgotten. Finally, they arrived in the basement and as soon as the doors opened the aroma from several different dishes had her stomach growling happily in response.

Fortunately, several other doctors were in the cafeteria, and after she and Mitch got their food, they sat in two completely different spots at the large table. When Mitch had introduced Grace, a handful of the other doctors greeted her and engaged her in conversation. Only occasionally did her eyes drift Mitch's way, and from time to time their gazes connected. Each time they both quickly glanced away, but not before a small burst of something happened in her chest.

She took the last bite of her Cobb salad while wishing he didn't affect her like that, but her mental desires and those of her body currently seemed to be on two completely different tracks.

The next morning, before Grace began her appointments at the Hunter Clinic, she took a cab to Kate's to visit Julie Treadwell. She'd thought about her most of the night, hoping and praying the surgery had put her back together well enough that she could deal with her new identity, hold her head high, and move on with her life.

One of the nurses smiled at her just before she entered Julie's room, and Grace returned the gesture, immediately recognizing her. The ward nurse was Charlotte, the attractive woman Grace had met at Drake's last night.

Julie sat up in bed, her facial bandages intact. The TV was on a fun, chatty morning show. She sucked a protein shake with added vitamins and minerals through a straw. Grace knew exactly what it was because she'd requested it in her post-op orders.

"Hi, Julie, how are you feeling today?"

"Not too bad. A bit like a mummy, but I know it's part of the package."

Grace smiled. "I don't want to disturb you, but I'd like to change your bandages."

Julie put down the drink immediately. "Sure." Her hands fisted in her lap. Grace could only imagine how nerve-racking waiting to see your new face would be.

"I'll let the nurse know what I need, then we'll get started, okay?"

Julie nodded bravely.

When Grace returned after asking Charlotte for the items she'd need, she had a hard bargain of which to convince Julie, "I'd like to suggest that you don't look at your face until most of the swelling and bruising has gone down. Maybe in a few days. Are you okay with that?"

"I'm not ready to look just yet anyway."

Grace took one of Julie's hands, the fist loosening as she reached for it, and squeezed. "You've been through a lot with the cancer. We'll take this one step at a time." Julie's eyes filled and brimmed with tears.

Charlotte brought in the new dressing materials, and Grace pulled the bedside curtains closed and got started cutting the gauze with her bandage scissors. She'd decided to keep this dressing change between her and the patient. She started at the forehead and carefully worked her way down from there.

Once some of the dressings came loose, she made a point of schooling her expression, of not showing any reaction to what she saw. Yes, Julie looked stitched up like a quilt, and the post-op edema distorted her features, but overall Grace was very happy with her appearance. As things settled down, the swelling would lessen and the stitches would dissolve or come out, and Julie would look human again. Her nose looked great. Grace continued snipping away at the bandages while thinking and planning. After Julie was completely healed, Grace would discuss erasing some of the remaining scars through laser treatments.

In fact, she'd already talked to Leo Hunter about having a few treatments on a particularly troublesome scar near her neck herself. Laser treatments had worked wonders for many of her patients; why shouldn't she try them?

She came to the upper-lip portion of the surgery and was very pleased with her work and almost smiled, then finished removing the remaining gauze. Mitchell's lip job looked superb...and strangely familiar. He'd gone beyond the call of duty and augmented Julie's lower lip as well, to make them match up in the best way possible.

The upper lip picked up where her philtrum groove left off in what she'd describe as a classic cupid's bow. He'd plumped up the lower lip, but hadn't overdone it. These lips looked as natural as hers.

The oddest feeling came over Grace while looking at the au fait mouth. Where had she seen that style of mouth before? She smiled. Coming from Hollywood, the talented Mitchell Cooper had probably duplicated some famous starlet's lips just for Julie.

CHAPTER THREE

FRIDAY MORNING THE entire staff of Hunter Clinic gathered at eight a.m. for the weekly staff meeting in the large and luxurious employee lounge. Grace took a seat beside Ron Whidbey and pediatric surgeon Abbie de Luca.

"We've had a very busy week," Leo said, taking charge, glancing at a printout, "with another full schedule for next week." He looked up and scanned the entire group. "I've heard some concerns about being overbooked, yet no one has come to me to complain. Though there has been evidence of people still crashing on the couch in my office."

He cleared his throat. That got a laugh that rippled around the room, and Ethan looked especially guilty, scratching the back of his neck and looking at the ceiling. "So if you're feeling you need some time off, make an appointment and we'll talk about it." He looked specifically at the nursing staff. "I don't want to overextend any of you."

Grace glanced around the room, but didn't see Mitch. An odd mix of relief and disappointment confused her. *Make up your mind, you're either interested or not. Sheesh.*

Leo then picked up a notepad and read from his planned notes.

"There have been some reports of staph infections in another London clinic. I've hired an infectious-diseases specialist to tour and assess our procedure rooms, even though we haven't had any such outbreak. I just want to be careful. So if you see a man with glasses and white hair wandering about, that will be Dr. Richard Thornswood. As always, we expect everyone to practice meticulous sterile technique, and Lizzie will have a separate meeting with our environmental-services staff to make sure they are also following all safeguards to the T with cleaning, disinfecting, and disposal."

Next, Leo invited Rafael de Luca to bring everyone up to date with a short talk on the latest developments in identifying and treating cleft palate in vitro.

Grace was transfixed by the level of knowledge of everyone on staff. Her concentration was soon interrupted, though, when Mitchell made a late entry and took a nearby seat.

No longer able to concentrate on what Rafael was talking about, she became totally aware of Mitch sitting to her right, one row forward. The vantage point gave her the chance to study his rich dark hair, how it waved ever so gently along his neck and kissed the collar of his forest-green shirt. She could only imagine how green his eyes would look with that shirt—

"Grace, would you like to stand up?" Leo said, jolting her out of her pleasant dream state.

"Oh, yes, certainly." She stood and waited expectantly.

Leo gazed at her as if it was her turn to talk, but as

she hadn't been paying attention for a few seconds, admiring Cooper and his glorious hair instead, she didn't have a clue what he wanted.

Feeling a blush on her cheeks, she decided to come clean. "I'm sorry, what did you want me to do?"

A few people chuckled, and that made her feel embarrassed and nervous. She cast a lightning glance at Mitch and found his sweet, sympathetic smile, and calmed the slightest bit.

"I just wanted to introduce you to those who haven't had a chance to meet you yet. Why don't you tell us a little about your background?"

With that, she composed herself and told her history in as short and concise a way as possible. Hating to be put in the spotlight, she forced a benign smile and pretended she enjoyed this exercise in awkwardness.

She'd worn a red mandarin-collared silk top with black slacks today, and her doctor's coat covered her arms. She didn't need to worry about her scars showing. Leo Hunter was the only person at Hunter Clinic who knew about her condition, and had even promised to take a look at the problematic scar above her clavicle after the staff meeting.

"We heard your first surgery went splendidly," Leo said, prodding her along.

"Oh, yes, thanks in no small part to Mr. Cooper." She smiled at him.

"Lips, lips, lips," Iain chanted, making everyone titter.

Evidently Mitch had quite a reputation.

Her gaze landed on Mitchell, who looked nonplussed by the teasing. He sat straight, ignoring Iain, instead smiling at her, as if silently cheering her on. She couldn't help but think about Julie Treadwell's surgery. She'd racked her brain on where she'd seen that mouth before, how similar it looked to her own when she'd studied herself in the mirror. Was he really that talented, or was it a wild coincidence that she was making far, far too much of? Of course it was.

When she'd finished her introduction, she nodded gratefully to Mitch. Shortly, after a few more announcements, Leo dismissed the meeting. Mitch stood and turned, looking right at her. In her gut she wanted him to come over and talk to her, but she felt a tap on her shoulder.

It was Leo. "I've got time to fix that issue we spoke about. Shall we go to a procedure room?"

"Oh, that would be great. Thanks," she said, seizing the moment.

She followed Leo out of the room, but before leaving she glanced back and couldn't help noticing a disturbed expression on Mitchell's face. Surely he wasn't jealous of a man who'd just gotten married?

Mitch overheard Leo invite Grace to a procedure room, and he watched them leave together. His heart sank. Was she having a little nip, tuck or Botox? Perhaps all three? Damn, he'd been so sure she'd never had anything done. His stomach went a little queasy over the thought of Grace having treatments done at such a young age. Little things led to bigger treatments, then more nips and tucks and more often. Bile soured his throat.

Her beauty was natural, and should stay that way.

He knew too well the sad story of women chasing their youth, one procedure at a time, until they wound up looking nothing like their former selves. Hell, he had a thirty-five-year-old patient with cat eyes and a tympanic-drum-stretched face scheduled for a knee lift this very afternoon to prove his point.

"Hey, Lips." Declan Underwood slapped Mitch on the back. The rugby-playing plastic surgeon nearly knocked him off balance.

He clicked into his office persona. "Hey, man, how's your weekend shaping up?"

"Great. Got a couple of games lined up tomorrow. You should bring Mia out to watch."

"Only if you can promise no blood or gore."

"Can't do that. Besides, my rugby team brings the clinic a lot of business."

"True. So true." He'd fixed a broken nose on more than a few of Declan's teammates over the last year. One guy with a caved-in forehead had been sent to the emergency room for more extensive exams. The last he heard, they'd had to drain a hematoma between his skull and brain.

Declan tipped his head toward the door through which Leo and Grace had just exited. "She's hot, don't you think?"

A new feeling displaced the caution and concern about her having a procedure done with Leo. Jealousy. Wow, just like that, red flames of anger shot up his spine.

He stiffened. "She's definitely a knockout," he said between clenched teeth. He was at work, talking to a colleague, he had to play along and not let on how he really felt.

The men smiled at each other in appreciation for the opposite sex in general. But, damn, Mitch couldn't let it go.

"Just one more thing, Declan."

Declan raised his dark brows in anticipation.

"I saw her first."

Now added to the wild stew of emotions simmering through him, Mitch had thrown total confusion into the pot. Hadn't his last office relationship ended in disaster? If he was looking for mommy material, he needed to stick with his plan, no matter how bored he was with the process.

Did he want Grace? Or did he want to run as far and as fast as he could away from her? At some point he'd have to make up his mind.

"Message received, Lips," Declan said, wandering off, giving the appearance of not being the least bit offended.

Six days later, having done a fantastic job of not seeing Mitch since last Friday's staff meeting—thanks to conflicting O.R. and clinic schedules and well-planned avoidance techniques—Grace stayed late at work to catch up on some paperwork.

The laser procedure Leo had performed on the buckling scar on her chest was smoothing out and healing beautifully, and she thought about asking him to touch up a few other spots in the near future.

Her phone rang.

She answered, and the person introduced herself.

The Cumberbatch case she'd been assigned on her very first day at the Hunter Clinic was proving to be high profile.

She was surprised that the call was from a tabloid journalist with a long list of questions about Britain's favorite bad-boy punk rocker. She refused to disclose anything and soon as she hung up needed someone to bounce her concerns off.

Sitting in her office that late Thursday afternoon, knowing Mitch was just around the corner—because she'd heard his door open not less than a half hour ago—she decided to finally pay him a visit. After all, she'd been at the Hunter Clinic going on two weeks and he was her next-door neighbor. Yes, they'd seen each other at the staff meeting last Friday but hadn't spoken to each other, just passed a meaningful glance or two each other's way. It was high time she popped in...for a strictly business matter.

She took an extra few moments to smooth her hair, which she'd worn down today. She checked her make-up, or what was left of it, and applied a new layer of lipstick. Then she retied the colorful scarf she wore with a double-loop wrap around her neck, loose yet high enough to cover her scars. She'd skipped her usual turtleneck today and wore a long-sleeved, boat-necked, white silk top over her black straight-legged slacks, so she needed that scarf. Besides brightening up the out-fit, the scarf also picked up the yellow plaid bow on her work flats.

With butterflies winging through her chest, she headed out of her office.

She waited at his door, which was already open. He

proved to be in deep thought, poring over his computer and some notes on his desk. And, damn, he looked gorgeous all thoughtful, strong and silent. She stood for a moment, watching, enjoying the view. Slowly his gaze drifted from the computer to the doorway.

"Knock, knock," she said.

His face brightened, and he stood. "Hi. Come on in."

The genuine welcome made a little happy spot crop up in her chest, until he schooled his expression to all-business mode, making her doubt he was happy to see her. Mitchell looked handsome, as always. His hair was mussed, with one lock dangling over his forehead, and she had the urge to run her fingers through it in the guise of fixing it, but practiced restraint.

"Have a seat. Can I get you some water or coffee?" It sounded more like obligation.

"Oh, no, thanks." She took a chair opposite his desk, wondering why he'd gone from warm to chilly as he sat down again. *May as well get right down to business, then.* "Say, have you gotten any calls from the local press about Davy Cumberbatch?"

"Nope. Have you?" He discovered and fixed his errant lock of hair with a quick raking of fingers, and she felt she'd fallen off the job by not doing it for him. Silly thoughts, really, but, still, they kept cropping up. Of course she had no right to touch him since they were merely colleagues, though adventurous pod people would always look out for each other. Damn, now he'd gotten her thinking like that again.

The quick memory of their one evening together and the fantasy of touching his hair converged and gave her a little thrill. She forced both thoughts out of her mind and herself back on topic.

"Just dodged a few questions from someone saying they were a journalist from *Talking London*," she continued.

"That rag? Nothing but a gossip paper." He pushed back from his desk. It made the muscles tighten around his upper arms beneath his white polo-style shirt. She shouldn't have noticed but… "You didn't give them any information, did you?"

"No, of course not, but I wonder how they got my personal office number?"

"They're devious, those guys."

"It was a woman, actually."

"Well, be careful. They hound us a lot as we do cosmetic surgery on the rich, royal and famous. Should have warned you about it. Davy Cumberbatch is a biggie over here."

"I suppose they've run out of stories to print about his barroom brawl," she said. "Shown all the gruesome pictures. Now they want the lowdown on how we intend to fix him."

"Guy got his face mangled in that fight, didn't he? Half of it was caved in." He laced his fingers and put his hands behind his head. Did he have a clue how distracting these poses were? "What he expects us to do is going to take a miracle."

"I thought that was our specialty here at Hunter, to make miracles happen. Every day." She quoted the clinic pamphlet. Rather than stare at him, her gaze drifted around his office as she'd never been in it before. He had a striking modern art painting on one wall—

she hadn't a clue what it depicted—his diplomas and awards on another, but his solid oak desk was reserved for one single picture frame. It faced him, and Grace wanted more than anything to turn it around and find out who he valued most in life—who got center stage on his desk.

She hoped it was a dog, not a woman. She could deal with him loving his pet.

"Miracles are one thing but rebuilding a face to look like Elvis is a whole different ballgame," he said, still all business.

A light laugh escaped her mouth. Mitch had a knack for putting things in perspective. "I thought he only wanted Elvis's chin, nose and cheeks. And he wanted you to give him Mick Jagger's lips." She considered calling him "Lips" like a few other guys in the clinic, but thought better of it.

"Talked him out of that one. He's down for the whole Elvis package now." Mitchell began to warm up to her, breaking a smile and softening the tension around his eyes. Maybe it was the topic.

"Wise decision. So when do I meet him?" She crossed her leg and laced her hands around one knee.

"He's currently in rehab. That was the stipulation the Hunter Clinic had before we'd take him on as a client. He has to dry out first."

"Another good call." She bobbed her head in agreement.

"Should be out next week." Mitch consulted something on his cell phone. "Yes. Here we go. Next Monday seven p.m. we'll have our consultation meeting."

"Having a meeting after hours won't necessarily keep the paparazzi off his trail."

"True, but they don't have to find out why he's coming here."

"Won't it be obvious?"

Mitch made a mischievous expression, the first she'd seen since the night in the pod at the Eye, or maybe it had been in that elevator at the restaurant, nailing her with his playful green eyes. She'd missed that expression more than she cared to admit. "You don't know about our room, do you?"

"Room? What room?"

"Our ophthalmology room." He used air quotes around *ophthalmology*. "That's how we treat famous people without the press catching on and exposing their plans. Do it all the time for royalty…and actresses and ballerinas and…" He grinned and winked, and it almost made her forget to breathe. "We'll bring Davy in following a press release from Lexi about how he's developed a torn retina due to the fight, then we'll have our consult. See how badly he messed up his face and discuss all the options. Send him out with another prepared statement that we performed laser surgery to repair the retinal tear."

She found herself smiling along with him. "So clever."

"The Hunter Clinic has been doing it for years."

"Still, I can't help but think my abilities could be used for better purposes."

Mitch sat straight and still. "Ah, Gracie, you've forgotten our adventurous-pod-people oath."

Finally, he'd brought that up again! Knowing he

hadn't forgotten made her glad. But the look she gave him, tossing her gaze toward the ceiling, conveyed she'd reached her limit on pod-people jokes, even though it was nice to have Mitch back on full form. If she hadn't been taken aback by him calling her Gracie, the name her little sister, Hope, had used to call her, she would have used words. *Not that tired joke again. Really, Cooper.*

Well, if he was giving her a nickname, she needed to come up with one of her own for him. She wouldn't dare go for the garish "Lips", but if the one she had in mind was good enough for Leo, it was good enough for her.

"Apparently, *Cooper*, I have forgotten that oath."

She saw a glint of amusement in his deep eyes when she called him Cooper. Yes, he liked that.

"Fix the rich to help the poor." Now, there he went surprising her again. This time with his valor.

"Kind of like Robin Hood?"

Their eyes connected and every thought about work, nicknames, and oaths—no matter how spot on it was— flew out the window behind him. She noticed his five-o'clock shadow and thought how sexy it was, wondered what he looked like first thing in the morning with messed-up hair to match.

"A bit."

She needed a moment to recuperate.

They'd finished their conversation about Davy Cumberbatch. He'd called her Gracie, she'd called him Cooper. He'd reinforced the Hunter Clinic mission statement, which was a new twist on Robin Hood, along with their pod-person oath—young adventurers unite! Their meeting with Davy C. was scheduled for next week. There really was no reason to stick around. *Get up. Do it now or you'll embarrass yourself staring at him too long.*

She stood to leave, shifting her position so she had a better angle to see the photo on his desk. "Well, I'll buckle down on studying The King's face, and come up with the cheek, nose and chin implants before next Tuesday, then." At least that would give her something to do on her second weekend in London. Alone. "I imagine Davy Cumberbatch will want to see what I have in store for him."

Her gaze slid in line with the photograph. It wasn't a woman. Or even a dog. Yippee, and thank heavens. It was a beautiful little girl.

Unable to stop herself, she smiled and picked up the frame. "Do you mind?" She didn't wait for his okay. "Who's this lovely little princess?"

His eyes lit up with pride. "That's my Mia. My baby girl."

Grace lifted a single eyebrow. "She's not a baby any more, Cooper. I hate to tell you. My gosh, she's sweet looking." A round face with huge eyes smiled happily at her. Loads of light brown hair curled around her head. Mia had the kind of cheeks Grace wanted to pinch. Or kiss.

"You're right about that. She turned five in March. She doesn't like to be treated like a baby anymore either."

She smiled, enjoying his fatherly frustration. "Do you get to see much of her?" He'd told her he was divorced, which meant he probably had to share time between his ex with his visitation days and all.

He looked confused. "Uh, every day."

"She lives with you, then?"

He'd gone back to shuffling papers around his desk. "Yes, I've got her full-time."

"Oh." What was she supposed to make of that? He was divorced, not a widower, so why would he have full custody of his child? "So she's already acting all grown-up, huh?"

He lifted his brows in agreement, passed a quick glance to the ceiling. "Drives me and the nanny crazy, too."

Since things weren't adding up the way she'd expected, she may as well take advantage of the opportunity to find out as much as possible about him and his living situation. "What's your nanny's name?"

"Roberta. She's a regular Mrs. Doubtfire, and thinks Mia is the granddaughter she never had…which would be impossible because she never had a child herself."

Grace wanted to pump her fist in the air with this new bit of information. There wasn't another woman in Mitchell's life—his ex-wife was completely out of the picture—just an adorable kindergartner plus a plump, middle-aged nanny—that was, if she truly was a Mrs. Doubtfire type.

Still, the news buoyed her spirit more than she had expected. She smiled at Mitch and put the picture frame back on his desk, not wanting to make too big a deal about it, though she had a thousand other questions spinning around in her mind she'd like to ask like, *how long have you been divorced? Who left whom? Why are you the one with full custody?*

She leaned on her knuckles, edging forward as if he

were a giant magnet and she a helpless piece of metal. They smiled playfully at each other.

He glanced at her mouth, and Julie Treadwell's recent surgery came to mind. There really was something about that mouth that seemed so familiar. Grace pressed her lips together, suddenly bashful about them and wondering why Mitch kept staring in that vicinity on her face. He got an I'm-a-naughty-boy flash in his eyes, as if he knew that she suspected what he'd done, and he didn't care! Was it her mouth? The thought, coupled with his flashing eyes, gave her a bout of tingles.

Thankfully the scarf she wore covered her chest under the thin white silk fabric. Their subtle moment stretched on and Grace felt the tips of her breasts tighten. She'd have to be the first to look away, any second now...before she embarrassed herself.

Too late.

Colleague. Colleague. Colleague. All business. Business. Business. Adventurous pod people no more.

"Okay, then, I'll leave you to your work." She should have cleared her throat first, she sounded way too husky for five in the afternoon. She stood straight, leaving his desk behind. "I'll study up on rocker Davy's face, see if he has what it takes to become The King."

"Don't worry, we'll make him a hunk-a-hunk of burning love." Why did he always resort to humor when things got heavy? She glanced back at him, pretending his joke had landed on deaf ears. "We're a great team, you know."

Were they a great team? Gracie and Cooper? Could she bear working with him all the time, having to keep that safe distance when desiring so much more?

"Nice scarf, by the way," he called after her, when she made it through the door.

She left his office smiling, but the spell was short-lived. There were so many mixed messages from Cooper, none of which she could ever possibly follow through on, and everything made her head spin.

What did it matter if Mitch was free, she could only dream about being with someone like him since she'd never, ever, let anyone close again. She couldn't bear to see the shock or pity on any man's face once they saw her scars. Once had been enough. Never again.

She walked back to her office and plopped behind her desk with one thought she simply couldn't let go of. Where was Mitch's ex-wife? He'd said he was divorced the first night they'd met. The wife wasn't dead. Now she'd seen his beautiful child, Mia. The pressing question was, why any woman in her right mind would let a man like Mitch and a daughter like Mia go?

Mitch stared at the door where Grace had stood. He inhaled the lingering fruity, refreshing scent she always wore. The fragrance did crazy things to his thinking and libido and took him off in all the wrong directions.

He'd done a miserable job of keeping her at arm's length just now.

Gracie. Really, Cooper?

Without trying, they'd moved on to the nickname stage. He was grateful she hadn't chosen Lips. Giving nicknames was something friends did, and they couldn't be friends. Not with the feelings she stirred up inside him just by sitting across from him.

They couldn't be lovers because they worked together and he'd learned from his mistakes, plus he couldn't put things out of balance for Mia. He'd given up gorgeous women, had put his superficial side on hold for good. Mia had been through enough at such an early age, and she deserved a stable, normal mommy.

But he couldn't get the image of Grace leaning across his desk out of his mind. He had to imagine her cleavage, though. Why did she always keep herself covered from neck to knees? She was blessed with a beautiful body—he'd seen the curves—so why did she work so hard to hide everything? He hadn't seen those beautiful legs again since her first day on the job.

Plus all the extra clothes she wore made it harder to imagine her naked...still, he had, just that morning in the shower.

Mitch ran both hands through his hair. What the hell was he supposed to do about Gracie?

Mitchell got the memo about the 8:00 a.m. Friday morning meeting in Leo's office just after Grace had left on Thursday afternoon. The blip on his computer helped him stop thinking about her—not to mention thinking about her naked—and the meeting memo also ended his brief enjoyment over teasing her. Against his better judgement, it was something he'd quickly become fond of in the short time she'd been at the clinic—teasing Grace. And it had to stop. He'd have to go against all his natural instincts where she was concerned, and continue to keep that arm's length between them. He'd made sure to avoid her the last several days. He hated the thought, but knew it was imperative if they were to continue working together.

Upon his arrival at the clinic on Friday morning, he went directly to the meeting. Across from Leo's desk sat the large and quiet Ethan. Though the younger of the brothers, Ethan's life experience, including his injuries, had made him look like the older of the two. It was no secret around the place that the brothers had issues still simmering between them. Sometimes their strained relationship made Mitchell feel uncomfortable.

"Ah, Cooper, I'm glad you're here," Leo said as Mitchell took a seat next to Ethan. Mitchell and Ethan nodded at each other but didn't shake hands, then Mitchell greeted Leo with a smile. "Coffee?" Leo offered a stainless-steel canister.

"No, thanks. Already had mine," Mitchell said. Tension crept up his spine regarding the meaning of this meeting, and he wasn't sure how to read Ethan's withdrawn body language today. Had he done something wrong? Ethan drank from a mug and in between swallows seemed to be pondering something floating inside the coffee cup, reticent as always.

"Well," Leo said, "I wanted to bring you both up to date about some future plans. As you know, our clinic wants to support Fair Go, the charity Olivia Fairchild—a pediatric plastics nurse who used to work here—has started in Africa." Leo poured himself more coffee. "In order to help as many children as possible, I've decided to bring Olivia over for a period of time. I don't know how long it will end up being, actually." Leo looked cautiously at Ethan, and Mitchell also glanced at him, noticing Ethan's grip tighten around the coffee mug. "Until we can afford to eventually go as a team to Africa, we'll have to bring the children here. And she's got a special case she'd like to start with. Unfortunately, she can't adjust her schedule just now." Ethan glanced up. Leo nailed him with a stern look. "So you may as well get used to the fact that one way or the other you'll be working with her, Ethan."

Ethan put his mug down and stood. "Fine with me." He turned and headed for the door but stopped there. He stared at the floor. "Do whatever you have to do. The kids need our help. They come first. Count me in." Then he left. Leo cleared his throat and glanced at Mitchell, who was trying to figure out why working with this doctor should be a concern to Ethan.

"Look, you deserve an explanation, but it's a long, long story," Leo said, as if reading Mitchell's mind.

Mitchell understood Ethan had been through a lot, and could be described as moody at times, but he'd never been rude or obstinate with him. He'd always been professional and Mitchell could see how much he cared about his patients. Mitchell had nothing but respect for him, felt he was a top-notch surgeon. Leo, on the other hand, had seemed to suffer the brunt of Ethan's demons since his return to the family clinic. Mitchell had also overheard many heated arguments behind closed doors since his arrival at Hunter Clinic, and took that into account.

Leo took a drink of his coffee, tension pressing down his brows. "It's a long story, but the basic fact is there's some history between us and Olivia." Leo took another drink. Mitchell understood that the Hunter brothers were limping along and trying to mend their relationship. What Leo meant by "history" between the three of them gave Mitchell pause. Could it mean what he thought? If so, that gave a whole new meaning to family feud.

"Maybe I will have some coffee," he said, and Leo poured him a cup. He took a long warm draw on the rich drink, and waited for the rest of the story.

"I'm sure you know that Ethan will do anything as far as humanitarian efforts go, so, like he said, I know he's on board with whatever Olivia wants to do, whenever she wants to do it. Fair Go is a great organization. I have my suspicions about what may be eating at him, but it's not for me to say." Leo took another drink.

Mitch wanted to be respectful of the brothers and their issues. He also knew Leo well enough that if he wanted to share the full story, he would. He drank his coffee and kept quiet.

"There's one more thing." Mitchell looked up. Was he about to hear the big secret? "And this is just between the two of us." Mitchell gave his nod of confidentiality. *Finally, after being here four years, he's opening up to me. I feel like this is taking our business friendship to a new level.* "Whether my brother wants to admit it or not, he's got a heart." Leo rubbed his eye with the palm of his hand, tried to smile but failed miserably. "If you think he's in a bad place now, just wait until Olivia arrives. I suspect her return will be tough on him, so if you think he's moody now, this is just a warning."

Mitchell put his cup on Leo's desk and stood. "I'll take that on advisement, and won't take any fallout personally." He reached across the desk and shook Leo's hand.

He wanted to thank him for filling him in, but the fact was Leo hadn't disclosed anything. He was a private man, and Mitchell shouldn't have expected him to open up to him beyond the bare essentials. Ethan would be forced to deal with a woman from his past, and Leo had simply wanted to warn him about it. Obviously, something major had happened between the Hunter brothers and this Olivia person, but what it was Mitchell couldn't fathom a guess.

The Hunter Clinic did great work on many levels, yet where the personnel's private lives were concerned, well, emotionally the place was the pits.

"Oh, and Cooper? We've got an explosion survivor on his way over from Ethiopia. One of Olivia's Fair Go children. Lost part of his face and an ear. His name is Telaye Derege. As I mentioned earlier, Olivia can't rearrange her schedule to be here just yet, so I'm assigning you and Grace to him." He tossed a pile of papers at Mitchell. "Here are the case notes. Take them home and study them over the weekend. You two can tackle the boy after the Cumberbatch case. It'll probably take that long for clearance of all the travel documents."

Mitchell picked up the notes, wondering how in the hell he was supposed to keep Grace at arm's length if they kept being assigned the same cases.

He left Leo with more questions formed than answered, and returned to his office.

Just before he entered, he saw Lizzie round the corner. He silently flagged her down and waved her into his office. If anyone knew the whole story, being the new Mrs. Hunter, she would. He waited inside his office until Lizzie joined him then closed the door.

"I've got a question for you."

"Sure. What do you want to know?" she said.

"I've just come from a meeting with Leo, and I'm trying to figure something out."

"Really. What has Leo done now?" She smiled with the understanding look of a woman deeply in love.

"Well, we all know about Fair Go and how we want to give the organization our support."

She nodded, her carefully shaped brows arched earnestly.

"But I've just been informed that Olivia Fairchild herself will be coming to the clinic. When Ethan heard that, he got up and left the meeting, as if she was the last person on earth he wanted to see. And Leo said something about it being a long story and there was some history between the three of them. Then he warned me that Ethan might be a bear to work with once she arrives. What the heck am I supposed to make of that?"

By the expression on her face, Lizzie seemed to know exactly what Mitchell was referring to. "I don't want to break Leo's trust, but I know how much he respects you as a colleague and a friend. He's not very good at opening up, and I can see why you're confused." She touched his arm. "I know I can trust you, Mitchell, and you deserve to understand why Ethan might be tough to work with for a while, so I'm going to tell you what the issue is."

She perched on the edge of the chair across from his desk. He leaned against the desk, legs outstretched and arms folded. "The short and sweet version is that the 'history' Leo's talking about is a love triangle."

Mitchell drew in his chin then shook his head. Brothers? "What?"

"Both Leo and Ethan had a thing for Olivia a long

time ago. Ethan won, then just as quickly broke Olivia's heart. Having spent time with Ethan when he was recuperating, I know he still carries a great deal of pain and guilt from his time in combat, and there were people he cared deeply about and lost during his tour of duty. I suspect having Olivia here at the clinic will force him to remember some things he may want to forget, and he may have to face the fact that he once really cared for her. It's not my place to say anything more, but I hope that helps a little."

"Yes. Thank you. I don't want to delve into places I don't belong, but you've given me more angles to consider."

"Anytime, Mitchell."

"Oh, and Lizzie, how are those honeymoon plans going?"

Her soft brown eyes nearly twinkled at the mention of her delayed honeymoon. "Fantastic. Never in my dreams did I ever think I'd have a wedding like that, and now the most incredible honeymoon. I won't bore you with all the details, but it will be unforgettable, I'm sure of it."

"That's great. Just great. I'm looking forward to hearing all about it when you get back."

She smiled. "Believe me, I'll be telling everyone about it." She paused and a tiny smile crossed her mouth. "Well, not everything."

With that she left Mitchell to his thoughts. A love triangle? Holy smoke, never in a million years would he have come up with that. It was true that women found Ethan mysterious, and from the ladies' scuttlebutt around the water cooler at the clinic, sexy as hell.

Leo was also a fantastically handsome guy, not that Mitchell normally noticed such things but in Leo's case it couldn't be denied. Mitchell had always gotten the idea that Ethan was more of a love-'em-and-leave-'em guy. That Olivia must be some woman to have gotten under his skin.

With his interest piqued about what to expect from Olivia Fairchild, he went over what else Lizzie had told him. Olivia would bring back memories Ethan probably wanted to forget about from his time in combat. Mitchell could only guess what he'd been through.

And he thought he'd had it bad. He shook his head, thought about the woman he'd lost bit by bit through plastic surgery, his ex-wife. He'd stuck by her even through her transformation, only then learning she'd fallen in love with his business partner back in California, the only man Mitchell had allowed to do all her surgeries. The two people he'd trusted most had stabbed him in the back and run off together. The rush of memories turned the rich coffee he'd just shared with Leo bitter as ashes in his stomach.

CHAPTER FOUR

ALEXIA ROBBINS KNEW how to be persistent, and Grace was feeling the full force of her won't-take-no-for-an-answer attitude.

Friday afternoon, Grace had just gotten back from the Lighthouse, having assisted on a pediatric cleft palate and extreme nose deformation case with Ethan. Besides being highly impressed with his surgical skills, she noticed how meticulous he was on every level. His team was kept on their toes at all times as he was a man willing to think outside the box when it came to solutions. He'd probably gotten that skill set from his years in combat in mobile surgical units.

The surgery had gone on far longer than she'd expected. She was tired and all she wanted to do was finish her paperwork and head for home to take a nice long bath. But there stood Lexi before her desk, determination flashing in her bright blue eyes and with notepad in hand.

"You've been dodging me, Miss Turner." Lexi put her hands on her hips in mock anger.

"*Moi*? I've been in surgery all day."

"I'm talking about yesterday, and the day before that."

"Surgery and surgery. I'm sorry." Truth was, she *had* been avoiding Lexi and her interview request almost as much as she'd avoided Mitch because of his irresistible charm.

"It's just a few questions. I do it with all our new staff."

Lexi wore the most fashionable clothes, and today was no exception. Her short dress fit to a tee, accenting her curves, and the flashy blue-and-bright-green pattern drew out the color of her eyes. What Grace would give to wear an alluring neckline like that....

"Our clients expect to know all about you."

That would never happen! Grace's mind raced for ways to answer her questions without really revealing anything. "Okay. Shoot." *As in you may as well shoot me because I hate interviews!*

"Lovely." Lexi sat in the white leather chair across from Grace's modern glass and wrought-iron desk.

"I'll answer your questions if you'll answer a few of mine—deal?"

Lexi didn't need long to think about the offer. "Deal. Now, firstly, what is your educational background?"

Grace ran down the list of her universities and medical schools, skipping the part about having to take a year off to recover, then all her awards and certificates.

"Ever married? Any children?"

"Never married. No children. Though I was engaged once," Grace said, without thinking. She hadn't thought about Ben in ages. Even now, after all these years, the thought of him twisted her stomach into a knot. "Once upon a time."

Lexi lifted the thick-lashed lids of her dazzling blue

eyes, made up to perfection, gauging the meaning of her response. "Care to elaborate?"

The fact that the guy couldn't accept her after she'd been burned? Hell, no. There would be no elaborating. "Not really."

"I understand."

Could anyone understand? Grace had been through a half dozen skin grafts, she'd finally been given the okay to get up close and personal with her fiancé again, but he'd taken one look at her naked—her breasts and neck covered in webbed and mottled scars—and, as hard as he'd tried, hadn't been able to hide his horror.

"Pets?"

"Pardon? Oh, none. Look, I'm afraid I'm really boring, and people may worry about my stability if we continue." Grace tried to make light of her situation.

"Oh, don't think a second about it. It's hard to pick up and move to London from Arizona. Besides, we're just getting to the good part."

Grace chewed her bottom lip, letting anxiety overtake her, wishing she'd never agreed to the interview. Moving on from heartrending, what could the "good part" possibly be?

Mitch popped around the corner of her office door, his mouth formed to ask a question. Grace and Lexi stopped and glanced his way.

"Oh, uh, never mind. Just had some news to catch you up on."

"Yes?" She wanted more than anything to hear that news, anything to put off this horrible interview. Next Lexi would be asking to take a picture, the second-most dreadful thing Grace could think of after an interview.

"It can wait," he said, and off he went.

Damn, there was no getting out of the rest of the interview now. How could she concentrate, wondering what his "news" was?

"Have a nice weekend." Lexi quickly settled back into the rhythm of their interview. "Tell me about your most amazing reconstructive surgery experience."

Ah, finally something she could shine about....

She smiled, relaxing into her thoughts, and laced her fingers together over one knee. "When I first began my reconstructive-surgery fellowship, I was fortunate enough to be chosen by my mentor to be on her special surgical-reconstruction team. She was one of seven plastic surgeons, along with several other surgeons, led by another woman doctor, taking part in one of the earliest face transplants in the world. Maybe you heard about it? The whole procedure took twenty-two hours…"

Lexi's eyes widened with interest as she scribbled with all her might on her writing pad, her diamond engagement ring gleaming in the overhead lights.

Grace paced the length of her apartment for a third time on a Friday night. She was too tired to go out to eat, especially by herself, and had settled for canned soup with toast. The soup was warming on the stove and the bread waiting for the toaster. Keyed up from a busy week, especially that day's intricate surgery and Lexi's interview, knowing that next week she'd meet her first high-profile patient, she'd soaked in the tub without relief. Feeling a bit in between things, she was restless yet not tired enough to go to bed. Besides, it was only seven o'clock, and she hadn't eaten her supper yet.

She'd blown her opportunity to turn the tables and get the lowdown on Mitchell from Lexi. Something told her there was quite a story behind his divorce and unusual custody arrangement. Maybe he'd married someone famous? As adorable as Mia was, her mother had to be gorgeous. Of course, having such a good-looking dad as Mitch had a lot to do with it, too.

She sat on the couch and fiddled with the TV controller, not having a clue what programs or channels were available on British television, settling on an international news station which was focusing on Spain at the moment, but, whatever, the news would act like white noise and she'd have to make do for now.

Her intercom beeped.

She jumped, never having heard it before. What was that about?

She crossed the room and pressed the button. "Yes?"

"Uh, it's Mitch. Have you got a few minutes?"

The sound of his voice sent a platoon of nerves marching through her. The one thing she'd felt relaxed about for the weekend was being guaranteed she wouldn't have to be near Mitchell Cooper, wouldn't have to fight her interest, or the reaction of her body, whenever he was near. Now, it seemed, he'd followed her home.

Since she hadn't been successful at getting him out of her mind, she may as well let him in!

"Mitch? Oh, uh, of course I've got time." The guy had come all the way to her apartment, she couldn't exactly refuse him. "Let me ring you in."

The moment she'd pressed the Open button she made a beeline for the bathroom to brush her hair and check her makeup. There was none there! Oh, my. She snatched her gloss and brightened her lips with a few dabs. Then she headed straight to the closet for a thin teal-green sweater to cover her arms. Shoot, she didn't have a turtleneck on so grabbed the nearest scarf, trying to remember how to tie a simple slipknot. She doubled up the scarf and wrapped it around her neck, then slipped both ends into the loop, with fumbling fingers. The result looked haphazard, but it would have to do.

Just as she finished with the scarf, her doorbell rang. Remembering she'd put on comfortable sweat pants after her bath, she groaned. Cripes! She slipped across the carpet to answer the door, turning off the TV on the way and only then realizing she was barefoot.

Mitch smiled when she opened the door, the vision of his strikingly handsome face taking her aback, as it always did at first glance. He wore an old brown leather bomber jacket over his tailored yellow shirt, brown slacks and loafers. He'd removed his tie and the collar was open at his throat.

Her eyes drifted downward to where he held a tiny girl's hand—the beautiful child from the picture. The sweetest-looking thing she'd ever seen.

"Hello!" she said, all thoughts of how she was dressed disappearing. "You must be Mia."

Mia's eyes lit up. "Hi!"

"Sorry," Mitch said, looking at his daughter. "Should have introduced you first. My apologies, Mia, it wasn't polite of Daddy to forget you."

"That's okay." She sounded so grown up.

While his eyes were in the vicinity of his daughter, and the carpeted floor, Grace realized he'd noticed her bare feet. Besides her hands and face, this was the only "naked" part of her he'd ever seen, and it felt intimate. Really intimate. A slow, warm trail sprang from the soles of her feet to the backs of her knees and kept heading north. She wanted to turn under her bright pink-tipped toes and rush off to put on some shoes.

The moment stretched on a bit too long, and Grace wished Mia would save the day.

Still looking preoccupied with her feet, Mitch flapped a pile of papers at her. "I'm sorry to invade your Friday night, but I thought you'd like to see these case notes on our next patient as soon as possible."

Our next patient?

"Come in," Grace said, after the initial shock let up a bit. "Come in."

"Nice digs," Mitch said, after taking a quick inventory of the living room.

"What beautiful flowers!" Mia had rushed to the coffee table where the calla lilies remained. The same ones that had welcomed her almost two weeks ago— they looked worse for wear, a little droopy with browning edges. The ones Grace kept meaning to throw out. Yet Mia found them beautiful.

Grace smiled, loving the child's enthusiasm, wishing she could tap into it herself.

"They're called calla lilies, Mia, and I think they're pretty, too." She glanced up and saw a beaming Mitch, looking on with adoring fatherly eyes, and wanted to hug him.

Mia quietly repeated the name of the flowers, "Calla lilies, calla lilies," as if memorizing the new words.

"Oh." Remembering her makeshift dinner, Grace

dashed for the kitchen. "Pardon me while I turn off the stove."

The open-style apartment made the kitchen easily viewed from the living room.

"Didn't mean to interrupt your dinner, too. Sorry."

"It's only soup and toast, but I can make grilled cheese sandwiches if you're hungry."

"We've just come from dinner, thanks." He followed her into the glaringly white kitchen.

"I'd like a grilled cheese sandwich!" Mia spoke up, hot on her father's heels.

Mitch looked surprised. "You just had chicken and salad, honeybee, how can you still be hungry?"

"I'm a growing girl?"

Grace laughed and Mitch reluctantly joined her. She loved the way he called Mia "honeybee". So sweet.

Mia, realizing she'd become the center of their attention, grinned. "That's what you always say, Daddy."

Grace went right into action. "Two grilled cheese sandwiches coming up. Do you like tomato soup, Mia?"

"Yes."

Grace smiled at Mitch, who shrugged.

"Then we'll both have a bowl. Can I offer Daddy a sandwich and some soup, too?"

"Thank you, but no. Unlike my daughter, who left most of her dinner on the plate, I'm full."

Grace went back on task. "You can sit right here, Mia, on this stool." She moved and then assisted the child onto the kitchen stool placing it near the small breakfast bar and the stovetop. "Can you stir this soup for me once in a while so I can make the sandwiches?"

Mia's eyes brightened and she reached for the long wooden spoon. "Yes."

Her voice was sweet and serious and it touched Grace's heart. What a precious child Mitch had.

A dreary dinner alone had taken on a new, welcome and completely enjoyable turn. She'd been kept so busy on the job that she hadn't realized how people-starved she'd been since moving to London. Back home, her Friday nights were often spent eating out with her sister. She really missed having someone to share things with—wished she could talk to Hope about Mitch and her mixed-up feelings about him, too, but the seven-hour difference kept her from picking up the phone and calling home whenever she wanted.

Her smart yet lonely apartment had seemed to come to life since Mitch and Mia had walked in the door.

Mitch watched Grace move about the kitchen with ease. She knew how to fend for herself, and he liked that. He liked the fit of her workout pants and the extra treat of catching her barefoot. She had pretty, slender feet, and the pink toenails were downright sexy.

Mia lit up under Grace's natural warmth and kind indulgences, as she carefully stirred the soup, Grace nearby, making sure she wouldn't burn herself or spill anything. Maybe she had nieces and nephews, and was used to being around kids.

"How'd you find out where I live?" Grace asked.

"I had to bribe our beloved receptionist, Helen."

"Ah. Did she give you my phone number, too?"

She sent a subtle message: call before popping in next time. Truth was he'd been afraid she'd put him off if he called first, and he'd really wanted to see her tonight. All through dinner bits of memories about Grace played out in his mind. Mia had gotten impatient at one point, tapping his hand and saying, "Daddy, Daddy, Daddy, don't forget about me!"

"I, uh, forgot to ask, but that's a good idea. We should exchange phone numbers since we'll be working together so much."

After his meeting with Leo, being told he'd be working with Grace on Telaye Dereje's case, he'd had a perfect excuse to stop by.

"Makes sense," Grace said. "Remind me before you leave and we can put each other's numbers in our cell phones."

He liked that idea, as he watched Grace grill the sandwiches and Mia stir the soup. Things grew quiet.

"What's your favorite dinner, Mia?" Grace asked out of the blue.

"Ice cream." Mia raised her shoulders and twisted her little body in delight, then mischievously glanced at her father. "Sometimes Daddy lets me have ice cream for dinner."

Grace's eyes, so blue, so beautiful, went wide. "Ice cream." She gave him a you-are-so-busted glance.

"Now, Mia, that was only for your birthday," he said, saving face. He really was a conscientious father and worked hard at the job, and he didn't want Grace thinking he was some kind of flake, spoiling his daughter by giving in to her every whim.

Grace grinned at him, understanding in her eyes. "I think a birthday is a perfectly acceptable time to have ice cream for dinner." She'd already started to grill the sandwiches and had flipped the first one. "I think I'll have ice cream for my next birthday, too."

"When's that?" He took the opportunity to fill in some of the blanks about Grace Turner, reconstructive surgeon. He looked her up and down. Why was she still wearing a scarf around her neck in her own home yet her feet were bare?

"October. I'll be thirty-three, if you're curious."

"Wow, that's old!" Mia said.

He grimaced and pinched his temples with his finger and thumb, then shaded his eyes. "Now, Mia, I'm much older than that."

"How old?" Grace seemed to jump at the opportunity to find out his age, too, and for some reason that made him glad.

"Thirty-six. Won't be thirty-seven until next January."

Grace gave a deadpan glance at Mia. "Now, that's old." Mia covered her mouth and giggled, and stirred the soup with the other hand.

"Okay, okay, ladies, let's move on."

Grace finished the grilling, ladled out two small bowls of soup and Mitch helped carry the sandwiches to the table.

"Are you sure you don't want anything?" she asked.

"I'm fine. Thanks." Just before sitting down to eat, they had another meaningful glance into each other's eyes, the kind that made time stop while swimming through her pale blue stare. He needed to ground himself or he'd start getting all kinds of bad ideas about what he'd like to do with and to Grace Turner. And though he'd once been drawn to beauty like a moth to flame, he'd given up women like her, finding most of them to be vain and superficial. Not so the case with Gracie, though.

"Mind if I talk about the new case while you eat?" he asked.

She blew over the soup on her spoon before tasting it. "Not at all." Grace seemed far too natural to be vain.

While Mia ate like she hadn't been fed all day, embarrassing him no end, and Grace daintily nibbled her sandwich and sipped her soup, Mitch filled her in. The boy had some kind of blast injuries and was from Ethiopia. Plans were being made to fly him over through Fair Go.

Grace listened intently.

Sitting at a table, like they were a family, clutched him around the chest, forcing him to realize how important it was. How he missed it from his childhood, and had never come close to being a family with Christie.

Was Mia lonely for a family? She certainly shined under Grace's attention. Maybe he should ask her out strictly for Mia's sake?

After they ate, he helped with the dishes, against Grace's protest.

"So, I was thinking," he said, drying the nonstick grill pan, "Mia and I are going to the park on Sunday, would you like to come along? You know, get you out of the apartment and show you some of London. What do you say?" He hadn't felt this nervous asking a woman out since he'd first moved to Hollywood and started noticing A-list models. Especially since it was a woman he'd vowed to keep at arm's length for his own good.

She gave him a surprised expression, then glanced

at Mia, who'd started clapping, then she tossed him a not-fair-how-can-I-refuse gaze. "Sure. I don't have any plans and it's supposed to be a beautiful weekend, according to the TV weather report."

"Great. Let's have breakfast out first. How about I pick you up at ten?"

"Uh, okay."

It was a dirty trick—how could she say no in front of his daughter?—but he didn't care. Mia liked her and so did he. Damn it. He wanted to spend more time with Grace, whether it was a good idea or not. Today he'd indulge his weakness for beautiful women. Besides, now he knew where she lived.

Before they left they exchanged phone numbers. Against all better judgment, now that he had her number, he may as well use the information.

Grace closed the door and glanced around her apartment. It was as though someone had dimmed the lights. Things looked duller and her energy level had fizzled since Mitch and Mia had left. Amazed how much they'd brought into her life, she smiled and went around shutting off the lights.

He was a good man and a good father. Mia was a special child who blossomed under her father's attention. But where was her mother? Not once had Mia said anything about a mother. Most kids shared how Mommy did it this way, or how much they liked the way their mother made them grilled cheese sandwiches, but not a peep about a mother from the darling. How long had Mitch's wife been out of the picture, and did little Mia ever have contact with her? Where was Lexi when she needed to pick her brain?

Grace shook her head. It wasn't up to her to figure everything out, no matter how curious she was. What mattered was how much she liked Mitch and the bright and curious Mia.

Grace's heart swelled with affection for both of them, and it caught her off guard. She might not be able to get involved in their lives as much as she'd like, but she sure as hell could be a friend to Mitch and especially to Mia, who needed a mommy, not a nanny.

Sunday morning, and Mitch arrived as planned at 10:00 a.m., looking fantastic in jeans and a T-shirt. It fit snug and afforded Grace a view of his flat stomach, broad chest, and an in-the-flesh view of the muscles she'd been admiring on his arms all week. Mia wore denim overalls and her hair was in a curly ponytail, high on the back of her head—obviously Daddy's go-to hairdo.

Grace had thrown on jeans and a gray turtleneck. Thankfully, it was a brisk morning, and she wouldn't have to explain why she'd covered up. Again.

In the past, if someone simply had to know why she dressed the way she did, she'd mention her burns. Expecting to end the subject right there, she'd then notice the tsk-tsk expression on whoever it was, and the look would make her crazy. She'd learned well to keep her scars a secret.

Already, it was important to her never to have Mitch give her that tsk-tsk look, or feel sorry for her in any way. So far he hadn't seemed to catch onto the way she carefully kept herself covered. Thank goodness.

"Are you ready for breakfast, Gracie?" he asked.

"Why, yes, Cooper, I'm starving. How about you, are you hungry, Mia?"

"I'm starving, too!" Grace wasn't sure that Mia knew what the word meant, but Mia had mimicked it perfectly with the exact inflection she must have heard in *her* voice. Besides mimicking, the child liked to clap about things, too. This time, Grace found herself imitating Mia, clapping right along.

"Yay," she said, suddenly more enthusiastic about having breakfast out than she could ever remember in her entire life.

"Great, because I'm taking you to our favorite waffle café, and they serve a lot of food."

"Sounds heavenly."

"By the way, you look beautiful today," he said.

Grace almost tripped in her tracks to his car. "Thanks." How should she handle the compliment? "You don't look half-bad yourself." She'd take the superficial route.

He gave her half a smile, letting her know he was okay with her brushing off his flattery.

Seriously, though, he thought she looked beautiful in her jeans and gray turtleneck? When was the last time a man had told her she looked beautiful, or she'd felt beautiful?

Meanwhile, he looked like a men's magazine-cover model, which distracted Grace from the deep discussion with Mia about her latest favorite animated film, something about balloons and children flying to another land where everything was pink and toys could talk....

Forty-five minutes later, looking down on the largest Belgian waffle she'd ever seen, smothered in sliced bananas, and inhaling the marvelous scent of the bananas and fresh maple syrup imported from Maine, she indulged herself in the first bite. She thought she'd gone to taste heaven. A moan of delight escaped her throat.

"Sounds like you're enjoying that a little too much," Mitch said, an envious glint in his eyes.

"You knew what you were talking about," she said, covering her mouth because she hadn't finished chewing. "This place is great."

"Glad you like it." He hadn't bothered to shave that morning and the stubble, combined with his sincere smile, almost had her moaning again, but for an entirely different reason. "By the way," he interrupted her dreamy thoughts, "I thought we'd do something really fun after this."

Her mouth was filled with a second bite of delicious waffle so all she did was look at him.

"I've been meaning to take Mia on one of those amphibious land/boat tours of London since we got here, and have yet to find the time. I thought today would be perfect."

Mia squirmed in her chair with excitement and did her usual clap.

Grace, with her mouth still full, clapped along. She glanced at Mia, and when Mia gave a wide smile, food and all, Grace did the same.

"Girls, get a hold of yourselves." Mitch played along, acting disgusted but obviously loving Grace coming down to his daughter's level.

Why was hanging out with Mitch and his daughter so much fun?

An hour after breakfast, Grace, Mia and Mitch boarded a bright yellow amphibious boat, along with a load of other people. They scrambled to sit toward the front, Mia carefully placed between them. Grace couldn't help feeling like they were a family, and she let herself pretend for a few seconds that they all belonged to each other. It felt too wonderful and scared her. *Don't daydream like this. It will only hurt later.*

"Why are you quiet?" Mia asked.

Grace snapped out of her mixed-up feelings, jumping right back into the here and now. "I'm so excited about this adventure, I needed a moment to say thank you."

"Who did you thank?"

Mia's direct questions forced Grace to think. She gave it a second then smiled at Mitch. "I guess I should say it out loud, then, shouldn't I? Thank you, Mitch, for inviting me along today."

The corners of his eyes crinkled as he smiled, those sea-green eyes piercing right to her center. "I'm really glad you came."

Mia clapped. Grace's good mood swelled with the child's natural enthusiasm.

For the next hour and a half they rode by the usual London tourist sites—Buckingham Palace, Westminster Abbey, Big Ben, Trafalgar Square—and finished up by splashing the big barge-type boat, that was first used in World War II on the beaches of Normandy, into the Thames for an up-close look at the Houses of Parliament.

Mia clapped and squealed as they launched into the water, and Grace laughed along with Mitch. The driver had taken on a ridiculous personality during the trip, Drake McDuck, making everyone laugh and carry on like they were kids again. Forcing them all to say "quack-quack" any time he mentioned his name, which was constantly! Grace couldn't remember when she'd last had so much fun. Then her mind jumped back to two weeks ago and the night she'd first met Mitch, when he'd taken her to the adventure playground.

The thought of having someone like Mitch in her life both scared and appealed to her. But having someone meant opening up and she couldn't do it. Not that he was asking anyway.

A distant amphibious boat created a wake that rocked and rolled theirs. Mitch enjoyed watching Grace's eyes open wide, just like his daughter's. He laughed when Grace and Mia squealed in unison and grabbed hands. Mia was usually shy and withdrawn around grown-ups, but not with Grace. They'd taken to each other right off, as if they'd known each other for years. Seeing how Grace genuinely enjoyed his daughter's company touched his heart. She wasn't faking it, everything about her was real.

When had he felt so lighthearted, so free of burdens lately? He couldn't remember, but looking into Grace's crystal-blue eyes, how they shone with joy against her creamy skin and dark hair, he wanted to grab her and kiss her.

But he knew better. He wouldn't ruin it for Mia. She'd made a new grown-up friend.

After the tour, they grabbed some vendor snacks and walked down to the Jubilee playground again. In broad daylight it was filled to overflowing with children and parents, and the noise level made it hard to talk without yelling. He'd liked it better the night they'd had the place to themselves.

Grace smiled at him. A lot. From across the playground while she pushed Mia on a swing. From the monkey bars as she stood beneath Mia, ready to catch her if she fell. And crawling along behind Mia in a long cylinder replicating a hollow tree trunk, her face lit up the day like the sun could never do.

A tight and sudden clutch in his chest brought him to his senses. It was so apparent how much Mia needed a mother, how she shone under Grace's attention. Every child needed a mother, yet it was the one thing he couldn't give his daughter. It wasn't Grace's job to fill in the blanks in his life. He'd fouled everything up by getting swept away by Christie's beauty. He'd been naive when he'd first opened his medical practice with Rick, his best friend from medical school in Southern California. He'd fraternized with the Hollywood crowd, simply because he'd been able to. Sure, he'd gone into plastic surgery to make big bucks, taking into account that Hollywood and glamour went hand in hand. Suddenly, he and his partner had been the big deal in town, and he'd been seduced by beauty everywhere, the kind of beauty he could make with his own hands.

There was an old saying about Hollywood stealing a person's soul, and for the five years he'd had his practice there, he'd lost his. He'd left the family life and values of his youth behind to explore the superficial and vain side of things. The prettier the women had been that he'd dated, the happier he'd been...or so he'd thought.

Until he'd chosen the most beautiful woman of all,

having been completely captivated by her looks, and somehow not seeing past the perfect facade to notice something much greater had been missing. Once they'd married he'd tried to go back to the way things had been when he'd grown up. Marriage meant a family with children. But that approach had proved to be a disaster. And his precious Mia had suffered the cruelest of all costs—a detached mother.

He shook his head and focused back on Grace, currently running and laughing with Mia. She was a busy surgeon, in a new city, probably just getting her bearings. It wasn't fair to expect anything from her. It wasn't safe either. What if Mia got too attached to Grace?

She was a business colleague, and that should be all. He'd have to pay for his mistakes and poor choice of a business and personal partner by himself.

An anxious reflex drilled through him. Had he made a mistake, asking Grace out today?

"Can we go to the pagoda?" Mia rushed him, catching him off guard. The Chinese Pagoda in Kew Gardens was, for some reason, his daughter's favorite place.

"It's getting kind of late, honeybee."

She used her surefire approach and jumped up and down, while saying, "Please, please, please?"

"I'd love to see Kew Gardens," Grace said. "That is, if it isn't cutting too much into your plans for the rest of the day?"

Mia clapped.

"On one condition, Gracie."

She stood there looking lovely and sun-kissed from a highly cooperative London day. It was all he could do not to reach out and hug her. "What's that?"

"We stop for some Chinese takeout and have a picnic while we're there."

"I'd love to."

Mia cheered. "Yay, we're going to the pagoda."

Later, Grace thanked Mitchell for a perfectly lovely day, when he saw her to the front of her building. Mia had fallen asleep, and rather than leave her in the car he hoisted her into his arms. So zonked was she from their long day spent entirely outdoors, that the child rested her head on his shoulder and he carried her as naturally as any father worth his salt.

He smiled and mouthed, "You're welcome," not wanting to wake Mia.

Somewhere around the time of the playground, he'd changed. His mood had shifted and since then he'd seemed cautious, withdrawn even.

Had she done something to offend him? Maybe she'd pushed it by agreeing to go to Kew Gardens with them, when it was clear he was ready to call it a day. She wanted to ask what she'd done, but it wouldn't be fair to grill a guy with his daughter like a sack of potatoes on his chest and shoulder.

She'd let her hair down and enjoyed every minute of their outing, something she hadn't done with a man since she'd been burned. Mia was such a fun child, she rarely fussed, and she actually listened to reason. He'd done a great job of not spoiling her but making sure she knew she was loved, and Grace wanted to tell him so, but, again, now just wasn't the time.

Sometimes actions spoke louder than words ever

could. The man had gone out of his way to show her a good time, and she appreciated it with all her heart.

Too bad he was holding his sleeping daughter. She went up on tiptoe, anchored herself by balancing her hand on his free arm and kissed his cheek.

"I'll always love London because of the way you shared it with me," she whispered.

He looked baffled, as if he couldn't think of a proper reply.

She laughed quietly and shook her head. Men were funny that way. She'd been too honest, and scared him off. Oh, well, at least he knew how she felt.

"I'll see you at work tomorrow," she said, then opened the door to her building without giving him another glance. "Tell Mia good-night for me."

"Will do. Say good-night, Gracie."

She grinned. "Good night, Gracie."

When she closed the door, she leaned her back against it, fighting off the strong desire to know Mitch and his beautiful child more. But one other thing inched into her thoughts—could the reason he blew hot and cold around her be because of unresolved issues with his ex-wife? What if he still loved her?

Then why was he in one part of the world and she in another? Hell, she had proved to be a lousy snoop. She'd spent the whole day with the man and didn't even know if his ex lived in London or the States.

She sighed—even if there weren't any concerns hanging things up on his end, there could still never be a possibility of them becoming close because of her issues—then she pushed off from the door and headed for the elevator. That about summed up the sorry state of her life—seeing wonderful relationships, longing to have one for herself, but knowing she never could. And she was really getting sick of it.

Damn Mitch for rubbing it in her face.

CHAPTER FIVE

MID-MONDAY MORNING, Mitchell barreled into Grace's office in the clinic with knit brows, looking frustrated. Fired up, as her daddy used to say. Even while obviously testy, she found him appealing. She quashed the thought, switching to all business, as she'd promised herself to do last night, lying in bed, staring at the ceiling, unable to sleep. Thanks to spending the entire day with him!

"I can't believe the hacks out there," he said, stance wide, hands on hips, scrubs fitting deliciously.

"Out where?"

"Do you know what I spent my morning doing?" The O.R. cap brought out that extra bit of blue in his otherwise green eyes, making him even more devastatingly appealing.

"What?"

"Fixing a botched plastic surgery job on a twenty-two-year-old, that's what." He paced the small space in front of her desk. "The guy mangled her lips, making her look like a duck. She had a smile like the Joker from that movie. Grotesque. And why would a surgeon agree to do a face-lift on someone just out of their teens? I tell you, sometimes I don't get our profession."

She considered his anger, threw in some of her own, then thought about their jobs and the oaths they'd taken when they'd become doctors—do no harm. She also thought about something that had been weighing on her mind since she'd been assigned a certain high-profile case.

"Isn't that what we do? Whatever people want? Not the duck-lips part, or the botching-up part, but don't we agree to do whatever our rich patients want? Isn't that what we promised to do for Davy Cumberbatch?"

"This girl is neither rich nor demanding. She's naive, and that hack took advantage of her wanting to look beautiful."

But Grace's direct comments stopped his thunder for a couple of seconds. He stopped pacing and pulled in his chin, as if he hadn't considered the comparison of Hunter Clinic to hacks ever before.

"You said it yourself," she said. "Fix the rich to help the poor? Or something along those lines." She didn't back down.

Maybe she didn't want to let him off the hook because she was still upset with him for tilting her world sideways, for making her see what she could never have. A family. A love of her life. It wasn't in the cards for her, and the Sunday outing with Mitch and Mia had driven that point home. Yes, she was upset with him for making it so clear, and right now she'd make him squirm on a professional level as penance.

"What we do," he said, stepping closer to her desk, balancing on his hands and leaning in, "is completely different from that. Sure, we try to keep the wealthy looking fresh and young as long as possible, but we don't mangle their faces in the process. We give people what they want without making them caricatures of themselves. We know where to draw the line. This guy was a hack. He took this young woman's hard-earned money and botched the job on her face. It took me twice as long to fix his mess as I'm sure it did for him to throw in those lip implants. How can he live with himself?"

She remembered the first case she'd ever scrubbed in on in plastic surgery, how nervous she'd been that she might ruin someone's appearance for life. Her own scars could at least be covered, but what could a person do when their face was ruined? Like the lady who'd had her face nearly ripped off by her pet dogs, and who'd needed a face transplant. She sometimes wondered why people took the chance with cosmetic surgery, but understood there were hundreds of reasons. The business of beautifying people was thriving, and that wouldn't likely change in the future. It was merely a sign of the times.

"Do you ever wonder what makes a woman of her age seek plastic surgery?" she asked.

His frustrated expression turned stone cold. "I've been trying to figure out why women flock to it for years."

"And men."

He nodded his agreement. "Haven't come close to an answer yet."

The fire returned to his eyes, and she found him sexier than ever, leaning over her desk, engaging her in a philosophical discussion on the pros and cons of cosmetic surgery, lip jobs and hacks. She had the urge to grab his tie, pull him close, and kiss him silly.

But she didn't.

Then she noticed he was studying her lips again, and she had a crazy idea. What if he'd "fixed" the botched-up lip job to look like hers? Now she'd gone off at the deep end, imagining things she wanted to believe. That Julie Treadwell mouth repair may have looked similar to her lips, but the rest, him doing it on purpose, was all a crazy fantasy she'd made up. She shouldn't flatter herself like that. Didn't deserve it. But maybe later she could visit Julie and check out her theory anyway.

"As far as Davy Cumberbatch goes, I see your point." Mitch had simmered down on the anger scale, but something else smoldered in his eyes. "Not many people would call me on it, though. So thanks for pointing it out."

How many men, surgeons no less, ever admitted they were wrong? She really could fall for this guy if she wasn't careful.

"By the way, you look really beautiful again today." Out of the blue he'd focused on her appearance.

"Now you're just buttering me up. What favor do you want?"

Didn't he get it? Once he saw her hidden scars he'd change his mind about her in no time flat. That's how it had been with her ex, and it would be the same with Mitch.

"I'm serious." He engaged with her eyes until she thought she might squirm in her chair, but suddenly he snapped out of it. "When Lucy Grant comes out of Recovery, I'm going to give her a stern talking to. Her face was good enough just the way it was. Now that she has more realistic-looking lips, I hope she doesn't use this face-lift, lip-job experience as an entry-level drug, so to speak."

Back in her residency, Grace had read several psychology journal articles on people becoming addicted to plastic surgery procedures, and they'd influenced her toward specializing in reconstructive surgery over cosmetic. She figured just about anything in life could become addictive...like gazing into the depths of Mitchell Cooper's eyes.

That frustrated look came back to his face. Something stirred beneath the surface of his thoughts, and the jump in his pulse rate was almost palpable in the air. This case had really gotten under his skin, and she could tell he needed to talk more about it. She wished she had time to be there for him, but her job and patients came first. That was the whole reason she'd come to the Hunter Clinic. "Maybe we can talk later," she said, as she prepared to leave for Kate's. She was due to fix a nasty cheek scar from a car accident on a young woman who was getting ready to head off to college in the states for the summer.

He mumbled something unintelligible in a discontented tone.

For some crazy reason, even that made her smile. He was passionate about his job and had a tendency to wear his emotions on his scrubs. A lovely change from most men she'd known. Bottom line, the guy had way too much influence over her state of mind....

But later never came. When Grace finished the surgery that afternoon and returned to the Hunter Clinic, she stopped by Mitch's office, and he was already gone.

That wouldn't stop her. She wanted to see him. Besides giving him another chance to vent his frustrations, she also had some questions about Davy Cumberbatch and their scheduled meeting tomorrow night.

She wandered out to Helen in the reception area.

"I was looking for Cooper, I mean Mitch. Cooper. Any idea where he is?"

The middle-aged, always-meticulously-coiffed-and-made-up receptionist had a curious twinkle in her gray eyes in response to her question. *I know you're wondering why I should want to know, but it's none of your business. Besides, as his business colleague I have a right to know where he lives. Oh, quit looking at me like that and just tell me already.*

"He had to pick up his daughter early today, as it's the nanny's night off."

How should she go about this? Mitch had gotten her home address out of Gwen, why couldn't she get his out of her, too? Sure, she had his phone number in her cell phone now, she could call him and ask him her questions, but she'd rather talk to him face-to-face. He'd seemed so disturbed about the botched job on the young woman, and they'd barely scratched the surface of the conversation when she'd had to leave.

Not to mention those questions about Davy's consultation.

Truth was she wanted to know where he lived. She wanted to see Mia again, even though she'd talked to herself just last night about not getting too close to either of them. It had only been twenty-four hours and she already missed the child. And Mitch. Besides, today was another day, and she sensed Mitch needed her to bounce his thoughts off.

Wasn't it practically her duty?

And if she went to his house, she preferred to make it a surprise visit, like he'd done—what goes around comes around and all. Being painfully honest, *she* wanted to see *him* look surprised for once.

"Here," Helen said, as she finished scribbling something on a piece of notepaper with the chic Hunter Clinic logo at the top.

Grace pulled out of her thoughts and looked at it—an address, Mitch's address. She hadn't even asked yet. Was she that obvious? "Thank you!"

From the coy Mona Lisa smile on Helen's face, apparently she had been.

Grace stood outside the door of the Marylebone Street house. She liked the quaint appeal of the traditional mews-style home— flat front, two stories, all white except for the front and garage doors, which were a dark and vibrant blue. There were lots of windows to let in daylight, and a huge green vine growing up the beam beside the porch up to the second floor, then branching out and going wild along the second story. A ledge underneath the front window held a long flower box, full to the brim with plants and bright colors. The man seemed to have a green thumb, and overall she was impressed by Mitch's taste.

She hoped he was there, having come all this way in a taxi and already having sent off the driver. Maybe she should have had him wait? In this out-of-the-way

London neighborhood, it would be hard to find another cab. But wasn't that what cell phones were for?

Maybe she should have called first. Doubts added up as she cast her glance down the street at the cab growing smaller and smaller. This wasn't the brainiest plan she'd ever hatched, but…

The door swung open, and there stood Mitch in jeans and a green T-shirt, making his eyes look unbearably emerald. His surprised expression soon turned welcoming. "Gracie! I didn't expect to see you again today."

"Well, Cooper, you seemed so irritated earlier I wanted to make sure you didn't come home and take it out on your daughter."

He laughed. "Like that would ever happen."

She knew, without knowing him really well, that he didn't have a mean bone in his body. Especially when it came to his daughter—the guy was a pushover.

"I hadn't even knocked. How'd you know I was here?"

"Saw the cab through the window. Got nosy."

"Okay. Well, anyway, I sort of accused you of being a hypocrite earlier and that wasn't my intention at all," she said, suddenly feeling the need for a full explanation. "I was merely pointing out certain aspects about our jobs that could be examined more."

"It's after hours, Gracie," he said, leaning on the doorframe. "Quit sounding like a professor and come inside."

She flushed, having taken the dry, intellectual route instead of his emotions-on-the-sleeve approach.

"Come on." He motioned her inside. "Mia will be thrilled you're here."

What about you? Are you thrilled I'm here, too? The words were foremost in her mind and on the tip of her tongue as she stepped over the threshold, but she didn't dare utter them. Why did her mixed-up feelings for Mitch make her so damn insecure?

"Have you had dinner yet?" he asked, breaking into her twisted thoughts. "I could throw something together for you." He swaggered down his entryway like a man who knew he was king of his castle. "You know, return the favor."

"I grabbed a sandwich from the buffet at the clinic just before I left. Thanks." The clinic provided just about everything the employees needed, including an exercise pool in the basement and a lounge fully stocked with food.

She glanced around his small but inviting home. It lacked the touch of a woman, with a high technological feel using glass, metal and leather rather than overstuffed cushions and colorful swatches of fabrics. But there was plenty of evidence that a child lived there. One entire corner of the living area was furnished with the latest sturdy plastic playhouse equipment complete with a minitreehouse beside it, big enough for Mia to crawl up into. Wow. Grace had never seen anything like it.

"Gracie!" Mia's usual dainty voice cranked up in volume when she barreled down the hall and discovered Grace in the living room. "Did you come to see me?"

"Of course I did." Without thinking, Grace bent over and lifted the five-year-old, and swung her round. "I missed you already."

The child's gorgeous smile nearly broke her heart.

Mitch stood nearby, a mixture of sex appeal and fatherly pride rolled into one gorgeous package.

An emotional flutter gripped her inside. Maybe it had been a mistake to come here. She'd ignored her better judgement, found an excuse, and insinuated herself right back into their lives. Exactly the opposite of what she'd resolved to do. What the hell was the matter with her?

"Can I get you a drink? Some soda or wine? Tea?"

A bit on edge, she made a snap decision. "You know, a glass of wine doesn't sound half-bad. White, if you have it."

"Coming right up." He was in his socks, and he quietly padded off to the kitchen.

Mia pulled Grace to her play area. "Want to see my house?"

"I sure do. Do you live here all the time?"

That got the reaction she'd hoped for out of the little girl, who giggled. "No. I have a real bedroom. Want to see it?"

"Maybe later, after I'm through visiting with your daddy. But why don't you show me your favorite toy?"

"Okay!" With that Mia ran back down the hall, disappearing behind a door.

Grace took the moment to scan the rest of the living room. Mitch definitely liked modern art as there were several bright splotched paintings decorating his walls, similar to the one in his office. Her gaze zeroed in on a small frame on a smoked-glass table top beside a black leather recliner. In the frame was a photo of a young woman. A beautiful young woman.

Grace's heart sank. Was this his ex-wife? She was

a woman worthy of being a famous model or actress. Perfect bone structure like that was rare. She wanted to pick up the picture and study it more closely, but didn't. With a father like Mitch and a gorgeous mother like this—if that's who she was—no wonder Mia was so adorable.

"Here you go," he said, from behind her.

She swung round, startled. "Oh, thanks." She'd been caught staring at the picture, so she may as well fess up. "Is that your ex-wife?" she said, before her filtering process kicked in as she sat down. It was none of her business, why had she asked? But it was too late, she had.

Mitch flattened his lips into a straight line. A resigned expression took over from the earlier welcoming one. He nodded. "Yes."

He'd fallen far short of clarifying why the portrait had been put in such a prominent place, and must have sensed she needed more of an explanation.

"That was taken a couple of years before Mia was born, when we first got married."

"She's lovely, Mitch." Her heart ached to say it, but it was true. Deep-seated insecurities came out of hiding, giving her a defeated and depressed feeling. She tried to hide it. She'd gone from prom queen in high school to nerdy med student in college, and then…the burns, and that progression had shattered her confidence.

After loving a woman as beautiful as this, how could a man settle for a scarred mess like her? Then one more thought popped up, and it hurt even more.

Did he still love his ex-wife? Why else would he leave her picture out?

A distant sad twinge invaded his gaze as he studied the photograph along with her. "Seems like a lifetime ago."

Mia came running back into the room. "Here's Koko, my favorite teddy bear."

"Oh, let me see him. May I hold him?" Grace set down her wine and reached for the black stuffed animal with a red plaid ribbon around its neck, hoping she'd hidden her true reaction to Mitch's unclear explanation about the photograph.

Mia kissed the bear's head and handed him over. Grace rocked him like a baby and poked his stomach while sitting him on her lap, anything to get her mind off that picture. "Aw, he's adorable."

Mia stood close and patted her bear's head gently, like a doting mother. Grace loved the smell of her—fresh children's shampoo mixed with a day of playing. She could have just as easily snuggled with Mia in that chair as the bear.

Satisfied her favorite toy was in good hands, Mia dashed off to play with her other toys in the corner. Mitch sat nearby in a chair exactly like the one she was in, and drank a large glass of water. She took a sip of wine, finding it light and fruity, wishing she was drinking it under different circumstances.

"You're probably wondering why I stopped by," she said.

"You were quite clear about it at the door."

"I'm not being snoopy or anything, I promise. I just got the feeling you needed a little more time to vent about your case today. We were cut short by my schedule."

Half his mouth hitched into a smile. "Ah, yeah, well, I blew that out of my system, thanks to you."

"We're coworkers, and we need to be there for each other. I feel like I could do the same with you, if I needed to."

"Definitely."

She took another sip of wine then set down the glass. "Mind if I pick your brain a bit about Davy?"

"Not at all. What's up?" Mitch leaned forward in the chair, forearms resting on his thighs, looking upward beneath a creased brow. She could hardly think with those eyes staring her down.

"I don't see how his narrow face can support such high cheekbones. You know—that Elvis look he's after."

Mitch bit his lower lip, and blew out a short breath. "I've been thinking about what you said earlier, about how we were doing the same thing with him as that hack I was griping about today did to my patient."

Oh, she'd touched a sensitive note after all with that observation.

"And you're right. Just because some rich rocker wants to look like Elvis, it doesn't mean we have to help him out. I've decided I'm going to talk to him tomorrow night, see if we can get him to back off a little from that extreme makeover he's looking for."

Grace wished she'd come from home so she could have brought her laptop and the graphic she'd made of how Davy's face would look by overlapping the Elvis features on it. It wasn't a good look on his narrow face. Not at all.

Knowing she'd influenced Mitch into changing his

mind about giving in to the guy's every whim made her feel valued and respected—a part of the Hunter Clinic team.

"But if we don't give him what he wants," she said, "what's to stop him from going somewhere else, getting really botched up, and leaving us scrambling to find funds to bring more children to the clinic pro bono?"

Mitch opened his mouth to say something when the beeper hooked over his belt went off. He glanced at the number. "I've got to get this one."

He got up and went in search of his cell phone in the kitchen. She heard muffled talking in the other room and shortly he returned with a torn expression on his face. "Damn, my patient is having some bleeding issues, and I need to go and have a look at her, but I'm in a bind with Mia as Roberta is off tonight."

"You need someone to watch her? I can do that."

"Are you sure?"

"I'd love to, and I don't have any plans tonight other than laundry. That can wait another day."

Relief trickled over his face, changing his worried expression. "I can't thank you enough."

"Don't even think about it."

He went over to Mia, who was busy feeding Koko in the tree house. "Daddy has to go back to work for a little bit, honeybee, but Gracie's going to stay with you. Okay?" He bent and kissed the top of her head.

Mia clapped. "Yay! Bye, Daddy."

"Talk about not feeling needed," he said, half teasing and obviously half insecure.

"I'll take good care of her. Don't worry. I just hope it's nothing serious with that girl."

He pushed his stockinged feet into his loafers and grabbed his keys. "Me, too."

And before she could say another word, he was out the door.

Mitch rushed home as soon as he was sure Lucy Grant was stable. The butcher job that the first plastic surgeon had done on her had already caused scar tissue to form and he'd had to remove some tissue before he'd put in the new lip implants. The mouth, being rich with vasculature, had bled easily and combined with the fresh surgical swelling had made the evening-shift nurse worry it might be a drug allergy. He did a thorough examination of the surgical site and discovered a leaking vessel, put in one stitch and all was well, but the patient would have extensive bruising and swelling for a couple of weeks.

Almost three hours later, he opened his front door, and headed down the short entryway to discover Grace and Molly asleep in each other's arms. On the sofa, they looked like a sleeping variation on the Madonna-and-child portrait.

Rocked to the core at the sight, he put out his hand and leaned against the wall, just staring at them. He'd made a huge mistake leaving Grace with Mia to bond even more. All his daughter had talked about the rest of Sunday evening had been Gracie, Gracie, Gracie.

This wouldn't do. He couldn't let this go on, yet he'd

opened the door and invited her in when Mia had already been under her spell.

He needed his head examined over that decision.

The most disturbing part of all was that he was just as deeply under Grace's spell, only much, much deeper, than Mia.

CHAPTER SIX

MITCHELL REALLY SHOULD wake up Gracie and carry Mia off to bed. Yet he stood there, looking at them from across the room like two parts of a puzzle perfectly fit together on his couch. Grace's long, dark hair feathered across the top of the sofa on one side, and pooled together with his daughter's chaotic brown curls on the other. He took a few steps forward for a better view. A long-forgotten yearning for a complete family prodded his memory. Having given up on that dream ages ago, he pushed it away.

Not gonna happen. The last mommy-material date had bored him to tears.

A guy was supposed to learn from his mistakes. Grace was in a demanding profession and didn't have time for Mia. Twice now he'd seen her go off with Leo to the procedure room for God knew what. For all he knew, she was already well on her way to becoming a plastic surgery junkie, like his ex.

It didn't ring true. She'd been the one to bring up Davy Cumberbatch and cautioning about unnecessary surgeries. And nipping and tucking ad nauseam really didn't seem Grace's style.

A book had fallen from Grace's hand—it rested on one of her thighs. He recognized the cover. *The Tale of Misty Do-Right in the Battle of the Wrongs*. It was his and his daughter's all-time favorite story, a fun way to teach ethics, and had awesome illustrations. Now she'd shared it with Grace. It was a clue how special Grace had quickly become to Mia, and the thought worried him.

Snuggled tightly under Grace's other arm, Mia's head rested on her chest. No doubt his child listened to Grace's slow and steady heartbeat, finding comfort in her sleep. Like mother and child.

The distant ache grew stronger. Mia had missed out on this special kind of closeness with her birth mother... and that was all Christie had turned out to be.

The sight of Grace and Mia entwined like family nearly bowled him over.

He combed fingers through his hair, trying to figure out what to do. Wake them up or enjoy the snapshot in time a moment or two longer? Because if he followed his gut, for the sake of Mia's already broken heart, this couldn't happen again.

He'd let Grace creep under his skin, and as overwhelmingly appealing as she was, especially considering her easygoing relationship with his daughter, he knew it wasn't worth the risk of letting her into his life. It wasn't worth the risk to his heart, or his daughter's. Theirs had both been thrashed by Christie.

It was his responsibility to guard his daughter from ever having her heart broken again. When she grew up, she was sure to get enough of that on her own. For now, at least, he could protect her.

His gaze drifted to the photo of his ex-wife—the woman who was nothing more than a stranger to him now—wondering why he even kept it around. Yet he knew it was for Mia's sake, when she asked about her mommy. Maybe he should put it away. Maybe she'd quit asking and finally forget. Maybe he could prevent the inevitable day when his daughter asked, "Why did Mom leave us, Daddy?"

He had to protect Mia from being hurt and disappointed by a mother figure. Thankfully, the child was too young to remember the devastating blow when Christie had failed to bond with her own baby and made her choice to leave. Both of them.

Grace must have sensed Mitchell's presence, as she stretched and opened one of her eyes. Without a word, in consideration to his daughter, she raised a hand in greeting and mouthed, "Hi," not the least bit self-conscious about being caught asleep in the intimate snoozing embrace.

"Hi," he whispered, moving closer, putting his doctor's bag on the table. "Nice nap?"

She smiled. "Very."

Mia stirred.

Mitch rushed to the couch and picked her up. "I'll put her to bed before she wakes up and gets her second wind. Then w—I'd be up all night." He'd almost slipped and said "we'd".

Grace followed him down the hall and into Mia's room, rushing ahead to pull back the bedcovers in preparation for his girl. What a team.

He was so used to doing everything for Mia himself, it felt as though Grace was invading his territory.

Except he kind of liked her helping out, and wasn't that how most parents did things? Together? He'd never had the luxury of that. What must it be like?

He watched his daughter hunker down on the mattress, burrowing back into a deep and peaceful sleep as he tucked the covers beneath her chin.

Grace had tiptoed out already, as if understanding he needed this special moment to say good-night to his daughter. *His* daughter. He kissed her forehead lightly, marveling, as he always did, at her preciousness.

Grace deserved an explanation about why he guarded his baby girl so carefully. Maybe one day he'd tell her. What was that old saying—there was no time like the present?

After closing the door except for a crack so the hall light could filter in, as was their habit, he walked back to the living room, thinking how best to approach the subject.

Grace sat on the couch, looking at him expectantly. She seemed to sense his every mood change. "Everything okay? Did she go back to sleep?"

"Like a rock. Thanks." Nervous energy caused his hand to shoot to his scalp again, and though he tried to stop them, his fingers seemed to have a mind of their own, tunneling through his hair.

"I hope you don't mind the messy kitchen, but we baked."

"You baked?"

"Rice Krispies treats. Not really baking, I suppose, but something a five-year-old can help with."

He grinned. He'd left Grace alone with his daughter for two hours and they'd baked together. He should have known she'd put the time to good use. "I hope you saved me some." He loved the marshmallow, butter and cereal bars, hadn't had one in years.

"Of course. Mia set aside a plate of them just for you."

The thoughtfulness of his daughter never ceased to impress him. Now, if he only knew what to do about Grace.

"How was your patient?" She must have picked up on the shift in his mood, assuming it was about the post-op issue. Why would she suspect the change was about her getting too close to Mia, when he'd done nothing but encourage their interaction.

"Fine. She'd bled a bit more than expected, had loads of edema, and it freaked out the nurse. She thought she might be hemorrhaging."

"I'm glad it wasn't anything serious."

Her eyes drifted around the dim room then onto the picture of his wife. He understood that picture—right in the middle of his living room—didn't make sense. It wasn't like she could avoid looking at it.

He walked over and picked it up. "I suppose you're wondering what happened to Mia's mother."

"I won't lie. The thought has crossed my mind." She tried to smooth over her reaction by seeming nonchalant, and he was grateful. She had every right to wonder.

He sat next to her on the couch, prepared to tell her most, if not all of the story. He owed her an explanation as to why he'd flirted with her then pushed her away.

"I come from a big family, two sisters and two brothers. I'm smack in the middle. I'd always assumed I'd have lots of kids when I got married, too. But I dated a model, and the thought of having children put terror in her eyes." He raised Christie's picture to accentuate his point. "But I was crazy about her." He shrugged as his gaze roamed the living room, anything to avoid looking into Grace's eyes—as if she'd see all his darkest secrets. "I convinced her to marry me, and expected this perfect little life to play out."

Suddenly thirsty, he got up and went into the kitchen to grab himself a beer. "Can I get you something to drink?" he called out.

"I'm fine, thanks."

He popped the lid, went back to Grace and sat next to her on the couch. He offered her a drink from his can, and surprisingly she took a sip and handed it back. When he took a swig, it occurred to him that this was as close as they'd come to touching each other.

He'd missed the closeness of being with a woman. Grace looked on with inquisitive eyes, her lower legs tucked under her hip. Though normally guarded about his sad and warped tale, he knew he owed her some kind of explanation for his situation—single dad with child and a nanny, mother not in the picture.

"When I brought up the subject of kids, my wife, Christie, kept putting it off. She kept modeling."

Mitch took another drink, gave Grace a serious glance. She sat transfixed, completely ready for him to open up and tell her the rest of the story. He didn't plan to tell her everything, because the whole story was too bizarre, just enough to satisfy her curiosity.

She reached for his can and took another drink. The act of sharing a beer felt more intimate than it should, but it had been so long since he'd sat in his home with someone other than his daughter on the couch. He wanted more from Grace than she could feasibly give, especially if they were to remain colleagues. Therefore, there could never be more. End of story.

He played with the threads on her thin long-sleeved sweater. Maybe if he explained why he was so cautious about letting people close to him and Mia, she'd finally explain why she kept herself covered from neck to knees all the time. And what she'd been having Leo fix for her.

"So Christie turned twenty-nine. She swore thirty was breathing down her neck the very next day. She wanted Botox. It was ridiculous. She didn't need it. We started fighting about it." He sent Grace a cutting glance. Waited for her reaction. She played it safe and schooled her expression, obviously wanting him to continue his story. "She said everyone who modeled used it."

He glanced at the photograph, the last one he had of her before she'd started having procedures done. It still ached to think of the transition she'd made in her appearance, how he no longer recognized her.

"Then she got pregnant. I was ecstatic. Thought she'd get over that bit about striving for perfection in her looks." He gave her a rueful smile. "Boy, was I wrong. You'd have thought she'd been given a death sentence with the pregnancy. I honestly feared for our baby's life in the beginning."

Grace reached across and squeezed his knee in empathy. He patted her hand in thanks, enjoying the warmth of her skin. Though that wasn't the reason he'd opened up to Grace. He'd never use his sad tale to ma-

nipulate another woman. No. He genuinely liked and
cared about Grace, and it was the strangest feeling.

"As the months went by, she couldn't cope with her
body. Fell completely apart. I had to fly my two sisters
down from San Francisco to L.A. to take shifts watching her, so she would eat and not harm herself or our
baby. Hell, I wanted a healthy baby. She had to gain
weight. That's how it works, how things are intended."

He drank more and handed the can with the last part
of the beer to her. Surprisingly, she finished it with a
mini-chugalug, obviously not wanting to steer his story
off course or cause another delay.

"Christie insisted on a bikini cut C-section. She
wanted our baby delivered as soon as feasibly possible
so she wouldn't have to get any bigger."

He gave her a doleful smile, and she returned an
encouraging look. *Go on*, her eyes seemed to prod.
There wasn't a hint of judgment in her sympathetic
blue gaze. Her fingers were folded and touching her
chin as she leaned against the couch and listened intently. She looked like an angel with dark brown bangs
and such kissable lips.

"Everything changed for me once Mia was born. But
not for Christie. She didn't even try to bond with our
daughter. All she wanted was liposuction. We hired our
first nanny then, and Christie simply handed over our
child. I did as much as I could for our Mia, but I had to
work, too. Sometimes long hours. I took off a couple
of months in the beginning and got pretty damn good
at the daddy stuff. Christie just didn't show any interest. She was self-centered and aloof. I worried how it
might affect Mia emotionally later on in life."

He got that stomach cramp he always felt when he thought about Christie. On reflex, his palm drifted to his abdomen and rubbed. Grace took his hand and laced her fingers through his. He squeezed back, and the cramp let up the slightest bit.

He inhaled a ragged breath as the worst of the story was ahead. "Our marriage barely limped on, but I married for better or worse, and I'd taken those vows seriously. Most days I thought I was a fool, but…"

"You're an honorable man, Mitch. Don't ever beat yourself up for that," she said, squeezing his fingers more, making him want to pull her close and hug her for understanding so well. But he kept his distance.

"All I did was focus on Mia and work. Christie just seemed to drift out of our lives like a cold breeze. Then one day she walked out on us. Just picked up and left."

Grace covered her mouth with her hand. "Oh, my God."

"Crazy, right? I couldn't believe it." The betrayal had cut deeper than anything he'd ever experienced in life. At first, some days he hadn't thought he could breathe or live, but he'd had a daughter to look after— to be there for. He'd forced himself to carry on. Mia was his saving grace.

His eyes connected with Grace's. Could she be his other saving grace—from loneliness? Would he be crazy to let another beautiful woman close? Suddenly, everything seemed so confusing.

"Is that what brought you to the Hunter Clinic?" Her sweetly husky voice brought him back to the moment.

"In a roundabout way." He clutched the empty can and slowly but consistently strangled and smashed the aluminum. "I'd had it with all the Hollywood fakery, you know? The last thing I wanted my daughter to do was grow up surrounded by that and become superficial and self-centered like her mother. I want Mia to always know she is beautiful to me both inside and out, no matter what the blasted mirror or society says."

She gave another empathetic nod. God, he wanted to kiss her. Totally inappropriate at the moment, but there you go; he wanted those lips, the ones he'd been obsessing about since their night in the pod. *Keep on track, Cooper.*

"I'd heard about the Hunter Clinic and contacted Leo. He invited me to join. California law says you can't take a child over a state line without the consent of the other parent, let alone to another country." He gave a wry laugh. "I don't know why I was surprised when Christie didn't contest my plans. She didn't so much as lift a perfectly arched eyebrow over it. Never even came to say one last goodbye to Mia. She simply didn't give a damn."

Grace clutched her chest as if heartbroken along with him over Mia's bad luck in the mother department. He'd stopped blaming himself for choosing such a self-centered person to marry, hoped he'd change enough in the character-reading department before he'd ever invited anyone else into his life.

He'd tried to keep a distance from the emotions roiling inside him as he told the story. He hadn't opened up to anyone but his sisters about it, and it had been so long ago, and he still hadn't told the entire story tonight. Because it was too gruesome to go into. He rubbed his chest, where it still hurt like hell whenever he relived that chapter of his life.

"I packed up my daughter and made a vow that she'd never know rejection like that for the rest of her life."

Things went dead quiet. He stared at the carpet, found a small red plastic toy piece and picked it up. Set the empty and smashed beer can on the table. Anything to avoid Grace's somber stare. He felt it on the side of his face, though, and knew that eventually he'd have to look at her.

She touched his shoulder and squeezed it. "You did the right thing. Mia is an amazingly self-assured girl, and it's all thanks to you."

He glanced up seeing her total acceptance of his decision to bring his daughter to another country, leaving her mother far behind. And it meant everything to him.

But Grace was too close. Her mouth was right there....

Grace's body went hot with emotion as Mitch unraveled his story. He was a strong, admirable man for going to bat for the innocent party, his daughter. She'd never met a man like that. Mia was the most important person in Mitch's life, as every child should be to their parents.

He'd veiled his hurt by acting imperturbable, but she sensed his pain, experienced it as if it had happened to her. Her heart wrenched for both Mitch and Mia. Wanting nothing more than to comfort him, she leaned in, at eye level with his sad downward-looking eyes. His hand went to her cheek, and slowly his gaze lifted to her mouth. He traced her lower lip with the pad of his thumb, scattering warmth along her jaw. It trickled down her throat and reaching deep into her chest.

His careful yet steady gaze traveled higher, to her eyes, and seemed to ask the question, was this all right, he and her sitting on his couch, touching each other?

Only a second passed for her to make up her mind. Yes, it was. In fact, she wanted to kiss him.

Evidently, he'd beat her to the decision, as his mouth covered hers in the sweetest, sudden embrace. The physical connection sent a shock wave throughout her body.

They straightened up on the couch, leaning against the cushions, as she wrapped her hands behind his neck, pulling him nearer, pressing her lips closer, enjoying the last of his day-long scent and that evening stubble.

His warm, soft kiss almost made her forget how messed up she was. How she couldn't let anyone close. Ever again. But right now she didn't want to think about those tired old excuses, she was too wrapped up in the moment and only wanted to think about kissing Mitch.

He angled his head so their mouths fit just so, then moistened the crease of her lips with the tip of his tongue. He shifted again to feather tiny kisses around her lips and over her face, on to her earlobe for a quick nip and tug, then back to her mouth to kiss deeper, releasing a chill bomb. She relaxed, slipped into his rhythm and need, met his tongue with the tip of her own, as all resistance to his bold kiss melted away.

She sighed into the feel of his lips as he took her mouth over and over, marveling that they were kissing, and tasting the beer they'd shared, fully aware she wanted so much more with him.

But she could never have a future with a man like Mitch. With any man, especially Mitch. It was senseless to kiss him, to start anything, even though this first kiss would be tattooed in her mind for the rest of her life.

Why toy with the affections of a man with whom she couldn't be completely open? Why taunt Mitchell, who deserved a normal woman, something she could never be. He'd already met his quota of messed up, distant and damaged women with his ex-wife. That was enough for his lifetime.

She let her thoughts pull her out of the moment. Far back in her mind, she couldn't help but think he still loved his ex-wife. Why else would he keep her picture out all these years?

Mitch clutched her arms—she sensed his passion shift from exploration to need. Or maybe he'd felt her hesitation as her thoughts had wandered again and again to his ex. His kisses grew hungry, desperate. They seemed to chase after her as she mentally withdrew. His need frightened her. She could never be what he wanted. If she stayed here, he'd expect more than she could give. She couldn't bear to see the disappointment in his face if he saw her burns. It would rip her heart out.

Though she longed for the comfort and thrills his lips promised, she needed to keep it real. For her sake and for his. Kissing was an entry-level drug—it led to desire and ultimately to sex. Grace Turner didn't get naked with men any more.

She broke away from his lips, struggling to catch her breath. "No wonder they call you Lips." She hoped to lighten the mood, to smooth over the sudden end to their make-out session.

"I'd rather you didn't call me that," he said, touching her, pulling her close again.

She hadn't a clue how she'd find her way home, but she needed to get away from Mitch. She'd call a cab as soon as she could think straight.

Since the attack, it wasn't in the stars for her to live a normal life so why pretend?

"I have to get home," she said, pulling herself away from his arms.

His eyes betrayed the confusion and sexual desire he struggled to hide. "Why, Grace?"

"We can't do this, Mitch." She stood and rubbed her folded arms as if she was freezing. "It's not a good idea."

"I'm just kissing you."

Grace straightened her clothes, trying with all her power to gather her composure. "That seemed like a hell of a lot more than just kissing." She gazed at him, but couldn't withstand his smoldering stare, so she looked away. "I guess I'm not ready, then."

Her eyes found the front door and focused. She'd get to her cell phone and call that cab company. Leaving was her only hope to save face. *Get out of that door. Leave. Now.*

"I'd never push you to do anything you didn't want to." He stood and moved toward her.

"I know, but I might be the one to push myself." She inched away.

Mitch's confused expression intensified, bordering on hurt. She owed him an explanation, didn't dare give it. He'd never understand. Besides, the way he'd looked so sadly at his ex-wife's picture earlier when he'd told her the story, the way he still kept it around as if continuing to pine for her, Grace had a deep suspicion that he'd never stopped loving her.

Not even in a perfect world, under ideal circumstances—even if she were the person she'd used to be—there wouldn't be room in his life for her. His heart was still hung up on the mother of his child, and he probably didn't even know it.

She grabbed her purse off the adjacent chair and strode for the door, afraid to look back, fishing inside for her phone on the way.

She'd almost made it home free when Mitch's firm grasp on her arm swung her round.

CHAPTER SEVEN

MITCH'S MOUTH CAME crashing down on Grace's again. He kissed hard and rough this time, pushing her against the door through which she'd tried to leave.

He took her breath away, thrilling her as he fought to get her back where they'd just been, near enough to heaven to feel it. She let him have his way with her lips, not ready to end this dizzying moment. His hands skimmed every part of her arms, sides, and back as if he couldn't feel enough of her. The desperate kiss nearly broke her heart, as he seemed to pour into it every bit of emotion he'd held back during his story.

Grace understood his reckless need to have her, and it took every last bit of her self-control not to join him. To give in. To let him take her. If things had only been different...

She pushed away from his shoulders, dazed by his ragged breath and dire need for her. Intoxicated by his palpable desire, she forced herself to focus. This couldn't happen. They couldn't be together, no matter how right it felt or how mesmerizing his kisses were.

"I've got to go." Somehow she'd found her voice as she'd ended the kiss.

He swallowed, obviously practicing self-restraint, and backed off. But his eyes tore into her, stripping her naked. "Remember this." His commanding tone dropped over her like whiskey and honey. "Think about what we could have."

Even now, knowing she had to end it, the breath from his voice and the nearness of him sent chills across her shoulders and chest. Her tight breasts ached for his attention. Every part of her cried out for his touch.

She couldn't look another second at the messy-haired, smoldering-eyed, sexiest man she'd ever seen… or kissed. All she could do was turn the knob on the door and escape.

He might have physical needs, and she understood there was definitely chemistry between them. But as hard as it would be to open up to any man again, to stand naked, exposed and scarred before him, she especially couldn't open herself up to heartache with a man who still loved the mother of his child.

Grace had been dreading the Cumberbatch meeting on Tuesday night. She'd managed to avoid Mitch all day thanks to a heavy surgery schedule at Kate's, but now, after hours, they'd be forced to come face-to-face because of the consultation.

It seemed everyone had left the clinic. The building was quiet and almost spooky. She wasn't even sure Mitch was on the premises.

Not wanting to be late, she'd come right to the clinic after her last surgery, and still wore scrubs. She hadn't bothered to change into street clothes and had simply thrown on her knee-length doctor's coat from her office. Tucking a thin white cotton scarf into the neckline of her top, she turned up her collar then headed down the hall to the "special" consultation room.

The clinic records verified that many a famous person had sat in this very room waiting for various minor procedures, from royalty to politician to musician to actor to reality star. The list was long, and she'd promised never to divulge their names to a soul.

With nerves skittering throughout her body, and hot memories of their kiss racing through her mind, she opened the door to find both Mitch and Davy Cumberbatch already sitting at the meeting table. Someone may as well have suddenly rung Big Ben's bell from the rush of her anxiety taking on wings and flying free at the sight of Mitch. She needed to get a grip.

Oh, and there was Davy, too.

After taking a sip of bottled water, she offered a polite smile to both men, avoiding Mitch's penetrating eyes, then used her old charm-school training to walk across the room slowly and steadily, as if she had a book balanced on her head.

Mitch stood, looking at her as if he hadn't seen her since forever, ravenously eating her up with his eyes. His gaze ran hot, oozing with longing, then pulled back to a fully professional expression.

She'd been transported back to last night, was right there with him on the desire level, seeing him for the first time since their kisses. The mere thought sparked a pool of heat, its warm rivulets coursing throughout her body. Her cheeks grew hot. She needed another drink of water and took it before sitting down.

Finally, she looked at Davy, who hadn't bothered

to stand, just sat there like a prince without manners. Gaunt, his sallow skin showing the evidence of hard living and self-indulgence, it seemed hard to imagine the legions of loyal fans he'd made over the past three decades. The image she'd been working with on her computer must have been several years back, in a healthier time. That could prove to be a problem, and further reason for her to refuse him his wish.

"Mr. Cumberbatch, I'm a big fan, it's a pleasure to meet you." She'd take one for the clinic and lie through her teeth, mark it off as being a team player.

Life came back to his battered face. He smiled. "Hey, Doc." He glanced at Mitchell. "You didn't tell me about the hot doc."

Grace could tell Mitch had reverted to diplomatic skills for the sake of the Hunter Clinic, as she had. He forced a smile, though she'd glimpsed a flash of anger in his charm. "We don't like to divulge all our secrets. You can relate to that, right, Davy?" Mitch winked.

The sarcasm and condescension skidded right over Davy's over-dyed elfin-styled punk hairdo, which seemed a tad ridiculous on a fortysomething male in the first place. She couldn't quite bring herself to call him a man, since his reputation remained more in the petulant and spoiled-boy realm. The sad thing was, if she'd been bold enough to tell him what she really thought, he'd just laugh and take it to the bank. Why should he care what anyone thought of him, when he was rolling in dough from his well-documented antics?

Finally, introductions were over and Grace took a calming breath, fighting the need to use disinfectant on her hands. "Let's get right down to business, okay?"

Davy nodded. Mitch sat straight and stiff, palms opened and flat against the table, wearing a well-rehearsed poker face.

Grace flipped open her laptop and went directly to the graphic program and the file she'd created on Davy Cumberbatch.

She showed him his natural face, before the recent barroom brawl, then superimposed the mock-up of his surgical cosmetic requests. After a few magic key-strokes his face morphed into an odd combination of the artist formerly known as Cumberbatch and the king of rock and roll, Elvis.

She used her big-guns software to create a 3D effect then rotated the virtual head three-sixty degrees so he could see himself from all angles. It wasn't a pretty sight, far from a match made in cyberland. On the contrary, the image on the computer screen looked near grotesque. More like a cartoon character. Grace used this graphic to drive home her point.

"As you can see, what you think you want isn't in your best interest." Without waiting for the stunned expression to fade from his face, she flipped to another screen and a far more agreeable rendition of Davy the rocker. At least, she thought so. "In this version, I've toned down the heavy Elvis influence and allowed the natural characteristics of your face to remain, giving a hint of the king but not superimposing your face with his. We can also remove some of the adipose tissue from above and beneath your eyes to give you a more youthful appearance."

"Adi-what?"

"Fat. See here and here?"

She pointed out his puffy lids and bags, waited for him to take a look.

"I've also given you some nips here and tucks there…" she gestured toward his real-life jaw and cheeks then focused back on the computer screen "…slenderized your nose, shortened and shaped the tip in a more classical way, and made the cheek implants smaller than your original request. But they work very nicely, don't you think?"

She swallowed and looked his way. Davy narrowed his eyes and studied the second computer image, not saying a word—though he didn't look happy. He glanced at Mitchell, as if he'd step in and make things right, put the "hot doc" in her place.

Davy turned back toward Grace. "It doesn't look a bit like Elvis, does it?" He hit her with a deadly stare, and she refused to look away. She'd be damned if she'd let him bully her.

Grace braced herself for a fight. And she'd surely lose if Mitch took Davy's side and they ganged up on her. Did Mitch really believe in giving the patient whatever they wanted no matter how bizarre the outcome?

She took a breath and held it, using all of her control and concentration not to blink.

"I agree with Miss Turner, Davy." Mitch broke the standoff, utilizing his natural affable charm. She breathed again and shifted her eyes to his, wanting to thank him. "The second image is far more complimentary to you." He tore his glance away from Grace and homed in on Davy. "And though you won't look like Elvis, let's be honest—could anyone? The point I believe Miss Turner is making is do you want to be the new and improved Davy Cumberbatch or a caricature of someone else for the rest of your life? It's your call."

Grace wanted to hug Mitch on the spot. Oh, wait, that wouldn't be a good idea after last night. She flashed him a quick smile, but yanked it back immediately, not wanting to come off smug in front of the rocker. That would be like coming down to his level and there was no way she could compete with Davy Cumberbatch when it came to being pompous.

Davy slumped down in the luxurious white leather club chair, giving the impression of a defeated teenager. Sullen, looking as if he'd just swallowed castor oil. "You made me go through rehab for this? I told you I wanted Elvis, and I always get what I want." He spoke through clenched teeth, his ring-covered fingers tightly balled into fists on the table.

Grace instinctively moved back in her chair, bracing herself, as if another brawl might break out.

"Very well," Mitchell said. "I'll refer you to another top-notch plastic surgeon, one more willing to give you exactly what you want." Mitchell stood, and reached out his hand for a shake. "Unfortunately, it won't be here at the Hunter Clinic."

Davy took his time getting up, his lanky legs seeming a bit wobbly. He never completed the handshake, just blew off Mitch's proffered hand. Once he'd made it to his full height, several inches shorter than Mitch, he glanced upward with something short of hatred coloring his dark, tiny, deep-set eyes.

Then he glanced her way. The biting stare made Grace swallow hard, tightening her core. She would not let him get the best of her. Angry that she'd given him the power to make her feel uncomfortable, she got up and stepped close to him, then looked into those stabbing eyes. "I hope you'll reconsider." She tried her best to sound professionally earnest, hoping to overcome both his ire and the anger burning inside her. Why should she care? "I'll forward my graphics to your personal email. Maybe you'd like to have another look at them and think about how you'd like to look from now on."

He brushed her off, the mark of a man who had little regard for women outside of groupies, and then only because he wanted sex with them, and engaged Mitch's attention. "I'll think about it. Get back to you."

One moment a hot doc, the next she didn't exist.

The Hunter Clinic was known for professionalism, and though Grace wanted to knee the guy in his groin, she stood her ground and let Mitch take over.

"Oh, first I guess we'd better put an eye patch on you," he said. "Get our story straight about you having a small tear in the retina and needing our help in the ophthalmology room." He patted his pockets then glanced at Grace. "Do you have the prepared statement from Lexi?"

Mitch strode to the stainless-steel supply cart in the middle of the otherwise posh consultation area, found an eye patch then used tape to hold it in place on Davy's face.

While he did that, she made a quick scan through her emails. There it was, the PR statement. "Give me a moment and I'll print it out." With the click of a finger from her laptop, the copier in the corner of the room came to life and spit out one page, a short and sweet statement. She retrieved it and brought it to Mitch as he put the finishing touches on Davy's eye patch.

"There, you look like a regular pirate. Now, repeat after me. I had a small tear in my retina and needed laser surgery to repair it."

Davy refused—what else was new?—but nodded. "Got it."

Mitch took the proffered statement and escorted Davy out to where Grace assumed Davy's people waited, but not before passing her a look loaded with meaning.

She could barely take it.

Their kiss came clearly to mind, and her body reacted as if it was actually in his embrace again, feeling his lips pressed to hers. She forced herself to stop the silliness. It simply could never be between them. The only kind of partners they'd ever be was at work in the operating room.

But even seeing him only as a colleague, she still could have grabbed and kissed Mitch when he'd come to her aid just now. He'd given her opinion some thought and apparently agreed with her. The man respected her opinion. Surely there was a point where any good surgeon drew the line.

Her heart lurched as she thought of Mitch standing up for her. She smiled at his quirky sense of humor—Davy as a pirate, hardly!

Mitch Cooper was appealing on far, far too many levels.

The room seemed suddenly buzzing with thoughts and questions and feelings with which she wasn't ready to deal. The lights were too bright, and the room felt hot and stuffy with leftover Cumberbatch soiling the air. She had to get out.

With Mitch and Davy gone, she took the opportunity to close her laptop, grab her purse and slip out the side door, heading straight for home.

Yes, she was a coward for not sticking around to tell Mitch in person how much she appreciated him backing her up. But the thought of what might happen after last night's passion and the possibility of letting Mitch get closer again tonight scared her. What if she opened up to him, had sex with him, and he pretended her scars didn't bother him? When she knew with all her heart they would. How could they not?

His lies and pity would rip her wide open.

The paparazzi at the back of the building were out of control. Cameras flashed and questions flew their way the instant the bodyguard opened the alley exit to the clinic. The chauffeur made a beeline for the limo and the bodyguard protected Davy from as many clean shots at picture-taking as possible.

"Why'd you come here tonight, Davy?"

When there was no response they turned to Mitchell.

"Tell us why Davy was here, Doctor."

Mitch glanced at Davy, being rushed to his car, not saying a word. He decided to run with the preplanned script from Lexi. "Mr. Cumberbatch suffered an eye injury and needed some laser surgery to mend a small tear in his retina." There was more to read, about how the Hunter Clinic hoped they'd fixed his injury to his satisfaction, blah, blah, blah, but before they could ask another question, Mitch turned for the door. At that exact moment another flurry of flashing lights indicated the limo was leaving the premises.

Mitch looked back and watched Davy Cumberbatch drive off in his white limousine, with one over-enthusiastic gossip rag photographer hanging from the bumper.

"Get the hell off the car, you idiot." The bodyguard had stood up in the middle of the sky light and flipped the finger at the reporters. More cameras flashed. No doubt there'd be plenty of pictures for the gossip rags tomorrow. The limo sped up and left the alley.

Mitch closed the heavy door tight, bolted and locked it.

He still seethed with the way Davy had brushed off Grace's hard work. She had state-of-the-art computer programs, computer software that he certainly wouldn't be able to operate without weeks of tutorials. She must have spent hours and hours putting the presentation together. Yes, she'd been blunt with Davy, but kind; the guy had acted like a spoiled brat. He'd like to throttle the old rocker, but had simply stood and waved goodbye like a moron in the night.

Mitch made his way back inside, eager to see Grace again, wanting nothing more than to apologize for his entire gender. What an ass that guy was. When their eyes had first met before the meeting had begun he'd almost come out of his seat with desire. It had been years and years since he'd felt that way about a woman...not since his ex-wife.

He swallowed back the longing for Grace, especially after the way she'd made her quick getaway last night. She'd literally run off into the night, phone to ear, calling a cab and walking toward the corner crossing. He'd wanted to run after her, but hadn't wanted to leave Mia alone in the house. He'd called out to her, begged her to come back, but she'd refused.

"I'm sorry," she'd said. "I need to go."

From inside his house he'd watched for over ten minutes as she'd paced beneath a streetlamp, until finally the cab had arrived, and he'd been able to breathe properly again.

Their kisses had been filled with passion, reaching so deep inside him he'd almost felt they'd joined together. Now all he could think about was finishing the act they'd played out with kisses, only this time using the rest of their bodies.

He'd wanted her with every cell crying out for her mercy, and was almost positive she'd wanted him, too. But for some reason she'd lost it, pulled back. Damn, after the sad story he'd told her, could he blame her?

Unless she was afraid of being close to a man.

Maybe he could change her mind.

He rushed down the last few steps of the hallway. He grabbed the handle and opened the door...only to find the room empty.

Disappointment cut through him, triggering anger. Twice now she'd run off to avoid him. If he hadn't kissed her, felt how deeply she'd responded to him, he might think she wanted nothing to do with him. But he'd been there with her, kissing like the world might end tomorrow. Her heated response had stirred up the hunger he'd suppressed for years, making him lust after her until his bed sheets were damp and twisted from restless sleep.

He wouldn't take no for an answer without a really good reason, and she couldn't keep avoiding him forever. When she finally stopped running from him, he'd be there, waiting to take her to his bed.

He flipped off the lights, locked up the room and left the Hunter Clinic as fast as humanly possible. He planned to go directly to Grace's apartment to confront her, force her to see how right they were for each other, see where it led.

On the way to his car his cell phone rang. It was Roberta. Mia refused to go to bed until Daddy read her a story and tucked her in.

Grace dried her hair, the noise of the dryer helping to drown out her thoughts. She'd imagined Mitch during the entire shower, wondered what it would be like to be naked with him, to be touched by him. All over.

This had to stop. She could no more expose herself to Mitch than he could pretend her scars didn't exist. She forced a look in the mirror at her chest and arms with webs of white and pink marbling scars where the acid had eaten away her skin. She'd lost count of the number of skin grafts she'd had to endure those first few years. The pain, both external and internal.

What man would want to make love to breasts like hers? How would the roughened skin on her arms feel to Mitch's touch? Could he want her sexually after seeing everything?

She looked away, put on her robe and distracted herself by continuing to blow-dry her hair.

It never failed. Why did the phone ring whenever she used the dryer? Like right now. She wasn't going to fall for it because it would only be another false alarm. It always was.

On she blew and brushed her hair, forcing the waves into submission.

When she was done, she put special aloe-and-vitamin-E-extract lotion across her neck, chest and arms, especially around the recently touched-up section at the base of her neck and collarbone. Then she used her favorite vanilla-and-lavender cream on her legs. Feeling fresh after a long day at the hospital, she walked to the kitchen to make some herbal tea. She put the kettle on to boil and put a pyramid-shaped tea bag into her favorite yellow-flowered cup, then started shuffling around in the cupboard for something to nibble on.

The intercom sounded. She jumped.

A burst of nerves warned she couldn't get away from Mitch that easily. He was probably upset about how she'd pressed Davy Cumberbatch to be realistic with his cosmetic surgery. He'd probably only backed her up to help save face for the clinic, but had come here to have words about her performance at the clinic.

Or he was here about last night—and the passion they'd shared. The thought released pent-up tingles across the very skin she'd just loaded with cream.

After stomping out the quick desire to take the coward's way out by not answering, she padded across the carpet. She was a fully grown woman who needed to confront her issues head on. The list of reasons she would never become intimate with Mitch started with the fact he was still in love with his ex-wife, included her scars, and ended with the very major point that they worked together.

"Who is it?" She prayed she was wrong, and it wasn't Mitch but someone else.

"It's Mitch."

So much for prayers. She wasn't dressed. "You should have called first."

"I did. You didn't answer."

The damn hairdryer. "Can you give me a minute? I'm just out of the bath."

"Let me in."

He sounded nothing like the man she'd grown to know and adore. All playfulness was gone from his voice. He sounded angry. She *had* botched things up with Cumberbatch.

"Please," he finally added.

Without saying a word, she pressed the door release, heard it buzz and him quickly enter her building. She flipped up the collar and lapels on her thick white robe, tied the sash around her waist, rushed to the bathroom and grabbed a towel, throwing it over her shoulders, clutching it tightly to her throat.

She didn't need to be dressed to tell Mitch to forget they'd ever kissed. Or stare him in the eye and tell him she'd treat her patients the way she saw fit, no matter how famous they were. Whichever scenario played out, she was ready. She double-knotted the sash on her robe and for security's sake went immediately back to clutching the towel.

His rapid knock at the door forced her out of the bathroom. She needed to get it together before she faced him. Two feet from the door she stopped and took a deep inhale, a cleansing breath. She held it for a beat and felt her pulse slow the slightest bit. *Stay calm. Act like nothing has happened. Just another day on the job.*

She swung open the door. "Cooper! What brings you here?"

He looked her over, his lips pursed, eyes consuming her. She needed another cleansing breath, quickly!

He didn't bother to answer her, just walked into her apartment like he lived there. Maybe he'd been taking lessons from Cumberbatch.

"Well?" she said.

"Well, what?"

"I asked what brings you here?"

"I would have been here earlier if I hadn't gotten a call from Roberta."

"The nanny? Is something wrong with Mia?" Her sudden concern reminded her how much she'd come to care for the child.

"Just a minor catastrophe." For the first time since she'd opened the door he showed a glimpse of his usual self. "Couldn't find her favorite book for bedtime."

"The Tale of Misty Do-Right in the Battle of the Wrongs?"

He nodded. "You remember?"

"How could I forget such great literature?"

He smiled, studied her more. "You look beautiful tonight."

"You're out of your mind. I've just gotten out of the bath and my hair is a fright."

He grabbed the wrist she'd waved around to brush off his statement. "My eyesight is perfect." The hunger in his eyes almost made her believe him.

She took back her hand. "Stop it, please."

He hesitated then shifted back to serious mode. "Look, we need to talk."

"About?" She couldn't manage to hold her robe tight enough but didn't want him to notice her white knuckles, so she lightened her grip.

"Us."

The kettle had boiled and rather than respond to him she dashed to the kitchen, pretending she hadn't heard what he'd said. Us? Oh, no.

"Would you like some tea?" she called over her shoulder, but hadn't needed to raise her voice after all because he was right there, standing behind her.

"No."

She begged her mind to stay focused and her hands to function as she poured steaming hot water into her cup. "I really need to thank you for sticking up for me with that vile Cumberbatch earlier."

Silence.

"Did I blow it for the clinic?" She peeked over her shoulder, saw a man who wasn't interested in office chitchat, a man who looked as serious as hell.

"Why did you push me away last night? Why did you leave?"

She used the granite counter for balance before slowly turning round. Nothing like getting right to the point. *Tell him the truth.* "Because it doesn't make sense to get involved with a man who's still in love with his ex-wife."

Okay, so that was half of the truth.

Disbelief twisted his brows and wrinkled his nose. "How could you possibly think I still love my ex-wife after what I've told you?"

"Have you dated since moving to England?"

A sheepish look passed over his exquisitely hand-some features. "Yes. I made the mistake of getting in-volved with one of the nurses at the Hunter Clinic a few months after I arrived. Things didn't work out. She eventually changed jobs."

"And that was how long ago?"

"Look, I've dated a few women since then, nothing serious, but nevertheless. The thing is, I don't want to confuse Mia."

She swallowed the ball of emotion forming in her throat. "You still keep your ex-wife's picture out, and I saw how you looked at her. I was sure I saw love in your eyes."

"For a person who doesn't exist anymore! She didn't want our daughter, remember? How can I love a mon-ster like that?"

"She's not a monster, Mitch, she's a broken person. We're all damaged in some ways." She glanced at the angry scar peeking out from the sleeve of her robe and quickly covered it.

He shook his head and gazed at her with a pained expression. "You don't know the whole story. I thought I'd told you enough to make you understand. Obviously, I didn't go far enough."

This was her chance to get to the heart of the issue. If his ex-wife was so evil, she had to know. "Then why do you keep her picture out?"

"For Mia's sake. A child needs to know who her par-ents are. Christie is her mother."

She took a moment to engage his eyes. All she wanted to do was level with him, he deserved her hon-

LYNNE MARSHALL 151

esty. "Okay, but maybe you're still hoping she'll come back, be the mother Mia needs, the wife you still pine for."

Hadn't he alluded to that the very first night they'd met at the Eye, after they'd gone to the bar then he'd seen her off in the taxi? *"If it was a different time in my life. If circumstances were different. The thing is... it wouldn't be fair."*

It wouldn't be fair because he still loved his ex-wife.

"God, you are so wrong. You don't know what you're talking about." He sounded frustrated, and a little angry. "Christie isn't the woman in that picture anymore. She's a totally different person. Some freakish creation..." he used his hands as if juggling balls searching for the right description "...from a surgeon's scalpel."

Grace shook her head, not wanting to understand. Had someone cut up Christie's face?

"Just before she got pregnant, she started having little cosmetic procedures. Laser treatments on tiny old chicken-pox scars, Botox injections, skin bleaching—you name it, she wanted to try it."

Mitch walked to the kitchen table, pulled out a chair and sat, resting on his elbows. Grace leaned her back against the counter and sipped her tea, prepared for a long story and eager to hear every last bit of it.

"I told her she was perfect just the way she was, but she didn't see it. Every fine line was blown out of proportion to being her death sentence as a model. She wanted me to give her a nose job. When I refused, she wanted me to refer her to the best plastic surgeons, and when I fought her about having rhinoplasty, she snuck off to my partner."

Grace could imagine how infuriating it would be to deal with an already beautiful woman who wanted nothing more than to be even more beautiful. Especially if he was married to her.

Mitch stared at the tiled floor, as if reliving a horrible secret. He alternated rubbing his knuckles with his palms, first one hand than the other. She didn't know how he could possibly talk with his jaw muscles bunched so tightly.

"She kept sneaking off to Rick." He looked up, realizing she might need an explanation. "My business partner and best friend, by the way." He tossed her another quick glance loaded with hurt and defeat.

"Christie was never satisfied with how she looked after that first operation. I suspect she already knew she'd blown it and ruined what she'd been given naturally, but wouldn't stop. Could never go back. But, oh, how she tried."

Grace understood exactly what he spoke of—she'd seen it in far too many cosmetic surgery patients, which was exactly why she'd specialized in reconstructive surgery instead.

Mitch turned sideways in the chair, leaned forward, elbows on his thighs, hands locked and head down. "Her vanity astounded me at times, but that's what I got for only dating models when I was a bachelor. I was just as vain about my women as she was about her looks. Until Mia came along."

He glanced up, a look of shame and regret coloring his eyes.

"At least you saw it, Mitch, saw the superficiality of

it all. You became a parent, rose to the occasion. But last night you said Christie wasn't able to."

"God, no. Christie kept having more surgery, especially after Mia. I already told you that part but, damn, I just kept hoping she'd come to her senses before it was too late. And, honestly, it already was too late. She'd ruined her face, striving for perfection. Had at least three nose jobs." He scrubbed fingers through his hair. "I lost count."

He hung his head. Things went silent for a few moments. Grace didn't dare utter a sound, so as not to stop him. He needed to get this nightmare off his chest, and if all she could be for him was a friend and a sounding board, she'd gladly be that.

She studied Mitch, a gorgeous man on the outside, one who'd once been just as superficial as his wife, but who'd grown up when he'd become a father. She had to respect a man who learned the importance of being a parent, and the true priorities in life. They went much deeper than the skin. Oh, God, if only she could believe that about herself.

"After that, Christie was a stranger to me." He broke into her thoughts. "And she looked like a plastic doll instead of a woman. I had to let her do her thing or I'd have lost the mother of my child and my wife altogether. I thought I'd taken the high road, was doing her a huge favor by not throwing her out." He cleared his throat, stared at his shoes. "But the joke was on me. She left. Me. For Rick. The guy who kept whittling away at what was left of her natural beauty. My so-called best friend."

Grace stifled the gasp in her throat. Poor Mitch. He'd done the right thing and been double-crossed. This amazing surgeon before her was as broken as she was. She wanted to rush to his side and hold him, but that might send a message that she wasn't prepared to follow through on. Moisture formed in her eyes and she bit her lower lip instead of physically offering him comfort.

"Obviously I couldn't work with Richard as my partner any more. I sold him the business and left Hollywood." He looked up and noticed her tears. She saw how they took him aback, his thick lashes dipping and lifting in quick succession. He took a breath and let it out in a long and tired huff.

"If I have any feelings left for Christie, they are for who she used to be, that person in the picture, long before I realized how self-centered and selfish she truly was. That woman is long gone, probably never really was, and I can assure you I'm over her." He waited for Grace to look at him again. His eyes had softened, and the tension etched in his forehead had disappeared, as if telling his story had freed him. "Believe me, Grace, I am completely and truly over her."

"I believe you." She put her cup on the counter and took a couple steps toward him, taking his hand and squeezing it. The warmth from their laced-together fingers traveled up her arms.

"I need you to believe something else, too." He rose to be closer to eye level with her.

She tilted her head upward, delving into his steady gaze. How much more could there be to his heartrending story?

He lightened the grip and gently held her hands, then stared into her eyes until she thought she might faint from the powerful jolt it sent through her. She'd never noticed how his green eyes were outlined in a ring of dark hazel, and how his thick, short lashes clumped together in an almost sawtooth fashion. She could gaze into his eyes for hours and hours and never grow bored.

"Since I've met you…" He pulled her close and wrapped his arms tightly around her. She welcomed the warmth and strength of his chest. "I've come back to life." The words vibrated in his chest as he spoke with his jaw beside her head. "I trust my instinct again, and know that you are good and true, and beautiful inside and out." He kissed the top of her head then took her by the arms and moved her away enough so he could look into her eyes again. A tender smile gently curved his mouth.

"You've restored my faith in women."

Now he'd gone too far. "Oh, go on." She couldn't help herself, a tiny bubble of joy and disbelief slipped from between her lips. He'd practically claimed she'd saved mankind.

"I mean it, Gracie." He tilted her head so she could see the sincerity in his eyes, those beautiful dark-as-the-forest eyes. She stilled, taking in every word.

"Because of you I believe in love again."

CHAPTER EIGHT

MITCH CUPPED GRACE'S face and planted a kiss on her. She knew she should fight it, but though it had only been twenty-four hours since the last time, she'd already missed the feel and pressure of his lips. She'd missed the smooth glide of the inside of his mouth and the velvety feel of his tongue as he searched out hers. His flavor was passion and the faintest bit of wintergreen mixed with the herbal hibiscus she'd just sipped.

He tasted so good. She could kiss him for hours.

He'd bared his soul to her. Accused her of changing the world for him, as if she were a superhero or a goddess. Only the intimacy of sex would bring them closer, but she couldn't let herself think about that, getting naked, baring it all in front of him; she didn't want to ruin the moment.

The kiss took on a life of its own. Needful. Intense. Frantic. The towel dropped from her shoulders, and she didn't care. His mouth and strong jaw took control. She answered his delving tongue with explorations of her own, and he obviously liked her nipping and tugging on his lips.

His hands grazed her hips and squeezed. A tiny

moan escaped her throat, filling the otherwise quiet room with another heady sound besides their fierce kisses. His breathing went ragged; she nearly panted as her body came to life. Every nerve ending lit up, pulsing across her skin, leaving trails of tiny goose bumps. Warm jets of need invaded her secret lair. The weight of her robe became heavy and intrusive. If only she could take it off.

"I need you," Mitch said, pulling her hips close to his. His thickening length pressed against her, nothing but his clothes separating them. She parted her robe to bring him closer.

He was as emotionally damaged as she as. She knew the whole twisted tale. They were two wounded people with the chance to share a blissful timeout from the rest of their lives. Maybe together they could forget.

Could she trust him?

Why did she have to carry her brokenness on her skin? She wanted to scream out for the thousandth time at the sick bastard who'd meant to hurt her sister.

"Grace." Mitchell must have sensed her change. The inner turmoil threatened to ruin things again and again. No man could put up with it for long. He'd quit kissing her, loosening his hold, looking puzzled. "Have I done something?"

"No. This is good." All she wanted to do was go back to their kissing, back to forgetting everything else, if her mind would only cooperate, but he wouldn't let her.

"What's happened? I told you I wanted you and you tensed up. I don't want to push myself on you, but you've got to know how much I want—"

"Nothing's happened. Please, Mitch, kiss me." She

stepped back into his arms, but he wouldn't hold her. Oh, no, now she'd blown everything.

His gaze penetrated her eyes, as if searching for the truth. His stare slowly traveled down to her neck. He lifted the hair from her shoulder, folded down the collar of her robe where she knew a scar peeked above, and moved in for a kiss. She tensed again.

He stopped. "Is this what you've been seeing Leo about?"

Surprised, she nodded.

But she couldn't bear it. Soon he'd notice the extent of her scarred flesh. She had to think fast. She wanted nothing more than to make love with Mitch, for once to leave her mind out of it, let her body take control. But she couldn't let him see her for the first time like this, not under the glaring kitchen light.

Maybe in the dark…

She stepped back, shook her head, so her hair covered her neck again, then managed a smile. "Why don't we go into the bedroom?" Without waiting for an answer, she took his hand and led him across the kitchen, down the short hall to her room. She opened the door, smiled over her shoulder at the man she planned to lure into the dark. At least there, in the dark, she wouldn't be able to see his reaction when he realized how scarred she was.

She wanted this time with Mitch more than she could ever remember. Once outside her room, seeing the heat still in his eyes, she breathed a sigh of relief, knowing it wasn't too late.

Grace drew Mitch over the threshold, using only her fingertips. Once he was inside she closed the door and turned off the lights. But before she could remove her hand from the switch plate, his covered hers. Her fingers went still as he turned the lights back on.

Caught and cornered, she looked pleadingly at him.

"Talk to me," he said.

"What *don't* you want me to see?" *A surgical scar?* Mitch guessed. Was that what Leo had been fixing? "How shallow do you think I am?" He glanced toward her neck, remembering how she always kept it covered. Her motionless stare registered dread. He moved her thick, silky hair away again, and tried to pull the white spa robe from her shoulder. "Do you think a little scar can scare me off?"

Wild hands stopped him. He froze. She'd invited him into her bedroom, yet now he'd stepped over the line? He shook his head, confused but desperately wanting to understand.

"You don't know what you're saying," she said.

With tears brimming, she looked defeated and distraught, not anything close to the way a woman seducing a man would. The sight of her, nearly begging him to stop asking questions, made him feel queasy. What had he done but follow her into her bedroom and turn on the lights? Hadn't she invited him inside?

He pulled back his hands, holding up his palms, making a physical promise not to touch her right now. "Tell me," he whispered. "Tell me what I don't know."

She swallowed and looked down. All he wanted to do was hold her, tell her everything would be all right, but he wouldn't dare touch her again until he knew she wanted him to. Her obvious despair tore at his emotions.

She worried her mouth, as if fighting to hold in the explanation he demanded. Yet he had no intention of leaving without one.

Her eyelids closed halfway. She stared into nothingness. "I was burned by acid."

The words trickled out without a hint of animation.

Yet she may as well have hit him with a sledgehammer. Her matter-of-fact statement nearly threw him off balance. He leaned against the wall for support. Anger and pain twined and exploded in his gut. Something told him not to show the feelings roiling through him, that she needed him to be restrained. He fought his instinct to grab and hold her with all his might, to honor hers.

"Go on." His voice was measured.

"Twelve years ago my sister started college, and immediately fell in love with the wrong guy." She stood perfectly still, reciting her history. "Hope realized it too late, after the guy became obsessed with her. He questioned everything she did, was jealous of anyone else she spent time with, and essentially became a paranoid freak. She kept it to herself, until one night when we had an online video call and I could see how stressed out she was. I begged her to do something about it."

She stared toward the distant corner, numbness in her eyes, as though she was exhausted from reciting the events that had happened years before.

"I was already home for summer break and knew Hope planned to break up with Tyler just before she came home from university. She thought everything had gone well, until one day he showed up at our house, demanding to see her. To talk to her." Grace lifted her arms, the first body movement since she'd started opening up, and used air quotes around "talk to her," said it in a clipped, angry manner—the first sign of emotion since she'd begun.

"I didn't trust him and refused to leave the room. Hope told me to go, but as I suspected she only said it to appease Tyler, because I could see it, the terror in her eyes. I snuck around the back of the house and watched through the French doors."

Grace crossed the room and sat on the edge of her bed, looking wrung out. The ache in his chest got stronger, seeing the normally full-of-life woman he'd been so fascinated with these past few weeks look deflated and defeated. He forced himself not to run to her side, to keep the distance for her sake. Nothing must stop her from telling the whole story. He deserved to hear it and she obviously needed to get it off her chest.

She picked at her robe with one hand, clutching the collar with the other. "I couldn't hear them, but from my vantage point I could see the pleading, fear and anger on my sister's face. She was sticking to her guns and refusing to get back together with him, just like she told me she already had at school. My fingers were ready to hit Emergency on my cell phone."

She paused.

Mitch wondered if her mind tried to rewind and change the outcome, even as she told the story. He wished he had the power to do it for her.

"Tyler must have realized he couldn't bully her into getting what he wanted anymore. Then I saw him reach into his back pocket for a brown glass bottle." She stopped briefly, closed her eyes as if shutting out horrible thoughts, the burden of knowing what would happen next.

"I didn't know what it was, but he was a science major and instinct told me to bolt into that room and knock it out of his hand before he could do anything to harm Hope. I tried to push him away as he uncapped and splashed the acid. Hope jumped back. He shifted and aimed the bottle toward me." She clenched her eyes tightly closed, wringing moisture from the sides. "He got me instead."

Fury rose up in Mitch's gut. What monster could do such a thing? For the first time in his life he suspected he was capable of killing someone.

Tears streaked down her cheek. She'd done the noble thing of protecting her sister from a crazy person and had paid the price with her own flesh. Tiny pins pricked behind Mitch's eyes, moisture gathered and brimmed on his lids. He ached to hold Grace and tell her how beautiful she was, even as he imagined smashing in the face of the maniac who'd done this to her. His fists opened and closed. *Please tell me the sick bastard's in jail.*

Sensing she wasn't through, he used every fiber of restraint and held firm where he was, leaning against the wall, keeping quiet, knuckles nearly cramping.

"I missed a semester of med school during the trial, but was determined to make up for it once I'd healed. Since then I've gone through countless skin grafts and extensive plastic surgery. But nothing will ever take away all of these scars."

"It doesn't matter," he said quietly.

"Yes, it does." She pleaded with him with her stare. "I was in love and engaged to be married back then.

Ben was the greatest guy in the world. At least, that's what I thought. He'd stayed by my side throughout the hospital stay, coming every day, bundling up in gowns and gloves just so he could hold my hand when I was in isolation."

Her jaw tightened and her chin quivered. "But I was always bandaged up, and when we were finally together—" emotion bubbled from her throat, she fought it back "—he was horrified. Didn't want to touch me. Couldn't. I mean, why would he? I looked like uncooked meat back then." She hung and shook her head. "How could I blame him?" She bit her lower lip and swallowed. "I haven't been intimate with anyone since. Can't take the risk. Besides, who would want me?" She squeezed her eyes closed again. "I never want to see that look again."

Finally she glanced at Mitch, offering him a doleful smile. "I'm afraid you're still looking for perfection, and the sight of me will ruin things between us."

She'd finally said it: she was afraid to show herself to him. She was willing to make love to him in the dark, because she didn't want to see his reaction. Oh, God, how could he make her know he didn't give a damn about the status of her skin? It was her, her heart and soul, that he wanted.

"I'm a surgeon, Grace. I've seen it all. Nothing could shock me, surely you understand that?"

"Did you hear anything I just said?" A puff of air pushed through her lips. Her face contorted. She peeked out from between tightly clenched eyelids. "He couldn't look at me. My scars turned him completely off."

"I'm not him. You've got to trust me, my love. Whatever that jerk's name was, he didn't deserve you. All I see is beauty when I look at you. You've got to believe that nothing can stop me from loving you."

"I can't live through another rejection like that ever again."

He shook his head, his body covered from head to toes with chills. Overcome, emotion flowed so powerfully he couldn't speak. Only one thing occurred to him. He had to show her how he felt about her, how her inner beauty was a hundred times stronger than her scars. She was the most beautiful, authentic person he'd ever known and nothing, nothing—especially her scars—could ever change that opinion.

Mitch came to her. He looked at her as if she were the most beautiful woman in the universe. There wasn't a hint of pity in those sea-green eyes, shiny with moisture and empathy. It seemed all wrong, his sexy intent. How could he still find her attractive? But his determined expression almost made her believe him.

Trust flickered in her chest. "Don't pity me. Please, don't."

He dropped onto one knee as she sat on the edge of her bed, and took her hand, looking sincerely into her eyes. "How can I pity you when I love you? All I see when I look at you is the most beautiful human being I've ever met."

She went still. He knew everything and he still wanted her.

Without another word he turned her hand over and kissed her palm, then her wrist, sending warm ribbons up her arm. He eased up the long sleeve of her robe, and she didn't fight him. Wouldn't. She had nothing else to hide. He knew her story, what he was getting into, what he'd find—scars, scars, and more scars.

It didn't matter anymore.

He feathered kisses up the inside of her arm, stopping at the delicate spot in the bend of her elbow, taking his time, giving her undivided attention there. Contrary to what she'd believed about her scars all these years, she wasn't numb but felt every touch of his lips as he burned his way north.

Prickles tiptoed on nerve endings, up her body, erupting into tingles on the back of her neck and across her shoulders. Her breasts tightened. The natural-as-breathing response made her dare to believe again. She smiled just as Mitch's eyes drifted upward. Their gazes held and melded, and, as sure as she'd ever been about anything, she knew he still wanted her. From his smoldering stare, the message was loud and clear that he couldn't live one more second without making love to her.

She wiped the stale tears from her eyes and basked in these new feelings, her anxiety and doubt seeping out, the leftover resistance vaporizing one touch at a time. He released what was left of her clutch on the spa robe and slid it off, first one shoulder then the other, kissing the base of her neck, the top of her arm, the webbed white scars on her breastbone. And, yes, alive again, she felt all of it.

Grace held her breath, waiting for him to change his mind.

Instead, he cupped her jaw with one hand, fingered a clump of her hair with the other, and stared her down as if she belonged to him. "You're beautiful." His mouth bussed hers. "So beautiful."

He caressed her breast, gently lifting, admiring— kissing her there. And there. Making her almost believe she *was* beautiful.

She dug her fingers into his thick dark hair, as she'd longed to so many times before, and pulled his head to her chest. Feeling his breath against her skin, she savored the moment. He found her nipple, flicked with his tongue then kissed it, tugging lightly, releasing another wave of chills she wasn't prepared for.

She liked feeling unprepared, her head swimming with sensation.

She kissed his head, inhaling the rich sent of his hair, getting lost in the feel of his hands as they explored her ribs, her waist. Her belly. He didn't act like a man horrified by her scars—or a man who pitied her. The lights were on. He could see it all. And he seemed to worship her, like a man in love.

She let go of the last frayed threads of resistance, finally believing and trusting him, loving him back.

Now Grace wanted nothing more than to see Mitch as bare as she was. She bracketed his jaw with her hands and planted a deep kiss on his mouth then pulled his shirt up and over his head. He cooperated fully. Fire flamed in his eyes as he realized she planned to make love to him.

She ran her palms down his chest, loving the feel of his muscles and the light swatch of brown hair along his breastbone, admiring his broad shoulders and strength of him. He was nothing short of gorgeous.

They flew back to kissing like they'd starve if they

didn't. Her breasts pressed firmly against his chest, magnifying the heat between them, igniting a fire much deeper inside.

Midkiss she found the drawstring to his scrubs and loosened it, working the thin fabric over his narrow hips, discovering thick muscled thighs and a large bulge in his briefs. His briefs were black, and she liked that, but right now all they did was get in the way. She couldn't wait to tug them down, to see him.

Gone. Finally they were gone, and his full erection felt hard and heavy in her hand. His musky scent made her head spin.

As she explored the smooth skin of his shaft, he cupped her mound, soon discovering how alive and damp she'd become under his attention. Hot and antsy, she squirmed against his palm. A finger dipped inside. She moved against him.

Now her scent mingled with his and nothing would turn them back from sex. She wanted him more than breath and life. They held each other tight and stretched out on the bed. His mouth burned its way down to her stomach while his fingers worked her into frenzy. Soon his mouth replaced his hand, bringing a gentler, deeper touch, driving her wild with long, luxurious pressure. He squeezed her hips, dropping the gentleness and going deep, soon overpowering her. So under his spell, she came quickly and hard, rocking with the energy jetting up her spine and out to her toes.

She gasped her pleasure. "Cooper!" He squeezed her hips tighter, not letting up with his mouth until he'd wrung her to the core.

She thought she'd nearly died, and surely this must

be what heaven was like, free-floating over the bed in ecstasy for several long, intense moments.

When he was satisfied she'd completed her orgasm he rose, grabbed her and wrapped her legs around his waist. "I like it when you call me Cooper."

They grinned at each other and crashed onto the mattress with him landing back first, her on top. He smiled proudly, as if he'd just staked a claim, and she belonged to him to do with as he wished. She laughed and shook her head, completely intoxicated by his charm and amazing skills. *Take me, Cooper. I'm yours.*

She shifted her position, wiggled around his erection and clenched the insides of her thighs, rising up to the tip then back down. He groaned. Looked gorgeous doing it, too. "Please tell me you've got condoms."

She went still, wanting to throttle herself. Never in a million years had she ever thought she'd need them in London.

A sexy, though impish expression popped up on his face. "No problem. Hand me my wallet."

Though relieved, she lifted a brow. "For emergencies?" She dug out his wallet from his scrub pocket and handed it to him.

"Been carrying these babies around since the night I met you in the pod." He flashed a victorious grin and handed the first condom to her to do the honors. She laughed again, throaty and natural, marveling at how he always managed to make her lighten up, even now during sex. She couldn't remember ever feeling this relaxed around a man, even before her injuries.

She loved the feel of him as she slid on the condom, firm and throbbing under her touch. She loved the round sponginess of the rest of his assets, too, and stopped to enjoy the full package. He obviously liked that, growing high and tight from her touch.

The deed done, with condom in place she straddled him, guiding him inside while still raw from her orgasm. Immediately she lit up with heat and amazement at having Mitch inside her.

They joined tightly, slowly, easing into each other. She stretched around him, and though she was on top he soon took over the speed and rhythm, bumping up against her, prodding her passion—at this point she needed only minimal prodding.

He moved slowly and gently, then faster and firmer. She leaned her hands on his chest for balance and met every thrust, heat simmering and spreading up to her hips and fanning across her lower back. Frantic to increase the pleasure, she took back control, forcing him deeper, and working him over her most sensitive spots.

Lost in his body and all it offered, she threw her head back and panted with bliss, wanting the thrills to go on and on. His full, steel-like response took her to the edge, held her there suspended in unbelievable passion for what seemed like forever, until she clutched in another orgasm. Eyes tight, shimmering lights behind her lids, matching the fireworks ripping through her body, she collapsed over him.

Catching her, he rolled her onto her back and drove her further and further. His strength grew and forged on. She wrapped her legs tightly around his waist, urging him closer and closer still, feeling his pistonlike passion power on. A groan accompanied a millisecond falter in his pace—"Ahhh, Gracie"—just before he gave it all, pulsating and pumping into her.

They couldn't possibly be any closer than at this moment—she holding him tight, he resting on her chest, breathing like he'd run a sprint.

Scars were the last thing on her mind.

Only one thought had taken up resident there.

Love.

Gracie had fallen hopelessly in love with Cooper.

CHAPTER NINE

THE CELL PHONE blared. Grace rubbed her eyes to help her wake up and checked the clock: 2:00 a.m. A second cell phone buzzed from somewhere nearby, the sound unfamiliar. She reached for her phone. Ethan Hunter's name flashed on the screen.

"Hello?" she said.

"Hello?" Mitch echoed her response after fumbling in the dark for his cell phone, though he whispered.

Surprise gripped Grace for an instant, thinking maybe everything they'd done last night had been a dream. But, no, Mitch was there...in the flesh.

"Grace, this is Ethan." She clicked back into the moment and away from the gorgeous man sharing her bed. She'd had very little interaction with Ethan since she'd arrived, other than the one surgery, and needed time to focus on his early-morning call.

"Oh, uh, yes. Hello, Ethan."

"Sorry for the late call, but I tried to call Mitch and he isn't home. I wanted to let you know that our first Fair Go patient, Telaye Dereje, just arrived from Ethiopia a few hours ago. He's at the Lighthouse."

She heard Mitch talking quietly behind her. "Okay, Roberta. Thanks for letting me know. I'll call him right back."

"Oh, that's wonderful," she replied to Ethan.

"The thing is his injuries are more extensive than we first thought."

Her heart wrenched over the poor ten-year-old child who'd had part of his face blown off in an explosion.

"I've managed to schedule theater time and I'll be joining you and Mitchell there. By the way, I can't reach him. Have you any idea where he might be?"

"Oh." Well, what should she say now? Mitch might not want anyone to know about them. "I'll try to call him as soon as I hang up."

"Thanks. We've scheduled Telaye for seven a.m."

"I'll be there by five. That should give me time to go over his records. We can discuss our approach then. Are you at the hospital now?"

"Yes. Now that I know Telaye is stable, I'm going to take a quick nap. See you soon, then."

"Thanks, Ethan, for pushing this surgery along. I look forward to working with you."

"Same here." He hung up.

She glanced at Mitch, who looked sheepish for a nanosecond before pulling her into his arms for some kissing. "I hear you have a message for me?"

She kissed him back. "Yes, Mr. Cooper." She decided to attempt her fledgling British accent. "You're wanted in Theater at seven."

His devilish smile excited her. "Great. That gives us some time to play."

Their bodies crashed together for some quick, hot,

early-morning sex before they napped contentedly in each other's arms for a couple of hours more.

At 4:00 a.m. her alarm went off. She catapulted out of bed and set up the coffeemaker, completely forgetting that she was buck naked. Mitch walked up behind her, wrapped his arms around her waist and pressed her back and bottom firmly against his sturdy wall of muscle, sinew and taut flesh. God, she loved the feel of him. Her head rested back on his shoulder, and he performed an interesting breast examination while they kissed.

One hand traveled downward, over her belly and beyond, pressing and massaging. She felt him lengthen and firm up behind her, prodding between her cheeks. She encouraged him with slow hip rotations. And he was definitely encouraging her.

Forget the coffee, sex would wake them up.

Heated up, she turned round and he lifted her. She bound her legs tightly around his hips as he did an amazing maneuver and wound up inside her.

They'd had a long talk earlier after he'd used the second condom. Their sexual histories were clear and clean as neither had been with anyone in over a year and they'd both been checked for everything with their annual physicals. She was on birth control for no other reason than to regulate her periods, and Mitch knew that, too. Never in her wildest dreams had she thought the Pill might get used for its original reason in London.

With her legs locked around his waist, and him planted inside, he carried her to the bathroom, where she reached out and turned on the hot water in the shower. He utilized those few moments of waiting for the water to warm up by balancing her against the bathroom wall, kissing and thrusting. She never wanted him to stop or to put her down.

Once in the shower he dunked her under the warm water then against the cold tile, but she didn't care. She tipped her hips for better access and, as amazing as the sunrise, they gave each other the best morning gift ever created.

Soon realizing time had gotten away from them, they rushed through the rest of the shower, got dressed and headed for the door. She didn't even bother to dry her hair. Just before Grace could open the door, Mitch stopped her. He looked seriously into her eyes, like a man in love, then kissed her tenderly on the mouth.

"Good morning, Gracie."

She hummed her answer. "Good morning, Cooper." Never having felt so wonderful or alive after so little sleep in her life.

Mitch seemed to know all the shortcuts from her house to the Lighthouse Children's Hospital, just down the road from the Hunter Clinic, and had them in the car park in less than five minutes. Good thing she was staying so close by.

They grabbed some coffee from the doctors' lounge and soon met up with Ethan for a quick meeting at five a.m., exactly on time.

"So here's what we've got," Ethan said, getting right down to business after their early-morning greetings. "Our patient's jawbone, tongue and portions of his face got blown off and it's up to us to repair them."

"I understand we don't have time for harvesting bone and skin from Telaye's leg, like I'd normally do in a case like this," Grace said.

"No," Ethan agreed. "That would require several surgeries and a great deal of healing time in hospital."

"We don't have the luxury of time in Telaye's case," she said.

Ethan nodded his agreement. "Right."

Which meant that Grace's computer-generated models for periodic jaw reconstruction as the boy grew out of one and needed another would go by the wayside.

"What we have is a boy with a severe injury, which requires innovative scientific thinking in order to help." From the sleepless look of Ethan's eyes, Grace guessed he'd spent his night doing research and coming up with a plan. "The boy's deformities also call for us to rebuild what's left of his tongue," Ethan said.

"I was planning on doing that," Grace said, "and to transplant skin from Telaye's thigh to his mouth and jaw."

"Skin, including a vein and artery."

"Absolutely. We have to ensure a solid blood supply for the tissues to encourage regeneration. As soon as we're done here, I'll check which of his legs looks most promising for that."

"Good. You've measured the prosthesis on your computer program?"

She nodded. "It will be a perfect fit for now, and under the circumstances plus room to grow, I guarantee."

"Good." Ethan scratched the short military-style cropped hair on his head. "I've got a wild idea that I think might work due to our time constraints." He looked at Grace, as if testing her mettle. "Have either of you heard about the technique recently performed by two British surgeons on a woman with jaw cancer?"

"The one involving a bicycle chain?" Mitch asked.

"Exactly." Ethan's eyes brightened. "Here's what I plan to do—"

Grace had read about the amazing procedure in a medical journal in the States, impressed with the idea and how it had turned out. So far it had proved successful. This was the kind of out-of-the-box thinking that a field surgeon such as Ethan would come up with for survival's sake, and because he had studied all the latest techniques yet chose this one, she trusted his recommendation.

It could be risky, but Telaye was a growing boy, and a usual jaw replacement would require frequent updates as he grew. It could also be weakened with growth, thus the need for the bicycle chain for added support. Considering where he lived, it simply wasn't feasible for him to have regular surgical updates. This one surgery might be their only chance to help in his lifetime.

"So we all agree to take the risk?" Ethan asked.

Grace nodded. "For Telaye's benefit, yes."

"I'm only the lip man, but count me in, too." After listening intently to the entire conversation, Mitch chimed in and his overwhelming support meant the world to Grace.

Hours later the surgery was going well, but had so far been grueling. Under hot O.R. lights, with perspiration beading on Grace's forehead and upper lip, she inserted the titanium mandibular prosthetic measured perfectly to fit Telaye's jaw, yet still giving him some room to grow.

Next Ethan stepped in and inserted a device that looked like ordinary bicycle chain made out of titanium to fit around the reconstructed mandible to offer support and flexibility to the newly replaced jaw, and to add the benefit of expanding as the boy grew. Then he attached it with screws to the remaining natural bone.

Grace looked on at his expert surgical technique with fascination. It was as though he'd done this particular procedure hundreds of times.

Every once in a while her gaze drifted toward Mitch, they'd latch onto each other for a brief moment, and though covered by masks, O.R. caps, and splash shields, they still managed to communicate with each other. Her thought was, *I'm so glad I know you.* From the seriously sexy look in his eyes, she suspected he'd quickly done a replay of some of their recent escapades between the sheets, on the kitchen counter and under the shower. The fanciful thought made her grin, and the quick respite from the intense surgery gave her a new wave of energy.

Ethan finished his portion and seven hours into the surgery it was back to Grace to attach the thigh skin, vein and artery—which would take the greatest amount of time—to what was left of the boy's tongue. He might never speak perfectly again, but it would be a lot better than if they left his tongue as it was.

She finished up reconstructing the facial skin flaps over the chin, then turned the last part—lip reconstruction—over to the master, her new guy, the man she loved, "Lips" Cooper.

Utilizing the boy's most recent picture, all carefully

measured on the computer screen and set up in the O.R., Mitchell matched the mouth and lips to how the boy used to look. And did another amazing job.

Knowing that their patient was only ten, he'd normally be looking at more reconstructive surgeries as he grew. Under the circumstances, as he lived in a rural village in Ethiopia, they had to make the results potentially last a lifetime. If nothing more, they'd at least bought him several years of looking nearly as good as new, and a damn sight better than when he'd been rolled into surgery.

Truth be told, there was only so much they could do for Telaye, but all three surgeons agreed he looked fantastic when they'd completed surgery.

Eleven hours later, feet aching all the way up to her hips, Grace ripped off her mask, O.R. cap, gloves and gown, washed up, then collapsed onto a chair in the doctors' lounge. Mitch followed her in, having chosen to be in on the entire procedure, instead of joining the team at his appointed time, and he looked as tired as she felt.

He plopped down next to her and took her hand, aimlessly running his thumb along her knuckles and over her fingers. She mentally cooed, thinking how special it was to have a man supporting and soothing her. Only then did Grace realize she hadn't worn her cover-up. Her arms and scars were on display for anyone who cared to notice.

Ethan walked in, his dark hair spiking out beneath the O.R. cap, observing the couple holding hands and not giving a hint that it mattered to him. Or that he'd noticed her scars. He'd probably seen far, far worse in combat zones.

"Well, that went really well," he said, looking as haggard as she knew she did, though still managing to pull off that handsomely rugged appeal. He shook their hands. Mitch stood to shake his.

"I'm glad you're up on all the latest tricks," Grace said. "Who'd have thought bicycle chain could be the missing link to a stronger mandible replacement?"

"Nice one, Gracie," Mitch said.

She glanced at Mitch and shrugged, not having a clue what he'd meant. Had she said something wrong?

"Bicycle chain? The missing link?" He played imaginary drums on his thighs and hit the nearby table as a makeshift cymbal to accentuate the inadvertent punch line. "We'll have to work on your timing, babe."

"I think you're punchy." She shook her head at his silliness, loving every inch of him, quirky personality and all.

Ethan, on the other hand, pretended not to be amused by the joke, though the corner of his mouth lifted in an almost-smile. He'd quirked a brow when Mitch had referred to Grace as "babe", but didn't comment.

"Well, now that we've got the technique down, we'll use it for future cases," Ethan said, ignoring the play on words and Mitch's post-op letting off of steam with silly jokes.

"Absolutely," Grace chimed in. "I'm a believer."

He stopped, put hands on his low-slung hips, looking like a man who'd accomplished his mission and now it was time to leave. "Well, then. I'd say take the night off, you've earned it. See you back at the clinic tomorrow."

"Sure thing," she said, noticing it was a quarter past seven.

"See you there." Mitch spoke simultaneously with Grace.

Once Ethan had left, Mitch leaned near and kissed Grace. "Have I told you you're my hero?"

She pulled in her chin. "Your hero?"

"Yeah. You're a natural-born reconstructive surgeon. Gifted as all get-out. I feel honored to know you."

Beaming at his compliment, she kissed him back. "You're not so bad yourself, Lips."

They kissed again. "You know what I miss?" he said.

They'd had sex three times in less than twenty-four hours, and had just come off nearly twelve hours of surgery. How could he possibly—?

"I miss my Mia."

By Grace's calculations, it had been close to twenty-four hours since he'd seen her.

"Why don't you have dinner with us?" he said. "Help me put her to bed. She'd love to see you." He stood, then pulled Grace up by her hands. "All she talks about is when you're coming over again." He smiled brightly at her. "She's going to be thrilled when she finds out about us."

"Isn't it a little too soon to say anything?"

He shook his head. "When a guy meets the one and only woman ever meant for him, he doesn't have to worry about waiting to tell his other best girl in the world. When the timing is right, it's right. When are you going to believe that?"

Taken aback with Mitch's world-tilting words, spoken in such a nonchalant manner, Grace hesitated.

He grew serious again. "I know it's early between us, but besides you being my hero I'm in love with you.

I think I have been since the day I met you in that pod. I just wasn't quite ready for you then."

Relieved that he felt the same way she did, she rushed to his arms. "Mitch, I'm in love with you, too."

"That's a weight off my chest." He smiled and tugged her close, kissed her again. "Thank you."

"For what?"

"For helping me love again."

She savored the sweetest moment in her life, all aches and pains from the long surgery forgotten, just the natural feel of belonging in the arms of the most wonderful man she'd ever met.

"Ditto, Mr. Cooper. Ditto."

"Gracie! Gracie! Read to me!" Mia jumped around in her princess pajamas like a pogo-stick ride gone wildly astray.

It hadn't taken Mitch much effort to convince Grace to have dinner at his house. Roberta had prepared a delicious casserole for dinner, and she was famished. Mia had already had her bath, as she'd eaten hours earlier, and while Mitch and Grace quickly ate the chicken and wild rice with mushrooms and peas, she filled them in on her eventful day.

"What's that?" Mia said, noticing Grace's arms, since she hadn't bothered to cover them up.

"Oh." The observation took her by surprise. "Um, those are my burns."

Mia looked curious, as if she was looking at a bug up close. "Does it hurt?"

"Only at first. I'm okay now."

Without missing a beat, Mia bent down and kissed Grace's arm. "I kissed your hurt. Make it all better."

That was that. Mia had seen her scars, kissed them to make them better and moved on. So matter-of-fact. After Mitch had completely accepted her the way she was last night, and now with Mia doing the same, maybe it was time for her to move on, too.

Grace reached for the child and hugged her tight. She glanced over the child's shoulder at Mitch, who looked on with a somber yet touching expression. "Thank you."

As if a guy could only take so much of squishy good feelings, Mitch got up and started to clear the plates from the table, leaving the girls to do their thing.

After Grace and Mia stopped hugging, and Mia skipped off to her next great adventure, this one having to do with chalk and an easel, she followed Mitch into the kitchen. "Is it okay if I do the bedtime reading tonight?"

"Of course." He stopped making busy work, turning to her. "In fact, I think you should sleep over."

Mia had wandered into the kitchen right at the "sleep over" part and clapped then jumped up and down again. "We're having a sleepover! Yay. Sleep with me!"

Exhaustion and joy mixed together at being wanted by the two most wonderful people in the world, making Grace feel giddy. A laugh bubbled up from her throat. She glanced at Mitch, as he had been the one to bring up the subject of sleeping over. She'd let him tackle this one.

"Uh, Mia…" He got down on one knee, reminding Grace of how he'd done the same for her in her bedroom last night after she'd finally told him the horrible old nightmare. Gushy tender feelings invaded her, seeing him like that again. "I think Grace should stay in the guest room as she's our guest. Don't you?" he said.

Mia gave a full-blown pout for half a second, soon unfolding her arms and smiling, then she clapped again, having instantaneously worked out the solution. She beamed at Grace. "I'll wake you up so we can have breakfast!"

Mitch shot Grace a cautioning look, as if warning it might be the crack of dawn when they'd eat. Happier than she'd been in ages, all she could do was smile. In fact, she couldn't remember smiling this much since before her injuries.

"Okay. I'd like that."

Mitch mouthed, "You'll be sorry," and glanced toward the ceiling.

Mia rushed towards Grace, grabbed her around the thighs and hugged tight. "I love you, Gracie."

How could a kid make up their mind about someone so fast? Well, she and Mitch had made up their minds pretty darned fast. It had been just short of four weeks since she'd arrived in London. She didn't care what level-headed people might think about their whirlwind encounter, she bent over, welling up with precious feelings, and hugged the child around the head then kissed the crown, fresh with children's shampoo scent. "You know what?"

"What?" Mia looked up with those huge and fathomless eyes, just like her father's.

Grace made her own snap decision. "I love you and can't wait to have breakfast with you, either." If she was lucky, maybe it could be for the rest of her life, or until Mia grew up and moved away. Oh, but she'd let her mind travel too far ahead. For now she'd just take it one moment at a time. Besides, savoring each moment was the best way to live. Finally she understood that.

She kissed Mia and an obviously happy and proud Mitch took his daughter's hand and walked her to the bathroom. "Okay, now that that's settled, let's brush those teeth."

Grace had never felt more welcome in her life. She'd never felt she'd belonged anywhere since her accident before this moment either.

Mitch had told her he loved her. She loved him. His daughter loved her. Could life be any more perfect?

She glanced around the living room while Mitch helped Mia with her teeth. The grin that seemed to have been pasted on her face since the moment she'd arrived tonight grew even wider. That picture of Christie was nowhere in sight. She wanted to pump her fist in the air but restrained herself, taking the missing photograph as a very, very good sign.

A few moments later Mitch returned to her and they smiled easily and hugged. "It's your turn. Mia's waiting."

Thinking she'd stepped into a dream, Grace walked down the hall toward a little girl who adored her. She snuggled next to a squirming Mia in her bed and helped her settle down by putting her head in the crook of her arm, near her chest so Mia could hear her heartbeat while she read. The same technique she'd used the other night. She opened Mia's favorite book, the same one they'd read together before, when they'd fallen asleep in each other's arms. *The Tale of Misty Do-Right in the Battle of the Wrongs.*

Fifteen minutes later, with all the Wrongs conquered, Mia was asleep, and the long and difficult day had also caught up with Grace. She turned off the light and walked to the living room, in full yawn.

Mitch was waiting for her. He'd changed into a white T-shirt and bright blue athletic shorts that showcased those great legs. "Everything go okay?"

"Perfect. She's out to the world."

"You look pretty beat yourself."

"And that's not fair because you don't. What's up with that?"

After he gave an affectionate smile, he grew serious. "I know you'll think this is crazy, especially after the way I went after you last night, but I'm actually an old-fashioned guy. Are you okay with sleeping in the guest room?"

A quick, breathy and relieved laugh slipped out. "I'm so exhausted I could sleep anywhere. At this rate I'll be asleep before my head hits the pillow."

He reached for her, held her close and rubbed her back, and it felt so wonderful she thought she might fall asleep in his arms right there in the living room.

"As much as I want to sleep with you, it's for Mia's sake. I don't want her to be confused when she goes hunting for you bright and early, and you're not in the guest bed."

"I understand. And I think it's a good idea. Though you don't have to put me up here. I can go home."

"No, you can't." He kissed her neck. "I'm too tired to drive you home."

As she often did when in Mitch's company, she gave a light laugh.

"Mia isn't the only one who wants to see you first thing tomorrow morning, you know."

They kissed, and it was hard to pull away from his embrace. But she was beat and was glad she'd brought along her grab-and-go overnight bag, which she always kept at work, knowing she at least had the bare essentials. "Same here."

"In fact, I'd like to see you first thing in the morning for the rest of my life," he said, nuzzling her ear and kissing her jaw.

The statement blasted her heavy eyelids wide open. She pulled her head back and studied him. Unashamed of what had slipped out of his mouth, he smiled benignly.

"I'm just telling it like it is, Gracie."

She put her head on his shoulder and sighed. "I like how you think, Cooper." They swayed in their embrace a few moments, and certain parts of her body started coming back to life, but she was way too tired to do anything about it.

"And who says I can't come and cuddle with you for a while before I hit the sack?" He glanced at her, a hint of devilry in his eyes. "If you want me to, that is."

"I wouldn't have it any other way." The thought of falling asleep in his arms sounded like heaven.

He led her to the guest room by the hand. She followed happily behind.

"I can set the alarm and sneak back to my room before Mia gets up."

"You're a devious genius, Cooper."

* * *

The next morning, Mitch and Grace went to the Lighthouse to check on Telaye. The little boy with the bandaged and taped head looked alert and pain-free. Amazing.

"Good morning," Grace said, taking his hand. He couldn't speak but squeezed her hand and she smiled. She glanced at Mitch, who was smiling, too.

She understood the child didn't speak English, and the Lighthouse had brought in a translator.

"How is he this morning?" she asked the young Ethiopian woman.

"He is doing well. No complaints."

"Please tell him we are very happy to hear that."

She spoke to the boy and he looked at them. Grace smiled again.

Leo popped into the room. "Good morning. I've heard from Ethan you did a fantastic job."

"See for yourself," Mitch said.

Grace wondered where Ethan was, but was happy to see Leo in his place. Leo reached for their hands one by one and congratulated them. "You've made headlines today."

"We have?" Grace wondered how word had got out so fast as they all prepared to return together to the Hunter Clinic, a short ten-minute walk from the Lighthouse.

Just as they exited the room Lexi, being the public-relations maven, showed up dressed to the nines as always, looking ready for her close-up.

"Morning, everyone. Did you see the headlines? I contacted the papers last night, the minute Telaye arrived. Didn't know about that fancy-schmancy new technique you'd used until this morning."

Her huge pink diamond engagement ring never failed to catch Grace's eye. She wondered if her finger ever got tired holding up the ring. Or if she worried someone might try to cut off her finger and run off with the rock.

"Hope you don't mind, but I've scheduled a quick progress report with the press at the front of the hospital in a few minutes. Everyone wants to know about the bicycle chain. Anyone care to talk?"

Grace turned to Mitch with a look of dread. He shook his head. "Not me."

"Me, neither." Grace grimaced, feeling bad, but had to be honest. Facing the press was the last thing she wanted to do this morning. Besides, Ethan was the innovative one; she'd just done what she always did with mandibular prostheses—except for the new bit about rebuilding the tongue. She smiled inwardly with pride.

Having no takers from the surgical team, Lexi glared at Leo. "Leo?"

What could he say? He was the head of the plastic-surgery clinic. She'd put him perfectly on the spot. He flashed a dutiful, though still charming smile. "I'd be happy to, Lexi. Shall we go?"

They left Telaye's room as a group, knowing he was in good hands with the intensive-care Lighthouse nursing staff and the interpreter nearby to explain things to him as they cropped up.

Soon Mitch and Grace said goodbye and splintered off, taking the stairs instead of the elevator. Leo would handle the situation with command and charisma, Grace was sure of it. The only one who could explain the Fair

Go charity better would be Ethan, but he was nowhere in sight.

"Aren't Lexi and Iain supposed to get married soon?" Grace asked on the first flight down the stairs.

"I think they're taking off this Friday. They've decided to make it a private affair."

"That's probably a good thing, because Iain would have to fight off every man with eyes once they saw Lexi's sexy pink dress. Not to mention those six-inch pumps covered in crystals that she's planning to wear."

Mitch turned and gave her a look as if she'd slipped into a foreign language. Yeah, it was a girl thing dressing up for getting married, but such fun!

Grace thought about the silver sequins on the bodice of the pink chiffon dress Lexi had shared pictures of the first night Grace had gone to Drake's with the group. How the sequins started at the shoulders in stripes, worked their way down along the soft and dipping V neck, and gathered at the ribbon waist. How fabulous Lexi had looked when she'd tried it on for the girls at the clinic the day she'd bought it. She had a perfect figure and never flaunted her natural sex appeal. Grace realized she didn't have a drop of envy or insecurity over not having a figure like that. Since making love with Mitch, she'd never felt more womanly and wanted in her life.

"I heard Iain is planning to wear his family kilt," Mitch said. "Should turn a few women's heads, too."

They laughed, Grace thinking Iain would look fabulous in a kilt, and kind of sorry she wouldn't get to see him.

"Where're they getting married? Maybe I'll crash it just to have a look." She beamed a teasing grin.

"At Marylebone Registry Office, that's what I heard."

The thought of a private wedding sounded fine to Grace. When a person married their meant-to-be love, who cared where they got married? She was sincerely happy for Lexi and Iain.

"Too bad we won't get to see them all decked out," she said.

Mitch squeezed her shoulder. "Oh, if I know Lexi, there'll be pictures, loads of pictures."

She smiled, looking forward to seeing them, as they rounded the landing to the last flight of stairs to the first floor. Warmth flowed through her chest, and it wasn't just from taking the stairs. Life was good.

She loved how spring seemed to be breaking out at the Hunter Clinic, with Leo and Lizzie leading the way in marriage and now Lexi and Iain. Rafael and Abbie had seemed to have worked through their marital problems, too. And after what Mitch had hinted at last night, she had an incredibly positive outlook for her own future.

When they hit street level and pushed outside, it was sunny and fragrant from the nearby Lighthouse rose garden. They noticed the group of reporters gathered on the hospital entry steps. She smiled and shrugged her shoulders, Mitch did the same, and they turned and snuck off in the other direction, ditching the crowd and leaving the PR up to those best suited for it—Leo and the soon-to-be Mrs. Lexi McKenzie.

Could a day be any more perfect?

CHAPTER TEN

SATURDAY MORNING, MITCH insisted Grace go along with him and Mia for waffles and a special surprise. Even though she had loads of work to make up, she didn't put up a fight—she couldn't think of two people she'd rather spend time with. And since she'd been staying at his house ever since Wednesday, how could she refuse?

It had only been four short weeks since she'd arrived in London, yet a lifetime of troubles had already disappeared. She gazed around and smiled before getting into the car. It was a sparkling sunny day—trees green or in blossom, the air warm and fresh. Even the sidewalks were clean and the drivers polite. As they drove, she rolled down the car window to listen for tweeting birds. Funny how being in love adjusted the attitude that way.

They ate at the same restaurant Mitch had taken her to for breakfast her very first week in town. But once their orders of waffles arrived, Mitch kept checking his watch. Grace let it slide as she was enjoying the magnificent flavor of blueberries and waffles cooked to perfection.

Later, when Mia dawdled a bit too long over the too-huge-for-one-little-girl fluffy waffle, he encouraged her along. "Eat up, Mia. We don't have all day."

"What has gotten into you this morning?" Grace asked. "I thought you said before we left that we did have all day. Just the three of us, remember?"

"Not exactly," he said, wiping the syrupy corners of Mia's mouth, letting her know she was finished whether she really was or not.

"What's up?" Grace prayed there hadn't been an emergency add-on surgery scheduled that Mitch hadn't told her about.

He sighed. "I want to keep it a secret, if you don't mind."

Surgery? "Well, excuse me," she said, lifting her brows and making a playful, exaggeratedly offended expression. Could this qualify for their first tiff? If so, it was really fun.

He stood. "I'll explain soon enough."

So he was going all dark and mysterious on her. Okay, she could accept that. In fact, he looked pretty sexy that way. Since she liked surprises, she'd go along with his secret plans. Not that she had a choice. Besides, who knew, it might be fun—like just about everything else was with Mitch.

"Where're we going?" Mia had clicked into the conversation. She grabbed one last bite of waffle and shoved it into her mouth.

He checked his watch again. "Too many questions, honeybee." He put a wad of bills on the table, stuffed his wallet back into his pocket and helped Mia out of her chair. "Ladies, just follow me, okay?"

They both opened their mouths to say something.

He anticipated it and shushed them before either could make a peep.

Mia looked at Grace and lifted her shoulders, held them by her ears for a second, then burst into a giggle as they dropped. Grace shrugged back.

Mitch was asking her to trust him. Easy-peasy. She'd never trusted anyone more in her life!

"Okay, boss. Whatever you say," Grace said, saluting and taking Mia's hand and following Mitch's wide strides out of the restaurant.

He looked gorgeous as usual, wearing fashionable navy-blue slacks and a designer-brand pink plaid shirt that showed off his flat stomach and broad chest. She loved a man who wasn't afraid to wear pink. He'd rolled up the sleeves. His lightly hair-dusted forearms always struck her as sexy and strong, especially when he unlocked the car door and the sinews flexed ever so subtly.

Yeah, she was in lo-o-o-ve.

They were back in the car and traveling into familiar territory within ten minutes. "Oh, look, Mia, there's the London Eye!" Grace pointed out.

Mia oohed and ahhed, which always put a smile on Grace's face. She loved seeing things through a five-year-old's perspective, as if for the very first time. She smiled again and realized that a smile hadn't left her face in the last three days since she'd been camped out at Cooper's place.

Mitch parked in a nearby lot and they all got out of the car. "I guess I can't keep this a secret any longer. We've got reserved pod tickets for ten-thirty. After all, we are pod people, right? Have to initiate the young adventurer, too. Let's go." To save time, he picked up Mia and they quickly walked toward the ride.

Grace laughed to herself. They were perfectly matched pod people. But Little Miss Adventurer-to-be Mia looked both excited and maybe a little frightened about the four-story-high ride.

"It'll be fun, I promise," Grace said, patting her arm. "I was a little nervous the first time, too."

"Promise?" Mia looked at her with those huge, trusting eyes.

It was never a good idea to fudge the truth to a child, but in this case Grace was perfectly sure. "I promise."

That seemed to do the trick. Mia's little hesitation disappeared, quickly replaced by a wide smile.

There was a separate line for those with reservations, and after a short wait they boarded a pod. Mitch grinned at Grace as if they'd returned to the scene of the crime. He took her hand. Sweet, flirty memories floated through her mind. How he'd seemed so glum at first but soon after she'd struck up a conversation with him he'd switched to charming and fun! How lucky she'd been to get on that particular pod at that particular hour. What if she'd decided not to go that night, or if she'd let her doubts rule the day and had never spoken to him? How different things would have been.

As they started their journey upward, Mia's fears returned and she buried her head in her father's chest. He rubbed her back and hummed. What a great dad he was, and could the man be any more appealing?

She loved him. Without the hint of a doubt. Loved him with all her heart.

"Oh, look over there, Mia," Grace said, attempting to distract her. "That's Big Ben."

Mia peeked up, forgetting how high they were getting, and soon began enjoying the sights along with Mitch and Grace.

About fifteen minutes into the ride Mitch put Mia down and took Grace's hand again. She said a silent thank-you for the man who'd changed her world. His grasp was warm and sturdy, and somehow she knew she could always depend on him.

The pod was crowded and noisy, nothing like the night they'd met, but the magic still snapped between them. They'd staked out a corner with a good view and that was good enough for this girl.

Mitch bent down to Mia. "Remember what we talked about?" She got serious and quiet, as if not quite sure what he really was talking about. He whispered something into her ear, and her eyes went huge with understanding. She made an O shape with her mouth then pinched her lips tightly together, as though she might let out the big secret otherwise.

Thoroughly intrigued and entertained, Grace looked on. So happy to be a part of Mitch and Mia's inner circle, warm, fizzy feelings pulsed through her veins.

Mitch straightened and cleared his throat. "There's something that Mia and I want to ask you."

Now he had her attention full-on. Did he want her to move in with them since she'd been spending every night there? She could give up her furnished apartment in a heartbeat. "Okay."

At the serious look in his eyes, she went perfectly still, sensing something special was about to happen.

The London skyline faded into the background, along with the chatter from everyone in the pod. All she saw and heard were Mitch and Mia. Mitch took one of her hands and Mia took the other one. The hair on her arms prickled with anticipation.

Grace savored this little circle of three with the two most important people in her life: Mitch—the man who'd given her back her self-worth and sensuality, the man who'd shown her complete acceptance, and who'd taught her to love with abandon. And Mia—the child who'd awakened a mother's heart in Grace, then had stolen it.

Mitch nodded at Mia then looked into Grace's eyes. Love and sincerity intertwined in the sexiest eyes she'd ever seen. His lips spread into a tender smile, and he inhaled through his nose as if building courage. "Will you marry us?"

"Yeah, marry us?" Mia slapped a hand over her mouth and covered a delighted squeal.

So moved by the question and rush of full-blown emotion, tears raced to Grace's eyes. She wanted to mimic Mia and clap her hands, but held the wild and crazy feelings in, trying with all her might not to jump up and down.

Being hardly able to breathe and with her head swimming with joy, she answered.

"I'd love to." She looked first into the sparkling sea-green of Mitch's eyes, seeing an ocean of love there. Her hand trembled when Mitch took it, steadying her nerves instantly.

Though it was incredibly hard to tear her gaze away from him, she didn't want to leave Mia out for one more second, so she bent over and pulled Mia close. "I've waited for you all my life." The message could be applied to both of the Cooper clan.

Mia crinkled her nose. "Even before I was born?"

Grace laughed softly and nodded. "Even before you were born I hoped someday to have a child, and here you are."

"Here I am." Mia grinned. "And I get to be a bridesmaid!"

Laughing with unfathomable joy, Grace took both of Mia's hands and squeezed them. "Of course you do."

Mia chattered on and soon got lost in her own thoughts about what her idea of a wedding might be— something that involved swings and slides, ponies and bubbles and…

Mitch took Grace in his arms and high above the Thames and the London skyline he gave her a world-class kiss. Warm, slow, tender and passionate all rolled into one. A kiss of promise. The kind of kiss a guy gave a girl he planned to spend the rest of his life with.

And Grace believed in that kiss and, most importantly, she believed with all her heart in Mitch Cooper.

* * * * *

200 HARLEY STREET: THE SOLDIER PRINCE

KATE HARDY

For the Harley Street authors—I loved working with you! Also, special thanks to Chris Brooks for technical help with military stuff, and to Chris Craig for technical help with workout programmes following injury—much appreciated, guys :)

PROLOGUE

THAT WAS THE last of the men.

Safe.

Or were they? The rescue had been slightly too easy for Marco's liking. The insurgents didn't usually give up that quickly. And this definitely felt like a false sense of security, he thought as he drove the Jeep back towards base.

'Pedro, I need you to keep a close eye out on the way back. Anything that makes you even slightly uneasy, you tell me immediately,' he said to his second-in-command.

'Sir. You're expecting an ambush?'

'Maybe.'

Pedro had worked with him long enough to follow his train of thought. 'You're right. It was a bit too easy. They're prob—'

The word was cut off by a loud boom.

Bomb, Marco thought, and was about to slam on the brakes when the blast wave smashed into the Jeep, cracking the screen. Marco put his left hand up automatically to shield his eyes; even as he did so, he was aware of splintering glass spiking into his skin.

But he didn't have time to worry about the pain. The blast wave had made the Jeep slew. He tried to steer out of the skid, but the blast wave was just too strong and the car rolled.

Everything went into slow motion, and Marco's senses were working overtime. Everything felt magnified. The bang of the rest of the glass imploding, the scrape of metal, the salty, rusty smell of blood.

Finally, they came to a halt. Upside down.

Oh, great.

He knew they were a sitting target in the Jeep. They needed to get out—right now. It would take just one RPG fired into the fuel tank to blow them all sky-high…

Then again, Marco also knew that the insurgents preferred prisoners to dead men. Live prisoners would be much more useful to them. Especially if one of them was second in line to a throne—even if the throne in question was that of a relatively small south European country. Sirmontane still counted.

That was why it had been too easy. Because they'd known that Marco wouldn't leave his men, that of course he'd come to rescue them. That every single one of his team mattered to Marco; he wouldn't leave any of them behind to be tortured and hurt.

So, by coming to the rescue, by doing the predictable thing, Marco had put them all in danger. He cursed mentally. What an idiot. And he'd thought he'd been so clever, devising the rescue plan.

The first Jeep hadn't stood a chance. It had driven right over the bomb, setting it off. The pieces would be scattered everywhere, along with the remains of its occupants. There hadn't even been the usual warnings of large rocks or whatever blocking the narrow road; at least in those circumstances they knew that any possible alternative route was likely to be rigged and could check it out. The insurgents had been one step ahead, meaning that Marco's team had driven straight over a buried explosive device.

'Pedro? We need to get out. Now.'

'Uh…' came the response.

Concussion, probably. But Marco didn't have time to be sympathetic. 'We have to take cover,' he said urgently. 'Look, I'll come and get you out.' He raised his voice. 'Everyone in the back, be prepared to evacuate and take cover.'

His hand hurt. It felt like a thousand needles burning into his skin. But he'd deal with that later. First of all, he needed to get his men to safety. What was left of them.

It took an effort to shoulder the door open, but he did it. He went round to the other side of the Jeep to pull the passenger door open and help Pedro out when he realised that something was wrong. He couldn't bend the fingers on his left hand.

Which meant it was useless; he couldn't even hold a gun, much less fire one, in this state.

Blood was oozing out of his hand, leaving a trail that just about anyone could follow. He swore, ripped a bit off his shirt and wrapped it round his hand to stanch the bleeding, and used his other hand to yank the door open.

Pedro was still groaning, but Marco was able to get him out of the Jeep, then move to the back and help the rest of his men out. Once he'd got them hidden in nearby vegetation, he used his elbows to propel himself to a better vantage position. Hopefully they'd been near enough to the camp for the blast to have been spotted on surveillance equipment, and help would arrive before things got really sticky.

He could see insurgents swarming all over the Jeep, and Marco prayed to the God he'd stopped believing in that something would happen before they searched the area and found his team.

Amazingly, his prayers were answered: screeching tyres and rapid bursts of fire drove the insurgents off.

'Thank you,' he whispered.

He could hear people calling. Knowing it was safe to do
so, he yelled back. Got their attention. Help was on its way.
And finally the pain in his hand made him pass out.

CHAPTER ONE

MARCO CAME TO in unfamiliar surroundings, and tried to sit up. An arm held him down. 'Stay there, Capitán.'

'Where am I?' he asked.

'Back at base. In the hospital.'

Marco forced himself to focus. He recognised the medic from times when he'd treated some of Marco's team. 'Dr Herrera. How are my men?'

'We need to talk about you,' Dr Herrera said.

'We need to talk about my men,' Marco corrected. 'Were there any survivors from the first Jeep?'

'No, but all of those from your vehicle are safe. Some of them have impact trauma from the crash, but nothing too serious.'

Marco absorbed the information. 'OK. I need to talk to their families. The dead soldiers'. Tell them what happened. Apologise for not keeping them safe.'

'You need to listen to me,' Dr Herrera said, 'unless you want to lose the use of your hand permanently and be invalided out of the army.'

That got Marco's attention. Stop being a soldier? His mother would be ecstatic, he knew; but in his own view it was unthinkable. This was what he was born to do. 'Give me the bottom line,' he said.

'You have a flexor tendon injury.'

At Marco's blank look, Dr Herrera explained, 'The flexor tendons connect the muscles of your forearm to the bones of your thumb and fingers. They let you bend your fingers, and the extensor tendons let you straighten them again.'

Remembering what had happened when he'd tried to open the door of the Jeep, Marco tried to bend his fingers. His index and middle finger wouldn't move, and his hand hurt like hell.

Dr Herrera rolled his eyes. 'Well, you can see that for yourself. I take it the window came in and you put your hand up to shield your eyes?'

'Yes.'

'Some glass shards must have severed the tendons. They won't heal themselves, because the tension in the tendons causes them to pull apart when they're broken—think of them working like a bicycle brake cable.'

'So I need surgery?'

'Microsurgery. And it needs to happen within twelve hours. Twenty-four at most. The longer it takes, the more likely it will be that scarring develops on the ends of the severed tendons.'

'Which means?' Marco prompted.

'Bottom line: you'll get less movement back in your hand.'

It was enough to convince Marco. 'OK. Do what you have to.'

Dr Herrera shook his head. 'I won't be the one operating. You're going to need specialist plastic surgery as well, once the tendons have been stitched and the wound has healed. We have a twelve-hour window from when it happened to getting you into theatre. Say two hours getting you back here from the site of the bomb, seven hours between here and London and an hour's transfer between the airport and hospital…' He grimaced. 'I need you on a plane to London now.'

Marco frowned. 'My men need me.'

'You wanted the bottom line, yes? Right now you're not much use to them, and you'll be even less use if you don't get your hand fixed,' Dr Herrera pointed out. 'I want you on a plane to London so they can operate.'

Marco's boss, Comandante Molina, came striding in and clearly overheard the last bit. 'You know the rules, Marco. Medical orders outrank military ones.'

Royal ones, too, Marco thought grimly.

'Get on that plane and get fixed up,' Comandante Molina ordered.

'What about my men?' Marco demanded.

'I'll sort out the medical side and fix them up again, good as new,' Dr Herrera promised.

'And I'll talk to the families,' Comandante Molina said.

'You seriously want me to go London?' Marco asked with a grimace.

'To the Hunter Clinic. Leo and Ethan Hunter. They have an excellent reputation for treating injured soldiers. One of them used to be an army doctor,' Comandante Molina said.

The Hunter Clinic. Marco had heard that name before. Marianna—his older brother Ferdinand's fiancée—had visited the clinic earlier this year for a blepharoplasty. And she'd had other work done there, too. 'I thought they just did cosmetic stuff.'

'They specialise in reconstructive surgery as well as cosmetic surgery. Burns, microsurgery.' Comandante Molina folded his arms. 'They have hand specialists. Which is what you need.'

Well, if his boss was insistent on it, it didn't look as if Marco was going to have much choice in the matter. Even so, for the sake of his men, he gave it a try. 'Why can't I be treated here? Surely it's better for everyone's morale if I'm treated here instead of being flown out to London as a special case. I don't want everyone thinking I get treated differently just because of who my parents are.'

'It's nothing to do with that. We can't guarantee to hold the media off. Not now you've been injured,' Comandante Molina said. 'Though I admit that, yes, your mother has views on the subject.'

His mother hated him being a soldier on active duty, worrying constantly that he was in danger and would get hurt. Marco had had enough conversations with her on the subject. And the injury to his hand would make her worries increase exponentially. Giving a little ground now might make it a bit easier on his mother.

'She wants me out of here, doesn't she?'

Comandante Molina said nothing but gave him a sympathetic look.

'OK,' Marco said, resigned. 'I'll go to London. But only for as long as it takes to get me fixed. I intend to be back on duty as soon as possible.'

'Marco, your dedication has never been in doubt,' Comandante Molina said softly. 'And your men know you don't think of yourself as any different to them. If this was Pedro sitting here, not you, wouldn't you be demanding that he gets the right medical treatment in the right place?'

'You have a point,' Marco acknowledged.

'So listen to Herrera, here, and do what he tells you.'

Marco said nothing.

'While you were out cold I flushed your hand with saline to get the grit out and avoid infection setting in. I need to give you a tetanus shot now,' Dr Herrera said. 'Antibiotics are controversial but, given that you're travelling for hours to another country for surgery, I'd rather you had them now to avoid the risk of infection.'

'Fine. Do whatever you need to,' Marco said.

'Thank you.' Dr Herrera smiled at him. 'I've spoken to the surgeon in London. He doesn't want me to suture your skin as your palm is a mess. I'm just going to dress your wound so it holds until you get to London.'

He talked Marco through what he was doing: a petroleum-impregnated gauze for the first layer of the dressing, to stop the wound sticking to it. Then another layer of gauze, this time soaked in saline but with the excess fluid wrung out, to let any blood escape and avoid a haematoma forming. The third layer was gauze fluff for padding, topped by a loose wrap, and finally there was cast padding with a fibreglass splint to protect the wound from further injury.

'There's a helicopter on standby to take you from the airport to the clinic,' Comandante Molina said. 'We'll talk later.'

'Right,' Marco said wryly to his boss's retreating back.

He was pretty sure his mother would put pressure on his father now to make sure his tour of duty was over, and the injury—even though it wasn't life-threatening—would probably make his father agree and put pressure on Comandante Molina to give Marco an honourable discharge. And there was only one circumstance in which Marco would accept that.

'When the tendons are repaired and the wound's healed,' he said to Dr Herrera, 'is the injury going to affect the use of my hand at all? Can I still do my job?' And he knew the doctor would understand what he wasn't asking: would he be able to work alongside his men without putting them in danger because his hand would be too weak for the job?

'I'm not going to lie to you,' the doctor said. 'There may be some loss of movement in your hand. It's your flexor tendon that was severed, which means it's likely to affect the strength of your grip.'

Loss of movement. Loss of grip. His left hand. The hand Marco needed to steady a rifle or change a magazine in a machine gun.

And it also could affect him playing his guitar again; with a classical guitar, you needed a strong grip to press the strings against the neck. Playing the guitar was what always calmed Marco down and swept away the stress.

If he couldn't do the job he loved…well, then he could still do his duty to his family and his country. Marco had always known that one day he'd have to leave his military career behind and go back to his royal duties. But he hated the pressure of that world. And if he was going to lose the one thing that could always soothe his soul, what would his life become?

Eight hours later, Marco was in London, sitting in a waiting room at 200 Harley Street. Everything about the place was discreetly luxurious: polished marble floors, white leather sofas, chandeliers, soft lighting. It felt more like a luxury hotel than a clinic. Though, for all Marco cared, the clinic could have been a shack thrown up out of corrugated iron and bits of reused timber.

He just wanted his hand fixed.

And for life to be back as normal.

Preferably yesterday.

OK, so the surgeon who was meant to be sorting him out had been called to see a patient urgently. Marco could understand that. He knew he wasn't the only patient at the clinic. He probably wasn't from the richest family or the most titled family there, either; the little time he'd had to glean information from the internet had told him just how exclusive this place was.

But the longer he waited, the more use of his hand he'd lose. And he really wasn't prepared to accept that.

* * *

'But, Ethan, you're Leo's brother. Surely you should be the one to head the Hunter Clinic in Leo's absence,' Declan said.

Ethan shrugged. 'You're Leo's second in command.'

'But *you* have the Hunter name.'

Yeah. And didn't he know it. The albatross round his neck. 'Declan, you've worked for it. I don't have a problem with you being in charge.'

Ethan was aware that the other surgeon was eyeing him curiously. Probably wondering if he and Leo had had yet another row and this was Ethan's way of getting his own back. It probably had something to do with it. But Ethan knew that Declan would never ask. The Irish doctor was charming, yet he kept people at arm's length and he knew to keep out of other people's sore spots.

'And you're better at PR than I am,' he added.

'That's the Blarney Stone for you,' Declan said lightly. 'Ethan, are you quite sure about this?'

'It's the right decision for the clinic. And the clinic's what matters, right?'

Declan nodded. 'Then, thanks. I'm happy to do the job.'

'Good.' One problem down. At least for a little while. 'I have a patient to see. Catch you later?' Ethan asked.

'Laters,' Declan said with a smile.

Just as Marco was about to go and find someone and ask—very politely, and through gritted teeth—if they could give him any idea how much longer he'd have to wait, a man walked into the room.

Well, *limped*.

He was about six foot two—Marco's own height—with dark brown short hair, dark brown eyes, and stubble that Marco thought privately was just on the wrong side of what women found sexy. If this was the doctor and he didn't give a damn about his appearance, did it follow that he also didn't give a damn about his job? Or was this guy some kind of porter?

'Ethan Hunter,' the man drawled.

One of the Hunter brothers, then. Surgeon. The one who was going to treat him?

He didn't try to shake Marco's hand. 'Sorry to keep you waiting.'

Marco had the distinct impression that the other man wasn't sorry at all. There was an edge to his tone, though right at that second Marco couldn't work out why.

'And I'm sorry it's me you're seeing rather than my brother—he usually does the royals and celebs, but rather inconveniently he's gone on honeymoon.'

Royals and celebs, hmm? Suddenly it was clear: Ethan Hunter had an issue about that kind of lifestyle. He'd automatically assumed that just because Marco was the younger prince of Sirmontane he was an over-privileged, thoughtless and selfish socialite. And Marco was in just enough pain now not to be able to rise above it. If Hunter wanted attitude, then he'd get it. Every damn step of the way.

'So how did you do it?' Ethan asked.

'How do you think? Skiing, drinking with my celeb friends and guffawing so hard at the peasants I didn't look where I was going, fell over and severed my tendons,' Marco drawled.

Ethan gave him a level stare. 'How about the truth?'

Common sense kicked back in. Hunter needed to know what had happened because it might affect the way he fixed the damage. Dr Herrera should have briefed him fully, but then again maybe Hunter was the thorough type and didn't just take other people's words for granted. Marco himself never accepted a brief without asking questions to make sure that nothing had been missed. Maybe Hunter was the same.

'I was in a convoy of Jeeps. The one in front of me drove over a bomb. My windscreen imploded and I put my hand up to protect my eyes.' Judging by the mess of his hand, that was just as well—or he'd be blind as well as having a potentially useless hand.

'Bomb.' Ethan stiffened. 'I see.'

Interesting, Marco thought. Was this the brother who'd been an army doctor? Marco shrugged with the shoulder that wasn't strapped up. 'I was in Afghanistan.'

'You were a soldier.'

'*Am* a soldier,' Marco corrected. 'And I hate being cooped up instead of being where I belong, leading my men and sorting out that whole mess out there. Making a difference. Making things better. But...' He blew out a breath. 'I guess it's still no excuse for being rude to you just now.' He'd been unprofessional and let the pain get to him when he should have known better—both from growing up as a prince in the glare of the public eye, and then from his military training. Time to defuse the situation. 'I apologise.'

'I apologise, too,' Ethan said, surprising him. 'Just because you're rich and royal, it doesn't mean that you're...' He grimaced.

Marco knew exactly what he meant. It was something that he hated himself, particularly in some of the people who liked hanging around his brother. He gave a mock braying laugh, and grimaced back. 'Pampered.'

Ethan seemed to relax at last. 'Yeah.'

'You were out there, too?'

Ethan shrugged. 'That's not important.'

'When did you get hit?'

Ethan's eyes narrowed. 'What makes you think I was hit?'

Marco nodded at his own arm and Ethan's leg. 'Different limb, same kind of pain.'

They shared a glance, and Marco knew that Ethan Hunter understood the rest of it. The frustration of being stuck here when your heart was back there.

'What have they done so far?' Ethan asked.

'Flushed my hand to clean it, put on a dressing. I take it you were the one who said not to suture my palm?'

'Yes. Can you feel anything in it still?'

'I'm not sure,' Marco admitted. 'The pain's gone into a blur.'

'Was it just glass, or is there anything else I need to know about?'

'Glass, mainly. Maybe a bit of dirt. But Herrera cleaned me up.'

Ethan nodded. 'Glass isn't going to show up brilliantly in radiography. I need to give you a CT scan to make sure all the glass is out and nothing else is lurking in there, and then I'll do the op.'

The scan seemed to take for ever. But finally Ethan Hunter was satisfied.

'No more glass. Good. OK, what I'm going to do is open up the wound so I can find the cut ends of your tendon, and then I'm going to stitch them back together. I'll put a splint on to protect the repair. Your skin's a mess, so you might need plastics—we'll see what it looks like when your hand's healed. And you'll need physio to get that hand working properly again.'

'Right. So how long will I be in the clinic?'

Ethan looked thoughtful. 'This happened nearly twelve hours ago and you've flown a long way. I want you in here for the next twenty-four hours so I can keep an eye on the repair. Theoretically, then you could go home. But, given who you are and the fact that you'll have the press hounding you all the way between your place and here when you come in for treatment...' He rolled his eyes. 'And we can certainly do without them hanging round outside and getting in the way while they wait for a glimpse of you.'

Marco could do without that, too. 'I don't want the press knowing I'm in England. If the story blows, then I might not be able to resume my tour of duty. It'll put my men at risk.' The ones that were left. The ones that hadn't been killed, thanks to his wrong judgement call.

Ethan nodded. 'Then you're better off staying here for a while. You'll need to see the hand therapist in any case.'

Marco frowned. 'But if I do go home after a few days, can't the hand therapist come to me?'

Ethan gave him a look that said very clearly, *Stop being a spoiled rich prince.* 'You're not her only patient.'

'Of course. Sorry. Patience isn't one of my...um...virtues.'

That earned him half a grin.

'Thank you. For sorting this out.'

Ethan shrugged. 'You don't need to thank me.'

Marco knew why he'd said it. 'Because it's your job,' he said quietly. 'That's what you did out there, too.'

Ethan turned away so Marco couldn't read the expression in his eyes—which in itself told Marco a lot. He'd seen that a few times before, in other people. So he was pretty sure that something had happened out there and Ethan Hunter didn't want to think about it.

'I need to get you in the operating theatre,' Ethan said. 'I'll do the repair under a general anaesthetic because it's fairly complex. It should take about an hour; though it might be longer if I find more damage once I open up your hand.'

'I'd rather not be out cold.'

Ethan rolled his eyes. 'OK, Zorro, if you want to be a hero.'

'Zorro?' Marco narrowed his eyes at him.

Ethan didn't look away or flinch; he clearly wasn't fazed by who Marco was.

'OK,' Marco said, 'I admit I learned to fence at school, and I did some training with the Sirmontane international fencing team.' Not that he was going to boast about the gold medal he'd won. He didn't need to score points with Hunter.

Ethan shrugged. 'I picked the right name for you, then. Probably that's what your men call you when they don't think you can hear them.'

For the first time in what felt like half a lifetime, Marco heard himself laugh. 'Yeah, probably. OK. If you need me out totally, then fine. Do what you have to. But make it quick.'

'Is this your sword arm?' Ethan asked.

'No. It's my fret hand.'

'You play guitar, too?' Ethan feigned a yawn. 'You're such a cliché, Zorro. Do you dance flamenco as well?'

'Flamenco's dull. I prefer tango.' Marco waited a beat. 'You get better sex after a tango.'

Ethan grinned. 'Probably just as well you won't be playing guitar for a while.' Then he sobered. 'Don't flirt with my female staff, Zorro. Any of them.'

'As if I would,' Marco said, enjoying himself now. He had a feeling that he and Ethan Hunter could be friends. Scratchy friends, maybe. But still friends. Because they each understood where the other was coming from.

Another busy day ahead, Becca thought as she walked up the steps to 200 Harley Street. And that was just how she liked it.

Or maybe not, she thought, as she walked into the reception area to find the clinic's Head of PR in a smooch with her new husband.

'Put the surgeon down, Lexi,' she said with a smile.

'Very funny.' Lexi gave Iain a last kiss and waved him off to his consulting room. 'Actually, Becca, you're just the woman I wanted to see.'

'Oh, yes?' Becca asked carefully. Usually this meant that Lexi was planning a PR campaign and wanted to talk the staff into doing something crazy. If Lexi had been anyone else, Becca would have made a polite murmur and avoided her, but Lexi was one of the few people she'd grown close to. Not quite close enough to confide in her about the past, but she was the nearest Becca had to a friend.

'I wanted to give you the heads-up on our new patient. Well, he's going to be yours. He's in Theatre with Ethan right now.' Lexi shepherded Becca towards her office. 'He's a bit high-profile—'

'So we need to keep everything under wraps.' Becca rolled her eyes. She was familiar with the drill. 'Got it.'

'I know you're the soul of discretion—but I wouldn't be doing my job properly if I didn't dot all the *I*s and cross all the *T*s,' Lexi pointed out gently.

'I know.' Becca smiled at her. 'Sorry. I guess I got out of the wrong side of bed this morning. So tell me about my patient.'

'A prince, no less.'

Becca wasn't that impressed, knowing that the clinic had an A-list clientele. 'What's he in for?'

'Flexor tendon. He was injured on a tour of duty, so that's another reason we want it kept under the media's radar.'

'A soldier prince?' Despite herself, Becca was intrigued.

'Young, tall, dark and handsome,' Lexi intoned. 'Prince Charming.'

A heartbreaker, then. Becca had met the type before. And been stupid enough to get her own heart broken by one, at a time when she'd still been dragging her life back out of the gutter.

Most of the women at the children's aid camp in South Africa had fallen under Seb's spell; but, knowing that men couldn't be trusted not to hurt you, Becca had avoided Seb like the plague. She'd been so determined to stay in the safety of her shell. But Seb had been patient. He'd made her feel special, had spent time talking to her about everything under the sun. And finally she'd relaxed with him and let him bring her out of herself. In the process, she'd fallen deeply in love with him. Enough to give herself to him. She'd even let herself dream of a future with him…

And then he'd left. Without even saying goodbye. He'd abandoned her. And the lesson had been branded on her heart: the only person she could ever really rely on was herself. Which was why she'd kept people at arm's length and dedicated herself to her career ever since.

Lexi frowned. 'Are you all right, Becca?'

Wild horses wouldn't drag the truth from her. 'Sure.' She faked a smile.

Luckily it was convincing enough, because Lexi continued, 'Even covered in mud, and looking as if he hasn't slept for days, our prince is sex on a stick.'

Becca groaned. 'And here's you married for about five seconds. Shouldn't you still be in the disgustingly loved-up stage, too busy to notice other men?'

'I'm married, not blind.' Lexi grinned. 'And don't tell Iain I said that.'

Becca just laughed. 'Right. I have patients to see. Catch you later.'

After the operation, Marco woke in the recovery room. It was warm and comfortable and he wanted to go back to sleep.

Except then he threw up. Violently.

'OK. We've got you.' Gentle hands wiped his face clean and helped him sit up.

'I'm sorry,' he said to the nurse.

'Don't worry. It happens all the time.'

Right at that moment, Marco was really grateful for her kindness.

'You're round, then?' Ethan asked, coming over to him.

'Uh-huh.' And his mouth felt disgusting. 'Did it work?'

'We'll see.'

'My arm feels numb and floppy.' Which was enough in itself to make him panic. And it was at that point that he noticed it was propped up on pillows. 'Does this mean I can't use it?'

'It's completely normal for your arm to feel numb and floppy after an op. And the pillows are there to support your arm and keep it elevated—that controls any potential swelling. I want your arm up at shoulder level and your hand above your heart, and you need to use pillows to support your hand when you sleep,' Ethan said.

'Got it.' Marco still felt groggy. 'Though you might have to remind me again tomorrow. I'm not sure how much of what you're saying now is going to stay in my head.'

'Sure.' Ethan paused. 'When the anaesthetic wears off, it will be painful. So don't be a martyr, Zorro. Take the painkillers my team offers you.'

Marco had the distinct feeling that Ethan was talking from experience. What had happened to him in Afghanistan? Had he lost someone—a member of his team, or someone he loved? Did he blame himself for it, the way Marco blamed himself for losing some good men? Had he not taken painkillers as a way of punishing himself?

'So when can I use my arm?' Marco asked.

'The short answer is, you can't. If you try to use that hand before your tendons have healed fully, the tendons will split apart. And, apart from the fact that I don't like having to repeat work, a second repair won't be as effective as the first.'

Marco absorbed this. 'How long do the tendons take to heal?'

'A couple of months.'

Marco stared at him in disbelief. 'No way. You're kidding.'

'And that's only for using your hand for *light* activities. You drive a motorbike?'

'Car,' Marco said.

'Good. That'll probably be OK in a couple of months. A motorbike would take a bit longer.'

'Mountain bike?'

Ethan shook his head. 'Sports you can do a month after that. And then maybe you can start to do heavy activities, as long as you haven't had any problems with scar tissue.'

Marco stared at him, horrified. He couldn't possibly be serious? But Ethan wasn't smiling. 'So basically you're saying I take at least three months off and be a penpusher?' Do a safe job while his men faced all the danger. Be a spoiled prince, leading safely from well behind the lines. That *so* wasn't who he was. He sighed. 'That really doesn't sit well with me.'

'Tough. It takes as long as it takes.' Ethan shrugged. 'Don't get that splint wet. You'll need to bag it completely and tape the bag to your arm if you want a shower or bath. Swimming's definitely out—and you don't take that splint off until I tell you or your physiotherapist tells you. Which is probably a month from now, minimum.'

The more Marco heard, the less he liked. 'No exercise. That's not good. I'm going to lose muscle mass.' And fitness. Which would delay his return to the army even longer.

'No push-ups, no pull-ups, no burpees, no weight training,' Ethan said.

Oh, great. That was pretty much his workout routine out of the window. And it definitely confirmed that Ethan Hunter had trained in the army.

'Running? Any form of cardio?' he asked, trying not to let the desperation show in his voice.

Ethan shook his head. 'You need to use your arm muscles to hold your arm across your chest with your hand to the opposite shoulder. So you'll be off balance for running or using an elliptical.' He shrugged. 'No fencing, either, Zorro.'

Because with one arm strapped up he wouldn't be able to balance himself properly. 'So that's a no.' Marco rolled his eyes. 'I'm going to go insane.'

'Very probably, Zorro,' Ethan agreed. 'No horse-riding, no guitar-playing, no...'

'No sex?'

Ethan grinned. 'Not if you insist on being on top, no.'

'I think I hate you,' Marco said.

'No, you don't. I fixed your hand. And I'm good at my job.'

'You'd better be, Clavo,' Marco said through gritted teeth.

Ethan raised an eyebrow. 'Clavo?'

'It's Spanish for Spike.' Marco gestured with his free hand. 'Face. Attitude. The thing you use to cut people open.'

'Technically, that would be a lancet.'

Marco shrugged. 'Clavo will do. You're sure my hand's fixed?'

'Yes. Unless you do something stupid, like try to use your hand too early.'

Marco groaned. 'You're telling me that I'm going to be stuck here for a whole *month*?'

'I didn't say that. I said you'll wear the splint for a month. You'll have physio every single day. Several sessions. I want to make sure there aren't any contractures to your palm, so you need to do stretches and gentle work. You do what the hand therapist says, when she says it, and nothing else. Got it?'

'Because, if I don't, then my hand's gone for good.'

'That's about it.'

So he had no choice. 'OK. I'll do what you say. And the hand therapist,' he added with a grimace.

'Good. Think yourself lucky it wasn't a severed thumb, Zorro. I would've had to replace it maybe with your big toe, and stick leeches all over you.'

Marco gave Ethan a reluctant smile. 'Remind me, which century is this again?'

Ethan laughed. 'I'll have you know leech saliva is the best anticoagulant ever—it's a hundred times more effective than heparin.'

'So I've got nothing to do except pace this room?' And, for the umpteenth time, wish to hell he'd out-thought the enemy. Wish his men hadn't died. Wish he'd managed to get them *all* to safety.

'Like a caged tiger,' Ethan agreed. He paused. 'There's a gym in the basement. It's really for the staff, but patients can use it.'

'I thought you just said I couldn't run or do weights?'

'You can't. The treadmill and elliptical are both out of bounds, ditto all the free weights and the machines.'

'Right.' Everything he was most likely to use. 'Which leaves me what, precisely?'

'The static bike,' Ethan said. 'And *don't* use your arms.'

That was Marco's idea of tedious. A proper bike in the mountains, yes, with steep inclines and rough terrain to challenge him; a static bike, even if it had programmes to change the resistance, wouldn't challenge him at all. 'Great,' he said, curling his lip.

'You can do walking lunges,' Ethan said. 'But that's

bodyweight only. Just to be clear, that means not having a bar across your traps, and no using dumb-bells, even with your good hand. Got it?'

'Got it.' Marco rolled his eyes again. 'Marvellous.'

'And you can do squats—again, bodyweight only, with a stability ball against your back.'

'What? Like a total novice?' Marco asked in disgust.

'No, like someone who's going to have one arm strapped up so his balance is going to be out and he's not going to be stupid enough to risk damaging his tendons again before they heal. You cross your other arm across your chest like this—' Ethan demonstrated '—and at least this way you can keep your core strong.'

Which was something, Marco supposed. Bodyweight exercises. 'Floorwork?' he asked.

'No. But you can do sit-ups on the stability ball.'

Marco couldn't bring himself to say anything.

'It's better than nothing at all,' Ethan said, and there was a brief flare of sympathy in his eyes.

'I guess.' But Marco was pretty sure that this next month was going to be the longest of his life.

Becca pulled herself out of the pool and squeezed the water from her shoulder-length hair before padding through to the showers. One of the things she loved about working at the Hunter Clinic was the pool in the basement; a swim after work always got the knots out of her muscles and her head in the right place before she headed for her stint at the rehab clinic.

On her way out of the building, she glanced through the glass doors of the gym. There was a man doing lunge walks down the length of the gym; his back was to her, but given the evidence she could see of a strapped-up arm he was clearly one of the patients.

Dark hair, tall, just like Seb...

Her heart skipped a beat.

Stupid.

It had been years since she'd last seen Seb. *Years.* It was about time she put him out of her head and stopped thinking about him every time she saw a tall, dark-haired man. Particularly as he'd made it very clear that he hadn't returned her feelings. He'd left the children's aid camp in South Africa without so much as a word to her. *Dump and run.*

'Get over it, Becca,' she told herself sharply. 'You've got a new life now. And you don't need a man to make it complete.' Besides, she had work to do. Somewhere she was needed.

Shaking herself, she walked up the stairs to the reception area and out into Harley Street.

Over the next couple of days, Marco was thoroughly bored. He tried to be charming to the nurses who came to check on him, but he hated all of this. Being fussed over. Smothered. Suffocated.

Even the gym wasn't a respite. Yes, it meant he could still work out. Of sorts. But he would have been much happier using the top-of-the-range free weights available, lifting until he'd reached his maximum one rep and then pushing himself just that little bit more. Doing a novice type programme just wasn't satisfying. The only reason he'd been able to keep himself in check was the fear of rupturing the repair work on his tendons and being permanently without the use of his left hand. Three months would be tough enough. For the rest of his life would be unbearable.

'You hate this, don't you, Zorro?' Ethan asked when he dropped in to see Marco at the end of the day.

'Sitting here, being useless, when I know I'm needed elsewhere?' Marco scowled. 'Wouldn't you?'

'It's not the easiest thing to deal with,' Ethan agreed. 'You just have to learn to be patient.'

'Is that what you did, Clavo?' Marco asked.

'Just do as I say,' was the level response.

'So you didn't.'

Ethan shrugged. 'This isn't about me; it's about you.'

'I hate this,' Marco admitted. 'I'm used to doing things. Not just sitting here. And your gym is pure torture. All the things I want to use and can't.'

'Patience,' Ethan counselled.

Marco just scowled at him.

'Let's have a look at your hand.' Ethan inspected it, then smiled. 'Good news, Zorro. You get to meet your physio tomorrow morning.'

'So I can start exercising my hand?'

'You do,' Ethan said, 'everything she tells you. And no more than that.'

'Or I'm risking permanent damage. Yeah, yeah. You've already told me.' Marco took a deep breath. Damn. He was being rude again, and the doctor meant well. 'Sorry.'

'Frustration. It gets all of us at some point. Don't worry about it. See you tomorrow, Zorro.'

'*Hasta luego*, Clavo.' Marco sketched a salute with his right hand, and both men laughed wryly.

Becca was still thinking about what Lexi had told her about her new patient. Prince Charming. *Ha.* She'd met men like him before. The last time she'd made the mistake of falling for charm she'd learned the lesson well. In a way, she supposed that Seb had done her a favour. He'd left her at a crossroads. One way had led back to addiction, trying to wash away the pain with vodka—making her mother's mistakes all over again. The other way led to working hard and making the best future she could—

for herself, because Becca knew that she was the only one she could really rely on.

She'd made the right choice, and she wasn't going back.

Ethan had said that the Prince was bored. So no doubt he'd be super-charming to her, wanting a distraction from his situation. Fine. He could be as charming as he liked. She'd be sweet and charming back, for the sake of the clinic. But she'd also make very sure that there was a professional distance between them, because she had no intention of being the Prince's personal distraction.

The next morning couldn't come fast enough for Marco's liking. Even though he knew that 'morning' could mean technically anything from one second after midnight until one second to noon.

At last Ethan strolled in to Marco's room followed by a woman in a white coat.

'Zorro, I've got someone you're dying to meet.' He smiled. 'Becca, I'd like you to meet—'

The woman in the white coat stepped to the side and stared at Marco. 'Seb,' she cut in, her voice a hoarse whisper, and all the colour drained from her face.

CHAPTER TWO

'NO, THIS IS Marco—Prince Marco of Sirmontane,' Ethan said.

Prince? What? The man definitely hadn't been a prince when Becca had known him in South Africa at the children's aid camp. He'd called himself Seb. Nothing more. No surname, no nothing. And she hadn't asked for any more details because she'd had her own secrets to hide and hadn't wanted to trade them.

At least he looked as shocked as she felt. That was one thing.

'Becca. I didn't know you were a hand therapist,' he said.

'I didn't know you were a prince,' she said, a little more tartly than she'd intended. Bad move. She didn't want him to know that it bothered her.

'You know each other?' Ethan asked, looking surprised.

Oh, yes. In the Biblical sense, too. 'You could say that.' Though it turned out she hadn't really known Seb—Marco—at all.

No wonder he'd left without a word. He was a prince, not an ordinary guy, and obviously he'd just been slumming it at the aid camp—something to do between finishing university and starting whatever it was that princes

were supposed to do. Which made her relationship with
him worth even less than she'd thought.

And how the press would dine out on that if they knew.
A girl from the wrong side of the tracks, a girl who'd been
hooked on vodka and E, a girl who'd almost ended up in
the gutter…and she'd had a fling with a prince.

'Becca—a quick word?' Ethan said, gesturing to the
door of Prince Marco's—she couldn't think of him as just
Seb any more—room.

She went outside into the corridor with her boss.

'Clearly there's history here. Would you prefer someone
else to treat Prince Marco?' Ethan asked gently.

Yes, she would. She didn't want to treat the boy she'd
fallen in love with one dreamy summer. The boy who'd
played guitar to her under the stars and sung songs of love
in a language she didn't know. But she'd seen the emotion
in his face and known exactly what the words meant. The
boy who'd made her feel so special—and then left without
a single word, letting her dreams crash down round her.

But that was an emotional response. And Becca didn't
do emotional any more. She'd promised never to let herself
get in a vulnerable state again. Yet, two seconds after seeing Seb for the first time in seven years, she was a mess.
In shock that the past had come back to haunt her. Trying to process just how many lies she'd fallen for. Trying
to get her head round the fact that Seb—the man she'd
thought had been an ordinary boy—had actually been a
prince in disguise.

With an effort, she pulled herself back into professional
mode. 'I'm the hand specialist. It's my job to treat him.'

'Not if it's going to be a problem for you.'

She liked the fact that her boss was standing up for her.
Having someone in her corner felt good; it was something
she'd never known, growing up. But it also wasn't fair to
lean on Ethan and let him make excuses for her. Seb—

Marco—whatever he wanted to call himself—was a patient here. Given that he was royalty, no doubt he was only here because of the reputation of the Hunter Clinic. And Becca wasn't going to let any unprofessional behaviour on her part do anything to tarnish that reputation.

'It's not a problem, Ethan,' she fibbed. 'But thank you.'

'Sure?' he checked.

'Sure.'

'So just how *do* you know each other?' Ethan asked.

'We both worked at a children's aid camp. Years ago. I was still a student. He'd just finished university.' If that was true. For all she knew, that could have been another lie. She flapped a dismissive hand. 'It's not important.'

Ethan's eyes narrowed slightly. 'OK. But if treating him does turn out to be a problem just talk to me and I'll get someone else in to cover his case.'

'Thank you. But it'll be fine,' Becca said. Prince Marco wasn't going to break her heart again.

How could you break something that was already broken?

'I guess I owe you an apology,' Marco said when Becca walked back into the room.

'Why?' Becca asked. For being yet another man who'd used her and broken her heart? As if a European prince could give a damn about how an unimportant girl from an obscure family felt.

He grimaced. 'You know why.'

And of course now she was expected to make it easy for him. Be gracious about it. Or maybe she'd just act cool and casual, as if their summer fling had been just as unimportant to her as it had obviously been to him. 'There's nothing to apologise for,' she said, hoping that she sounded a lot more dismissive than she felt.

'I didn't tell you who I was, back then.'

'No.' She knew it would be hypocritical of her to be mad at him for that. She'd kept her own past a total secret—from everyone else at the camp as well as him. And nobody here at the Hunter Clinic knew about that part of her life, either.

'But I didn't lie to you completely. My name's Marco Sebastian Enrique Guillermo García.'

'Uh-huh.' Becca tried to maintain a semblance of cool. Though right at that moment she was remembering her first introduction to Seb, the guy who was to lead her team at the aid camp. She'd been nineteen and he'd been twenty-one, just graduated from university—well, unless he'd lied about his age as well. And Seb had been the most gorgeous man she'd ever laid eyes on. Tall, dark and handsome, with soulful eyes and a voice like melted chocolate, just a hint of a Southern Mediterranean accent. All the girls at the camp had been in love with him, and when he'd smiled at Becca she simply hadn't stood a chance. She'd fallen for him almost the second she'd met him.

She'd fought the attraction at first, knowing that men couldn't be trusted to do anything else but hurt you; but Seb had been patient with her. Gentle. He'd talked to her, skilfully drawn her out of her shell. It had amazed her that, despite the fact he could've had his pick of all the girls at the camp, he'd actually chosen *her*.

Fast forward seven years to now. There were shadows beneath those beautiful eyes—a combination of exhaustion and pain over the last few days, she'd guess—but Prince Marco was still the most gorgeous man she'd ever seen. And now he was a man, not a boy. The youthfulness had gone from his face, and he'd filled out from being a tall and slightly skinny youth to having hard, perfect musculature.

And his mouth… It still promised sin. The ultimate temptation. A mouth she could remember giving her almost unbearable pleasure. It would be oh, so easy to let herself act on the old attraction.

Well, she was just going to have to resist that urge, because the likes of him were definitely not for the likes of her. And she wasn't stupid enough to jeopardise her career for one of the few sweet memories of her past. She'd worked way too hard for that.

'My grandfather's called Sebastian,' he continued. 'I was named partly after him. So it made sense to use his name—one of my middle names.'

'What was wrong with calling yourself Marco?'

'It would've made it too easy for the press to make the link,' he said. 'And I didn't want everyone thinking that I was just some bored aristocrat slumming it.'

'Weren't you?' she asked, before she could stop herself.

'No,' he said softly. 'I wanted to make a difference.'

She could almost believe him.

Except... 'You left without a word.'

He sighed. 'I was called back to the Palace. My grandfather was ill. It would've been too complicated to explain.'

'And you couldn't have told me that you'd been called home because of a sick family member? You were *that* paranoid about the connections being made?'

'I didn't say that all my decisions have been the best ones—or the right ones,' he said, and looked wryly at his strapped-up hand. 'Or I wouldn't have this.'

'What happened?' she asked.

'Shrapnel. Well, glass,' he said. 'It severed a tendon.'

Which was pretty much as she'd been briefed. Patient: male, late twenties, royal, soldier, severed flexor tendon, needs physio work to regain mobility and movement in his hand.

The last thing she'd expected was for it to be the man

who'd broken her heart to the point that she'd sworn off relationships for good and focused on nothing but her career.

Which was what she should be doing right now. Professional was good: it would put some much-needed distance between them. 'Ethan said the repair was a success.
So now it's my job to get your hand mobile and working
properly again.'

'Is it going to be a problem, Becca?' he asked. 'Working with me?'

She shrugged. 'You're a patient, Your Royal Highness.
This is my job.'

Was it her imagination, or had she seen a flicker of hurt
in his eyes just then?

Well, tough. He'd hurt her. Badly. And, besides, she
was pretty sure it was his ego that was hurt and nothing
else. He might think of himself as Prince Charming, but
she had absolutely no intention of playing Cinderella. Or
fawning adoringly over him. She'd be cool and calm and
professional, and treat him just as she would any other patient. With care and kindness, and just a little bit of necessary detachment.

'You can drop the "Royal Highness" bit,' he said.

'What would you like to be called today?' The snippy
question was out before she could stop it.

He sighed. 'I guess I deserve that. Call me Marco. And
I hope I can still call you Becca.'

Oh, help. The way he said her name. That slight trace
of a Spanish accent, so incredibly sexy. It made her knees
buckle.

Resist, she reminded herself. This was a job. He was a
patient, and she had to treat him with the utmost professionalism. And he was also a prince. They had no possible chance of a future together, and she wasn't going to
wreck her career for just a fling.

'I guess. May I have a look at your hand?' she asked.

He indicated his strapped-up arm with his free hand. 'Help yourself.'

Gently, she removed the strapping and took the hand strap off the splint.

Seven years.

She'd changed. Back then Becca had still been a girl. Nineteen years old, a little shy. Beautiful.

Now she was all woman.

Even with her soft curves hidden beneath a sexless starched white coat, with that glorious auburn hair tamed back in a ponytail and those beautiful green eyes hidden behind wire-rimmed glasses, Becca Anderson was gorgeous.

Worse still, Marco knew what it felt like to kiss her. How her body responded to his when they made love. How her breathing changed just before she climaxed.

Ah, hell.

This was so inappropriate it was untrue.

Becca Anderson was his hand therapist, and Ethan Hunter had told him not to flirt with any of the female staff at the clinic.

Ha.

Flirting wasn't the half of it.

What would Ethan Hunter say if he knew just how far things had gone between Marco and Becca all those years ago?

Marco had to get a grip.

Which was half the problem; right now his left hand didn't have a grip. That was what Becca was going to fix.

And he needed to think of her as a medic. Not as a woman.

In fact, he needed not to think of her at all. Since he'd left her behind in South Africa he hadn't let himself think about her. Well, apart from the day after the doctor had

confirmed that his grandfather had come through the heart
bypass operation safely and would be just fine. Marco
had gone back to the children's aid camp, then. For her.

Except she'd left, two days previously, with no forwarding address.

The one girl who'd seen him for himself instead of as a
prince. Who'd made his summer feel full of magic. Who'd
made him fall in love with her shy, gentle sweetness.

He'd lost her. And he hadn't been able to track her
down, even with the help of a private detective; somehow
she'd managed to vanish completely.

And all sorts of things could have happened in the last
seven years. He glanced swiftly at her left hand. There
was no wedding ring, but that didn't mean that she wasn't
committed. She might not wear rings to work, given that
she was a hand therapist. She could have a family, now.
A child.

Besides, she'd made it very clear how she regarded
him now. *'You're a patient, Your Royal Highness. This
is my job.'*

So he needed to stop thinking about her, right now, and
do what he'd done for the last seven years: keep himself
busy at work, and then play just as hard with a string of
totally unsuitable women. Not let himself think about the
girl he'd left behind.

'You've made a real mess of this,' she said, examining
his palm. 'How did it happen?'

'Hunter didn't tell you?'

'Soldier, severed tendon.' She shrugged. 'So I'd guess
it happened in action?'

'My windscreen was blown out. I put up my hand to
protect my eyes.'

'No wonder you severed a tendon. You're lucky it didn't
sever an artery and you bled out on the field. Or it could've
severed your whole hand.'

'I know.'

Not that it made him feel any better. He'd been over and over what had happened the last two days and nights. Thinking about what he could have done differently. What he *should* have done differently. But it didn't change what had happened. Or do anything to lessen the guilt. He'd phoned every single wife, every single mother, and apologised for not taking better care of their loved ones while they were under his leadership. They'd all been grateful that he'd phoned, amazed that a prince would bother to share his memories of their husbands and sons. They'd cried. They'd even thanked him.

And it hadn't made a scrap of difference. He still hated himself for making those mistakes. For not bringing all his men safely home.

'Others weren't so lucky.' He sighed. 'Those who were injured have the best possible care. Those who…' There was a lump in his throat and he couldn't say the rest of it.

'Marco, you were in a war zone. People get injured. They die. You can't blame yourself for that.'

'They were acting under my orders.'

She shrugged. 'I take it other people were injured, or killed, following the orders of someone else?'

'Well—yes,' he admitted.

'And do you blame the officers for those deaths?'

He sighed. 'I guess not.'

'Then don't blame yourself. If it hadn't been your orders, it would've been someone else's. I think you're suffering enough without adding guilt to it. You just did your job, Marco.'

How had she become so wise? he wondered.

To his relief, she changed the subject back to his injury. 'The first few days of physio, you're just going to do some gentle exercises. These will help to prevent your tendons becoming stuck in your scar tissue.'

'Stuck?'

'Then Ethan would have to operate again. And the outcome might not be so good second time round.'

'Right.' He paused. 'I'm under orders to do what you tell me.'

She raised an eyebrow. 'And a prince takes orders from ordinary people?'

Score one to her. 'The rule is, medical orders outrank military orders.'

'What about royal orders?'

He shrugged. 'As far as I know, royal orders from Sirmontane only work inside my country. And right now I'm in your country, not mine.'

'Touché.' She sighed. 'Sorry. I don't mean to snipe at you.'

'But I lied to you about who I was. I can understand you being angry about that.'

'It's not so much that you didn't tell me who you were, it's the fact that you left without a word.'

'So did you,' he pointed out.

She blinked. 'I did not. You were the one who left, not me.'

'But you left the camp without a forwarding address.'

She frowned. 'How do you know that?'

'Because I came back for you when my grandfather pulled through his operation,' he said.

Her cheeks went pink. 'I didn't know that. And, anyway, what happened between us was obviously just the equivalent of a holiday fling. It was over *years* ago, and we're both very different people now.'

He caught her gaze and held it. Was it over? The attraction was still there, for him. And the way her pupils grew slightly larger when she looked at him made him think that maybe, just maybe, it was the same for her. 'Are we?' he asked softly.

'Yes.' She looked away. 'I worked hard to get this job. I'm not going to let anything put that in jeopardy. You're in London for a few days—maybe a few weeks, until your tendon is healed enough—and then you'll be back to doing whatever it is princes do.'

He raised an eyebrow. 'Which is?'

'How should I know?'

She sounded ever so slightly flustered.

Interesting.

Was it seeing him again? Had it brought back memories? Did she remember what it felt like to kiss him? Was she, like him, tempted to find out if it was still the same between them?

'And it's none of my business what you do,' she said.

'I was in Afghanistan,' he said softly. 'There's a media blanket in place to keep my regiment safe. They don't report anything about me, so my team isn't targeted. Nobody knows I was hurt out there, and nobody knows I'm here. Well, apart from my team back at the base, my family, and the clinic staff here.'

'And you want to keep it that way.'

He nodded. 'To keep my team safe. I guess the media will find out eventually that I'm here.'

'Not from me or anyone else at the clinic, if that's what you're asking. There is such a thing as patient confidentiality. And we're very strict about that, I can assure you,' she said crisply.

'Thank you.' He took her hand with his good hand, and squeezed it lightly before letting her go again.

Mistake.

Because his body remembered the feel of her skin against his. Intimately. And it reacted instantly.

Oh, hell.

Just as well she wasn't looking at anything other than his busted hand. He took a deep breath, willing his body to calm down. This wasn't what was supposed to happen. He was supposed to be following her instructions, not lusting after her.

'Now, you need to do these exercises every hour,' she said.

All businesslike and bossy. And Marco rather liked this new side of Becca. She was professionally confident, rather than the shy teenager she'd been.

'You need to keep the splint on, but you can take the hand strap off while you're doing the exercises. You start with three reps of this one.'

'Three reps?' He smiled. 'You sound like a gym instructor.'

She frowned. 'Stay out of the gym. Any pressure on this hand while it's healing and you'll be looking at permanent disability.'

'I've already had that talk from Ethan. Though he says I'm allowed in the gym to do sit-ups and squats with a stability ball, provided I keep my body balanced and don't use my left hand.'

'That figures,' she said. 'Bodyweight exercises only.'

'And walking lunges.'

She went pink again. 'So was that you in the gym, the other day?'

She'd recognised him without seeing his face clearly? That was even more interesting. 'I didn't see you there.'

'I wasn't there. Just passing the glass door on my way out of the pool. And I assume Ethan told you to stay out of the pool?'

'And put a bag over my arm when I have a bath or shower so I don't get the splint wet. Yup.' He looked at her. 'But I could spectate at the pool. Do you swim a lot?'

'It's in my schedule.'

So she wasn't going to let him push her into telling him anything about herself. Interesting.

'It's a cliché, you know,' he said, enjoying himself.

'What is?'

'Having a temper to go with your hair colour.'

'I don't have a temper.'

'Don't you, Becca?' he asked softly. 'Or are you just gentle with your husband and children?'

'My marital status is *my* business,' she said coolly.

Maybe, but at least now he knew what it was. If she'd actually been married she would've told him, to put him in his place. Or she would've turned into a proud *mamá* like his sister Arabella, ready to show off photographs of her children at the least excuse.

'Your first exercise, Your Royal Highness,' she said crisply. 'Use your right hand to curl each finger of your left hand down to the top of your palm.' She demonstrated with her own hand.

He couldn't help flinching as pain lanced through his hand.

'Did that hurt?' She didn't sound like a vengeful harpy. She sounded concerned. Caring. But in a professional capacity.

'A bit,' he admitted.

'Did you feel anything pull?'

'I don't think so.'

'Maybe,' she said, 'I need to massage your hand first, to warm up the muscles.' She frowned. 'I'd better warn you now that it might hurt a bit.'

'If it gets my hand working again and it means I can go back to work, then I don't care if it hurts,' he said. 'Do whatever you need to. I'm in your hands.'

She went very, very pink.

Yeah.

He could feel the heat rising in his body, too.

'Lie back with your palm upwards.' She sounded

slightly flustered and she was clearly making an effort to be professional.

OK. He'd behave. Even though what he really wanted to do right now was slide his good hand round the nape of her neck, draw her to him, and spend a very long time kissing her.

She pulled a chair round to the side of the bed. 'Tell me if anything hurts.'

Wild horses wouldn't drag that particular admission from him.

He closed his eyes as she massaged his hand. Yes, it did hurt; but at the same time it made his hand feel better. And he liked the feel of her skin against his. Warm. Gentle, yet firm at the same time. Soft. She was near enough for him to smell the light floral scent she wore. She'd always smelled of flowers in South Africa, he remembered. Roses.

With his eyes closed, and mercifully silent, Marco was a lot easier to deal with.

Maybe she ought to tell Ethan that she couldn't cope with her new patient. But then her boss might think less of her—and she'd worked damn hard for her job here. After South Africa she'd thrown all her energies into her studies, graduating with top marks and quickly gaining promotion at the hospital where she'd worked. She hadn't let any relationship get in her way.

Hadn't had another relationship since Marco, full stop.

Until today, that hadn't mattered. Work here and volunteering at the rehab clinic had been her life, and it was good. But seeing Marco again...it had brought everything back. The sheer passion he'd made her feel. The confidence his love had given her.

And then the bone-deep devastation when he'd abandoned her and she'd realised that he was yet another man who'd let her down.

OK. She could understand it a bit more, now she knew who he really was. Being in the public eye all the time must be draining and it would be hard to know who to trust, who would sell you out to the press.

But she would have kept his secrets.

Just as she'd kept her own. Nobody at the camp had known that she'd spent time in rehab at the age of sixteen. Nobody here knew about those things, either. The past was the past. OK, so she hadn't learned from her mother's mistakes, either with the drink or with the men she'd chosen. But she'd learned from her own mistakes. Really learned. She had no intention of repeating those mistakes ever again. No drink, no drugs, no men—and definitely no heartbreak.

'Better?' she asked when she'd finished massaging his hand.

'Better,' he agreed.

She took him through the first exercise again. 'Good. Now repeat.'

He was a fast learner; she didn't even have to talk him through it, the last time.

'Is that it?' he asked.

'Three reps,' she said. 'And now you do it again, but this time keep your fingers flexed. Use your muscles as you let go with your other hand.'

Again, he did exactly as she asked, and she didn't need to repeat the instructions.

'Good. Last time now,' she said. 'Touch your palm, just using the muscles of your left hand, and extend your fingers back so your fingernails touch the splint.'

He did as she'd asked him to do.

'OK. Now, is your wrist feeling stiff and awkward to move?' she asked.

'A bit,' he admitted.

'OK. Lift your hand up—' she demonstrated the movement '—and let it gently fall forward. Keep your fingers
relaxed. Good.' She gave him an encouraging and strictly
professional smile. 'Now, back the other way, still with
your fingers relaxed, so the back of your hand moves back
towards the splint. Better?'

'Better,' he said.

'Good. Last two—your shoulder and your elbow.
Stretch your arm above your head. Down. And again.'
She talked him through the shoulder stretch. 'Now, bend
and straighten your elbow. And again.'

When he'd done the last repetition of ten, she said, 'And
that's it for this session.'

'How often do I need to do this?' he asked.

Too often for her peace of mind, given that she was
going to be working with him. 'Hourly,' she said. 'So I'll
see you later.' Hopefully her common sense would be back
in charge before their next session.

'OK. And, Becca?'

'Yes?' She turned to face him. Mistake. Because he still
had that make-you-weak-at-the-knees smile.

'Thanks.'

'You're welcome,' she said, and fled.

When she got home from her session at the rehab centre
that night, Becca switched on her laptop and looked up
Prince Marco of Sirmontane on the internet.

There were lots of pictures of him with beautiful, eli-
gible woman—glittering socialites and A-list celebs. Models, actresses and singers. On a yacht at Monaco. At the
film festival in Cannes. Skiing in Sirmontane. He was
photographed with a different woman every time—and
Marco didn't even seem to have a particular type. Tall,
petite, slender, curvy, blonde, brunette, auburn...

The only requirement Marco seemed to have in his girlfriends was that they had two X chromosomes, she thought wryly.

All the gossip columns referred to him as the 'Playboy Prince' and speculated about who would be the woman to tame him. Unlike his much more serious older brother Ferdinand, who was first in line to the throne; Ferdinand was settled, engaged to Princess Marianna. The gossip columns described the older prince of Sirmontane as the perfect king-to-be.

Was that why Marco had thrown himself into his social life? Because he was only second in line always destined to live in his brother's shadow?

No, she didn't think so. Marco wasn't a spoiled brat or he wouldn't be a serving soldier. Besides, she knew that Ethan Hunter had little time for their A-list celeb clients, and yet she also knew that he dropped in to see Marco several times a day for a chat. Maybe they'd bonded over the fact that they both had a military career. But Ethan definitely wouldn't have bothered spending time with the Prince if Marco was shallow and vain and spoiled.

Prince Marco of Sirmontane was a puzzle.

And one that Becca needed to stay away from. For the sake of her own sanity.

CHAPTER THREE

ETHAN CAME IN to chat to Marco that evening and to check up on his hand. 'It's looking good, so far.' He paused. 'So how are you getting on with Becca, Zorro?'

'She's very good.' Marco raised an eyebrow. 'And bossy.'

Ethan smiled. 'Right, on both counts. That's why we hired her.' His smile faded. 'So how do you know her?'

'I worked at a children's aid camp in South Africa for a couple of months when I finished university, before I joined the army. She was there during the university summer holidays.'

Ethan gave him a narrow look. 'That's what she said.'

Marco shrugged. 'So you could say that we're old friends.'

'Such good friends, Zorro, that you didn't even tell her your real name?'

Marco sighed. 'Trust me, being a prince has its downsides. Half the time people don't see me; they see the money and the trappings that go with who I am. So I'm never sure whether people want to be friends with me for myself, or for what they think I might be able to do for them.'

Ethan nodded. 'That's the thing about being rich. Having socialites for parents.'

'You, too?' Marco asked.

Ethan gave him a rueful grimace.

'But you have a brother, right, Clavo? The one who's on honeymoon?'

'Yes.' Ethan sounded cagey.

Marco frowned. 'So you're not close.'

For a moment, he thought that he'd pried too hard and the surgeon was going to walk out. But then Ethan sighed. 'We have...issues.'

'That's tough,' Marco said. 'I'd be lost without Ferdy.'

'Your brother?'

Marco nodded. 'A lot of people think I should be jealous because he's first in line to the throne, but being the second son—the baby of the family, I guess, as our sister Bella's in the middle—means I get away with an awful lot more than he ever can. I can choose my own job, within reason. Ferdy's life is mapped out for him and he has no choice at all. He's the one with all the responsibility and the weight on his shoulders.' He lifted his chin. 'But I always have his back. *Always.* I would move the mountains of Sirmontane for him if he asked me. Even if my hand was still strapped up and I could only use one arm.'

'So you don't resent him being the eldest and the one everyone thinks is so wonderful?' Ethan asked, sounding curious.

Marco laughed. 'No. I guess I'm kind of glad it's not me. I wouldn't enjoy being king. It'd be like being boxed in. Obviously I'd do it if I had to, because it'd be my duty and I'd never let my family or my country down, but I'd hate it.' He shrugged. 'And, anyway, Ferdy *is* wonderful. He's one of the good guys, and I know if I was ever in trouble he'd be the first person I'd call.' He smiled. 'Ferdy understood why I needed to be on active service for our country, and he talked our mother round. If she had her way I'd be wrapped in cotton wool and not allowed out of the palace grounds. And Ferdy's the reason she's not here right now, smothering me to keep me safe and driving me nuts.'

'You're safe here,' Ethan pointed out. 'I know you have your bodyguard outside the door, but he also checked out our security system and he's happy with it. And nobody here will talk to the press.'

'I know, and it's appreciated.'

'OK. I'll let you get some rest. Oh, and Zorro…?'

Marco rolled his eyes. 'What?'

'Remember what I said. No flirting with my staff.'

Marco knew he was being warned off Becca.

The problem was the warning was too little, and way too late.

Breezy and light. That was how she had to be with Marco, Becca told herself as she walked to the clinic, the next morning. Brisk and breezy and light. Professional. Nothing in the slightest bit personal.

But it was so much easier said than done.

She'd spent seven years suppressing her feelings for him, seven years burying herself in study and hard work.

Yet that first time she'd seen him again it had been as if nothing had changed. As if she was still that young, naive girl in South Africa who'd fallen in love with a boy whose smile was full of sunshine.

But that wasn't who she was any more and he needed to realise that, too.

She nodded to the bodyguard outside Marco's room who, as usual, simply nodded back, and walked in, ready for the first physio session of the day. *Professional*, she reminded herself.

'Good morning. Did you have a comfortable night?'

'Yes, thank you.'

Marco was equally polite with her. Obviously he'd had

time to think about it and be sensible, too. Good. That would make it easier.

'How's your hand this morning?' she asked.

'A little sore,' he admitted.

Which might not be good. The last thing he needed now was an infection in the wound. 'Let me take a look.'

She sat down next to him and willed herself not to be affected by his nearness, to ignore that tangy sandalwood scent he wore, as she took his hand and released the strap on his splint so she could take a look at the wound.

But she then glanced at him and was lost. He was staring at her face almost as if he were trying to memorise it.

'Marco,' she said softly. 'Your *hand*.'

'Yes.' But now he was looking at her mouth. As if he remembered what it felt like against his. As if he wanted to kiss her again.

Oh, help.

Because now she wanted to trace the curve of his lower lip with the pad of her thumb. Feel how soft it was, how warm.

She never, ever behaved this unprofessionally with a patient. No matter how good-looking he was.

Then again, nobody had been as close to her as Marco. He was unlike anyone she'd ever met. There had been a time when she'd thought he could see into her soul.

And how stupid she'd been. How naive and pathetic.

With an effort, she pulled herself together. 'It's a little bit red. We need to keep an eye on that. I'll tell Ethan and see if he wants you to have antibiotics.' Gently, she put some aqueous cream on his palm and massaged his hand. 'Is that OK? Sore? Stinging?'

'It's fine. Better now,' he said softly, his voice a husky whisper.

This really wasn't fair. That accent, combined with that sexy, husky voice. It just blew her common sense away.

'I have another patient in fifteen minutes,' she said. 'We need to go through your exercises.'

'So you're not exclusively mine?'

She knew he was talking about the situation from a work point of view. Not personal. She dragged in a breath. 'No.'

'Uh-huh.'

He held her gaze for a moment, and she was pretty sure he knew what kind of effect he had on her. What kind of effect he had on most women, according to the gossip columns.

'You never said you were going to be a physiotherapist, Becca.'

'You never said you were a prince,' she pointed out.

'It was complicated.'

'How?'

He sighed. 'I wanted to be seen for *me* in South Africa. Not for my role. Using another name was the only way I could do that.'

It hadn't occurred to her before but, yes, people *would* see him firstly as a prince and secondly as a man. She could understand that.

Though he'd still hurt her. He'd been careless of her feelings. And that she couldn't forgive quite so easily.

He went through the first of the exercises she'd taught him and she watched the range of movement carefully, checking that the tendons were still working and hadn't stuck in the scar tissue.

'So what kinds of things do you treat?' he asked.

'Apart from people with tendon injuries like yours? All kinds of hand problems.' Talking to him about work made this easier. Gave her space. Stopped her doing something really stupid—like taking his hand and pressing a kiss into his poor, damaged palm. 'The Hunter Clinic does a lot of work with burns; as well as damaging skin, burns can damage nerves and I need to help with that and any post-op rehabilitation. I work with people who have carpal tunnel problems and RSI; not just on the physio side. Sometimes I do a site visit and I can recommend changes to the way a workstation is laid out, or alternative work methods.'

'So you prevent the problem happening in the first place?'

'Where I can, yes. Sometimes it's helping with sports injuries—I treat things such as ligament damage and skiers' thumb. Or maybe my patient has a progressive disease such as arthritis, which means their hands are painful and stiff. I can help them regain some mobility and movement in their hands, and work on pain management. I was thinking about doing an acupuncture course as well, so I can offer more than just a TENS machine or drugs for pain management.'

'Adding to your skills? Good idea.' He paused. 'What made you specialise in hands?'

She shrugged. 'The importance of touch, I guess.'

Wrong phrase—because now she was remembering touching him. Remembering the way he'd touched her, his hands caressing her; his touch had set her on fire.

'Making a difference,' he said.

Becca was hugely relieved that he wasn't able to read her mind. And now he'd given her another safe topic: *his* work. 'Like you—at least, I assume that's why you became a soldier.'

He nodded. 'I don't have the patience to be a medic and make a difference that way, but I'm good with systems— I learned that in South Africa. I can see ways to change infrastructures and make them work better for the people they're meant to help.'

'You were good at teaching, too,' Becca said, remembering. 'You were good with the kids.'

'I like children,' he said simply. 'They're straight-forward. No hidden agendas. You know where you are with them.'

That sounded heartfelt. She wouldn't have a clue what kind of pressure a prince would face, apart from having to live in the public eye so every single mistake would be picked up and magnified. But it sounded as if Marco was really weary of having to watch every single move and not knowing who was a friend and who was waiting for him to fail.

'You picked up their languages quickly,' she added, hoping to shift the conversation to something a little less painful for him.

'My parents always got me to learn a few basic phrases in the language of any visitors we had, so I could help make them feel at home,' he said. 'Not that I'm trying to boast, but it means I can greet people, say please and thank you and wish them a nice day in twenty different languages. And, actually, it's good to make that effort. I like seeing people relax and be themselves instead of trying to be something they think is expected of them.'

'Your English is perfect,' she said. 'I know nothing about Sirmontane—is English the official language of your country?'

'No—that's Spanish,' he said. 'Though I was educated in England.'

At one of the top public schools, she'd guess. Eton or Harrow or Marlborough. And then Oxford or Cambridge; the other thing she remembered from South Africa was that Marco was very, very bright. 'So tell me about Sir-montane.'

'It's on the Spanish border,' he said. 'It's a mountain-ous country—we don't have a coastline.'

'So it's cold?'

'In winter, it can be.' He smiled. 'Tourists come for the

skiing in the winter and for the lakes and the walking in the summer. We also have a thriving wine industry—it's hundreds of years old, from the days when monks used to let the wine mature in cisterns they'd hollowed out in the stone. And our dairy products are renowned. We have lots of cattle on mountainous pasture.' He grinned. 'I think our chocolate is better than Switzerland's, but then I guess I would say that.'

'Lizzie Hunter, our head nurse, is a total chocolate addict,' she said. 'Maybe you should get her to do a taste test. She'd give you an impartial opinion.'

'Don't *you* like chocolate?' he asked.

Oh, she did. But the idea of eating chocolate with Marco, being fed one morsel at a time—especially if he teased her, made her reach up to take the piece of chocolate between her lips...

She pulled herself together. 'I'm about to be late for my next patient. You're doing well. I'll see you in an hour to go through the whole lot again.' Swiftly and surely, she refastened the hand strap of his splint. 'See you later.'

Even as she left she knew how much she wanted to linger. It was probably just as well that she had an appointment with Mrs van der Zee to take her mind off Marco.

'Good morning. How are you today?' she asked as she ushered Mrs van der Zee into the treatment room.

'A little sore. But I know my Becca's going to make me feel better because you always do,' Mrs van der Zee said, patting her hand.

Gently, Becca removed the splint and examined the old lady's hand, mentally noting the changes since her last appointment. 'The swelling's definitely gone down, so I think that flare-up's over. Did you find wearing the splint at night helped you to cope better with the pain?'

The old lady nodded. 'Much better. And alternating the heat pack and ice pack helped, too.'

Ice for swelling and heat for comfort. 'I'm glad. Are you happy that we work on making your hands a little more mobile today?'

'Yes, that's fine.'

Becca massaged the old lady's sore hands, warming the muscles. She knew that you weren't supposed to have favourites, and she always gave her patients her best regardless of who they were, but Mrs van der Zee was special. Like the grandmother Becca had never had and always wanted: full of smiles and stories of the past.

'Let's start with your fingers,' she said. She talked the old lady through the exercise, showing her how to hold her hand so the fingers were straight and close together. 'Then I'd like you to bend the top and middle joints, keeping your knuckles straight. That's perfect. Now, slowly unroll them again, and we'll repeat it with the other hand.'

From there, she guided the old lady into making a loose fist while resting her hand, wrist and forearm on the tabletop.

'And now we'll work on your thumb,' she said. 'This first one will help you make the joint more stable.' She showed the old lady how to make her hand into a C-shape, as if she was holding a glass or a hand. 'And now we'll stretch it out.' She guided the old lady's hand into a neutral position. 'Try and touch the base of your little finger with the tip of your thumb.'

Mrs van der Zee tried several times and shook her head. 'It won't go that far, Becca.'

'With practice and time, it will,' Becca said. 'And you've done really well, so don't think you've failed. We know how far you can move your thumb now, and that's a really good baseline. We'll work to increase that range a little bit more every time.' She smiled at Mrs van der Zee. 'Last bit, now—we'll stretch your fingers.' Under Becca's guidance, Mrs van der Zee put her hand back in the starting position. 'Now make your first finger and thumb into an O shape.'

'I can do that,' Mrs van der Zee said with satisfaction.

'And now your middle finger.' Gently, Becca talked her through making the same movement with each finger. 'That's great. You're doing really well.'

'Is that it for today?'

'Nearly. Just the finger walking to go, and we're done. Put your hand flat on the table, palm down. That's perfect. Now, move your thumb away from your hand, keeping it in contact with the table. And now move your first finger towards it.'

Once the old lady had stretched each finger in turn and repeated the moves several times with both hands, Becca was satisfied.

'Lovely. You've worked really hard on that today, Mrs van der Zee. And if you try to go through that routine every morning, after you've massaged your hand, it'll make moving a lot more comfortable for you.'

'Thank you, dear.'

When Mrs van der Zee had left, Becca wrote up her notes, then glanced at her watch. Time to go back to Marco.

'How was your patient?' he asked as she walked into his room.

'That's confidential, I'm afraid,' she said with a smile.

'Of course.' He smiled back at her, then went through the arm and shoulder exercises she'd taught him.

She noticed this time that he winced when he lifted his arm above his head. 'Where does it hurt?' she asked.

'It doesn't hurt, exactly—my shoulder's a little stiff.' He looked resigned. 'I guess it's only to be expected with having a sling and my arm being held up like this.'

'Let me take a look,' Becca said, and gently took his arm out of the sling so she could remove his pyjama top.

The worst thing was it meant she was going to be skin to skin with him. Her fingers tingled where they touched him, and she felt her breathing going shallow.

Stop this, she told herself. *Think of him as just another patient. Be professional.*

But that tingle of desire wouldn't go away.

It was years since she'd last seen his naked, muscular back. Sculptors would fall over themselves to use him as a model.

And he was her patient.

Focus, Becca, she told herself sharply. *This is work.*

'Yes, your muscles do feel a bit tight. I'll loosen that up for you.'

Aqueous cream was the most unsexy stuff in the world. Plain, unscented, and easily absorbed by the skin. Not like oils, which would leave a sheen on the skin and then release a scent as it was warmed by body heat.

This was supposed to be a medical treatment.

She shouldn't be enjoying this anywhere near as much as she was.

And Marco was enjoying it, too. His breathing had changed; it was shallow, almost rasping. It had nothing to do with any kind of medical condition and everything to do with the connection between them, the burning need that sizzled as their skin touched.

He turned round and they looked at each other. His pupils were huge, and she was pretty sure that hers were the same. And that slash of colour across his cheekbones was echoed on hers.

Her mouth went dry, and she really couldn't help sliding the tip of her tongue between her lips to moisten them.

Marco leaned forward, slid his right hand to cup the nape of her neck, and brushed his mouth against hers. The kiss was light, gentle, dreamy—as if they were thousands of miles away from London, under a wide starry sky. Just as it had always been between them. And it felt as if fire-works were going off in her head.

'Becca,' he whispered when he broke the kiss.

She pulled away. 'Marco, we can't do this. You're my patient.'

He shrugged. 'I don't care.'

'I do,' she protested. 'I could get struck off for unpro-fessional conduct!'

'I'm not going to let that happen.'

Her lip curled. 'Right, and just because you're a prince you can order a professional body to believe that I haven't done anything against the rules? I don't think so.'

'We have unfinished business, Becca, and you know it.'

'I'm your hand therapist. You're my patient. You're in pain and you're vulnerable.'

'Yes, to the first, second and third. Absolutely not to the last,' he said crisply. 'My left hand might not be work-ing right now, but the rest of me is in full working order, I can assure you. I know what I'm doing, Becca. And I want you. I want to kiss you. Touch you. Make you feel the way I'm feeling right now.'

She dragged in a breath. *Oh, help.* She wanted him, too. Just as much.

But.

It was mad. A quick path to getting hurt again. How stupid of her to think that he wouldn't be able to break her heart a second time. Of course he could.

And would, if she didn't stop this right now. They didn't have a future. Couldn't have a future. He was a prince, and someone with her kind of past was totally unsuitable for him. The only thing he could offer her was a fling. Was that enough? Right now, she didn't think so.

She lifted her chin. 'I'm not going to be like the women you spend your time with.'

He frowned. 'What women?'

'I looked you up in the gossip columns,' she said.

He rolled his eyes. 'They're called gossip columns for a reason—the hacks write what they think their readers want to hear, and that can be a million miles away from the truth.'

'There were plenty of pictures of you escorting different women,' she pointed out.

'Which doesn't mean I slept with them or even kissed them.'

'Who you sleep with,' she said coolly, 'is absolutely none of my business.'

'Becca.' He drew her hand up to his lips and pressed a kiss into her palm, his mouth warm and soft and so sweet that it made her want to cry.

'We can't do this,' she said. 'This is a seriously bad idea.'

'It's the best one I've had in a long time. I haven't been able to get you out of my head since I saw you again.' He held her gaze. 'And it took me a long time to get you out of my head after South Africa.'

He'd thought of her after South Africa? He'd missed her?

Really?

The thought made her head spin. And it would be oh, so easy to give in to the demands yammering through her body.

Marco had been her first lover. And her last.

And she still wanted him.

But if she gave in to the hot tide of desire—what then?

Marco had nothing to lose. He was a prince. Sure, the press might write a few stories about him, but at the end of the day he could do whatever he wanted.

Whereas Becca had everything to lose. Her career. The life she'd built so carefully for herself. Without those what did she have? With nothing left, would she fall back into her old ways? Would the oblivion that a bottle of vodka could bring—and had brought in the past—be all she had in the future?

She couldn't afford to take that risk.

'No,' she said, loosening her hand from his and taking a step backwards in the hope that putting physical distance between them would bring her common sense back. 'You're a prince, I'm a physiotherapist at the best private clinic in London, and our lives are on totally different paths.' She lifted her chin. 'And if that's not enough for you, I might point out that you've already dumped me once. I don't repeat my mistakes.'

'I'm sorry I hurt you.'

He sounded sincere enough, but she didn't fully trust his words.

'I'm older now. Wiser.'

'But you still can't offer me a future.'

'Is that what you want?' he asked.

It was something she hadn't allowed herself to think about; instead she'd concentrated on her career, working her way upwards and filling her life with work. 'I don't know,' she said. 'Maybe.'

'One thing I learned as a soldier,' he said softly, 'was to take happiness with both hands. Live in the present, don't worry about the future or the past. Enjoy the warmth of the sunshine, the coolness of the rain. Just *be*.'

Where was he going with this?

'Maybe that's what we need to do right now,' he said. 'Forget the past. Don't worry about the future. Just enjoy the here and now.'

If this was the way he talked women into bed, no wonder the gossip columns were full of pictures of him dating.

'Excuse me. I have another appointment now,' she said, and fled to the safety of her office.

CHAPTER FOUR

BECCA WENT OUT at lunchtime, hoping that a walk would clear her head. It was actually sunny for once, and it might turn out to be the only nice day London had for the whole of June, so she wanted to make the most of it. Only she couldn't just enjoy her favourite summer lunchtime treat of heading over to Regent's Park and walking among the roses. All she could think of was Marco.

She had to face it: she was still attracted to him. He'd made it clear that he was still attracted to her. But it was pointless starting something that could never have a future. Why set herself up for the misery of having to give him up to his royal duty, once his treatment was over?

Besides, if he knew the truth about her, he'd run a mile. Her past could blow up in their faces and cause untold amounts of damage to both of them. The press would have a field day—and she hated to think what kind of headlines they'd think up.

The Prince and the Addict.

Prince Charming and Vodka-Ella—and maybe they'd put the E in a different colour, just to make the point.

It would embarrass his family, it would embarrass the clinic, and…just *no*.

Yet Marco's words stuck in her head.

Take happiness with both hands. Live in the present—

don't worry about the future or the past. Enjoy the warmth of the sunshine, the coolness of the rain. Just be.

Could it really be that easy?

Could they have a fling and walk away intact at the end? If they went into it knowing that it would have a definite end would it mean that neither of them would get hurt this time around?

The thoughts spun through her head, making her dizzy. She had no answers. No idea at all about what to do.

Part of her was tempted to discuss it with Lexi.

Then again, that would mean telling Lexi about all of her past. Not just the fact that she'd fallen in love with Marco before and he'd abandoned her, but the really hard stuff. The way she'd been brought up. The way she'd longed for love but had it taken from her time and time and time again. The way she'd fallen into that vicious circle of needing more and more vodka—and almost been dragged under by Barney.

She couldn't do it.

So it was better to try to keep her distance from Marco.

Marco didn't raise the subject when she called in to run through his physio exercises with him. Part of Becca was relieved; part was worried. Was she just a whim— something to amuse a bored, spoiled prince? Or was she being unfair to him?

She couldn't think straight when he was around, and it made her tetchy. She wasn't used to her world being turned upside down like this. She'd worked hard to keep everything on an even keel, and now everything seemed in jeopardy. The life she'd made for herself, her peace of mind and the walls she'd built round the ruins of her heart.

But on her last visit of the day he took her hand. 'Becca. When are you off duty?'

'You're my last patient,' she said. 'I just need to update my notes.'

'Uh-huh.' His eyes were unreadable. 'What are you doing this evening?'

Well, that was progress. He finally seemed to realise that she did have a life outside the clinic and that she might actually have plans that didn't involve him. Even if it wasn't really that much of a life, if the truth be told: her usual routine was work, a swim, and her voluntary work at the rehab centre, with the occasional team night out to make a change.

For the last year or so it had been enough for her.

Until Marco had walked back into her life.

And now she realised that she'd just been existing, not living.

'I have to be somewhere this evening—it's an arrangement I can't break,' she said.

'Boyfriend?'

She glowered at him. 'Do you honestly think I would've let you kiss me this morning if I'd been involved with someone else? Thank you very much. Why don't you just call me a faithless cheat and be done with it?'

Marco fanned himself. 'Wow. You are woman, hear you roar. I think you're more effective than a flame-thrower.'

Flame? Was this a veiled remark about her hair being red? She scowled. 'Don't make stupid clichéd comments about my hair, either.'

It upset her that she was letting him get to her like this. So much for keeping her cool. If she carried on like this, Marco would guess in seconds that she still had feelings for him. Feelings that she'd thought she'd buried but had still been smouldering without her permission. And now he was fanning the fires again just by being here.

'I'm sorry.'

His apology took the wind out of her sails. 'I'm sorry, too. I didn't mean to snap at you. It's just that I don't do this sort of thing.'

'Just so you know,' he said, 'neither do I. The press is very good at twisting circumstances.' He paused. 'I appreciate that you have other commitments, and I don't expect you to rearrange your life just to suit me, but do you have time to have dinner with me this evening?'

Even if she skipped her swim, she really didn't have time tonight. 'Sorry. Another evening, maybe?' When she could work out how to carve out some time in the evenings without breaking promises to the girl she'd been supporting at the rehab centre. Short of cloning herself.

'How about a cup of coffee, then?' he asked.

'I'm not playing hard to get, Marco,' she said softly.

'But you have a life outside here.' He sighed. 'And I'm being selfish. I should be grateful I still have one working hand and the use of both my legs. Other people haven't been so lucky.' His face twisted. 'Thanks to me, some of my team won't see their kids grow up.'

'You can't change the past,' she said, 'so why beat yourself up about it?' Though at the same time she was wryly aware of what a hypocrite she was; she was just as hard on herself for making mistakes.

'If I didn't care,' he said, 'I'd be less of a soldier. I'd be a monster.'

'There's a difference between caring and wallowing,' she said, 'and you're in danger of wallowing.'

He winced. 'You don't pull your punches, do you?'

She shrugged. 'You need something to occupy your head and stop you brooding about the might-have-beens.'

'A distraction.' He looked straight at her. 'You could distract me.'

She knew that. Just as he could distract her. 'I'm not offering.' Though she could feel her cheeks turning pink. It would be so easy to offer him comfort. And then, once he'd gone, he'd leave her bereft. She wasn't up for that.

'So what do you suggest?'

'I know it's difficult for you, not being able to do things the way you normally do.'

'It's making me a bit twitchy,' he said, and grimaced. 'When I'm stressed, I usually play my guitar. It's got me through any difficult times for years.'

She remembered him playing guitar at the children's aid camp. Songs that everyone knew and could sing along with, so he'd managed to take everyone's minds off things for a while. Pretty classical pieces that had taken her breath away. And then there had been the songs he'd sung privately to her.

'And right now I can't play. I can't use my left hand at all for at least the next month. I *hate* not being able to play. Or being able to do a proper workout in the gym. Or being able to do practically anything else I normally do to relax. As for not being able to do my job… Don't even go there.' He scowled. 'I really hate being so *useless*. Right now I feel like a waste of space.'

'I would offer you a massage to take the knots of tension out of your muscles,' she said, 'but, given what happened this morning, that might not be such a good idea.'

'Yes.' He dragged in a breath. 'I might have to kiss you again.'

The worst thing was, she knew she'd respond if he did. Slide her fingers along the back of his neck. Stroke his face. Tease his lower lip with her teeth, her tongue…

She shook herself.

'Look, I know it's tough—but you have to give yourself time to heal. It'll happen.' She paused. 'Just not as quickly as you'd want it to. And unfortunately you can't change biology. Nothing and nobody can make you heal any faster.'

'I know. I have to learn to be patient.' He rolled his eyes. 'Sadly, patience isn't one of my virtues.'

She wasn't so sure. He'd been patient with the children

in South Africa. And with her. Maybe it was just himself he couldn't be patient with.

'I'll see you tomorrow,' she said. And she'd have a quiet word with Ethan on the way out. Maybe he could think of something to help their patient.

Their patient. Marco had a professional relationship with her now, not a personal one. And she needed to keep that uppermost in her mind, rather than letting herself think of him as a man.

By the time Becca walked back into his room for his first physio session the next morning, Marco was a mass of seething frustration. He'd had a whole night to think about it. A whole night to remember what it had felt like, losing himself in Becca. A whole night to wonder what it would be like between them now they were older and had more life experience. He'd never found that particular sweetness when making love with anyone else. Now they were older, would it have changed? Would it still be as sweet? Or was he chasing some distant dream that could never be recovered?

He'd driven himself half crazy with wondering.

Even verbal fencing with Ethan at the end of the evening hadn't taken the edge off Marco's need for Becca. And he'd only just managed to convince the surgeon that it was the frustration of not being able to use his hand that was making him so edgy, not sexual frustration. The last thing Marco needed was for Ethan Hunter to pull rank and decree that someone else would have to treat the prince.

Marco wanted Becca.

In every single way.

And he wanted her *right now.*

'Good morning,' she said chirpily.

'Yeah.' He knew how grumpy and out of sorts he sounded, but he couldn't help it.

She raised an eyebrow. 'What's the matter, Zorro?'

'Don't *you* start with that ridiculous nickname. I get enough of that from Hunter.' He scowled at her.

'Oh, come on. The Spanish nobleman who's a freedom fighter and a dab hand with a sword?' she teased. 'Ethan's right. It's you to a T. You know, I was thinking about getting you a domino mask. I think you'd look cute in it.'

'Yeah, yeah.' He flapped his right hand dismissively.

She sat on the edge of his bed, next to the comfortable armchair he was occupying. 'OK. Tell me now. What hurts?'

His heart.

Which was even more shocking, because he'd never actually let someone get that close to him before. 'Nothing.'

She unhooked the hand strap and examined his palm. 'It's not so red today. That's good. OK. Now lift your arm up.'

'Why?'

'So I can see if there's any stiffness in your shoulder.' She gave him a concerned look. 'You're in a hell of a mood, Marco. Has something happened? Something with your team? You've had some kind of bad news from home?'

He hadn't even thought of Sirmontane for the last day. And that made him feel guilty. He'd been totally self-indulgent and selfish. Spoiled. Brattish. 'No.'

She sighed. 'I know you hate being hemmed in and unable to do much. But, as I said to you yesterday, it takes time for your tendons to heal and it's beyond the laws of physics to speed that up. You'll just have to find something else to keep you occupied.'

'Like what? Playing endless games of patience with a pack of cards?'

'Sure. Or maybe a jigsaw puzzle.'

He closed his eyes. 'I know you're trying to be help-ful, but really—can you see me doing a jigsaw puzzle?'

'I guess not,' she admitted. 'So what do you suggest?'

He opened his eyes again and looked at her. 'You could kiss me better.'

There was a long, long pause. And then she sighed. 'I've already told you I can't do that. You're my patient. Anything else is against the rules.'

'Rules can be broken,' he pointed out.

'Not these ones.' She bit her lip. 'Please don't make this any harder for me.'

So she found it tough, too? Oddly, that actually made him feel a bit better. A bit less alone in this. And even though it frustrated him that she clearly felt the same at-traction as he did but refused to act on it, he could respect that she wanted to keep her professionalism. 'OK. I'm sorry. I'll back off.'

'Thank you.'

She took him through the set of exercises, barely say-ing a word except to guide him a little more on the physio. Cool and calm and completely impersonal.

She hadn't always been like that. When he'd first met Becca she'd been sweet and shy. For him, she'd been like a breath of fresh air—she'd made him feel as if he could have anything he dreamed about. And he was sure he'd helped her, too; he'd brought her out of her shell.

Oh, hell. He'd thought he could do this. That he could back off and let her be professional and detached. But, actually, he couldn't. He wanted that breath-of-fresh-air feeling back. The warmth. The sweetness.

This was crazy. It had been tough enough to get over her last time. And he knew that all he could offer her was a fling, and that wasn't fair to her. He couldn't offer her any-thing more because he had a duty to his country and his family, and he knew he'd have to marry the same kind of woman as his brother was marrying. So for now he'd have to keep his dreams and his libido tightly under control.

Having Becca's hands on his skin really wasn't helping.

He needed a distraction.

Like *now*.

'Becca. Talk to me,' he said.

'What about?'

Anything. Everything. He picked the first question that came into his head. 'Is being a physio what you dreamed about doing when you were a child?'

'No.'

'So what did you want to do?'

'I can't remember,' she said with a shrug. 'It was a long time ago. How about you?'

He raised his eyebrows. 'My job was already pretty much decided for me the day I was born. Until Ferdy and Marianna have kids, I'm second in line to the throne of Sirmontane. There wasn't really another option.'

'I guess not.' She looked curious. 'So what was it like, being a prince and growing up in a castle?'

'Honest truth?' he asked.

'Honest truth.' She paused. 'And it counts as medically confidential, just in case you're worrying about that.'

So she'd worked that one out, at least. Marco was shocked by how relieved it made him feel. 'I loved the castle. The suits of armour, the paintings of knights, the pageantry of the guards marching up and down outside.' He sighed. 'I liked sitting on my *abuelo's*—my grandfather's—lap,' he said, 'and hearing about all the tales of old. The warrior kings, the old legends. I pretty much drank them in. I used to spend hours making cardboard shields and swords.'

She looked surprised. 'Wouldn't your parents buy you a toy shield and sword?'

He laughed. 'Of course they would've done, if I'd

asked. But a true warrior forges his own sword. And I guess it kept me occupied for a while. They knew if I was colouring in some intricate design on a shield, it would keep me out of mischief.'

'And being a soldier when you grew up was the closest you could get to being a knight or a warrior?'

'While still doing my royal duties. Pretty much,' he said with a smile. 'I've just never been one for sitting still. Ferdy was always fine, curled up with his nose in a book or drawing. He's fantastic at art. Visiting dignitaries were always pleased with him—a child who was seen and not heard.'

She raised an eyebrow. 'I take it you were the opposite?'

'My mother had to spend a lot of time apologising for me,' Marco admitted. 'I was a bit of a nightmare child, always doing things that I shouldn't—climbing trees, sliding down the banisters at the castle, that sort of thing. I was lucky that we had a fabulous nanny who adored us—and who still works for us, though obviously not as a nanny now.' He grimaced. 'But we also had a very stuffy butler, who didn't approve of me at all and was forever telling tales to my father.'

She smiled. 'And then you batted those incredibly long lashes, and looked up with those big brown eyes, and everyone forgave you.'

'I'm not *that* manipulative,' he said dryly.

'I didn't mean that. Just that you—well, you're charming. I'd guess that you were a hit with all the princesses.'

'The ones of my parents' generation, yes. The ones my age, no—up until the age of about ten they were only interested in boring girly things and they didn't appreciate being introduced to my pet frog. They actually called him slimy,' he said in disgust.

Becca laughed. 'And after the age of ten?'

'They wanted to talk about clothes,' he said. 'Tiaras.

Shoes. Lipstick. Dull stuff like that. The ones who liked horses weren't so bad, because they didn't mind getting a bit grubby or pretending to chase dragons. But the ones who were introduced to Ferdy as a potential future queen...' He shook his head. 'That's when I was *really* glad to be the second son. Because I'd hate to have to marry someone I couldn't talk to.'

Becca frowned. 'I've met Princess Marianna. She seemed very sweet.'

'She is—she loves Ferdy to bits and she suits him down to the ground. But she's not the type of woman I could be happy with.'

Becca couldn't resist asking, 'So what type of woman *would* you be happy with?'

'Someone I can talk to. Share ideas with. Share my dreams with. Someone who can think outside the box.' He looked almost dreamy as he added, 'Someone who's a breath of fresh air.'

Becca knew it was a dangerous question—one she shouldn't ask because she was pretty sure she already knew the answer—but she couldn't help herself. 'So, as the second son, can you actually choose your own bride?'

'As the second son,' he said, 'I don't have quite as much pressure to get married and produce an heir.' He grimaced. 'Though I guess I'm still expected to marry the right sort of woman.'

Any last little wisps of the dreams Becca might have secretly had—that *she* was the kind of woman he could talk to and share his dreams with, and that she and Marco could possibly recapture what they'd had in South Africa—vanished completely at his words.

Of course Marco would be expected to marry the right sort of woman.

Which meant royalty. Or, even if he did choose to marry a commoner, someone from an impeccable back-

ground who'd been to the right sort of school. Not someone
whose mother had forever sought her own Prince Charming and spiralled into drink and despair when he didn't
turn up. And definitely not someone who'd repeated her
mother's mistakes in thinking that the answer lay at the
bottom of a bottle.

'What about you?' he asked.

'What *about* me?'

'You never really told me much about yourself in South
Africa. I mean, helping at a children's aid camp—your
parents must've been proud of you for doing something
that would make a difference. Especially as it meant travelling so far from home in England.'

Her parents had both died by then. There hadn't been
anyone to care, or to be proud of her. 'I guess…' she said
neutrally, not wanting to tell him about that or see the
pity in his face.

'So you're an only child?'

'Mmm,' she said. It was true enough; she was the only
child of *her* parents. She had half-siblings she'd loved
dearly as babies, but their fathers had always taken them
away after the inevitable break-up of their relationship
with her mother and cut all ties with both Becca *and* her
mother.

And she really didn't want to tell Marco about all
of that. She wanted to keep the past where it belonged.
Buried. For good. 'I'm sorry. I have another appointment.'

'And it isn't fair of me to make you late.'

'I'll see you later,' she said, and disappeared.

What was she hiding? Marco wondered. He'd noticed that
whenever he brought up the subject of her childhood she
either changed the subject or vanished. It was clear that
she came from a much more modest background than his

own. But did she really think he was so much of a snob that he'd hold that against her?

He mixed with people from all sorts of backgrounds as part of his job, and it had never bothered him whether someone had been to the 'right' sort of school or if they spoke with a regional accent instead of being 'posh'. It was how you treated others that counted with Marco, not where you came from.

Maybe he could get her to open up to him tomorrow. Maybe.

CHAPTER FIVE

ON THE TUESDAY morning Ethan walked into Marco's room with Declan Underwood, the acting head of the clinic, looking grim. 'Well, Zorro, it looks as if someone's ratted you out,' he said. 'The paps are three deep outside, waiting for a glimpse of you. And we can hardly give our clients the discreet service they expect from us when there are hundreds of cameras out there.' He tossed a tabloid newspaper onto Marco's bed.

Marco glanced at the front page. There was a picture of him in uniform, taking up half the page, with the headline: *Wounded hero returns to London.*

He scanned the text swiftly. Just as he'd feared, they'd run a story about him rescuing his men in Afghanistan and how he'd got everyone out of his Jeep even though he couldn't use one hand.

He shook his head. 'I'm not a hero. I just did my job—I did what anyone else in my position would have done.'

Ethan looked sympathetic, almost as if he'd been there.

'And you know as well as I do it turned out not to be the right thing in any case. They'd rigged the road and men *died* because of me.' Marco scowled at the newspaper.

'Nobody from here broke the story,' Ethan said.

'Of course not. Apart from anything else, there are details here that only someone from the camp would know.

Or their families, maybe.' Marco sighed. 'I'm so sorry you've been dragged into this. I imagine this is going to cause you a few problems.'

'It's going to be a bit tricky for some of our clients,' Ethan agreed.

'So how do we get rid of the press?' Marco asked.

'You need to work with them,' Declan said. 'Give them enough to keep them on side without breaching any confidentiality issues.'

Ethan curled his lip. 'They make up what they want. And they'll dig until they find what they want to see.'

That sounded personal, Marco thought. Had the press trashed him in the past? Or maybe someone close to him? 'They do exaggerate,' he agreed.

'But if you work with them it'll lessen the damage. We need to build a relationship with the press,' Declan repeated.

'That's why I brought him here,' Ethan said. 'Declan's a lot better with them than I am. He's good with the blarney. Not to mention the fact that he sweetened them up last time we were papped by sending them tea and biscuits because it was cold.'

'I just want to do my job,' Declan said, 'and getting the press on our side means fewer delays.'

'You could give them a photo opportunity, Zorro,' Ethan said. 'Perhaps a royal wave from the balcony with your good hand—but do make sure they see the strapping for your war wound so they can see the work we've done on you.'

'Not funny, Clavo,' Marco said, narrowing his eyes. 'I don't give a damn what they say about me—but now the press blanket's been breached it means my regiment is in danger.'

'But everyone knows you're in London. There's no

point in anyone targeting your regiment as they know they're definitely not going to capture *you*,' Declan said.

'They can capture others and demand me in exchange,' Marco pointed out.

'As *if* your family would ever agree to that,' Ethan said, rolling his eyes. 'Get real, Zorro.'

'I need to go out there and calm the mob down,' Declan said, 'so our staff can actually get into the building. I think we need to tell them that, yes, you are here, Marco, and, yes, you've had an injury to your hand, but that I can't go into further details because of patient confidentiality; you're making a good recovery and we'll update them as and when we can; and you'd like them to continue their good work in being careful about what they report so they don't put your team's safety at risk.'

'That works for me,' Marco said. 'I'll call my father and tell him how we're handling it. You have a PR team here?'

'Lexi's the head of our in-house team,' Declan confirmed.

'My father's PR team will probably want to liaise with her. Oh, and it's warm outside, right?'

'Right,' Ethan said, looking mystified. 'Why?'

'Because it's not the right weather for tea and biscuits. Send the paps ice creams and cold drinks, and I'll pick up the bill.'

'Now, that,' Declan said with a smile, 'is a great idea.'

'I don't think anyone could miss the press pack outside the front door,' Declan said at the emergency staff meeting that morning. 'I've told them, with Marco's permission, that he's here, we've treated him for a hand injury, he's comfortable and he's making a good recovery. I've also told them that I can't give them any more information, because of patient confidentiality. So if any of them ask you for more, just smile and say he's comfortable, and you're sorry but you can't break patient confidentiality, and I'll update them as soon as I can.'

'Got it,' Becca said. But her stomach knotted in panic. If the press couldn't find a story about Marco, would they start digging elsewhere? Supposing they started researching the pasts of the staff at the Hunter Clinic? They'd broken the story about Ethan and Leo's father, years before. And there had been another story, about the rescue Ethan had been involved with in Afghanistan; Becca could still remember Leo's reaction to that. The shock. The hurt.

With a bit of digging, the press could find out about the sordid mess of her past—and that would cause shockwaves through the clinic. It would mean she'd have to resign. What kind of patient would agree to be treated by a former addict, even though she hadn't had a drink or touched any tablet stronger than paracetamol for more than seven years now?

And, worse, if they found Barney and he told them what he knew... Of course he'd leave his own part out of it, and the press wouldn't care what he'd done to her because they'd have their story. She'd have to leave the job she loved so much. She might even be struck off the professional register for something that had happened when she was still little more than a child. OK, so technically she'd been over the age of consent, but...

This wasn't *fair*.

Worry made her short-tempered. She was short with Marco when she went in to do his physio—even though she knew she was being grossly unfair, because it wasn't his fault that the press was doorstepping him. Though she noticed that he was equally short with her.

The last few days had been a sweet, romantic dream. They'd been cocooned in a bubble, where perhaps they could start to fall in love with each other again and everything would be perfect.

But now it was time to wake up, face reality, and know that it was over.

'I've spoken to my father,' Marco said to Ethan. 'And his media team has come up with a fix. Tell the press you've done such a great job of mending my hand that I can be discharged from the clinic and move out to my family's London apartment. So there'll be no point in the press camping out here any more, because they're not going to get a glimpse of me—I won't be here.'

'Thank you,' Ethan said. 'But we *haven't* actually finished treating you, have we? There's the small matter of physiotherapy. And if you don't keep up with the exercises, then you'll risk losing movement in your hand. As it is, I'm concerned about your grip. I'd advise very strongly that you continue your therapy.'

'So what do you suggest? If I come back here for treatment, you'll still have the press doorstepping you.' Marco paused. 'Unless your staff could visit me? Although, as you've already pointed out to me, I'm not Becca's only patient. I know my family's place isn't that far from here, but she still wouldn't have enough time to come to me, treat me, come back here in time for her next appointment, treat her patient, and then be back with me for my next physio. Not to mention doing all her paperwork. It wouldn't be fair to her.'

'That kind of routine's not doable,' Ethan agreed. 'But I'll talk to her. If she's happy to work with you on a one-to-one basis, and for you to be her only patient for the time being, then I can arrange a stand-in physio for the rest of her caseload.'

And maybe, Marco thought, once they were outside

the clinic Becca's professional distance might dissolve. In the times when she wasn't treating him they could grow closer. Be friends instead of patient and therapist. Maybe they could even become lovers again? He'd get the chance to discover who Becca had become—and maybe they'd sort out this thing between them and find out what the future held.

He damped down the surge of optimism. 'And if she's not happy to do that?'

'Then you get the stand-in,' Ethan said. 'And may I remind you—?'

'No flirting with your staff,' Marco cut in, rolling his eyes. 'I remember.' Strictly speaking, he wasn't flirting with any of the staff at the Hunter Clinic. But at his home…things might be different. Because then different rules would apply.

'Becca—a word?' Ethan said.

'Sure.' Becca followed him into his office. 'What can I do for you?' she asked.

'I thought you should know that our illustrious patient is leaving this afternoon.'

She froze. Marco was *leaving*? But he hadn't said a word to her.

This was South Africa all over again: he was going without even saying goodbye. Just as well she hadn't let him back into her life, or it would be dump-and-run for the second time.

She schooled her expression into neutral. 'Uh-huh.'

'Which means we're not going to be doorstepped by the press any more, and he'll get the high-level security he's going to need now the story's broken.'

'Of course,' Becca said, trying very hard not to let it

show how much she minded that Marco hadn't said a word to her about it in their treatment sessions this morning.

'But,' Ethan said, 'he hasn't finished his physio treatment. Which is where you come in.'

'Me?' She frowned. 'But, if he's leaving, it means he won't be treated here any more.'

'No. He'll be treated at the family apartment.'

She still didn't see what that had to do with her. If Marco was going back to Sirmontane, surely there were physiotherapists there?

'In London,' Ethan clarified. 'And I wondered if you could do it.'

She ignored the flare of hope. 'What about my other patients? I've got appointments booked in between his. And, unless this apartment's literally a two-minute walk away, I won't have time to treat anyone else—I'll be spending all my time travelling between his place and here.'

'Marco needs hourly treatments, which means basically having a personal physio,' Ethan agreed. 'So I can draft someone in to cover the rest of your caseload, if that works for you.'

'He asked for me to treat him?' She really hoped her voice didn't sound as breathless and squeaky to Ethan as it did to herself.

'I didn't give him the chance to ask for you,' Ethan said. 'I wanted to run it by you first. If it doesn't work for you, then I'll tell him he'll have to have a different physio. Royal or not, he can't order you about.' He shrugged. 'But you're good at your job, Becca. You're the obvious first choice, if you're happy to do it.'

Work one-on-one with Marco. No other patients.

It didn't seem real.

She remembered what he'd said. *Seize the day.* Could she be that brave?

'Yes,' she said.

* * *

'Ethan told me you'd agreed to treat me at home,' Marco said when Becca called in to go through his next set of exercises. 'Thank you.'

'It was the best solution for everyone,' Becca said, try-ing to play it cool. 'Sorry I was a bit short with you earlier.'

He shrugged. 'No worries. It always tends to get a bit tense when the press are involved.'

'So…um…do I turn up to your place tomorrow morn-ing at nine? It might be handy to know the address,' Becca pointed out.

He smiled. 'I was rather hoping I could tempt you to come over later this afternoon…say when you've finished work? And maybe stay for dinner?'

'Dinner?' Did he mean just dinner, or would he expect more than that? Her heart rate sped up.

'No pressure,' he said softly. 'I like your company.'

Becca wasn't sure whether to be disappointed that he didn't want to take things further, or relieved that he was letting her off the hook. 'Dinner,' she said again.

He paused. 'If you're not committed elsewhere.'

How could she tell him about her work at the rehab centre? Even if she told a slight fib and said she was vol-unteering there because they'd helped a close friend, and she wanted to give something back for her friend's sake, he was bright enough to guess that the 'friend' didn't exist—that *she* was the one who'd needed help from the rehab centre to wean herself off vodka and the other stuff Barney had introduced her to.

She really didn't want to tell Marco the truth about the whole sordid mess. She didn't want him to know just how low she'd sunk. She didn't want him to know how she'd been hooked. Even though the therapist had tried to persuade her that none of it had been Becca's fault—that with her mother's addiction and the kind of people who'd surrounded her Becca hadn't stood a chance—Becca had never quite been able to believe that. She still thought she should have been stronger.

'I need to make a phone call,' she prevaricated.

'OK.'

'So why aren't you leaving the clinic in the middle of the night?'

'Why would I do that?'

She spread her hands. 'We've had patients leave in the middle of the night before to avoid the paparazzi.'

He smiled. 'No, I want the press to *see* I'm leaving. Then they'll stop staking out the clinic and you can all go back to normal.'

'What about your arm? If it gets knocked in the middle of the crowd...'

He shrugged. 'That's what my bodyguard's for. He'll clear the way. So... Tonight...' He gave her an address.

Becca blinked, recognising the name of the road and the very exclusive development of houses. It wasn't that far from the clinic, but it was too far for her to go and see him and then come back to see her other patients between his appointments, even if she took a taxi between his house and 200 Harley Street. 'You live on the edge of Regent's Park?'

'Yes.' He didn't look in the slightest bit fazed by the question. If anything, he acted as if it was perfectly normal to live in the sort of house that cost more than a thousand times the average person's annual salary. Yet again Becca was aware of the massive gulf between their lifestyles.

'Come over after work,' he said. 'I'll tell Security to expect you.'

'Security?' she asked.

'There's a security gate. Visitors need to sign in. Are you walking or coming by car?'

'Marco, normal people don't tend to drive in London.

It's way too much hassle and parking's a nightmare. You either take public transport or you walk.'

'I could send Rafa, my driver, and the limo for you,' he offered.

'Limo?' She smiled. How incongruous could you get? 'Marco, I'm a physiotherapist, not a rock star or a famous actress. I'll get a taxi.'

'If you insist.'

'I do.'

'OK. Our place is about five minutes' walk from the gate. Just ring the front doorbell and Maria, our house-keeper, will let you in.'

A housekeeper, a driver... How normal he made it sound to have staff. Whereas she did her own housework and if she'd had a car she would've driven herself.

'Right. Now, let's take this hand strap off and see how much mobility you've gained in your hand since yester-day.'

'Yes, ma'am,' he teased.

Face the press. OK. He could do this.

Marco took a deep breath, pinned on his public smile, and walked through the front door of 200 Harley Street, his bodyguard at his side.

What felt like a thousand flashbulbs went off, followed by a babble of excited speech.

'Prince Marco, where are you going?'

'Why are you leaving the clinic?'

'Are you going back to Afghanistan?'

Marco held up his free hand. 'Guys, one at a time, please. Where am I going? To my family's home in Lon-don so I can finish recuperating. Why am I leaving?' He nodded at his left arm. 'Because, as you can see, I'm fixed. Or at least on the mend—it was a flexor tendon injury, so it will take a bit of time to heal. Am I going back? I hope so, but not until I'm fit. Because I can't—and *won't*—put my team at risk.'

More flashbulbs. More babbled questions.

'Hey, Marco, thanks for the ice creams and the cold drinks!' someone called.

He smiled back. 'My pleasure. I thought it might be a bit hot for tea and biscuits.'

There was a ripple of appreciative laughter. No doubt half the paps had also been here for the tea and biscuits episode Ethan had talked about.

'Thanks, guys. I'm going home now. And can I ask that you don't jog my arm, please, on my way to the car? My hand's still a little bit fragile.'

'You're a hero!' someone else called.

Oh, how he wasn't.

'I'm no hero,' he said quietly. 'I just did my job. It's not my place to talk politics, but in my view the real heroes are the ones putting their country back together and trusting they can give their children an education and medical treatment. The ones who are fighting for men and women to be treated equally.'

There were heads nodding in agreement as he spoke.

'Marco, will you have a string of beautiful women to mop your brow while you recuperate?' another one of them called.

Marco laughed. 'I'm afraid that's not actually in my doctor's orders. I just have to rest and exercise my hand as I've been taught.' He smiled at them. 'I'm sure you can all understand that I'm a bit tired right now—I'd really like to go home, and I could kill for a cup of coffee.'

There were sympathetic grins all round.

'My father's PR team will issue regular bulletins to tell you how I'm doing,' he said. 'And please remember that my team's still out there in Afghanistan. You were great at keeping them safe before with the media blanket. I'd really appreciate it if you could keep up the good work and keep them safe while I'm here in London.'

And finally, to Marco's relief, the press pack parted and allowed him and his bodyguard to go down the steps to Rafa, his driver, in the waiting limo.

CHAPTER SIX

REGENT'S PARK WAS a place where you'd go to have a picnic by the lake, or to visit the zoo or the gardens. The place Becca had desperately wanted to visit as a child, after reading *The Hundred and One Dalmatians* and discovering that Pongo the Dalmatian was walked there by Mr and Mrs Dearly. The place she sometimes went to in her lunch break, as they had the biggest collection of roses in London, and Becca had always loved the scent of roses.

It definitely wasn't a place where you actually lived. Not unless you were from a seriously wealthy background. The nearest Becca had ever come even to renting a house there was on a Monopoly board.

She went to the security gate, as Marco had directed; to her relief, the staff there were expecting her. She showed them her identity card from the clinic and her bank card, to prove that she was who she said she was, signed in, then walked round the corner to Marco's family home and stopped dead.

The house was amazing; it was part of a long, sweeping terrace. There were four floors, the walls were cream stucco and punctuated by huge floor-to-ceiling windows, and there were actually columns holding up the portico—real fluted two-storey-height columns, like the ones outside the British Museum, except with leafy bits at the top instead of scrolls. There was a wide wrought-iron balcony running along the entire length of the house on the first floor, and wrought-iron railings at the front of the house. Behind the railings were raised flowerbeds, and as Becca got closer she realised that the steps leading to the house were marble.

Wow.

Really, she felt as if she ought to be going to the servants' entrance rather than the front door. After all, wasn't that kind of what she was as the prince's physiotherapist?

Lifting her chin, she rang the doorbell.

A middle-aged woman that Becca assumed was the housekeeper Marco had told her about answered the door. 'Can I help you?'

'Hello, I'm Becca Anderson, the physiotherapist from the Hunter Clinic. I have an appointment with...' Help, how did you refer to a prince? She couldn't just call him Marco, the way she did to his face. His housekeeper was bound to expect a properly respectful mode of address. 'With His Royal Highness,' she finished miserably.

'Ah, so you're Becca—come in. I'm Maria, the housekeeper. I'll take you through to the Prince.'

Becca was surprised and relieved by the warmth of the greeting. She followed the housekeeper through the large black door into the hallway. There were marble floors that reminded her a bit of the ones at Harley Street, but there the resemblance ended.

She was used to discreet luxury from working at the Hunter Clinic, but Marco's family home was something else. Maria showed her into a room where the floors were polished parquet and there was a huge rug in the centre; it looked like silk and Becca was almost too nervous to stand on it, in case she put a mark on it or pulled a thread or something.

'Have a seat. The Prince will be with you shortly,' Maria said.

Everywhere in the room was incredibly neat and orderly. There was a choice of beautiful cream sofas to sit on, liberally spread with thick cushions and augmented by Louis XV tall-back cream-upholstered armchairs. There were also several occasional tables from the same period that Becca suspected were original pieces rather than reproduction, and several beautiful floral arrangements in crystal vases.

The lights were traditional chandeliers, which reminded her of the stunning Venetian glass she'd fallen in love with on holiday one year—the kind of stuff that had been way, way outside her budget. There was a gilt mirror over the mantelpiece, and the reflection had the kind of softness that told her it had to be very old glass—maybe several hundred years old, and handmade by a craftsman rather than mass-produced in a factory.

The floor-to-ceiling windows had cream damask drapes and a view over Regent's Park that took her breath away. *Imagine growing up here*, she thought. It was only a few physical miles away from the grotty seventh-floor flat where she'd grown up, but it was light years away emotionally. Here, everything was beautiful and light and airy, instead of dank and chipped or fraying.

The mantelpiece was marble and held a number of heavy silver-framed photographs. Becca couldn't resist being nosey and taking a closer look at the family portraits. In pride of place was what looked like a relatively recent photograph of the King of Sirmontane with his queen, two sons and a daughter; Becca could really see the resemblance between Marco and his family. Marco had the same dark eyes and hair as his father and brother and the same smile as his mother and sister. His older brother looked more serious, but there was a kindness in his face that Becca knew was part of Marco's make-up, too.

Another photograph showed Marco's sister in a wedding dress, with a man Becca assumed was her husband, and another showed them both in a garden with two toddlers, clearly theirs.

She could imagine Marco as an uncle. He'd be the first one on the floor with the children, building forts out of bricks and settling them both on his lap to read them a story.

Just for a second she imagined Marco as a father, holding his newborn child with a tender expression in his eyes. And she suppressed the thought ruthlessly. She wasn't ever going to have a family, and she most definitely wasn't going to have a family with Marco.

There was another photograph of an older man with the three children, though in this one they were much younger. She had a feeling that the older man was the grandfather who'd been taken ill while Marco was in South Africa—a feeling that deepened when she saw a picture of Marco as a child with the same man and a puppy, laughing and looking totally carefree. A picture that tugged at her heart.

'Good evening, Becca.'

She spun round, feeling the colour flood into her face at being caught snooping. 'I—er—sorry, I was being nosey.' Why hadn't she just sat down politely and waited for him as she'd been told to do?

'No worries. Help yourself.' He smiled at her. 'That's the family—obviously my parents, my grandfather, my sister Arabella, my brother Ferdinand, Bella and her husband Luiz, the twins, and that was my little dog Pablo. He was my sixth birthday present from my grandfather, and I loved him to bits.'

'Uh-huh.'

Marco here didn't feel like the Marco she knew. In

South Africa he definitely hadn't been a prince; he'd been just one of the other volunteers at the children's aid camp, super-handsome and yet kind and thoughtful with a heart of gold. And at the clinic he'd seemed just like any of the other patients. But here? Here, Marco was markedly a prince. Even the way he walked seemed different—seemed regal, somehow.

What on earth was she doing here? This place high-lighted just how unsuitable Becca would be as a prince's girlfriend. This was so far out of her own experience, it was untrue. She needed to keep that in mind and protect her heart. As soon as Marco was fit to go back to work, he'd leave—and after that one goodbye she'd never see him again.

'Would you like a guided tour?' he asked.

'Um…sure.' Though it felt almost like having a guided tour of an English country house that had been left to the nation by the family years before—a snapshot of the past. Somewhere you could only dream of living. Not some-where that people actually lived for real.

'I guess I should start with the front of the house. It was designed by John Nash and built nearly two hundred years ago; it's a listed building,' he intoned.

Well, of course—where else would a royal family live?

'It's my parents' base in London—obviously it's big enough for us all to be here together, including Bella's husband and the twins, plus any guests and staff.'

Becca didn't dare ask how many bedrooms there were. This was way, *way* out of her league.

'So, this is one of the sitting rooms.'

One of? Most people she knew had only one, and some-times not even that; in her own flat the sitting room did triple duty as her dining room and her study, too.

'This is the dining room.'

He took her through to the next room. Again, the windows were floor to ceiling, the large gilt-framed paintings on the walls all looked like original oil portraits, and the dining table was so huge that it could have seated an entire rugby squad and then some. The wood was beautifully polished and there were some candelabra at either end that might have been gilt but Becca had a nasty feeling that they were actually solid gold. There was another beautiful arrangement of fresh flowers in a crystal bowl in the centre.

'This is the library,' he said, showing her into the next room.

She caught her breath. 'Oh, I love this,' she said, unable to hold the words back. Like the other rooms, it had floor-to-ceiling windows, with bookshelves between them and covering one entire wall. There were comfy sofas in the centre, with reading lamps nearby, a low table with a chessboard, a grand piano, and also a couple of guitars on stands which she guessed belonged to Marco. This was a room that made her feel comfortable—where she could actually feel as if she belonged.

He sat down at the piano and picked out a melody with his right hand. 'It doesn't feel right, playing something without the harmony,' he said, 'but I guess this is better than nothing at all.' He stroked one of the guitars longingly. 'So how long will it be before I can play again?'

'You can't even lift a kettle for another six or seven weeks,' she said. 'I'm sorry, Marco. There isn't a nice way of saying this.'

'Tell me straight. I'm never going to play again?'

'Not *never*,' she said, 'but playing guitar means using a lot of pressure. It counts as heavy activity, so it'll be months rather than weeks or days before you can try, and even then you'll have to take it really easy. Play for a couple of minutes, rather than hours.'

'I guess I have to learn to take things slowly, or I'll do

more damage that even Ethan Hunter won't be able to fix it.' He looked utterly miserable.

Hating the fact that he was so unhappy and unable to resist trying to comfort him, Becca walked over and hugged him. She knew this was a bad idea—she ought to keep some professional distance between them—but how could she stand by when he was so dejected?

Marco wrapped his good arm round her and rested his forehead against hers. 'Thank you. I needed that. I just hate being so helpless and having to rely on other people to help me. I'm used to doing things myself.'

'Action hero,' she said softly.

He shook his head. 'I'm no hero, Becca. I just do my job, and I try to do it well.'

She guessed that Marco would be good at just about anything he did. Second best would never be enough for him.

'And this time I messed it up,' he said, confirming what she'd just thought.

He was so hard on himself. Why?

'I could hold the guitar for you,' she suggested. 'If you told me what notes to play, you could still do the strings with your right hand.'

His lips brushed against hers, a feather-light touch. She thought it was probably meant to be a token of gratitude, but all it did was make her tingle all over and want more. To the point where she could feel herself on the cusp of hyperventilating.

'That's such a sweet offer. Do you actually play the guitar, Becca?'

'Um—no,' she admitted. 'I never learned to read music or anything like that, and you're the only person I've ever met who actually plays an instrument.'

'Then I'd probably end up barking orders at you and getting frustrated because I couldn't explain myself well enough to you, and—well, I'd be horrible,' he said. 'And I don't want to be horrible to you. But thank you for offering. I appreciate it.'

He held her just a little bit closer, then released her. She guessed that he was just as confused about this as she was. Wanting to touch, to kiss, to lose themselves in each other; yet at the same time knowing it wouldn't be sensible.

When they went to the next room Marco took Becca's hand on the way, lacing his fingers through hers. Her skin tingled where he touched her.

Oh, help. This wasn't the deal. She was his therapist, not his girlfriend. South Africa was in the past, and it was staying there.

The study held more bookshelves and a polished oak desk with more family portraits in pride of place.

'This is Papá's, but Ferdy and I use it sometimes if we're here and he's not,' Marco said. 'The next two floors are just bathrooms and bedrooms,' he told her, leading her up the stairs again. 'But this is my favourite bit of the house.'

He led her up a last flight of stairs, released her hand and opened the door for her.

She gasped as she realised what it was. 'A roof garden. How amazing.'

It was stunning—flagged stone, with terracotta pots of sweet-smelling herbs and bright flowers, comfortable chairs and even a hammock. But the bit that took her breath away was the view: not just the whole of the park, but the middle of London itself, including iconic structures such as the London Eye and the Shard.

They were right in the centre of London, with thousands of people around them; and yet at the same time the garden was incredibly private. She assumed that the other houses in the sweeping terrace had some kind of roof gardens, too, but this one didn't seem overlooked in any direction.

'And then there's this. You don't get the same kind of view of the stars that we did in South Africa,' he said, 'because there's too much light pollution in the city, but it's still good to sit out here and look up at the sky on a summer's night.'

'This' referred to a spa pool, screened off from the rest of the garden by a trellis covered in wisteria.

'I thought maybe we could have dinner up here to-night,' he said.

'I've never had dinner on a roof garden before,' Becca said.

'Good. I think you'll enjoy this. Excuse me a second.' He took his mobile phone from his pocket and made a swift call in Spanish.

'Chef would like to know if you have any allergies or if there's anything you don't like?' he asked.

Becca couldn't quite process this. He had a personal chef? 'No allergies. I'm happy to eat anything.' And then a nasty thought hit her. 'But I'm not keen on puddings with alcohol.'

'That's fine. I'll make sure he knows.' He spoke rapidly into the phone in Spanish again. 'OK, Miguel. *Talué.*'

'What does that mean…*talué*?' she asked.

'It's bye-bye.' He wrinkled his nose. 'Basically it's slang, running the words *"hasta luego"* together. I guess it's like saying *ciao-ciao* in Italian instead of *arrivederci*.'

'Right.' She didn't speak Italian, either, apart from with the aid of a phrasebook.

He grimaced. 'Sorry. I didn't mean to show off. Chef will, though.' He grinned. 'I told him he can show off as much as he likes and do you a real Sirmontanean meal.'

She was still trying to get her head round this. 'You have a personal chef?'

He rolled his eyes. 'You make it sound far more snooty than it is. My parents have to entertain when they're here, and visiting dignitaries kind of expect their full attention rather than having my mother rushing off in the middle of dinner to check something in the kitchen.'

His parents. His family. Ice trickled through her veins. What if his family came over to be with him now he was out of the clinic? Would they think she was suitable to be his physio? They definitely wouldn't think of her as suitable in any other way.

The panic must have shown in her face, because he sighed. 'Relax, Becca. It's just you and me. My family is under strict instructions to stay away because I need to rest.'

Even though part of her was relieved, part of her felt a bit guilty. 'Isn't that a bit unfair to your mother? She must be worried about you.' In her shoes Becca would have been worried sick and desperate to see her injured son for herself.

Not that Becca thought she'd ever get married and have a family of her own. Her experiences with family had pretty much put her off taking that particular risk.

'I love my mother, I really do, but she drives me totally *loco*,' Marco said. 'She frets and she thinks up all the worst-case scenarios. If she had her way she'd wrap me in cotton wool, and that doesn't sit well with me—and then I end up rebelling and snapping at her, and then she gets upset, and then I feel guilty for being mean because I know she loves me as much as I love her, and...' He grimaced. 'Like I said, *loco*.'

It must be nice, Becca thought, to have a parent who cared that much about you instead of one who always put herself first and dumped you when the going got tough. Not that she had any intention of telling Marco about any of that. She didn't need his pity.

'We should do your physio,' she said.

'So when do I get to do the next stage of exercises?' he asked. 'The ones where I can start doing light work with my hand?'

'The next stage of exercises will be in about another fortnight. And another month after that before you do light activities.'

He groaned. 'Surely I can start using my hand *soon*?'

'Not even to read a newspaper,' she said. 'And using a knife is totally out of the question. That counts as heavy use, and that won't be until three months after the operation. Light use you can start two months after the operation. *Provided* you don't push it and set your progress back before then.'

'Excuse me a second.' He took out his phone and made another call in rapid Spanish.

She gave him an enquiring look.

'I asked Miguel—Chef—to make food I can eat with a fork,' he said, looking grumpy. 'This is worse than being a toddler. I hate the idea of someone cutting up my food for me.' He sighed. 'It's the lack of independence that's getting to me. Not being able to do things I've taken for granted for years.'

'Patience,' she counselled.

'Something I'm not very good at.'

'You were patient with the children in South Africa.'

'That was different.' He shrugged off the compliment. 'Ferdy—now, *he* has patience. Which is why it's so good for Sirmontane that he's the elder son and not me.'

'Do you mind that you won't be king?' she asked.

'No. I have so much more freedom than Ferdy.' He sighed. 'Though obviously I have royal duties. Things I can't neglect. Things that have to come first no matter how I feel about it.'

'It's the same with your hand,' she said lightly. 'You're

desperate to use it again—but you have to wait and the healing has to take place first, no matter how grumpy and frustrated you get.'

'Point taken,' he said dryly.

'Time for your exercises.' She talked him through them, watching him and making sure that he didn't push too hard, yet at the same time pushed himself hard enough to make progress.

They were halfway through the physio session when Maria came up onto the roof garden, carrying a tray bearing a silver teapot with a matching jug and sugar bowl, two porcelain cups, and a plate of delicate almond biscuits.

'Miguel's so happy to have you home, Marco—he's enjoying having someone to cook for other than just the two of us and Rafa,' she said with a smile. 'I'm happy to have you home, too, *hermoso*.'

He smiled at her. 'Thank you, Maria. Though I can assure you that they looked after me well at the Hunter Clinic.'

'It's not Harley Street that worried me,' she said pointedly.

Marco rolled his eyes. 'If Mamá has asked you to nag me about my job, I'll take that as read and you don't have to do it. I'm still in one piece, just a little bit battered, and Becca's fixing me up. She's bullying me, mind.'

Maria laughed and patted Becca's shoulder. 'Bully away, *hermosa*. He needs taking in hand. I brought tea, but if you'd rather have coffee I can bring you some—no problem.'

'Tea's lovely, thank you. It's very kind of you.' Becca smiled at her. 'Though, to be honest, I'd normally make my own tea, and I feel a bit guilty, having you wait on me.'

'Nonsense. That's what I'm here for.' Maria smiled again. 'Call me if you need me.'

'Thank you,' Becca said.

The almond biscuits were lovely.

'These are gorgeous. Can you tell Miguel for me?'

'Sure. They're traditional Sirmontane biscuits,' Marco said. 'They're usually served with coffee after dinner, or sometimes with morning coffee.'

'The tea looks more like an English tradition, though.'

He grinned. 'Yes. Like our neighbours, Spain and France, in Sirmontane we prefer coffee to tea.'

'Just remember you're not to lift anything with your left hand at the moment, even a cup as light and delicate as this,' Becca said, and took charge of the teapot.

Serving tea to a prince, with fine porcelain and silver. If anyone had told her a couple of weeks ago that she'd be doing that she would have laughed. How far away this felt from her real life.

They finished off the physiotherapy session after their tea, and then she was content to sit with Marco in the sunshine and chat about nothing in particular. Just being with him felt so good. And as long as she didn't let herself remember that she was in a multimillion-pound house with a prince, it felt *real.*

Dinner that evening started with tapas. 'Obviously, because we're on the Spanish border, we have similar dishes to Spain,' he said. 'And I like tapas. Lots of little tastes.'

There were dishes of olives, ham, cheeses she didn't recognise but which were totally delicious, and fresh bread. 'This is very nice,' she said, tasting each one in turn.

'And, best of all, I can eat it one-handed,' he said wryly.

The next course was a tender lamb stew, with saffron-scented rice and baby vegetables.

'Fork food at its finest,' Marco said with a grin. 'Miguel's done us proud.'

And then Maria brought up cinnamon-spiked *churros* with the most amazing chocolate sauce.

'Oh, my God. I've never eaten anything as nice as this,' Becca said.

He grinned. 'I told you Sirmontane chocolate's better than Swiss.'

'Lizzie's going to beg you for some of this,' she said, taking another bite.

'I'll get some delivered as a welcome-back present.' Marco laughed.

Finally they had bitter coffee, with the nicest dark chocolate thins she'd ever had in her life, and watched the lights come up over London.

'We could,' Marco suggested softly, 'have a spa bath.'

She shook her head. 'Nice idea, but I'm afraid I don't have a swimming costume with me.' Hers was back in her locker in the clinic.

He pursed his lips. 'What if I said you don't need a costume?'

Oh, the very idea of sharing a spa bath with him—skinny-dipping under the stars... It sent a shiver of desire through her.

'Marco, this—we can't—we shouldn't...' Her voice faded.

'I have no idea what you're trying to tell me, *hermosa*.'

'Oh, yes, you do. I'm your therapist. I can't be anything else.'

He took her hand. 'We're not at the clinic, now. Technically, you're not at work. You're having dinner with me.'

'A platonic dinner.'

'It doesn't have to be.'

'Marco, I'm not going to be just a distraction for you. I'm worth more than that.'

'I know you are.'

But he didn't relinquish her hand. Instead, he raised it

very slowly, turned it over so he could see her wrist, and pressed his mouth against her pulse-point. And she knew that he'd be aware of how much her heart-rate was speeding up—and precisely why.

'Remember what I said before?' he whispered. 'Forget the past. Don't worry about the future. Just enjoy the here and now.'

She wanted to. So very badly. It had been driving her crazy, keeping her distance from him and trying her best to be professional when all she wanted to do was rip his clothes off.

But...

'How can I?' she burst out.

'Becca,' he said, 'will you please just shut up and kiss me?'

She narrowed her eyes at him. 'Is that an order, Your Royal Highness?'

'No. It's a polite request. And I did say "please",' he pointed out. 'Or do you want me to beg?'

Oh, help. The pictures *that* put in her head. She dragged in a breath. 'I know I'm technically off duty, but you're still my patient.'

'Then consider me signed off, as of now,' he said.

'I'm afraid I can't do that. Only Ethan can sign you off, as your surgeon. Or maybe Declan, as the acting head of the clinic. And you'd be stupid to sign yourself off. Your hand...'

He groaned. 'Right now I don't care about my hand. This is driving me crazy, Becca. I can't stop thinking about you.'

The confession seemed dragged from him, and it made it easier for her to admit to him, 'I can't stop thinking about you, either.'

'I need to be honest with you. I'm not sure I can offer you a happy-ever-after. I have...well, responsibilities. I

still have to finish my tour of duty as a soldier. How do I
know that the next bomb won't be directly under my Jeep
instead of the one in front of mine?'

'Marco.' She stroked his face. 'Don't talk like that.'
She hated to think of him being badly hurt, or even killed.

'I'm not trying to manipulate you, Becca, or bully you
into having a fling with me.'

'Is that what you're offering? A fling?'

He blew out a breath. 'Right now it's all I can offer.
Maybe—I don't know. Maybe. I don't want to make any
promises I can't keep. That wouldn't be fair to either of
us. But I can offer you happy-for-now.'

Was that enough?

Either way, she knew that he was going to walk out of
her life in a few weeks' time.

If she said no, all she would have were regrets. In years
to come, would she wish that she'd been brave?

If she said yes, they could have some time together.
Build memories. Things that might sustain her and might
just stop her spiralling back into addiction again when
he left.

'Seize the day,' she said softly, and leaned forward to
kiss him.

How good his skin felt under her fingertips. How good
his mouth felt as it teased hers, tempted her, incited her to
bite his lower lip and kiss him back.

Despite only having one working hand, it took him
seconds to loosen her hair.

'That's what I wanted to see,' he said softly. 'Your hair
falling over your shoulders, just like it used to. Fire over
cream.'

Oh, God. How had she forgotten how damn sexy he
was? Even the way he talked to her made her feel wet.
Hot. Needy. Nobody else had ever made her feel this way.
It had been so easy to refuse dates, because the men in

question hadn't made her feel a fraction of what Marco made her feel.

He brushed a kiss against her mouth. 'Becca. I want to sit with you and drink champagne and look at the stars—well, as much as you get to see of the stars in London.'

'You're on antibiotics,' she pointed out, 'so that's not a good idea.'

'OK. You can drink champagne and I'll watch you,' he said.

Oh, help. She didn't want to explain all this. She didn't drink. Ever. She couldn't risk even one sip in case it pushed her straight back down the slope of addiction. 'No, it's fine. I'm not one for champagne,' she said hastily.

'Pimm's, then?' he suggested. 'Or a cocktail? Miguel makes wicked cocktails.'

Worse and worse. It looked as if Becca was going to have to tell him a certain amount. But she had no intention of letting him push her into a more detailed explanation. 'Actually, I don't drink,' she said. 'Sorry.'

Marco looked intrigued.

The only way she could think of to take his mind off the subject and stop him asking questions was to kiss him. And she was quivering by the time Marco broke the kiss.

'Let's get in the pool,' he said.

'You're not going anywhere near that water without a plastic bag over your arm. You can't get the splint wet. Or the dressing.'

He laughed. 'You're so bossy.'

'Someone has to be. Right now you're exuberant, bored, and full of bright ideas,' she said.

He kissed her lightly. 'Guilty on all three counts. But my bright ideas are great.'

'Another day,' she said. 'When I can make sure I tape up your arm properly and I have something to wear.'

'I'll hold you to that,' he said, and the expression in his

eyes made desire lick all the way down her spine. 'OK. Second bright idea. How about you stay here tonight? I remember what it was like, waking up with you in my arms. It might be nice to do that in a comfortable bed instead of a sleeping bag.'

Becca was tempted. Deeply tempted. Though she knew it was a bad idea. The closer she let him get now, the more she was in danger of getting in too deep and ending up hurt again. Making love with him would be one thing; but allowing him a deeper intimacy, like she had in South Africa—that was one risk too far.

'I don't have so much as a toothbrush with me.'

'Not a problem. Our guest bathrooms are well stocked.'

'I don't have any clean clothes, either.'

'Maria can laund—'

She stopped him by pressing one finger gently against his lips. 'Marco, I'm not used to this way of life. I don't have staff. I've always looked after myself. I'm not comfortable with making other people clear up after me. And I don't expect anyone else to launder my clothes for me.' Colour crept into her face. 'Plus…I don't want her to think…well.'

'That you're my lover?' He raised an eyebrow. 'Maria's a woman of the world. Married, too. You've probably guessed that Miguel's her husband. And, despite me teasing her earlier, she's not my mother's spy. She's the soul of discretion. She's been with my family for years—since before I was born.'

'Was she the nanny you told me about?'

He smiled. 'Yes.'

That certainly explained Maria's easy relationship with the Prince and the way she teased him and fussed over him.

'I just feel awkward about it, Marco,' she said.

'OK. So how about,' he said, 'I see you tomorrow—you stay for dinner and bring a swimming costume with you?'

She bit her lip. 'I need to be somewhere tomorrow evening.' To do the volunteer shift she'd skipped tonight.

He stroked her face. 'I don't want you thinking I'm just bored and using you to distract me. Because I'm not. I want to be with you, Becca.'

It was so very tempting.

'I'll sort it out,' she said. He wouldn't be in London for much longer. She'd make the most of the time they had together. 'But I need to go now, Marco.'

'I'll ask Rafa to drive you home in the limo.'

She shook her head. 'I don't need a limo. I'll get the tube. The station's not far from here.'

He sighed. 'I'm not trying to control you, you know. I just want to make things easier for you.'

'I'm fine.' She smiled. 'Don't fuss. I'll see you tomorrow.'

'Mañana,' Marco said, and kissed her, taking his time and heating her blood to the point that she almost, *almost* changed her mind and agreed to stay.

'I'll see you out.'

As Marco closed the front door behind Becca, so he didn't have to watch her walk away, he knew she was right. If a limo with blacked-out glass took her home the neighbours would ask questions, maybe start talking. A word to the press here, a car number plate given there, and connections would soon be made.

He needed to keep his links with her out of the public eye and out of the press. Not because he was ashamed of her—of course he wasn't. She'd always been cagey about her own background, and had been even cagier since she'd discovered he was a prince, so he was guessing that she came from a very modest family. But money didn't bother him. It was how people treated others that mattered to him. You could be as high-born as you like and still be a low-life.

No, he wasn't ashamed of her. It was what the press could do if they found out about her that bothered him. He'd seen for himself how easily the press could hurt people—how public criticism had chipped away at the confidence of his sister-in-law-to-be Marianna. He didn't want that to happen to Becca. So keeping her secret would be the best thing he could do for both of them.

CHAPTER SEVEN

MARCO FOUND HIMSELF looking forward to seeing Becca, and he loved the fact that she'd talk to him about everything under the sun. Except one thing: she was seriously secretive about her past. She changed the subject every time he asked a question about her. He knew absolutely nothing about her family—were her parents still together, still alive?

'You're a puzzle,' he said.

She frowned. 'I'm not with you.'

'I know nothing about you.'

'There's nothing much to know.' She shrugged. 'I'm a physiotherapist, I specialise in treating hands, and that's about it.'

'So this thing in the evenings that you do—is it a course? You mentioned that you were thinking about studying acupuncture.'

'No, I'm not studying acupuncture yet—I'm still in the process of choosing a course.'

He noticed that she'd switched the subject again, and she hadn't told him what she was doing in the evenings. Why wouldn't she open up to him? Did she think he'd hurt her? And how could he get her to trust him?

Though at the same time he knew she was right: he

couldn't offer her a future because his duty to his family and his country had to come first.

Yet he needed her.

And he thought that she might need him.

Somehow they'd manage to find a way to make this work.

Somehow.

'I can't stay for dinner, but is the offer of the spa pool still open?' Becca asked, later that day.

'It most certainly is—OK, so it means we don't get to see the very few stars you can see in the London night sky, but we can watch the clouds going past instead. How about after lunch?' he suggested.

'That'd be great.' She gave him a shy smile that left him tingling. 'I brought my costume with me. And a bag for your arm, and tape.'

'That's good.'

'But, for now...'

'I know, I know,' he said. 'Exercises.'

In the middle of the afternoon Marco changed into his swimming trunks and Becca taped up his arm to make sure that his splint wouldn't get wet. He climbed into the pool and settled back next to her with a contented sigh.

'This,' he said, 'is paradise. I love London.'

'Wouldn't you rather be in Sirmontane, in the mountains?' she asked.

'Not when I can't ride a bike or go skiing,' he said wryly. 'Of course I love my country, but there's something special for me about London. There's music, there's drama, there are museums and art galleries—you can eat foods from practically any country in the world, walk in the park, dance in the middle of a fountain. . .'

'Well, *you* can't dance in the middle of a fountain—

not unless you bag your arm up like that, and I think that might cramp your style a bit,' she teased.

He laughed, pulled her close with his good arm and kissed her. 'I don't think it cramps my style at all.'

'No?' she teased.

God, he couldn't resist her. 'No.' His expression grew hot, and this time his kiss wasn't all sweetness and gentleness. It was demanding and enticing and promising, all at the same time. He needed her to know how he felt. Needed her to feel the same way.

Nobody else had ever made Becca feel this way—as if she were going up in flames every time his skin touched hers. It had been so easy to refuse dates because the men in question hadn't made her feel a thousandth of what Marco made her feel.

'I need to see you, Becca,' Marco said, tracing the edge of her swimming costume with the tip of his forefinger. 'And nobody's going to interrupt us. This is just you and me.'

She couldn't resist him any more. 'Yes,' she whispered.

It took him a second to slide the straps down her shoulders. And then he was cupping one breast, his thumb stroking her nipple and making her gasp.

He dipped his head and took her nipple into his mouth.

Becca shuddered as he sucked. 'Oh, my God.' It had been way too long since she'd felt anything like that. Since she'd let anyone touch her in this way. And how strange it was that they were both older, changed by their experiences—and yet their bodies reacted the same way they always had.

'You like that?' he asked.

'Yes,' she breathed.

'Good.' He stroked her abdomen and she knelt up, arching against him.

'I'd forgotten how good we are together,' he whispered. 'How you feel. Like warm silk.'

He slid one finger underneath the lower hem of her swimsuit and drew it along the length of her sex. The second time he did it she was quivering. And when he pushed a finger deep into her, she was glad that he'd jammed his mouth over hers again because she couldn't help whimpering in sheer need.

All coherence left her as her body began to tighten round him.

'Better?' he asked softly when she'd come back down to earth.

She felt the colour flood into her face.

He simply grinned. 'It's good to know that it's still like that between us.'

'I...' She shook her head. 'I don't know what to say.'

He kissed her softly. 'Then don't say anything.'

But she didn't want him thinking that she was cheap. Because she wasn't. 'I don't normally do this sort of thing.'

'Neither do I,' Marco said dryly, 'no matter what the press like to think.' Then he frowned. 'Are you telling me you haven't made love with anyone else since we were together?'

'No.'

Guilt flooded through him. 'Because of me?'

'Partly,' she said, but he had a feeling that she was trying to let him off the hook.

'I hurt you that much?'

She shrugged. 'I was young. I guess we both were. And in a way you did me a favour. It meant that I concentrated on my studies instead of letting someone distract me.'

Even so, he'd hurt her to the point where she hadn't trusted anyone else. Maybe she'd dated, but she hadn't let her boyfriends go anywhere near this far.

'I'm sorry,' he said. 'I didn't mean to hurt you.' And

wasn't he in danger of doing that all over again? Only offering her the here and now? He dragged in a breath. 'Becca, I...'

'"Seize the day", you said.'

'But that isn't who you are. You're careful. Guarded.'

'Now who's overthinking it?'

Her tone was light, but he was sure she was masking something.

How was he going to persuade her to trust him with the rest of her, not just her body? When they made love they were on the same page. But Marco knew that wasn't enough.

'I have to go,' she said.

He wasn't so sure that she really needed to go, but he also knew if he pushed her now he'd lose any chance of getting close to her and really finding out what was in her head.

'OK. I'm not going to push you.' He paused. 'Will you stay for dinner tomorrow?'

'I'll see what I can do.'

'And maybe,' he said, 'you could stay over.' At the panicky look on her face, he said, 'No pressure. You can stay in one of the guest suites, if you prefer.'

Though he really wanted to spend the night with her in his arms. He wanted to wake up with her and know that the day would be better because she was in it. Or maybe he was asking too much.

'I'll see,' she said, and left to do whatever mysterious thing she did in the evenings.

The next morning, doing the limited exercises he was allowed to do in the gym was a form of torture, Marco decided. So was sitting in the library. Usually it was his favourite room in the house, but not when the guitars he couldn't play right now were in full view, reminding him just how limited his movements were.

The only bright spot in his day was the fact that Becca would be spending it with him; and there might be a chance that she would stay for dinner as on the first night.

Whether he could persuade her to stay overnight was another matter. She'd been reluctant, the night before, and she kept mentioning these mysterious commitments, but clammed up if he asked her about them.

He could put tabs on her easily enough, and find out what she did that way. But having her followed like that would feel wrong. He'd much rather she told him herself, of her own free will.

Clearly she didn't trust him. Now he'd got to know her again he could understand why. He'd left her before, in South Africa, not wanting to explain because everything was too complicated. And he'd been too young and thoughtless to realise just how much that had hurt her.

Now they were both older. Wiser, maybe.

Except Marco knew he was in danger of really losing his heart to her. He liked the woman Becca had become— kind, yet at the same time efficient and good at her job.

If only she'd been born royal. Then it would have been so easy for both of them.

It had always been made clear to him that he had a responsibility to his country. That he should marry royalty and consolidate his country's relationship with that of another country. Royal marriages were based on duty first: respect and love had to learn to grow later.

With Ferdy being engaged to Princess Marianna, it had taken the heat off Marco; but Marco also knew that it wouldn't be too long before the pressure was back. Especially as this tour of duty with the army was likely to be his last.

Whatever this thing was between him and Becca, it

couldn't last. He'd have to give her up. Even though it would feel like ripping part of himself away.

Marco seemed thrilled when Becca told him that she could stay for dinner. And even more thrilled when, just after lunch, she mentioned that she'd brought an overnight bag with her.

'You're really going to stay?'

'If the offer's still there.'

He kissed her soundly. 'It is. Though I meant what I said about no pressure. You don't have to spend the night in my bed.'

She felt the colour flood into her face. 'What if I want to?' she whispered.

His eyes went really dark and he caught her lower lip between his. 'That,' he said huskily, 'would be a bonus.'

She'd already noticed that his accent changed when he was excited; he sounded much less English and much more Spanish.

Right now, she really wished he had two good arms. She loved the idea of him carrying her to his bed. And she had a feeling that he'd like that idea very much, too.

'Exercises,' she said, more to calm herself down than anything else. Marco tempted her too much.

'Sure.'

But she noticed he winced slightly.

'Let me see,' she said, and checked his palm. 'If that gets any redder over today, you're going back into the clinic to let Ethan have a look at it, and the paparazzi can do what they like,' she said.

'You think it's infected?'

'I think,' she said, 'we need to be careful.'

And not just with the condition of his hand.

He lay with his head in her lap while she massaged cream into his hand, taking care to be gentle enough not to hurt him yet firm enough to make a difference to the sore, tight skin.

'Thank you,' he said softly when she'd finished, and pressed a kiss to the tips of her fingers.

'Any time,' she said, stroking his cheek.

Even without Marco carrying her to his bed, Becca found herself swept away by the whole romance of sleeping with him. This time it was nothing to do with canvas and a slightly lumpy sleeping bag and everything to do with a four-poster bed, the softest and deepest pillows she'd ever seen, and cool cotton sheets with a thread count so high that the material felt softer than silk.

And, more to the point, she'd brought condoms. So this time they could really make love. Recapture the old closeness.

'I can't stop thinking about you, Becca,' he said, the admission ripping from him. 'About us. And it's driving me crazy.'

In answer, she leaned forward, just far enough to touch her mouth to his. Gently, softly. It started out all sweet and reassuring, but Marco wrapped his good arm around her, drawing her closer, and the kiss spiralled into hot, aching need.

She wasn't sure who started undressing whom, or how much help she gave him, but it seemed to take seconds until they were both naked.

'Do you have any idea how lovely you are?' he asked huskily.

She felt the colour bloom in her cheeks. 'I'm ordinary.'

He stole a kiss. 'Your judgement's off. There's nothing ordinary about you. You're beautiful, Becca.'

'You're not so shabby, yourself.' Her voice sounded husky to her own ears.

Marco traced the line of Becca's collarbones with his

fingertips; she shivered, arching her back and tipping her head so he could kiss the hollow of her throat.

He needed her so much. He wanted to touch her. Taste her. Make her feel as desperate as he did.

She shivered. 'Marco...'

He wanted her all wide-eyed and flushed with passion. Like she'd been when he'd touched her in the spa pool. When she'd fallen apart in his arms.

'I'm having a hard time taking this slowly,' he warned.

She traced his pectorals with the tip of her forefinger. 'Me, too.'

'Good.' He was so dizzy with need for her, he couldn't think straight. 'I'm in your hands,' he whispered. 'All yours.'

'All mine,' she repeated, and her mouth and eyes turned so sensual that he caught his breath.

She smoothed her hands across his bare chest and the pads of her fingertips teased his skin, making him ache. He wanted more. Much more.

She leaned forward and pressed a hot, open-mouthed kiss against his throat; he arched his head back, giving her better access, and closed his eyes in bliss as she nibbled her way across his skin. God, her mouth felt so good. And he wanted her to dip lower. To take him into her mouth and ease the ache.

Her hands stroked over his pecs, his abdomen. 'You're gorgeous.'

'And I'm aching for you.'

'Are you, now?' She looked incredibly pleased with herself. 'I need you to put that sling back on. Your hand needs support.'

He couldn't help groaning with impatience. 'You drive me crazy.'

'Oh, I intend to,' she said, her voice husky and making

his pulse kick up a notch. 'But I don't want you undoing all the hard work we've put in so far. Sling. *Now.*'

He sighed, and let her put the sling back in place. 'I could really do with two hands to do what I want to do with you.'

'Tough. You've got one. Improvise,' she said, giving him a wicked look from under her lashes.

Slowly, slowly, he dropped to his knees, stroking her abdomen. 'You feel nice.' He moved closer and nuzzled her skin. 'You smell nice.' He traced a circle round her navel with the tip of his tongue. 'And you—' He was aware that she was shaking, and stopped. 'What?'

'I'm trying to work out if you're doing the three monkeys or the three bears.' Her eyes were lit with amusement.

She'd been *laughing*?

'That was supposed to be sexy,' he said, giving her a pained look.

She just laughed at him. 'You should've worn the domino, Zorro,' she teased.

'You like the idea of being seduced by a masked hero?' he asked.

She stopped laughing then and caught her breath. And then she traced his lower lip with the tip of her index finger.

He moved to catch her finger between his lips and sucked. Hard.

'Ohhh.' It was a high, breathy sound. Sheer desire. And his whole body responded to it.

He kissed her throat, nuzzled the hollows of her collarbones; she quivered 'Your *hand*,' she said, looking at him and then looking at the bed.

'Then I guess you get to be in charge,' he said, and pulled back the covers and lay back against the pillows.

She swallowed hard, then retrieved a condom.

'Marco, I...haven't done this for a while,' she said.

'It doesn't matter.' But he was glad she'd reminded him. So he could hold himself back, take it slowly for her. Make sure that she was ready for him. 'Come here.'

Looking suddenly as shy as she had all those years ago, the very first time they'd done this, she walked over to the bed. Sat down.

He sat up again and stroked her face. 'Stop worrying,' he whispered. 'I think we both need this.'

'Yes.' Her green eyes were huge.

He kissed her, very slowly, lingering until he felt her breathing change. And then he lay back, drawing her with him.

She straddled him, and he could feel the heat of her sex against his skin.

'Now?' he whispered.

'Now.' She rolled on the condom with shaking hands, then slowly eased herself down on him.

This felt perfect. 'You feel amazing,' he whispered, pushing deeper. 'It's like the very first time.'

'Yeah.'

Her voice sounded shaky. Was she crying? He stopped moving and shifted slightly so he could look her in the eye.

'Are you OK?' he asked softly. 'Really OK?'

She nodded, clearly not trusting herself to speak.

'If you want me to stop, Becca, then I'll stop. It's fine to change your mind.' He touched her cheek with the backs of his fingers.

'It's just—it's been a while for me. And I wasn't expecting…' Her voice trailed off.

'Neither was I,' he said. And although he wanted her, very badly, he knew she needed reassurance before anything else could happen. 'Do you want me to stop?' he asked quietly.

She shook her head. 'I don't want you to stop.'

'I don't want to stop, either.' He lowered his mouth to

hers in a warm, sweet, reassuring kiss. He could feel the softness of her breasts against his skin, the hardness of her nipples—and he loved being wrapped in her warm, sweet depths.

Pleasure spiralled through him and he slowed everything right down, focusing on the pleasure; he could tell it was the same for her because she gasped and bore down on him, letting him push deeper.

And then he felt her body tighten round his, pushing him into his own climax—and it was sweeter than anything he could ever remember. Sweeter than even their first time. It felt as if he'd just found something he hadn't even known was missing—but now he knew what it was he was complete.

'My Becca,' he whispered, and sat up so he could wrap his good arm round her and hold her close.

She rested her forehead against his shoulder. 'Marco.'

They just stayed together for a while, holding each other close, enjoying the closeness. And then finally he said softly, 'I need to deal with the condom. But I'm telling you now: I want to go to sleep with you in my arms. I need you close.'

'That's fine by me,' she said softly.

Becca woke the next morning, curled against Marco's side. He was lying on his back and her head was resting on his right shoulder. She gently eased herself away so she didn't wake him, and propped herself on one elbow so she could watch him sleeping.

Asleep, relaxed, he was beautiful—and he was all hers. She didn't have to share him with anyone. It was better even than in South Africa, because there they'd both been busy and had been needed by other people; here it was just the two of them in their own little bubble.

She knew it was going to end and she ought to keep

her heart more guarded, but at the same time she knew she still loved him. She needed to be with him for as long as she could.

If only things could have been different. If only she'd had a different life growing up. Maybe if her past had been squeaky clean his family might be able to overlook the fact that she didn't have royal blood—but her past was far from squeaky clean. She'd been in a rehab clinic at sixteen. And you couldn't change the past—you could only do your best to hide it.

Later that day, Becca noticed Maria wincing in pain as she put the tray on the table.

'Maria, would you sit down for a moment, please?' she asked.

The housekeeper looked slightly worried. 'Is there a problem? Something wrong?'

'I think that's what you could tell me,' Becca said gently. 'Remember what I do for a living—OK, I'm a hand specialist, but before I specialised I learned about the rest of the body's systems, and I think right now you're in pain.'

Maria gave a dismissive flap of her hand. 'It doesn't matter. This sort of thing happens when you get older.'

'Arthritis?' Becca guessed.

'My hip. And the tablets don't work as well as they used to,' Maria admitted. 'Maybe I should go back to the doctor and see if he can give me something else. But, please—don't tell Marco. I don't want the family to think I can't do my job and pension me off. I love working here.'

'Marco's in the gym and, knowing him, he'll be there for a while,' Becca said. 'If you wouldn't mind me examining you, I might be able to give you some exercises to help with the pain.'

'Really?'

'Really. One of my favourite patients has arthritic hands. I give her exercises to help with the mobility and the pain, and I've seen a big difference over the last six months. I can do the same for you.'

Maria looked close to tears. 'That's so kind of you, *hermosa.*'

'It's the least I can do, seeing how you've spoiled me since I've been here,' Becca said.

Gently, she examined the older woman, getting her to go through a range of movements so she could see where the trouble spots were. She'd just finished teaching Maria some exercises when Marco came back into the room.

'Good morning, Maria,' he said. 'Am I too late for coffee?'

'It's cold now. I'll get you some more,' Maria said.

'It's my fault. I made her sit down and talk to me,' Becca said with a smile. 'She's told me loads of scurrilous stories about you as a child.'

'I was a perfect child,' Marco protested, laughing.

'A perfect monster, yeah,' Becca teased. 'You told me yourself how your mum had to apologise for you all the time. Making little princesses kiss your pet frog.'

'I didn't make them kiss my pet frog. I just put him on the chair next to them.' He grinned. 'They were annoying. And it stopped them pestering me to play dressing-up games when I would rather have been climbing trees.'

Maria laughed. 'He was a bit of a tearaway.'

When Maria had left, she looked at Marco. 'Can I talk to you about something?'

'Sure.'

'And it won't go any further than you?'

He frowned. 'What's wrong?'

'I need that promise first.'

'OK. I promise.'

'Thank you. There's just something I've noticed. Maria

doesn't have a lot of help, and her job's physically quite demanding.'

He looked at her. 'Are you saying this with your work hat on?'

'Pointing out that some work systems might need improving? Yes,' she said. 'Though don't you *dare* say a word to Maria.'

'Patient confidentiality?' he asked softly.

'I,' Becca said crisply, 'am not answering that. But I was just thinking there must be a way to make things a bit easier for her, but doing it tactfully, so she doesn't feel that you all think she's no longer competent.'

'I think,' Marco said, 'I get what you're saying—and also what you're not saying. And, yes, in that case, we need to be tactful. She's been with the family since Ferdy was a baby. She's part of us. That's not ever going to change and I'll make sure she knows it. But I agree, she needs more help. I should have noticed.'

'Why would you notice? You're a prince.'

'I'm a soldier,' he corrected. 'And I look at systems all the time. How things work. I should take more notice in my own home instead of being complacent and thinking that this is the way we've always done things, so this is the way it's always going to be. I'll talk to Mamá and get it sorted.'

'Good.'

'That's teamwork,' Marco said, and gave her a high five with his right hand.

'Talking of work,' Becca said, 'now you've finished being a gym rat, time to do your hand exercises.'

'Yes, boss,' Marco teased, and let her release the hand strap on his splint.

Whatever Becca's mysterious commitments were, she'd clearly managed to change her schedule because she actually agreed to stay overnight every night for the next week. Though Marco noticed that she insisted on going home before dinner and doing her own laundry. Although in some respects it annoyed him, because it was so unnecessary, at the same time he liked Becca's sense of independence and the fact that she wasn't afraid to say no to him.

It made him realise that he was falling more and more deeply in love with her. And that wasn't fair to either of them, because he still hadn't worked out how he could fit her into his life along with his royal duties.

Or maybe, he thought, he was just getting a bit stir-crazy at being cooped up here. Maybe they needed to go out and escape all the worries and just have a bit of fun. It couldn't be somewhere too public, because they'd be caught on a camera lens, but he knew somewhere they could go.'

'Tomorrow night,' he said, 'let's go dancing.'

She looked surprised, then wary. 'Dancing?'

'At a club.'

'But—isn't that a bit, well, public?'

'It's an exclusive club in Soho, owned by friends of mine.' He smiled. 'Mardi's. Short for Mardi Gras—they play mainly Latin music. Samba, salsa, tango.'

'Your kind of music?' she guessed.

'Absolutely. And it's somewhere that our privacy will be respected, because my friends will be careful for us.'

She smiled. 'You're asking me out on a date, Prince Marco?'

He shrugged. 'If you like.'

'You and I—we've never been on a date,' she said thoughtfully. 'Not even in South Africa.'

'Then maybe it's time we did.'

She bit her lip. 'Marco, we...'

He pressed the tip of his forefinger to her mouth, very

gently. 'I know. But we agreed—we'll live for the moment. And I want to dance with you, Becca.'

She looked thrilled. And then wary again. 'I, um, don't really do clubs normally. So, um, I don't think I have anything suitable to wear.'

'That's easily sorted. What size are you?'

He eyes widened. 'What?'

'What size are your shoes, your clothes?'

'No way am I going to wear a dress that one of your women left behind,' she said, sounding disgusted.

He laughed. 'I wouldn't insult you by suggesting anything like that. Apart from the fact that I don't normally bring women here, the only women within twenty years of your age who leave stuff here are my sister Bella or Ferdy's fiancée Marianna. Although they're both about the same size as you, their styles aren't the same as yours.'

'Uh-huh.'

'And, just for the record, the press exaggerates hugely. I don't date anywhere near as much as they like to make out, and I'm quite picky about who I sleep with, too.'

'Sorry.' She sighed. 'I'm not good at this relationship business.'

'Neither am I,' he said softly. 'I've made my share of mistakes. Look at what happened when I rescued my men. I made the most stupid tactical error. And other people paid for that.'

Mistakes.

This was her cue to tell him about the massive ones she'd made.

But she knew that if she told him the truth about her past, he'd start to despise her. Besides, she'd moved on from those grim, dark days. It was better to keep her own counsel.

'I'll sort you out something to wear,' he said. 'I need your dress size and your shoe size.'

'So, what? We find something on the internet and you get the stuff delivered here?'

'Better than that,' he said with a grin. 'Leave this with me.'

It wasn't until the next morning that she discovered what he meant, when Maria showed a couple of men holding armfuls of bags into the sitting room.

'Your Highness—I hope we've come up with a selection you'll like,' the first man said, bowing.

Marco had organised a shop to come to them?

And then Becca recognised the logo on the bags. A luxury department store. A place where the celebrity clients of the Harley Street clinic all had accounts, no doubt, but it was way out of Becca's league. She was too stunned to say a word.

'I'm sure you've covered everything,' Marco said with a smile. 'Thank you for being so accommodating. As you can see, I'd find shopping a little tricky at the moment.' He indicated his strapped-up hand.

'We're always happy to help, Your Highness,' the man said. 'Shall we call by this afternoon to collect what didn't suit?'

'That would be perfect. Thank you so much.'

No wonder the newspapers called him Prince Charming. Because he was.

When the shop's staff had left, Becca sat down on one of the sofas. 'Marco, please don't think I'm ungrateful, but I wasn't expecting this. I'm afraid my salary doesn't run to designer originals.'

'It doesn't have to. This was my idea, so it's my bill.'

She frowned. 'I don't expect you to buy my clothes, Marco.'

'Becca, this isn't about being a control freak and telling you what to do—I just wanted to do something nice for you, buy you a dress and shoes so we can go dancing. Is that so very bad?'

She grimaced. 'Sorry. Now I feel like a spoiled brat having a tantrum.'

He laughed. 'Trust me, I've seen spoiled women having a tantrum—and that didn't even come close.'

'It just feels weird, having a shop come to me instead of the other way round.'

'My mother and my sister do this all the time,' he said.

'Royal privilege?'

'More like valued customer privilege—they spend a lot of money at this particular store, and the store looks after them so they don't take their custom to a different store. Either they get stuff brought here, or the store opens for them outside normal shopping hours so they can go shopping in peace. I'm pretty sure they do that for other customers who spend a lot of money with them, too.'

'I guess,' Becca said, still feeling awkward.

He shrugged. 'If it makes you feel better, this way it's safer for me—if we go shopping in actual shops, supposing someone knocks into me and damages my hand?'

She coughed. 'Right, and that's not going to happen at all if we go dancing tonight?'

'It's not,' he said, 'because we're going to a small and fairly exclusive club.'

The one owned by his friends. No doubt from the moneyed set. Where she wouldn't fit in.

As if he guessed her fears, he said softly, 'Becca. This is just you and me, getting away from it all for an evening. Besides, I loathe shopping. I hate dragging round the shops. The chances are there will be someone tailing me in the hope of getting a story, and would you really want pictures of any underwear you bought splashed all over the tabloids, along with a lot of speculation?'

She'd hate being in the spotlight. And the idea of the press finding out anything about her made her bone-deep terrified. 'No.'

'Come on. Let's have a look at what they brought.'

The bags contained dresses, underwear, shoes, and accessories—in lots of different styles and colours. 'This is amazing.'

'So do I get a fashion show?' he asked.

She raised an eyebrow. 'Does this mean you're going to choose my dress?'

'No, *you're* going to choose the dress, but I want the fun of seeing you in every single one of them.'

Becca was surprised to discover just how much fun it was, dressing up and walking up and down the sitting room while Marco looked on thoughtfully.

Finally she chose a classic little black dress, shoes that were high enough to be elegant and yet low enough to dance in, and a small evening bag that was just big enough to contain her phone, keys, and some money.

'There's something missing,' he said. 'Ah, here we go.' He took a pile of boxes from another bag and started opening them. 'Diamonds—no, they're cold and you're all about warmth.' He opened another box. 'How about this set of black pearls? Look at the lustre; you can see your reflection in them.'

Diamonds and pearls? This didn't seem real. Becca rarely wore jewellery, but when she did it was costume jewellery.

Then Marco opened another box. 'No, this is the one. Just like your eyes.' He held up an emerald choker.

A chill ran through her. 'Aren't emeralds supposed to be unlucky?'

'No. That's just because they're more fragile than other stones and are more likely to chip.'

She narrowed her eyes at him. 'And how do you know so much about jewellery?'

'I had a misspent youth.' He grinned. 'OK, my grandmother has a few emerald pieces and she told me.'

Again, Becca was reminded of the differences between them. Nobody in her family had ever had jewellery, let alone 'a few emerald pieces'. As far as Becca knew, her mother had pawned her engagement ring and wedding ring so she could spend the money on alcohol.

She pushed the thought away. They'd agreed to live for the moment. And this was a night out at an exclusive club where they'd be safe from the crowds. 'Thank you.'

CHAPTER EIGHT

THAT EVENING, WHEN Becca emerged from the bathroom with her hair pinned up and the emerald choker round her neck, Marco looked at her, his eyes widening.

'You look stunning. Not that you don't look beautiful every day,' he added swiftly, 'but I've never seen you all dressed up to go out before. That dress suits you.'

'Thank you.'

'I've been thinking—it's probably easiest if I go first, then send Rafa back for you.'

She frowned. 'Why are we going separately?'

He grimaced. 'Because it's easier.'

'How? We're leaving from the same place and going to the same place, so it makes sense to share the transport.' Then understanding dawned. 'Marco, you said we were going dancing—on a real date. Have you changed your mind? Am I not good enough to be seen with you in public?'

'It's nothing to do with that.' He sighed. 'Look, my life is pretty much like a goldfish bowl. There was a media blanket when I was in Afghanistan but it's back to the usual free-for-all now. I just want to spare you from that.'

She went cold. Did he know about her past? Had he found out, somehow? His family's security team had probably investigated her and discovered the truth.

'It's just not much fun being hounded by the press, that's all,' he said softly. 'I've seen how much it's knocked Marianna's confidence. I guess I'm trying to protect you.'

So maybe he *didn't* know the truth about her, then. She just prayed she could keep her secrets until their fling was over.

'I'll go first, then meet you in there. Rafa will drive you,' he said, and kissed her swiftly. 'You look lovely. And I can't wait to go dancing with you. See you shortly.'

Was this the right thing to do? Becca wondered. Plus it would be really intimidating, meeting him in a strange place where he knew everyone but she would know nobody.

But Marco had been getting twitchy for the last couple of days. Maybe it would settle him, seeing his friends.

She went to chat with Maria in the kitchen while Rafa drove Marco to the club.

'Look at you, *hermosa*! Gorgeous,' Maria said, resting her hands on Becca's shoulders and looking at her.

'Thank you.'

'You're good for Marco, you know,' Maria said. 'Not like those fluffy women who chatter on about nothing and only care about their clothes.'

If only. Becca wrinkled her nose. 'I'm not under any illusions that it's going to last, Maria. I'm not from the right background.'

'Love always finds a way,' Maria said. 'And you love him, don't you?'

'I've loved him for years,' Becca admitted. 'I never got over him when he left me last time.'

'This time,' Maria said, 'it will be different.'

Becca knew it wouldn't be—how could there possibly be a happy ending for her and Marco when they came from such different worlds?—but she smiled at the older woman and pretended to agree.

Then Rafa came into the kitchen. 'I'll take you to the Prince,' he said.

Becca baulked when he opened the door at the back for her. 'Would you mind very much if I sat with you, instead?'

'It's a scary lifestyle the Prince leads, yes?' Rafa smiled at her. 'Sure, come and sit with me. I don't mind.'

He drove her to Soho and parked just outside the club.

'Are you going to be all right? Would you like me to walk you in?' he asked.

'No, I'm just being pathetic. I'll be fine. But thank you for being kind, Rafa.'

'No problem, *señorita*. Have a good time and I'll see you when you're ready to go home.'

She nodded. 'Marco will ring you?'

Rafa smiled. 'I wait here until you're ready.' Clearly he could see that she was about to protest that he shouldn't have to hang around, because he said gently, 'I have the radio for company. It's fine.'

'Then thank you. I'll see you later.'

She walked up the stairs to Mardi's and took a deep breath. It was ridiculous to feel so nervous; but at the same time she knew that she didn't fit into Marco's world.

He'd said the club was owned by friends of his. She hoped that they would at least be polite to her on the surface, for his sake. It would be awful if they were mean and sneered at her.

She took another deep breath and pushed the door open.

The club was amazing. From outside it was a nondescript building, but inside the walls were painted a deep burgundy, and there were fairy lights everywhere. It made the place look magical.

There was a band playing on the small stage—a singer

with a guitar, another guitarist, a double bassist and a drummer—and people were dancing. The floor was shiny black with lots of tiny lights set into it so people could see their feet as they danced.

She scanned the room, looking for Marco. He was over by the bar; he lifted his good arm in greeting, and she nerved herself to walk over to him, knowing that the people standing with him would be scrutinising her.

'Good evening, Becca,' he said softly, and kissed her. 'I did wonder if you'd chicken out.'

She shook her head. 'I couldn't do that—what if you knocked your arm and needed urgent physio?'

He laughed. 'No, I just need you.' He stroked her face. 'Come and meet my friends. This is Rupert and Henry— they own the club. They were at school with me,' he explained.

'Hello, dear girl,' Rupert said. 'Delighted to meet you.'

'Enchanté,' Henry said, and kissed her hand.

'And this is Seraphina and Talia.'

Rupert and Henry's girlfriends? she wondered. They were incredibly elegant—reminding her of Audrey Hepburn on a really stellar day—and she felt totally out of place.

'Oh, I love your shoes,' one of them said.

'And your nail polish. Such a gorgeous colour.'

They both smiled at her—and then suddenly everything was all right. She'd been worrying about nothing.

She learned that Seraphina and Talia were both Rupert's sisters, and that Rupert and Henry were life partners as well as business partners.

'Marco bailed them out last year when the club was about to go into receivership. He won't let them pay him back until they're totally on their feet again. He's really one of the good guys,' Seraphina confided.

'He certainly is,' Rupert said, clearly overhearing the

last bit. 'We used to call him El Príncipe at school—The Prince.' He smiled. 'Though when he met my sisters and everyone else's we changed that to El Príncipe Azul—Prince Charming.' He grinned. 'He was a hero to the rest of us, though—he stopped one guy bullying one of the little ones, even though he was four years older than Marco. Nobody's quite sure exactly what he did or said, but we know it involved a sword.'

Becca blinked. 'A sword?'

'And the school needed to buy a new mattress,' Henry added.

'You're telling me Marco killed someone?' she asked in a shocked whisper.

'Not quite, dear girl—wrong fluids. The guy wet himself to the point where the mattress was ruined.' Rupert smiled. 'Mind you, he never bullied anyone again after that.'

'Did he get into trouble?'

'Marco?' Henry grimaced. 'Um, yes—you can't exactly go round threatening people with swords, even if you *are* being a hero. The head confiscated his sword and banned him from fencing practice for the rest of the term—but we all knew the teachers were on his side about it.'

'Interestingly,' Rupert added, 'the bully left at the end of term and never came back.'

Becca wasn't surprised that Marco had helped a bullied child. It was totally who he was: protective and kind-hearted.

'You do know he's a serious fencer—that he's an international champion?' Henry asked.

Becca looked at Marco. 'I had no idea. You never said.'

Marco rolled his eyes. 'Honestly, it's not that big a deal.'

'A gold medallist, no less.' Rupert described a huge circle on his chest. 'Only our Marco would say it's no big deal. And you know when celebs open things by cutting ribbons? Well, El Princípe here does it with a sword.'

'Sabre,' Marco corrected dryly.

'It's still awesome—and he wears a dress uniform and looks...' Rupert fanned himself and grinned. 'Well. Such a shame you only like women, El Princípe Azul.'

''Fraid so.' Marco grinned back.

Becca smiled. 'Hey, Rupert, do you know what his surgeon called him at the clinic?'

Marco groaned. 'If you tell them that, Becca, they'll never let me live it down.'

'Too late, dear boy,' Rupert said. 'You have to tell us now, Becca, or we'll come and criticise your curtains.'

She couldn't help laughing; she liked Marco's friends immensely. 'I'm sure you'd never be so mean.'

'Come on, what did the surgeon call him, Becca?' Rupert asked, wagging his finger at her. 'Tell us. Tell us now.'

She paused for maximum effect. 'Zorro.'

Henry hooted in delight. 'How *perfect*. Wait a second.' He disappeared, and came back with a domino mask. 'Come on, dear boy, put it on.'

Marco gave him a pained look, but did so.

'Doesn't he look perfect? El Princípe, the freedom fighter—Zorro.' Henry looked pleased with himself.

Rupert looked at Marco. 'Hmm. Does the surgeon know about the medal, I wonder?'

'No—and you're not going to say anything to him, are you, Becca?' Marco said.

Becca just smiled. 'Tell me more, Henry.'

'Ferdy, now, he was the serious one who was top of the class at everything, but Marco here was the cool guy—the one who managed to make his uniform non-regulation, and he played lead guitar in a band,' Henry said.

That didn't surprise Becca in the slightest.

'Everyone's sister fell in love with him,' Rupert said,

with a stern look at his own sisters, 'and he had hordes of girls trying to sneak into school to see him.'

'He's good at everything he does,' Henry said. 'If he wasn't such a nice guy, you'd have to hate him for it.'

'Oh, enough.' Marco flapped a dismissive hand. 'I'm going to get drinks. What's everyone having? Rupert, Henry, look after my girl,' he said, once he'd taken the list of what everyone wanted to drink.

Becca found herself surprisingly happy to be left with his friends. They weren't being nice to her for Marco's sake; they were being nice because they *were* nice.

'I haven't seen him smile like that for a long time,' Rupert said. 'You've made a difference to him, Becca.'

She gave him a rueful smile. 'We don't come from the same world. I'm under no illusions here.'

'It doesn't matter where you come from,' Henry said, 'it's who you are that matters, how you treat other people. Marco believes that, too.'

Becca thought, *If only that could be true.* But her past was always going to get in the way. The only thing she could do was to make the most of now, store up the memories for the rest of her life.

'So we're dancing the tango tonight?' Marco asked when he returned with the drinks.

'You can't do it with one arm, Marco,' Rupert said.

'Yes, I can.'

Rupert rolled his eyes. 'Not if Becca hasn't done it before—unless you take the girl's part and let her lead, that is.'

Marco just grinned. 'Yeah, right. That's *so* going to happen.'

'Can I show you the steps, Becca?' Rupert asked.

She looked at Marco, who sighed. 'Rupert teaches this stuff for a living, so I guess he'll do a better job than I would.'

Rupert laughed. 'I should jolly well hope so. Especially as right now you only have one arm! Come on, Becca, darling. Now, the tango is all about stalking. See how El Príncipe here is looking daggers at me right now? That's how a man's meant to look in the tango. And here we go. Slow-slow, quick-quick.' He talked her through the basic steps. 'And at the end, when you turn round, you stamp your feet—it's great when someone has spent all day annoying you and you can stomp about like this.'

She laughed. 'You think Marco spends all day annoying me?'

'Dear girl, he's a soldier and he orders people about. Of *course* he's annoying.'

And to think she'd been worried about coming here tonight. Marco had been right, after all—she was enjoying this, had relaxed, and was really having fun.

'And there's a lovely little move where you snap your head to the side—oh, but wait, the sling.' Rupert grimaced. 'It might not be kind to him. I don't want to hurt him.'

'Perhaps we'll leave that one for now,' she said.

'OK. But you can do the corner. Marco, no promenades, OK?' Rupert instructed.

Marco just rolled his eyes.

'Let's go through it again, dear girl. Marvellous. Now he can dance with you holding you only with his right hand.' He looked thoughtful. 'But the tango is special. We're not ready to dance that yet. We'll warm everyone up with some salsa first.'

Marco took off the domino mask and put it in his pocket.

'You have to wear it for the tango,' Henry said. 'I ought to see if I can find you a cape.'

'Great idea. Then we can make him do the Paso and wave the cape about,' Rupert agreed.

'Oh, please.' Marco rolled his eyes. 'Next thing you'll have me waving a sword about.'

'Now, there's an idea,' Rupert said with a grin.

'Becca, tell them I'm unbalanced with my arm like this,' Marco pleaded.

'Unbalanced, hmm?' Henry made a mocking circle with his forefinger on his temple.

Becca couldn't help laughing.

'I give up,' Marco said, and kissed her.

Becca was having a great time. Marco taught her the basic salsa steps, and she even recognised the music—*Living la Vida Loca* and *L'Americano.*

'Now, Rupert would tell you that the salsa is a party dance. Obviously if I had both arms working properly I could teach you different steps and the arm movements, but…' He grimaced. 'Not tonight.'

She smiled. 'I'm glad you realise that will have to wait, bec—'

'Because it's not light work for my hand,' he cut in, using his good hand to make the sign of someone talking too much at her. 'Yeah, yeah. Heard it a thousand times.'

'Ah, so he's finally listening,' she teased back.

She was so glad he'd brought her here. This wasn't her usual kind of scene, but she enjoyed it, and nobody commented or tried to push her into having alcohol when she asked for sparkling water. She liked his friends, too; they seemed warm and genuine and really cared about him. And they were interested in her job, too; although when one of the girls asked for her advice about RSI Marco cut in gently, 'Hey, guys, she's off duty.'

'I don't mind. Call me at work,' Becca said, 'and I'll sort it out for you.'

They were taking a break from dancing when a woman sashayed over to them. She looked familiar, though Becca couldn't quite place her.

'Darling, how lovely to see you,' she said to Marco, and draped herself over him.

'Anastasia.' Marco was polite but seemed distant.

Anastasia kept glancing at Becca, but didn't ask to be introduced and pretty much ignored her, concentrating all her energies on Marco.

That was when the penny dropped. Anastasia must have dated Marco at some time in the past. Becca was about to make an excuse that she needed the toilet, but Marco's fingers tightened round hers, as if he'd guessed that she was desperate to go and was asking her to stay.

Eventually Anastasia gave up trying to persuade Marco to dance with her, and left in a bit of a huff.

'Sorry about that,' Marco said. 'I didn't know she was going to be here tonight.'

'Is she an ex?' Becca asked softly.

He nodded. 'It was over months ago, but she wasn't too happy when I ended it.'

Becca knew how that felt—and she also knew she'd feel that way again.

'Becca—don't overthink this,' Marco said. 'I liked her when we dated, but there wasn't a real spark between us. It's not like how...'

She caught her breath—was he going to tell her how he felt about her?

Did he feel the same way about her as she did about him?

'Not like how things are between us,' he said softly. 'You're so different from the other women in my life.'

He could say that again, she thought wryly.

'There's something about you,' he said, 'something pure and innocent.'

Oh, help. He couldn't be more wrong.

'That's what drew me to you in South Africa, I think,' he said. 'You're not tarnished by life.'

Yes, she was. She'd been in rehab at sixteen. She'd seen the darkest sides of life. She'd watched people pour their lives away.

'I admire you,' he said, his eyes dark with sincerity. 'Really I do.'

How would Marco react if he knew the truth about her—if he knew that every day she had to remind herself to breathe and never, ever let her life spiral back to where it had been? He wouldn't admire her then. Nobody in their right mind would admire someone who'd skipped school in favour of vodka.

Maybe she should break it off now, before he could find out the truth about her and she saw his feelings change and crumble into dust.

And yet they'd agreed this was happy-for-now. They both knew their fling would have to end when he healed enough to go back to his royal duties. Was it so wrong of her to want to cherish these last few days together, to eke out every precious moment?

'Becca?' he asked softly. 'What's wrong?'

She was saved from having to answer when Henry came over and patted them both on the shoulder. 'It's time to tango. You need to wear your mask.'

Marco rolled his eyes but put the domino on.

When the music began, they went onto the dance floor.

'It's not the same with only one arm, but one day I'll dance with you properly,' Marco promised. 'For now, I'm afraid this will have to do.'

The music was incredibly sensual. Becca found herself picking up the beat easily after Rupert's earlier tutorial, especially as Marco guided her with his good arm and used his body to make her move the right way. He talked her through the steps: slow-slow, quick-quick, swaying along.

Then a spin. 'Quick-quick, turn; quick-quick, stamp—and we do it again,' he said.

Then they found themselves in the corner of the dance floor. Marco leaned over her and drew his hand into the small of her back, making her arch backwards. For a moment Becca's heart skipped a beat and she thought he was going to kiss her. But then he pulled back, guiding her with his good hand to lean over him, before repeating the move so that he was leaning over her and his lips were just millimetres from hers.

It took her breath away and the mask made everything ten times worse, because it made him look like a movie star. Sexy as hell.

He danced her round the corner and along the next side of the room, keeping her close and his thighs thrust between hers.

'Oh, my God, Marco—I had no idea you could dance like this,' she said.

'I love the tango,' he told her. 'It's the same stance as boxing—but I'm more of a lover than a fighter.'

He was both, she thought. A lover and a fighter—for freedom and truth and decency.

And she loved every single bit of him.

She was shocked by how hot the dance made her feel—how much she wanted him. And it decided her: no, she wouldn't tell him about her past. She'd take these sweet, stolen moments as they were and not spoil them.

When the dance ended, he kissed her lingeringly.

'Marco—can we go home?' she asked.

He gave her a slow, sensual smile, as if he knew what she was really asking. 'Great idea. Let's go home.'

CHAPTER NINE

MARCO AND BECCA said a quiet goodbye to Henry and Rupert, then left the club wrapped in each other's arms. But the second they stepped outside the front door flashes started popping in their faces.

On instinct, Becca covered her face. This was just like the press pack outside the clinic when the news of Marco's injury broke. Except this time they appeared to be focused on him.

And on her.

Panic flooded through her. She prayed they hadn't caught a picture of her face. If they found out who she was they'd reveal her past to the world and, worst of all, to Marco. The man she'd lied to.

She had to get out of here.

Now.

Just as she was about to run, Marco clamped her to his side. 'Keep your head down and don't worry—just walk. I'll protect you.'

No, you can't protect me, she thought. *Nobody can protect me. Not now.*

Marco's bodyguard—who'd been so discreet that she hadn't even noticed him at the club—materialised on the other side and cleared a path to the car.

The noise levels were unbelievable. People were all

talking and yelling at once, and she could barely make out the words; it was just a babble of noise. Flashbulbs were still going off, lighting up every step they took. What? Were they waiting for her to trip and fall over? For her skirt to fly up and show her knickers? They were like a crowd of teenage bullies, going on and on and on, and never shutting up. Pushing and pushing and pushing.

'Who's the girl, Marco?'

'Who's your lady friend?'

'Are you going to leave us a glass slipper, Cinderella?'

And the comments were interspersed with mocking catcalls and whistles, no doubt designed to make her look them in the eye so they could get a clear picture of her face.

'Ignore them. They're simply trying to get a reaction,' Marco said.

Just like playground bullies, she thought.

Except Marco wasn't going to be able to protect her as he'd protected the little boy at school by facing the bully down, because you couldn't face down the press. They'd find their story and twist it and twist it until they got their sensational headlines and their sales, not caring whose lives they wrecked in the process.

They just about made it to the car.

'Take me home,' she begged as she closed the car door on the rabble outside. 'Please take me home.'

'Rafa, back to Regent's Park, please,' Marco said.

'No, I want to go to *my* home,' Becca said, close to tears. 'They'll follow us to your place—if I go back to mine I can disappear and they won't find me. They don't know who I am so it'll all blow over.'

He took her hand. 'Becca, even if Rafa breaks a few speed limits, it won't make a difference. Some of the paps have motorbikes, so they will be able to keep up with us. And do you really want to be doorstepped at your place?'

She thought of how the paparazzi had been at the clinic, blocking the whole street to get a picture or a quote about one of their celebrity patients. That would be unthinkable in her quiet little street.

'At least at my home you'll be protected. You won't be out there on your own.'

She felt sick. Maybe she ought to tell him the truth about her past, right here and now—but she just couldn't face seeing the disgust in his eyes if he knew what she was and what she'd done.

She hadn't cried since the day she'd found out Marco had abandoned her without a word in South Africa. She'd thought she'd cried out all her tears then—but now she found herself sobbing, unable to stop.

Marco hated feeling so useless. There was nothing he could say or do to make this right for her. He knew she'd seen the paps in action before, given that the Harley Street clinic where she worked treated celebrities, but nothing could prepare you for actually having it happen to *you*. He'd been used to it all his life, but he knew it must be overwhelming to someone who wasn't used to living in the public eye.

When they got back to Regent's Park, he made her a mug of hot milk and shooed Maria away. 'No, of course I haven't done anything to make her cry. It's shock because the press followed us. Don't worry, I'll look after her.'

Becca didn't drink the milk. All she did was cry silently.

'Talk to me, Becca,' he begged, seriously worried. 'You're blowing this out of proportion. Once they work out who the mystery girl is they'll have their story. They'll run on for a bit about the prince and the physio, and then it'll die down. There might be a couple of headlines—

Who's that girl? or something like that—and then they'll find someone else to annoy.'

She shook her head and just looked at him in mute appeal.

He didn't understand why she was reacting this badly. What did she have to worry about? It didn't matter that she wasn't a socialite.

'Come on, let's go to bed,' he said. 'And, no, this isn't me trying to take advantage of you. It's me saying I want to hold you and make you feel safe until you fall asleep.'

To his horror, more tears streamed down her face.

'Becca, talk to me. What's wrong?'

She shook her head, clearly unable to get the words out.

'If I didn't have a busted arm, I'd carry you,' he said.

She looked horror-stricken at that, no doubt worried that he'd hurt himself.

He brushed his mouth lightly against hers. 'Come on, let's go to bed. Everything will be fine in the morning.'

He lay there with her curled against him. He knew she was still crying because he could feel the warmth and wetness of her tears against his skin, but he didn't know how to fix this, what to do or say. He just held her and hoped that he was right about the press and all would be fine in the morning.

All the same, he slept badly. Becca was clearly exhausted as he could hear her breathing, slow and deep; she wasn't faking sleep.

Unable to settle, he got up early, without waking her, and checked the news sites on the internet.

As he'd expected, there were a few *Who's that girl?* headlines.

But then he hit 'refresh' and saw the headlines of the story change.

My Nights of Shame with Prince's Lover...

What?

Marco flicked through the reports. They seemed to be focused on a guy called Barney, telling how Becca had been drunk out of her mind on vodka. According to him, she'd taken tablets to get high, then spent a sordid night with him.

No, this had to be some kind of mistake. Becca wasn't like that. She wasn't a wild child. The girl he'd met in South Africa had been sweet and shy. She'd been a virgin, for pity's sake. You couldn't fake that…could you?

And Marco knew for a fact that Becca didn't drink. He'd offered her champagne and cocktails and Pimm's, here on the roof garden, and she'd told him straight that she didn't drink. She'd drunk only mineral water last night at the club.

Then again, this could explain why she was teetotal. Because she'd had problems with drink before, now she couldn't trust herself with so much as a single sip of alcohol.

More news reports were coming through, all saying the same. Some had different levels of detail, but all of them said she'd been a wild child as a teen.

Why hadn't she told him?

Did she really think he would judge her for something that had happened years ago, when she was still little more than a child? Did she really think that he hadn't made some stupid mistakes himself?

He scanned another page and a fact leapt out at him.

Barney was in his late forties.

And if this had happened when Becca was sixteen, ten years ago…

What the hell had a man in his late thirties been doing with a teenager less than half his age?

Something about this wasn't right. Had the guy been grooming her? Had he been the one who'd given her the drink and the drugs?

Right at that second Marco wanted to hunt this Barney down. He wanted to pin the guy to the wall, with the tip of his sword at the scumbag's jugular vein, and demand some real answers.

And he was furious for himself for not protecting Becca. Why had he been so stupid and pushed her into going out for a night of fun at Mardi's when she'd been reluctant to go in the first place?

Henry and Rupert were loyal to him, he knew, and would have been more likely to create a diversion for the press to keep their attention off him rather than rat him out. But there had been someone else at the club who'd had an axe to grind, especially given that he hadn't gone there alone. He was pretty sure he knew who'd tipped the press off. There was nothing he could do about it now it had happened, but he could make Anastasia apologise to Becca and then warn everyone that he knew what she'd done, so they knew Anastasia couldn't be trusted and they'd need to be careful what they said and did around her in future.

He felt as if he'd been sucked into the middle of a seething cauldron of guilt, anger, and despair. He was guilty and angry with himself that he hadn't been able to protect Becca from all this spite and that she'd been hurt; he was angry with Becca that she'd kept something so huge from him; and he was despairing because he realised now that he'd been working towards the idea that his family might accept her as his life partner, but he knew all this mess would close the conservative royal circles to her. Anyone involved with the monarchy had to be totally squeaky clean. And even though Becca had been very young at the time it had happened—and he was damn sure she hadn't been the instigator of the drink, drugs and sex stuff—the mud was still going to stick.

He heard the door to the library close and looked up.

Becca was standing there, fully dressed, looking pale and drawn and incredibly nervous.

Becca could see that Marco was reading something on the internet. If her phone hadn't been out of charge she would have checked the news herself. But she had a nasty feeling that the truth was out now. All of it. In every deeply shameful detail.

She couldn't tell from his expression how he felt about it. He'd said last night that he admired her. Now, would he despise her?

'Are you all right?' he asked.

She nodded, and swallowed hard. 'It's in the papers, isn't it? Everything?'

'Yes.'

The story must have travelled round the whole world before breakfast. And now everyone knew just how bad her past had been.

'Why didn't you tell me?' he asked.

'I couldn't—I was...' The words stuck in her throat. 'I was ashamed,' she whispered. 'So ashamed.'

Just as she could see now that he was ashamed of his relationship with her—and she couldn't blame him for it. After all, she'd just dragged his name into the mud along with hers.

'You should have told me,' he said.

Becca knew she was being unfair, taking out her shock and fear on him, but she couldn't help the anger bubbling over. 'Why? So you could judge me and find me wanting?'

'No. I'd never do that.' He stared at her. 'But I'm hurt that you didn't trust me. That you didn't feel you could tell me the truth.'

'It wouldn't have changed anything, would it? You can't change the past. I was a drunk and I went to rehab. Telling you wouldn't make me *not* have been a drunk. And I'm not a drunk any more. So what was the point of rehashing the past and telling you?'

'Because at least then I would've heard it from you. I wouldn't have had to find out from some spiteful, scurrilous article.'

That was true. But right now she couldn't think straight. The fear and the misery were uppermost. 'What's the point?' she asked. 'This thing between us—it's always been a fraud. Right from the start, in South Africa, when you lied about who you were. And this time round we couldn't even conduct a relationship in the open—it had to be kept a secret.'

'That's not fair,' Marco said. 'I wasn't the only one who wanted to keep it quiet. It suited you, too.'

Because she'd been an idiot and tried to hide from the truth. She should have known better.

'And,' he said, 'I might point out that I took you to meet my friends.'

She scoffed. 'We didn't even go to that club together. You went first, and I followed.'

'Because it was easier that way.'

'Easier for *you*. Do you have any idea how it felt, having to walk into a room on my own where you knew loads of people and I knew nobody?' Her eyes met his. 'You've lived such a privileged, pampered life—you have absolutely no idea what the real world's like.'

'Says the woman who works in a clinic catering to the rich and pampered,' he snapped back.

She flinched. 'We do a lot of charity work at 200 Harley Street. It isn't all facelifts and cosmetic procedures.'

'No?'

'No, it damn well isn't! You should know—they treated *you*. And I might not even have a career there any more.'

The one thing that had been certain in her life and now

it wasn't. Fear of what was going to happen next made her bones feel as if they'd turned to liquid.

'Now all my past's been dragged up people aren't going to want me to treat them. I might even be struck off the register for unprofessional behaviour. It's all right for someone like you—you've got a family behind you, people who have your back. The only person I can really rely on is me—and I'm not going to be able to save myself from this.'

She shook her head.

'I can't stay here any more.' Not being so close to him, and knowing that he could never be hers any more. It was too much for her. She wanted out.

'You can't go. The paps are knee-deep outside,' he said wearily.

Not *Don't go because I love you and I want you to stay,* she noticed. He was worried about his *reputation,* not her. How had it come to this? How had all the love just leaked away overnight to leave them with nothing?

'I'll take my chances with them.' She lifted her chin. 'You know as well as I do it could never have worked out between us. We would never have got together in a million years. A prince can't date an addict—even a reformed one. But this time, Marco, this time *I* get to be the one to walk away.' Even though walking out on him was going to be like ripping her heart out.

How stupid she'd been to let herself fall in love with him all over again. With a man she knew was out of her reach, a man she could never have. They'd been living in a bubble, and now it was time to face the truth. It was over.

'Don't bother sending my stuff after me,' she said. 'Just throw it away. I don't want it any more.' Not when everything would be soaked in memories of him.

* * *

As Becca walked out, Marco was too shocked to stop her or follow her.

She clearly wasn't going to listen to his side of things.

Just when he'd been sure that he'd found someone who actually loved him for himself—someone who'd loved him before she even knew that he was a prince—he realised that he hadn't.

If she'd really loved him then she would have known she could tell him anything and it wouldn't matter.

The fact that she'd kept such a dark secret from him just proved that she didn't trust him—and if she didn't trust him, then how could he trust her?

So maybe she was right and it was better this way.

Maybe he should just let her go.

Because you couldn't give someone a royal order to love you. You couldn't order them to feel something they didn't feel.

And she was right, too, about them never getting together in a million years—they came from such different places. This was a reality check. The bubble had burst.

The only thing was, he didn't want it to be over.

And he didn't see how it could be anything *but* over.

Angry, hurt and just a tiny bit bitter, Marco sat at the piano and, one-handed, played all the saddest music he knew—music of pain and heartbreak and misery. And even then it couldn't express how he felt because he couldn't add in the bass, the deep notes of despair.

Becca left everything behind in the house at Regent's Park except her handbag.

Marco hadn't come after her. How stupid she'd been to hope that he'd care enough to follow her, that he'd ask her not to go and tell her they could work something out. The fact that he hadn't just proved that she'd just been a diversion for a bored prince while he waited for his hand to heal.

The press were waiting outside for her.

This time she wasn't going to let them make her cry. Or run. They could all go to hell, as far as she was concerned. Because she really didn't care any more. She didn't care about anything. Because she didn't have a heart left to care.

She just ignored the cameras flashing and the questions being yelled at her and strode through the park until she got to the Tube station. She was relieved that she already had a season ticket and didn't have to worry about buying a ticket. She lost some of the press pack in the morning rush hour as she went through the ticket barrier, then quickened her pace and took the left-hand side of the escalator so she could rush down in the middle of a pack of commuters instead of being trapped in one place. As she was halfway down the escalators, she felt the cool breeze signalling that a train was coming in and quickened her pace again. It didn't matter that the train was going in the wrong direction; she could sort that out later. She heard the station announcement telling passengers to mind the doors, and managed to squeeze on to the train.

Thank God none of the press pack was quick enough to follow her. No doubt they'd all been barged out of the way by irritated commuters.

Becca stayed on the train until it stopped at Embankment. Then she joined the throng of commuters, changed over to the Circle line, and caught the Tube through to Paddington. Hopefully the press wouldn't have managed to dig up her address yet.

She kept her head down as she left the train, but there was no sign of waiting paparazzi. Relieved, she headed for her flat and locked the door behind her.

Safe at last.

But just what did she do now?

Technically, she was still working one to one with Marco, so her caseload at the clinic was still being covered and she didn't have to worry about missing any appointments. But she knew that the rest of the staff would have seen the news. She couldn't just pretend that nothing had happened; she had to face it.

Just…not quite yet.

It was still early, officially before the start of the main day at the clinic, so with any luck she'd get the answering machine instead of the receptionist and could leave a message to buy herself a little more time and work out what to say. How to explain. How to apologise.

To her relief, the answering machine kicked in. 'Sorry, it's Becca,' she said. 'I'm not feeling well. I'm not working today. I'll keep you posted. Sorry.' Aware that she was gabbling, and not wanting to risk that someone would hear the message as she was speaking and pick up the phone, she hung up.

A few moments later the doorbell rang. Marco? Her heart leapt at the thought.

She picked up the Entryphone. 'Yes?'

'Becca Anderson?'

It was a voice she didn't recognise—and there was the kind of hubbub in the background that told her some of the journalists had managed to get hold of the electoral roll and found her details on it. Of course it wouldn't be Marco. He didn't even know where she lived.

She didn't answer the journalist, and hung up without pressing the button to let anyone in.

The doorbell rang again and again, but she ignored it.

No doubt now they were after her side of the story, to

see if they could fill in any juicy details that Barney had left out.

Well, tough. They weren't going to get it. She had nothing to tell them.

Becca spent the next three days holed up in her apartment, not answering the phone or the door or emails, and keeping her mobile phone turned off most of the time. When she did turn it on, she deleted all messages from Marco without reading them and just ignored the ones from work. She still couldn't face talking to anyone. Not even Lexi, who'd left several messages before Becca's answering machine was filled to the max, and then texted her saying she was there whenever Becca needed to talk.

What should she do now?

The first thing would be to resign. The stories about her were just too awful; if she stayed, her reputation would drag down the clinic. Patients wouldn't want to be treated by someone like her. But leaving the clinic meant she'd have to give up her flat, too. She wouldn't be able to afford it without a job. And where was she going to find another job? She still wasn't sure if she'd be struck off the register for unprofessional conduct, but even if she wasn't she could hardly ask for a reference. Without a reference she'd be unemployable. All her dreams, all her future—gone.

And the worst bit was how much she missed Marco. Last time round she'd been a naïve teenager. This time round she was a strong, independent woman. She'd made exactly the same mistake. And, this time it hurt more. Missing him was a physical ache. The rest of her life stretched out in front of her, and there was nothing left to fill it. Just a black hole where she wished Marco could be.

And all the time the press remained camped outside the block of flats. In the end, she disconnected the Entryphone because she was tired of the constant calling.

When Becca finally managed to slip out of the back entrance to her block of flats, without the paparazzi following her, she went straight to Harley Street.

'Is Ethan in?' she asked Helen, the receptionist on duty.

'Yes, he's in his office,' Helen said. 'Are you all right, Becca?'

No, she wasn't all right, and she didn't think anything would ever be all right again. She gave the receptionist a sad little smile in answer, went to Ethan's office and rapped on the open door.

He looked up from his desk. 'Becca, you look like crap,' he said bluntly.

'I'm sorry I let you down and went off sick,' Becca said. 'I wasn't really sick. I just couldn't...'

'It's OK. I understand,' he soothed her.

She took a deep breath. 'I'll resign.'

'You most certainly will not,' Ethan said. 'You're an excellent hand therapist and we don't want to lose you. Your resignation is not accepted.'

'But all the stuff in the papers...'

'I don't care—well, I do,' he said, 'because I hate to think that you had such a rough time growing up, and I'd like to scoop out that Barney's heart with a rusty blunt scalpel.' He smiled at her. 'And, believe you me, I'd have to fight for my place at the front of the queue to do that.'

She stared at him, not quite believing this.

'Look, I know what it's like to have a parent who drinks.'

She nodded. She'd heard the rumours, even though it had all happened years ago—which was also why she knew the stories about her would run and run and run.

'It's not pleasant. And look at you now—you've pulled yourself out of that world. It all happened years ago, and it's totally not relevant to what you do now.'

'But won't the patients—well—prefer not to be treated by someone like me?' Becca asked.

'Are you kidding? Mrs van der Zee has been ringing every day to see if you're back yet, and she's not the only one—they're all worried about you.'

Becca felt the tears well up and blinked them back.

'You belong here,' Ethan said, 'and we've got your back, Becca. You're one of us.'

She really belonged?

Really, *really?*

She couldn't trust herself to speak, at first, but eventually she managed a broken 'Thank you.'

'Anyway, where the hell is Zorro? Why hasn't he protected you from the monsters in the press?' Ethan demanded.

'We— It's over,' she said in a whisper.

Ethan said something very pithy about what Marco was lacking.

'That's not quite fair, Ethan. I was the one who walked out on him.'

'But he should've come to get you back. He's an idiot and he doesn't deserve you.' Ethan narrowed his eyes. 'And I told him not to flirt with my staff. I thought he'd understand that meant anything further than flirting was way off limits.'

Becca couldn't say anything to that.

'Right. Lexi will help deal with the press—we'll get this sorted and minimise the damage. And we want you back to work, so go and scrub your face. When did you last eat?'

'I can't remember,' she admitted. Since the story had broken, she hadn't felt like eating.

'Well, you can't live on fresh air. Go down to the buffet and grab some breakfast—I don't want you fainting on anyone—and then get in that white coat and back in your office, OK?'

'OK.' It was so, so much more than she'd hoped for. So much more than she thought she deserved. 'Thank you.'

Funnily enough, eating breakfast did make her feel better. And so did the fact that every single member of the clinic dropped in to see her, give her a hug, and say that they were on her side.

'You idiot. Why didn't you tell me?' Lexi hugged her. 'You know what I do for a living. You know I could've spun this for you and saved you from all the nonsense.'

Becca was too close to tears to answer.

Lexi hugged her again. 'And we're friends, right?'

Friends. This time, a tear trickled down her cheek. 'I think so,' she whispered.

'I know so,' Lexi said. 'Even though you always keep so much of yourself back.'

'I'm not used to having friends,' Becca said. 'When I was little…' She dragged in a breath. 'People got sick of my mum being late to pick me up from playdates. And they noticed that she smelled of drink. So they didn't encourage their kids to be my friend. I was always the child in the class who didn't get invited to any of the birthday parties.'

Lexi stroked her hair. 'That sucks.'

'It's how it was. It was my life.' She dragged in a breath. 'It wasn't so bad when I was a teen. You know how kids like to rebel against their parents—so my home life didn't stop them being friends with me. Or *trying* to be. Nobody ever taught me how to make friends. I wasn't very good at it.' She looked away. 'Then I started drinking. I wasn't nice to be around. I was an embarrassment to everyone.'

'The teen years are hard,' Lexi said softly. 'Harder still if you don't get support from your parents.'

Becca narrowed her eyes. 'That sounds personal.'

'It is. The way you look…' Lexi shook herself. 'Enough of that. But the important thing is not to stop believing in yourself. Look what you did. You were dragged into the kind of world a teenager should never be dragged into. And you got yourself out of it. You studied hard, and you got yourself a really good job. You're stronger than you think.'

'Right now I don't feel strong. I feel stupid.' Becca blinked away the tears. 'What was I thinking, having an affair with Marco? He's a prince. Of course the likes of him aren't for me.'

'Why not?'

Becca found herself telling Lexi the whole messy story. How she'd fallen in love with 'Seb' at the camp and he'd broken her heart. How she'd met Marco again at the clinic and they hadn't been able to stop themselves falling all the way back in love. And now… 'He didn't ask me to stay or say he'd help me fix things.'

'Did you give him the chance to ask you to stay?' Lexi asked.

'Maybe not,' Becca admitted. She bit her lip. 'He was pretty angry because I hadn't told him the truth.'

'Angry because you hadn't trusted him, maybe,' Lexi said.

'That night, just before the press lay in wait for us, he said he admired me. That I was sweet and innocent and untarnished.' She closed her eyes. 'Now he despises me.'

'Did he say that?'

'He didn't have to.'

'Does it not occur to you that there's a lot to admire about you?' Lexi asked. 'Look at the way you've overcome your past.'

'That's just PR spin,' Becca said.

'No. It's the truth. Look at yourself properly, Becca. You've got so much to give. And Marco has a point. What happened wasn't your fault. You were a child. People were supposed to look after you, not drag you down into the mire.'

'I could've said no.'

'When was the last time you had a drink?'

Becca thought about it. 'Before rehab.'

'Years ago. Exactly. You're strong, Becca. You're amazing. And that's what Marco would've seen if you'd trusted him with the truth. I don't know him that well, but what I do know is that he has integrity. Give the man a chance. Trust him—and then you can really move on from your past.'

'I think it's too late for that.' Becca shook her head. 'I'm totally unsuitable for him. His parents would never approve.'

'His parents,' Lexi said, 'are surprisingly down to earth. And they're very easy to work with in PR terms. You need to take that step forward, Becca. Trust yourself. And trust him. I know it's easier said than done, but think about it.' She hugged Becca again. 'I'll see you later, with my PR hat on, and we'll get a few things sorted. But, for now, just remember I'm here. As your friend.'

The lump in her throat was so huge Becca could hardly speak. 'I will,' she whispered.

Becca's first patient of the day was Mrs van der Zee.

'Are you sure you still want me to treat you?' Becca asked. 'After all the stuff in the press?'

'Which no doubt they exaggerated to sell more filthy copies.'

'Not that much,' Becca said. 'I was addicted to vodka and E.'

'You were sixteen, still a child, and it wasn't your fault,' Mrs van der Zee said. 'That man has a lot to answer for. I think every parent in the country wants to find that man and make quite sure he can never do anything like that again.'

Becca felt the tears well up again. She hadn't expected people to be so kind.

And it made it hurt even more that the one person she'd wanted to believe in her, root for her, had just abandoned her and left her to it.

Mrs van der Zee hugged her. 'It'll work out, love—don't you worry. And I think that prince of yours needs a good kick up the backside, war hero or no war hero.'

That earned her a watery smile. 'He's one of the good guys.'

'Well, he should be here protecting you and making the press go away,' Mrs van der Zee said. 'Now, shall we get started?'

Becca wouldn't answer a single one of Marco's calls, and either the clinic was protecting her or she'd totally gone to ground. All the curtains in her flat were drawn. The door hadn't been answered when he'd sent a discreet box of chocolates to apologise—because he knew damn well that the press would make a big deal of it if he sent a huge bouquet that she refused to accept. Being Becca, she *would* refuse to accept it.

The only reason that he hadn't gone to get her himself was because he knew that it would make the press speculation much, much stronger, and they'd make her life even harder. At times like this he really hated his background and wished that he was just an ordinary man who wouldn't be noticed going about his day-to-day business—that he could put things right without every movement being scrutinised in the public eye.

But the worst bit was the huge hole in his life now Becca wasn't here. He hated being without her. The future was just lonely and bleak, stretching out for eternity.

Nothing but his duty to sustain him. And that would be his royal duty; he had to be honest and admit that the injury to his hand would make it next to impossible to go back to active service in the army. Anything less than full fitness would put his men in jeopardy, and he wasn't prepared to be that selfish.

Just his royal duty, and no Becca to help him through it.

Then again, if he had Becca in his life it meant he couldn't have his family. He couldn't bring disrepute on the monarchy and the mud would most definitely stick, even though Becca was clearly clean of drink and drugs now.

If he stayed as Prince Marco, he'd be without the love of his life.

If he became an ordinary man, he'd be without his family.

Why couldn't he have come from an ordinary family so none of this would matter? What was so wrong with wanting love *and* your family? Why couldn't you have both? There had to be a way. There just had to be.

And he couldn't sort it out in England. He needed to be back in Sirmontane and talking it over with the two people who could help him make it happen. He needed them to understand how he really felt. And maybe, just maybe, they could work it out.

Four hours later, Marco walked into his parents' drawing room in the castle.

'My son.' Elena, his mother, greeted him with a hug. 'You look absolutely terrible.'

He rolled his eyes. 'Thanks, Mamá.'

'I'm your mother. I'm not going to lie to you.' She hugged him again.

Alfonso, too, hugged Marco. 'Your mother has been worrying about you.'

'I'm healing.' He indicated his left hand. 'I get to do more this month.'

'Not just about your injury. We've read the papers,' Elena said.

And no doubt they thought the worst of Becca. 'She's not like the press paint her,' he said. 'She's not a wild child at all. She's brave and she's managed to overcome her past—she's worked hard and made a good career for herself. There's a lot to admire about her.'

'I agree, the press are spinning it,' Elena said, surprising him. 'She was vulnerable when it happened. Still a child. And it wasn't her fault that she was led into the darker edges of life.'

'I agree, too. And as for Barney, I'd horsewhip him myself,' Alfonso said.

The guy who'd groomed her. 'I'll kill him,' Marco said.

'No—and we don't want another incident like that one with the sword at school,' Alfonso said. 'You're not a hot-head in the army. Don't be a hothead outside it. Think before you act. How many times have I told you that?'

'And how many times haven't I listened?' Marco asked wryly.

'You are who you are.' Elena smiled at him. 'So you knew Becca before you met her at the clinic?'

'I first met her in South Africa, at the children's aid camp.' Marco grimaced. 'Then Abuelo was taken to hospital. I went back for her when the doctors said he would pull through, but she'd already left South Africa. Vanished.'

'And you didn't tell her where you were going in the first place, did you?' Elena asked, rolling her eyes. 'Why are boys so hopeless when it comes to communicating?'

'That's why we get married, *cariña*,' Alfonso said, kissing her. 'So our wives can do it for us.'

She flapped a dismissive hand. 'This is about our son, not you.'

'Though Papá has a point,' Marco said dryly.

'Yes, I suppose he does.' She sighed. 'Sometimes, Marco, for a man who can be so bright, I wonder how you can be quite so stupid. Do you know that Becca is still involved with the rehab centre that helped her?'

'How do you know that?' he asked, surprised that his parents seemed to know a lot more about the situation than he did.

'We've been working with Lexi at the clinic,' Alfonso said.

'Becca's a volunteer at the rehab centre,' Elena explained. 'She talks to young girls like she was, girls who are addicted to drink and worse, and helps them find their way back to a happier life.'

The penny suddenly dropped. That was the 'commitment' Becca had been so vague about. And of course she wouldn't have been able to tell him about it, because then she would have had to explain why she helped there.

And now for the crunch issue. The one that could divide him from his family. But he needed it to be out in the open.

'Becca's the only woman I've ever really loved. The woman I want to spend the rest of my life with. I know it's all a mess, and lots of people are going to think she's totally unsuitable to be a princess. But I'm so miserable without her.' He bit his lip. 'I've been thinking about it. I'm prepared to give up being a prince, if that's what it takes to make her acceptable as my wife. But I don't want to lose my family. I don't want to have to choose between you. And that's why I came home. To talk to you. To see if there was a way I could still be your son but be with the woman I love.'

'My darling boy, you would *never* have to choose between us. We're your parents and we will always love you, no matter what you do and even when you make us worried sick. We want you to be happy,' Elena said. She tutted. 'Alfonso, I told you he was stupid. How could he think such a thing?' She cuffed Marco's good arm.

'So you would accept Becca,' he said carefully, 'as my wife?'

'We think she's a shining example of strength and grace, someone who's lived through hard times and come out the other side to help others who fall into the same traps,' Alfonso said. 'And other European princes have married women who are not of royal birth. This is the twenty-first century. There isn't the same issue over class that there was for my father, or my father's father.'

Hope flared in Marco's heart for the first time in days. 'With Becca at my side I'll be a better man. A better prince.'

'A better soldier?' Elena asked dryly.

He shook his head. 'I have to be honest. My hand will heal, but I might never regain the full range of movement or grip. I won't be able to do my job properly, and I won't put other people at risk just for the sake of my pride. I'm prepared to accept an honourable discharge, or just finish my tour of duty as a pen-pusher. And then that's it. I'm back in the fold and ready to begin my royal duties.'

Elena hugged him. 'For that alone I would gladly accept Becca. Because having her in your life will take you out of danger.'

'Small problem,' Marco said. 'She's not talking to me right now.'

'So you think she'll turn you down?'

'I'm going to eat humble pie,' Marco said. 'And I'm going to tell her how I really feel about her. And then, with luck, she'll agree to make me the happiest prince in the world.'

'Go, *niño*,' his father said, 'with our blessing.'

Elena coughed. 'We'll be going to London, too.'

Alfonso frowned. 'Why?'

'To meet our future daughter-in-law.'

'Mamá, much as I love you, I'm not having that conversation with Becca in front of you,' Marco said.

Elena laughed. 'Of course not. But I'm looking forward to meeting her. And you can tell her that, too—not in an intimidating way, but in a welcoming way.'

Marco smiled. 'That's a royal order I'd be very happy to carry out.'

'I'll call Carlos and have the plane sorted out,' Alfonso said. 'And you need to do your exercises and then rest your hand, *niño*.'

CHAPTER TEN

FIRST THING THE next morning, Rafa drove Marco to the back entrance of the Hunter Clinic, and Marco slipped inside.

The receptionist looked at him. 'Can I help you, Your Highness?'

Either she recognised him from his stay at the clinic, or she'd seen the newspapers. Given the slight coolness of her tone behind the politeness, he had a nasty feeling it was the latter. Of course everyone here would be protective of Becca.

'I was, ah, hoping to see Becca Anderson.' He indicated his strapped-up arm. 'I'm due a physiotherapy session.'

'I see. If you wouldn't mind waiting over there, Your Highness, I'll see if I can find her for you,' the receptionist said, gesturing to the waiting area.

Marco sat down on one of the plush white leather sofas. He ignored the glossy magazines on the low coffee table; right at that moment he couldn't concentrate on anything. He just needed to see Becca.

But would she agree to see him?

He looked up hopefully as he heard someone come down the corridor. Except the tall male figure wasn't the one he wanted to see.

Ethan Hunter looked grim. 'Shall we go to my office, Your Highness?'

Oh, hell. He wasn't here to have a fight. He was here to make things right.

'Sure,' he said, and followed the surgeon to his office.

Though he declined to have a seat.

'So what you do want, Your Highness?' Ethan asked.

Marco sighed inwardly. It wasn't just his relationship with Becca that he'd messed up; he'd crushed his burgeoning friendship with the spiky ex-army doctor, too. 'I need to see Becca,' he said.

'Uh-huh.' Ethan gave him a level stare. 'I told you not to flirt with my staff, but you completely ignored me. In fact, you did more than that. So, tell me, why the hell should we even let you back here?'

'Because I need to see Becca.'

'I don't give a damn who you are—prince or no prince, you hurt Becca, and that's not acceptable. We have a zero tolerance policy and no money or celebrity or royal status will ever change that.'

Marco knew he deserved every bit of the reprimand. 'I screwed up,' he said softly. 'But, hand on heart, Clavo, can you tell me you've never made a mistake? Can you tell me you've never hurt a woman? Someone you loved? Because everything around you got messed up and the right words wouldn't come out?'

Ethan said nothing, and Marco knew he'd hit home. Whatever Ethan Hunter had done probably wasn't quite in the same league as the way Marco had messed up, and it certainly hadn't been done on the stage of the world's media circus, but all the same Marco could tell that the surgeon knew what it was like to get it badly wrong.

'I need to see Becca,' he repeated. 'I need to apologise to her properly. I need to tell her that I love her and I don't give a damn about where she comes from or what she's done in the past—it's the present and the future that matters. Who she is now.'

Ethan didn't look convinced.

Marco drew in a breath. 'I know she doesn't have family to look out for her, and the people here at the clinic and the rehab centre are the nearest she has to a family. I'm glad you're all looking out for her—and I can assure you my intentions towards her are completely honourable.'

Ethan was silent for so long that Marco thought he'd blown it.

But then the surgeon nodded. 'Just so you know, if you do anything to upset her or hurt her, I'll come after you myself. Limp or no limp.'

'I'm not going to hurt her,' Marco said. 'I'm going to grovel. And I just hope she can find it in her to forgive me and give me a second—no, a third chance.'

'Three strikes and you're out, I'd say.'

Marco gave him a wry smile. 'I'd better make sure I get it right this time.'

'Yeah, you'd better. She's in her office,' Ethan said. 'I assume you know where that is?'

'I do. And thank you.'

When the surgeon had left, Marco went down the corridor to Becca's office and rapped on the door.

She looked up, as if to welcome in a patient, and her face went white. '*You*. What are you doing here?'

'I believe I have a physiotherapy appointment,' he said. 'Phase two.'

She shook her head. 'I'm not treating you any more.'

'I can understand why you'd rather not treat me,' he said carefully, 'and I'll accept your decision—but will you please listen to me before you make that decision?'

Her eyes narrowed. 'Like you listened to me?'

'Technically,' he said, 'you didn't give me the chance to listen to you. You blew up and stormed out. And, yes, I know I should've run straight after you and stopped you leaving. I was a fool. I let stuff get in the way.'

She said nothing, but at least she hadn't thrown him out.

'I don't care about your background, Becca. I don't care where you came from or what happened in your past,' he said. 'Well, I *do* care—I hate that you were treated so badly when you were a vulnerable teenager, by someone who should've looked after you instead of dragging you down—but what I mean is that the past doesn't matter. I love the girl you were when I first met you, and I love the woman you are now.'

'You love me?' she said. 'But nothing can come of it. You're a prince and I...' She blew out a breath. 'Well. The press labelled me a wild child.'

'Because they know only half the story. Something that someone fed them. By the time I've finished talking to them they're going to see you for exactly who you are,' he said. 'A brave, talented woman. Someone who's a real role model—someone who's come through adversity and built a decent life for herself. I'm proud of you.'

She curled her lip. 'You didn't seem proud the other day. You were angry.'

'I was, but not with you,' he said. 'I was angry with myself. I should've protected you better. And I should've seen for myself that you can fit into my world. You're good enough, Becca. More than good enough.'

'What made you see it differently?'

'Being without you. Because it was like a black hole. I saw my future without you, and it was so bleak and lonely and miserable.' He looked at her. 'My parents have been talking to Lexi. Nobody's broken any confidences—but they did tell me that you volunteer at a rehab clinic. And

I'm guessing that's your way of paying back for the way you were helped.'

She frowned. 'Yes—but...' She looked confused, unable to take things in. 'Your parents?'

'They hold you in pretty high esteem,' he said. 'I guess what I'm saying is if you'll have me, and put up with the royal engagements and media circus that kind of have to go along with me, then...' He had nothing to lose, now. So he'd tell her just how he felt. 'Becca, you make me a better man. I feel complete when I'm with you. I know I've hurt you, more than once, and I'd like the chance to make that up to you. Will you marry me?'

'But—what about the drink and the drugs? I'm totally unsuitable for a prince's consort or what have you.'

He shrugged. 'Everyone makes mistakes. Sometimes they're helped to make those mistakes, dragged into it by someone else. It's in the past. You can't go back and change it. But you can learn from your mistakes, put them behind you—and you've gone one step further than that, because you're helping other people who've ended up in the same trap you were in. And they'll listen to you because they know you've been there and come out the other side so you understand what it's really like. It takes someone really special to do that, to help people like that. So will you marry me?'

She bit her lip. 'Marco, I can't give you an answer. Not while this is all hanging over me.'

'I hope you know that you have my family's backing. And the backing of everyone here. And I'd guess it's the same at the rehab place. You're not alone,' he said softly.

'I was alone for a long time,' she said, suddenly looking very young and vulnerable.

He held out his free arm. 'If telling me the whole story will help you, I'll listen. And I won't judge,' he said softly.

* * *

Would telling him the whole story help her?

At least it would mean they had no more secrets. No more lies between them.

She stood up from her chair and walked round to his side of the desk. Let him hold her.

All these years of standing on her own two feet and now, for once, it felt good to have someone to lean on.

She dragged in a breath. 'My dad died when I was tiny. It was an accident. My mum didn't cope very well—she wanted someone who'd look after her and love her, the way he had. I had a lot of "uncles", but she never seemed to find the right one. And in the end she started drinking to help her forget how unhappy she was.' She looked at him. 'And I mean hard drinking. Half the time she forgot I was there, too. I learned to make a jam sandwich before I could even write my name.'

'Oh, Becca.'

She shrugged. 'Plenty of people have it as bad as that. They don't have much money; bread and jam's cheap, it fills you up and it doesn't need cooking.'

He stroked her hair. 'OK. I'm not judging.'

Though she could see in his eyes that he was angry on her behalf.

'It doesn't get better,' she said. 'But I understand why, now. My mum was lost. She couldn't find her way out. I guess she was needy—and it was too much for a new partner. Every time she met someone and I thought it was going all right, because she was going to have a baby and we'd be a family... Well, she found it hard to cope when the baby cried. Then she'd drink. Pick fights. Then her partner would get tired of her drinking and leave. And that would make her feel worse, and the only way she could feel better was to drink enough to make her forget.'

'Hard on you.'

'Not just me. I've got, what, four or five brothers and sisters. Half-brothers and sisters,' she amended. 'Not that I've seen any of them since they were two years old. Their dads got custody—well, what with my mum's drinking, it was probably better they lived with their dads than with us.'

'What about you? Didn't any of them try to take custody of you?'

She shrugged. 'I wasn't their child. They didn't want me.'

'But why didn't you get taken into care? Surely the authorities knew from the court cases that your mum was drinking and not looking after you. Didn't anyone speak up for you?'

'There wasn't anyone to speak up for me.' She shrugged. 'It was OK. I managed. I mean—it hurt that nobody ever invited me to birthday parties, but I understood why. The other mums didn't like my mum. She'd get drunk and try to flirt with every man in sight.' She sighed. 'We did OK until I was fifteen—and then she started seeing Barney.' She bit her lip. 'He started putting vodka in my lemonade. I didn't realise what was happening at first—you can't taste vodka, can't smell it. But it quickly got so I felt I needed something. He talked to me in the kitchen one night, and I must've said something because he gave me a drink. It made me feel better. So I had more. And I…I was horrible when I was drunk. I fell out with the few friends I did have, because of my drinking. And drinking more helped to blot out how miserable I was.'

Marco looked at her. 'You were *fifteen*. Too young to drink.'

'Too young to buy it for myself from a shop or a pub, and too young to drink in a public place,' she corrected. 'But it's harder to police what goes on behind closed doors. There were lots of underage kids at the rehab centre.'

'So he let you drink vodka. He encouraged you.'

'And then one night he kissed me.' She closed her eyes briefly, remembering how disgusting she'd found it. How he'd slobbered over her. How she'd wanted to scream herself sick when he'd put his hands under her clothes but she'd been too scared to make a noise, because Barney had told her to keep quiet or her mum would be upset.

But her mum had been upset anyway.

'My mum caught us, and he told her...' She dragged in a breath, still outraged by how easily Barney had lied, and how her mother had actually believed him. 'He said I came on to him. She accused me of trying to steal her boyfriend, and she threw me out.'

Marco stroked her hair. 'Where did you go?'

'I didn't have anywhere to go,' she said. 'I'd fallen out with everyone at school because of the drinking, so I couldn't ask to stay with anyone. I thought I was going to have to live on the streets. I was just walking round, trying to see a doorway where I could shelter for the night. But then Barney came after me. He said he'd look after me. That I could stay at his flat. And he had a spare room.' She bit her lip. 'I thought he felt guilty about what he'd done and was trying to be nice, helping me out. I thought he was going to soften my mum up a bit so she'd let me go back home and I'd stop crying round his flat. Except...'

She looked away.

'That wasn't quite what he had in mind. He said he had something for me, something that would make me feel better. And he gave me this tablet.'

'You took it?'

'I was drunk at the time. Of course I took it.' She swallowed hard. 'And then a couple of weeks later, when he'd given me more and more, he said I owed him for the drugs I'd taken. And the vodka. I didn't have any money. He said I could—I could pay him in kind. Give him my virginity.

And…' Oh, this was so hard to say. 'He was going to film it,' she whispered. 'Make money from it. Sell it to people who wanted to watch.'

Marco held her close. 'Oh, my Becca. I want to kill him. Very, very slowly. The traditional death from a thousand cuts.'

'He didn't actually do it,' she said. 'Because I told him I couldn't do it, it was the wrong time of the month. And he said as soon as—as soon as I was clean, he'd do it.'

Marco held her tighter.

'But I went to school that day,' she said. 'I'd been skipping lessons. I didn't care about school any more. But for some reason I felt I had to go in that day. We had a Personal Development class. There was a woman there from the rehab centre, giving us all a talk about drugs. After the talk I asked to leave the classroom to go to the loo, but I followed her out to her car, and I asked her to help me get into rehab—to help me get away from Barney. And she told the school I was going with her, and she took me to the rehab centre. They helped me get off the vodka and the drugs.'

'What about Barney? *Please* tell me she skewered Barney. That he was put in prison for what he did.'

She shook her head. 'He said I was lying. It was my word against his. He said I'd tried it on with him and he'd turned me down because I'd only just turned sixteen, and he said I was just trying to get my own back by smearing his good name.'

'How could the police let him get away with it?'

'I had no evidence. It was all circumstantial. Like I said, it was my word against his.'

'But surely your mum stood up for you and told them what he did?'

'She was still angry with me. She said nothing.'

'Oh, Becca.'

'I never lived with her again,' Becca said. 'The rehab centre found me a place to live, and got me made a ward of the court so I couldn't be taken anywhere without their permission. Barney couldn't come and get me. And I was determined I'd prove their faith in me, that I'd make something of myself. I passed my exams—I crammed everything at the last minute and my grades weren't brilliant, because I'd had a year of skipping classes and being drunk, but I passed enough to go on to sixth form. I did better with my A levels, earned a place at university. The rest you know.'

'You truly are amazing,' Marco said. 'And I'm so proud of you.'

She blinked back the tears. 'I'm *not* going to cry.'

'Only happy tears, from now on,' he said. He stroked her face. 'Did you make it up with your mother?'

'Not really. After she split up with Barney she drank even more. She ended up with oesophageal varices. One day, she bled out. It was just before my A levels.' She swallowed hard. 'The emergency department called her neighbour, who called me—I'd given her the details in case Mum ever changed her mind and wanted to see me. So I was there at the end. But she didn't forgive me, Marco.'

'Because she couldn't forgive herself, maybe,' he said. 'She knew she'd let you down, hadn't looked after you properly. And she'd introduced you to Barney. She'd let him do what he did to you. She couldn't forgive herself for it, and she couldn't tell you that, so she just made you feel that it was your fault—and it *wasn't* your fault, Becca.'

'I wish we'd made up,' she said. 'And it scares me. Maybe there's an alcoholic gene in my family. My mum never said why we never saw my grandparents, but maybe one of them was an alcoholic. So was she. So was I.' She took a deep breath. 'And I always said I'd never get mar-

ried, never have a family, because I don't want to pass
that weakness on.'

'Firstly,' Marco said, 'you're very far from weak. You're
strong. Yes, you were supported by the rehab centre, but
you were the one who took that first step and asked for
help. By sheer determination, you got yourself sorted out
and away from all the mess of your life. Secondly, you're
not your mother. You wouldn't ever abandon your children, and you'd steer them away from drink and drugs.'
He dropped to one knee. 'As for marriage? I hope very
much that you'll reconsider that and marry me. Be the
perfect modern royal escort.'

'I'm not perfect,' she said.

He smiled. 'Don't you see? That's what makes you perfect for the job. You're human. You're brave. And you can
move on from mistakes you've made. But...'

Her eyes widened. 'But?'

'This is the third time I've asked you, now. If you don't
want to get married, then I'll respect that. Provided that
you'll live with me. Be my love. Be part of my family. Because I don't ever want to be without you again, Becca. I
need you with me. I love you.'

She dragged in a breath. 'But how can your family ever
accept me? I'm from the *gutter*.' She shook her head. 'I
love you enough to walk away and let you find someone
suitable. Someone who'll make you happy.'

'I don't want to find "someone suitable".' He grimaced
as he made quote marks with his good hand. 'I want you.
You're the one who makes me happy, Becca.'

'You don't have a choice. You're a prince of Sirmontane.'

'I do have a choice. And, before you even start thinking it, no, I don't have to choose between love and duty.
I'm free to choose you.'

She couldn't let herself believe it. Dared not let herself

hope. 'There's no way your parents will be able to accept a former addict as your partner.'

'Yes, there is.' He sighed. 'Look, come and meet them. Then you'll see for yourself.'

'Meet them?'

'I'm under royal orders to tell you that they want to meet you. Not to be intimidating, but welcoming. Actually, I have a feeling you'll get on incredibly well with my mother. And then,' he said, 'your doubts will all be put to rest and you can do what we both want and agree to marry me.'

He was right—it was the only way she could be sure. Except she was pretty sure that she was the one who had it right, not him.

'OK.'

Marco grabbed his phone from his pocket and called his mother. 'Mamá ? No, she said no. Not until she's met you and Papá. OK. Yes, here would be good. *Talué*. Yes, I love you, too.' He laughed, and put his phone back in his pocket. 'Righty, Ms Anderson. One bluff thoroughly called.'

'Your parents are coming here?' she asked.

'If we go to Regent's Park we'll have to run the gauntlet of the paps.'

'And so,' she pointed out, 'will your parents, if they come here—and that's not fair. We'll go to them.'

'OK. I'll tell them to stay put.' He rolled his eyes and made two more calls. 'All sorted. Rafa says the back entrance is the quieter one, so we'll use that one.'

So much for quiet. The paparazzi were three-deep. Flashlights popped as Marco helped Becca into the car, and there were ribald comments and calls of, 'Are you giving the prince some *special* treatment, Becca?'

She remembered what Declan and Lexi had told her about dealing with the press: be polite, be gracious, and don't let them see that they've got to you. So she just smiled, said nothing, and got in the car.

She felt unbelievably nervous about meeting Marco's family. What if they didn't like her, after all?

Marco, as if guessing how tense she was, simply held her hand. 'It's going to be fine.'

How could he be so sure?

The drive to Regent's Park was over way, way too soon.

But at least Maria the housekeeper was there to meet her with a hug. 'Lovely to see you back, *hermosa*.'

'You, too, Maria.'

'Your parents are in the sitting room,' she told Marco.

'Thank you, Maria. Maybe we could have some coffee in a little while?'

Oh, help, Becca thought. *Please don't let me spill it all over that expensive silk carpet.*

Her nervousness grew exponentially as they walked up the stairs to the next floor and Marco opened the door to the sitting room.

What on earth did you say to the King and Queen of Sirmontane? She should have asked Marco in the car about formal addresses. Too late, now. Hoping that she was doing the right thing, she swept into a low curtsey when they were standing in front of Marco's parents. If a prince was Your Highness, his parents must be the next rung up. What did people call the Queen of England? Hmm… She couldn't call a king 'ma'am', could she? She was just going to have to wing it.

'Good morning, Your Majesties,' she said.

Marco coughed. 'How come you never curtsey to me like that?'

She looked up at him and rolled her eyes. 'Because you don't deserve it.' The words were out before she could stop them.

Oh, no. Why had she said something so *stupid* in front of Marco's mother?

But, to her surprise, Marco's mother burst out laughing. The Queen of Sirmontane stood up and held her arms open. 'Now I know you're definitely the right girl for my son. I did have my doubts.'

Because of the press?

The question must have shown on her face, because the Queen of Sirmontane explained, 'When you curtseyed to us. But, no, you're exactly what he needs. A breath of fresh air. He's absolutely right about you. Welcome, Becca.'

Oh, my God.

She was being offered a hug *by a queen*.

This couldn't possibly be protocol.

But the fact that she was being offered a hug proved that Marco was right, that his family had already accepted her. It made the last barriers of fear round her heart melt. So she stood up and hugged Marco's mother right back.

'Sit down with me, *hermosa*,' Marco's mother said, sitting down herself and patting the seat of the sofa next to her. 'Now, I'm Elena, and this is Alfonso.'

First-name terms with a king and queen.

This didn't seem real.

'Maria's been singing your praises,' said the King— Becca didn't quite yet dare to think of him as Alfonso. 'She says you've helped her a lot.'

That business with her arthritic hip. And Becca had been sworn to secrecy about it. 'I don't want to be rude, Your Majesty, but may I plead patient confidentiality?'

Elena smiled. 'Of course you may. But she's told us everything. And I'm cross with her for not saying something before, because we could have sent her for treatment much earlier and got her some more help.'

'There's something about this house and extremely

stubborn women,' Marco said, lounging back on one of the tall-back chairs and giving his mother an insolent grin.

Elena gave him a speaking look and ignored him. 'So Maria will have more of a supervisory role in future,' she said. 'Thank you for helping her, Becca.'

'It was my pleasure,' Becca said, meaning it.

'And we would like you to know that we would be very happy to welcome you to the family,' the King said.

'Even though...' There wasn't a way to put it tactfully. 'After all the stuff the papers said about my past?' Becca asked.

'The way you've come through adversity would inspire a new generation,' Elena said, surprising her. 'And your example might also give Marianna—Ferdy's fiancée— back some of the confidence that the press has chipped away.'

'I agree,' Alfonso added. 'I think you'll be good for us, Becca. You've made Marco happy. And steadier than he's been in quite a while.'

'I am *here*, you know,' Marco said, sounding pained.

'And we're your parents, so we can talk about you in front of you,' Elena said crisply. 'Always. Even when you're a white-haired grandfather yourself and we're ancient crones.'

Alfonso coughed. 'Since when can men be crones, Elena?'

'You can be an honorary crone, then. Add it to your titles,' Elena said.

Becca couldn't help laughing. She really, really liked Marco's family. And to think that she'd been afraid they'd be stuffy and formal. Lexi had been right about them: they were down-to-earth. Elena was wonderful. Brisk, no-nonsense, and with a rapier-sharp sense of humour. And Marco had been right, too: Becca had the distinct feeling that, in the future, she and Elena would be good friends.

'Now we've got that sorted, I think Becca and I need a quiet chat,' Marco said, and stood up. 'Excuse us, O ancient crones-to-be.' He took Becca's hand and pulled her to her feet. 'We'll be back shortly. Because I am *not* having this conversation in front of you, Mamá.'

'Spoilsport,' his mother grumbled. 'Becca, I want a full report.'

'You'll get it,' Becca promised with a smile.

Marco took Becca up to the roof garden.

'So can you see it, now?' he asked softly. 'That my parents are very happy to accept you in my life.'

She nodded. 'I like your parents. Especially your mum.'

'Mamá,' he said, 'can be a bit full-on. And she's horrendously bossy.' He smiled at her. 'They say that women marry men like their fathers. I guess it's the same for men.'

She looked at him. 'Are you calling me bossy?'

He grinned. 'I love it when you're bossy. But sometimes I want to be the bossy one.' He dropped to one knee. 'Becca, I don't have a ring to offer you right now, because I want the fun of choosing it with you. But will you do me the honour of being my wife, the love of my life and the centre of my family?'

Being the centre of a family. What she'd always secretly wanted and always feared she'd never have.

And, best of all, waking up with Marco every morning, knowing that it would be a good day because he was there and he loved her as much as she loved him.

She knelt down to join him. 'Yes,' she said, and kissed him.

EPILOGUE

One month later

'READY?' MARCO ASKED BECCA.

'Ready.' She smiled at him and stole a kiss. 'My first ever royal engagement. Well, royal-to-be,' she amended.

'It still counts as royal,' Marco said. 'And I can't think of a better place for it,' he added as he helped her out of the car outside the rehab centre.

'Be careful with your arm,' she said. 'You're only just allowed to do medium activities with that hand.'

'Yes, dear,' he teased. 'You can nag me about the exercises later. Stop worrying. I'm fine.'

Thanks to a donation from the royal family of Sirmontane, the rehab unit had been able to set up a new physical therapy room to help their patients.

Cameras flashed as Becca got out of the car. She waved and smiled at the paparazzi, who'd decided since the news of the engagement broke that she was their darling rather than their demon. Instead of calling her Wild Child Becca and sneering at her, they'd nicknamed her Princess Braveheart and cheered her on.

The fact that at her last press conference she'd spotted that two of the journalists were shaking their writing hand,

and taken them to one side and taught them exercises to relieve the pain, had only made them love her more.

Marco was rather less thrilled that the press had also taken to calling him Prince Zorro, but he put up with it for Becca's sake. If she was happy, then his world was all right.

They did the tour of the rehab centre, as agreed—but it took rather longer than planned because Becca stopped to talk with every single one of the young patients. And every single one of them was smiling when she left them, knowing that they were understood rather than judged.

His wife-to-be, Marco thought, was a real shining star.

'I'm delighted to declare the physical therapy room open,' she said, and posed with the oversized scissors in front of the ribbon for the press. Then she smiled and cut the ribbon. 'And may everyone who uses this room find their inner strength, too.'

Like she had.

Marco was so proud of her. She'd come so far. And, just as his parents had predicted, she'd inspired a new generation—across Europe, not just in Sirmontane and England. And politicians finally seemed to be noticing the problem of addiction among teenagers and were setting up more rehab units to help them find their way back.

As they came back to the royal limo, one of the press called, 'Kiss her, Prince Zorro!'

He smiled at Becca. 'I guess that's telling me my royal duty.'

He kissed her, to cheers from the crowd.

'I'd just like you all to know,' he said, 'how proud I am of my Princess Braveheart. And I can't wait to marry her in four months' time.'

In the cathedral next to the palace in Sirmontane where

he'd been christened, his parents had been married and his father had been crowned.

He kissed her again. 'I love you, Becca. Now and always.'

She kissed him back. 'And I love you, too.'

* * * * *

LET'S TALK
Romance

For exclusive extracts, competitions
and special offers, find us online:

f facebook.com/millsandboon

⊙ @millsandboonuk

🐦 @millsandboon

Or get in touch on 0844 844 1351*

For all the latest titles coming soon, visit
millsandboon.co.uk/nextmonth